Praise for Murder, Mess, and the Tangerine Dress

"**Fantastic Series Beginning** . . . Hijinks, snark, disruption, and chaos ensue when Izzy touches her client's tangerine dress and sees the woman's deceased husband who warns her that his wife is in mortal danger. Rankin-Esquer has created a quirky and fabulous group of friends and family who battle over order and chaos and who manage to solve a tricky mystery before time runs out. Kudos for another great group of players and funny adventures."
—Wendy Adair, award-winning author of *The Broken Hallelujah* and the Brentwood Women Mysteries series

"**Loved Every Page of *The Tangerine Dress*!** Professional organizer Izzy Bishop is the perfect mix of quirky and relatable—and you can't help but root for her. In fact, all the characters shine in their unique, lovable glory—especially Izzy, who navigates her world with a mixture of humor, grit, and genuine warmth."
—Ann Huchingson, acclaimed TV and novel writer

Also by Lynn Rankin-Esquer

My Paperback Cape: The Unlikely Odyssey of a Bookworm

The Unmooring of Mrs. Mango

Murder, Mess, and the Tangerine Dress

An Order Out of Chaos Mystery — Book 1

Lynn Rankin-Esquer

XandL Press
California

Murder, Mess, and the Tangerine Dress: An Order Out of Chaos Mystery – Book 1

Copyright © 2025 by Lynn Rankin-Esquer. All rights reserved.

No part of this book may be reproduced in any form or by any electronic or mechanical means, including information storage and retrieval systems, without written permission from the author, except for the use of brief quotations in a book review.

ISBN: 979-8-9918987-0-6 (eBook)

ISBN: 979-89918987-1-3 (Paperback)

Cover Design: David Bloom

Dedicated to everyone who ever longed to make something and put it into the world. And to the two best creations to come through me, Elle and Xavier.

Chapter 1

"Toto, I have a feeling we are not in Kansas anymore," said Vivi, peering out the windshield of her ancient but spotless Forerunner. We were a few miles from my house, but decades of generational wealth apart. Just over the Berkeley hills beyond the San Francisco Bay, the mansion we were winding our way towards had a killer view, old-money elegance, and privacy that came at a steeper price than the hill we were climbing.

"I love *The Wizard of Oz* as much as the next person, but you just called me a dog," I said. "That's low."

"Don't bite the hand that drives you to work," said Vivi, laughing.

Unlike me, Vivi could always find her keys, which is why she was driving me to my organizing job on her day off.

"No neighbors in sight," I marveled. Looking up through the ancient live oaks twisting into a canopy over us, I had a moment of feeling out of time. And a sense of trespassing. Which was silly—I had an appointment.

"What's one percent of the top one percent?" asked Vivi. "I think that's what we are looking at here."

"You can do it. You know that, right?" I said to Vivi.

She shot a sideways look at me, confused by the change of topic. "What do you mean?"

"You are going to get through this stuff with your mother. You are strong, and I'm here for you."

Vivi shook her head while staring ahead at the curving driveway. "You're uncanny. I just got off the phone with her before I picked you up."

I shrugged. "It just comes." Vivi's mother's health was fading, and they had a complicated relationship. Sometimes I could feel it weighing on her.

Vivi laughed. "I appreciate it. Just don't ever use that skill for evil."

"Stay and help me," I begged, shoving my mascara and brightening cream back into my bag. Vivi made everything more fun, even cleaning out closets and garages.

Vivi snorted. "Izzy Bishop, you're adorable. Mediterranean women do not miss waxing appointments. I'm not going hairy just because your sister stresses you out. We're in our forties now; maintenance is not a luxury anymore."

Vivi was not only my best friend, she was now my co-worker, having joined me in working for my sister's organizing company, Order Out of Chaos. Vivi was a natural at the job; I was more of a pity hire. Coerced, actually—thanks, mom? Despite her four sons, a husband, and two dogs, Vivi's house stayed magazine-worthy, while mine looked . . . let's go with "pleasantly cluttered."

So right now, I was the one headed to work late, hastily dressed, long blond hair in an untidy ponytail, makeup slapped on in the car, while Vivi was headed to a waxing appointment, looking like she was on her lunch break from her corner office at *Vogue*. Her caramel-highlighted brown hair smoothly framed her face, her jeans hugged her generous curves like they were designed for her (they were), her ostrich belt and matching spiky boots perfectly complemented her creamy silk shirt.

"I told Lauren I don't work Mondays. Boundaries," said Vivi, giving me a side-eye. "Maybe try them out some day."

"I'm trying," I said. "A lot."

"You fail a lot, too," Vivi said, with an affection that took the sting out of her words.

"So, I like pleasing people. Remind me why we are friends?" I joked.

"Because I know you better than you know yourself, and I'm the only one who will tell you the truth," said Vivi. "Like, maybe you didn't try super hard to find your car keys?"

"I did! Can't help it that I'm Izzy Bishop, the disorganized organizer." Talk about a poor talent–job fit.

"Let's not sugarcoat it," said Vivi. "You had a hideous accident. Anyone would be anxious. Have you been on the highway yet?"

"Haven't needed to be," I lied.

My disorganization was lifelong. My driving anxiety was newer. Who wouldn't be anxious after totaling a car and ending up in a coma?

Vivi flicked her eyes. "Right," she said, slowing as we got to the half circle of intricately patterned brick driveway in front of the house, a multi-storied, multi-winged expanse that wouldn't have been out of place among the Newport, Rhode Island, mansions.

I looked in the sun visor mirror. "Were you going to tell me about the blob of mascara?" I said, wiping at my eyelid.

Vivi shrugged. "Probably." She stopped alongside a truck labeled on all sides with "Jacko's Plumbing." "Try not to set anything on fire," she added as I got out, her perfectly glossed lips failing to hold back a smirk.

"That wasn't my fault!" I said.

"It never is." Vivi waved as she pulled away.

"Sorry I'm late," I said, sailing into the plush bedroom suite of Joanna Sullivan, today's Order Out of Chaos client. Crap. Piles of clothes were heaped on every surface, the closet almost bare. The organizing had begun without me.

Order Out of Chaos had built a reputation as the local, affordable Marie Kondo, with a promise to (mostly) painlessly declutter and organize homes into a beautiful, simple lifestyle. Even though we were getting the mansion ready for a charity gala, Lauren insisted a proper cleanout started in the bedroom. Something about waking up in a clear space leading to a clear head. I wondered what that would feel like.

Lauren, my boss and—even worse—younger sister, slightly tilted her head, not disturbing a hair in her subtly highlighted, angled blunt cut. She glanced towards the clock beside the bed and stretched her lips in what would look like a smile to anyone outside of family. I've known her since I was seven and she came home as a red-faced bundle in our mother's arms thirty-five years ago, so I wasn't fooled.

"Of course, you had to take care of those drop-offs first," lilted Lauren—a lie, but it was important to her that our clients trust our punctuality. An organizer who couldn't even organize her time was a failure right out of the gate.

I saw her glance at my messy hair, then down at my outfit, and her lips pressed tighter. Lauren was always perfectly plucked, shaved, made up, blown dry, creaseless, prepared. Her purse was the professional organizer's version of a first-aid kit. Need a Band-Aid, a hair twisty, a zip tie, a wall anchor, a craft knife, a tape measure, a tampon, a stud finder, a liquid IV packet? It was in there. Lauren never misplaced her car keys. Or was late.

"Work with Joanna on the dresses," Lauren said, pointing to a pile on the bed that had to be five feet high.

Joanna dropped the sequined dress she was holding, bustling over to hug me. "Izzy!" she exclaimed. "Now the fun really starts!"

Joanna's face radiated with smile lines, the natural aging of an attractive woman taking no extreme measures. In her early sixties, she wore her blond- and gray-streaked hair cut short with a bit of natural wave. Along with the yoga pants and loose, long-sleeved top she was wearing, she gave the impression of an active, vivacious woman.

Looking over Joanna's shoulder as we hugged, I noticed that Lauren's spine looked extra stiff. It wasn't my fault people liked me more than her. "Get to work," she mouthed behind Joanna's back.

Joanna gave one more squeeze and stepped back, almost tripping on another huge pile of clothes ranged along the floor at the foot of the king-sized bed. Joanna pointed at the clothes she'd just tripped over. "We're leaving the workout stuff for last. I just keep accumulating!" Her eyes were bright. "I like having different outfits for pickleball and tennis and jazzercise and all that. I mean, it's what I wear every day."

She was cheerful but looked tired, not an uncommon reaction to Lauren. Not a good sign since we had barely three weeks before the gala that was the reason for this entire house overhaul. Lauren had a very detailed plan, so if we could keep up with her energy, the place should be completely ready.

"Very important to recognize the function and importance of the clothes!" said Lauren in a light tone. I've worked with her enough to know she was horrified by the number of workout outfits and would do her best to cull it at least in half, if not quarters. I was excited to see Joanna defy her.

"Heyo," a booming voice sounded through Joanna's bedroom door. A smell of sewage preceded a large man clad in a filthy gray uniform.

Joanna released me and turned towards the man lumbering towards us. "Yes, Mr. Jacko?"

"More complicated than I thought," Mr. Jacko said, head shaking. "Those pipes are ancient, galvanized, and just breaking apart everywhere. And whoever put that shower in didn't slope it properly."

Joanna winced. "It's always something in a house this old."

"It's a lot of somethings," said Mr. Jacko, his face bright with anticipation. He rubbed his sleeve across a dripping nose, adding a smudge of dirt to his already unclean face. "Just need your permission to proceed."

Joanna shrugged, "Whatever you need to do."

"I don't want to interfere," said Lauren. "But perhaps Mr. Jacko could provide you with an estimate?"

Mr. Jacko gave Lauren a dirty look. "We haven't needed that in the past. Maybe you stick to your business, and I'll stick to mine."

Joanna looked uncertain. "Probably a good idea?" she said faintly.

"I'll put something together," Mr. Jacko muttered. "After I get the leak stopped. Might not be today. I'm moving slower than usual." With that, he turned around and shuffled out on flapping dirty boots, leaving behind the smell of fetid water and worse.

I picked up a beautiful tangerine-colored dress to display it for the thumbs up or thumbs down and felt a blast of cool air on the back of my neck. The cool air turned into a buzz in my head and the left side of my vision got dark. What the heck? Was I getting a migraine? Having a stroke?

I struggled to keep focused on the bedroom in front of me but was overwhelmed by a series of images, like I had fallen into a dream. A small dance floor, under the stars, twinkly lights strung overhead, white-linen-covered tables nearby. Flowers everywhere, people standing around the dance floor, clapping and smiling. A giggling Joanna wearing the tangerine dress stared happily into the eyes of a slim, gray-haired man as they danced.

I've always been intuitive but had never experienced a sudden scene like the one flashing through my head. It felt foreign and intrusive and as if it was flowing out of the dress. I dropped the dress, and the images faded, but the man stuck around. I felt horrifyingly disoriented, as if I had time-traveled and body-traveled. I couldn't shake the feeling I had just been looking through the eyes of a gray-haired man, staring at Joanna at another point in time.

Up until now, my intuitiveness did not involve such clear scenes or other people. It was more that a thought would come into my head and I'd say it without thinking, like when I was six and told my mother not to worry; the baby was ready to come now. She stared at me with watery eyes and, not long after, joyfully told me I was going to have a little brother or sister. Or the time I screamed "Wait!" at a green light, only to see a huge tractor trailer come screaming through the intersection right where our car would have been.

Those had always just seemed like hunches. Channeling a *person* was completely new, if that's what this was.

"Izzy?" said Joanna. I must have looked like a zombie, standing still and staring into space.

"Izzy?" said Lauren, right beside me now.

"Oh, uh, yeah, nice dress," I said, pointing at it. I was afraid to touch it again.

Joanna picked up the dress and beamed. "This was actually my wedding dress. I did the whole white dress thing in my first marriage. Thomas and I were both so happy to find love again we decided to throw out all the boring traditions. My Thomas." Her eyes crinkled in sadness. "The reason for the Heart Gala, of course."

I knew that we were preparing her house for a heart disease charity gala and that it was in her dead husband's honor.

My chest stabbed in pain so badly it took my breath away. Not a stretch to know that Thomas had died from a heart attack.

"So, uh, what did Thomas look like?" I asked, still feeling out of it, like I hadn't fully made it back to this place and time.

Joanna gestured towards pictures on the built-in wall shelves. "That's him."

It was the man in the images. I had just inhabited a dead man. Or he had inhabited me. In fact, he was still hanging around—I could feel him. This was a whole new development.

"Ahh, Sunny, so beautiful," I said, my voice deeper, almost accented.

Joanna went still. "What did you say?"

"The dress is so beautiful," I said, struggling to understand what was happening. I felt oddly detached from myself.

"You said 'Sunny,'" said Joanna.

"I did," I said. "The color must have seemed like a sunset or sunrise." I realized the words hadn't been mine. Must have been Thomas. There was no way I was letting anyone know that I thought a ghost was around. It made me seem like a wackadoo.

Lauren was on her knees, putting shoes that had made the cut into clear plastic boxes. "Beautiful! Definitely keep that dress, we can put it at the front of the closet if you'd like."

Be careful. Thomas's words appeared in my head. It wasn't like I could see him in front of me—it was more that I had an image of him and then words appeared almost like they were on a screen. And then feelings passed through my body that weren't mine. Love, sadness, more love, and then a swirl of danger around Joanna.

And then, oddly, an image of me pushing Joanna out the French doors on the side of the suite.

Go away! I begged silently.

She shouldn't be in here. Thomas's words floated through my head.

Joanna's eyes filled with tears. "Thomas called me Sunny, but never around people."

Lauren nudged my ankle from her spot on the floor, eyes boring into me with a silent command to focus. "Joanna, you have such lovely things!" Lauren said. "I can see why it's so hard to pick what to get rid of."

"In fact, he found this dress! Said the color reminded him of me." Joanna swirled the dress and the light caught the little sparkles woven into the material of the full skirt. "I felt like a princess."

I could feel Thomas's love flowing towards Joanna. It was so strong I was surprised she couldn't feel it. Then I saw her face light up. Maybe she *was* feeling it.

It was too much; I needed to regroup. Get rid of this ghost and find some focus.

"I need to use the bathroom," I said.

"You can use the powder room down the hall," said Joanna, eyes lingering on me, like she got a sense of Thomas being around too but was doubting herself.

Lauren followed me, grabbing her big bag. When we got to the hall, she pulled out a bottle of Excedrin and dry-swallowed two. Ever efficient. "What was going on in there?" she asked.

I shrugged. "Just got distracted."

"I'm going to need you to focus. I've got a headache coming on, and we need to keep moving on this." Lauren looked uncharacteristically uncertain. "I hope I haven't taken on more than I can manage.

"No worries, we've got it, Lolo," I said, trying to calm her with her childhood nickname.

A soft smile flitted across Lauren's face and, for a second, she was my little sister, not my boss. "Right, we can do it. Just stay focused, okay?"

I peed and washed my hands. Stop whatever this is, I begged my reflection. I was fine with the kind of sensing that made people feel cared about, like asking Vivi about her mother. I wanted nothing to do with channeling ghosts or whatever weirdness this was.

No chance of its stopping, though. On my return, I was pulled towards an open door just beyond Joanna's room, like a huge magnet had been turned on and I was a flimsy paper clip incapable of resisting it. My chest constricted in pain, and the words *"Go in there!"* appeared in my head, not so much like a sound but like it was my own thought. I could almost feel Thomas's hands on my back, pushing me towards the room.

I'm looking, Thomas. Back off.

Great. I was talking to a ghost.

I peeked in to find a medium-sized bedroom, with a trail of tools and plumbing materials leading to what I presumed was the bathroom where Mr. Jacko was working. I heard some mutters and curses from that direction. It smelled of mildew, and a fan whirred somewhere out of sight. It didn't look scary, but I felt waves of fear crashing over me. Was it Mr. Jacko or the room?

"What's in the room next door?" I asked Joanna when I got back to her bedroom.

"Spare room. One of the many." Joanna waved her arm, presumably referring to the size of the house. "I moved Thomas's stuff in there. I just haven't . . . wanted to let go."

"Maybe we should work there next," I said.

No! Thomas didn't like that idea at all.

Huh. Why send me to the room and then push me away?

"The bathroom flooded into the bedroom, and the carpet is wet, so maybe after it's dried out?" said Joanna, sinking down onto the bed, wiping her hand across her brow. "I'm not feeling so great," she said. "Kinda tired. I wonder if I'm getting sick."

"We'll be quicker than you think," said Lauren, and Joanna pushed herself back to standing.

The Give-Away bags filled, as the huge pile of dresses on the bed shrank and then disappeared. We hung the tangerine dress in the front of the closet so she could see it first thing, but then hung the rest of the dresses she was keeping at the back of the closet since Joanna said she rarely got dressed up. We were working on the sweaters mounded on the couch (Fit? Wear it often? Have duplicates?) when Lauren got a call. She picked up, stepped out of the room, and then came back.

"I've got to run over to Peaches' house for a moment. You guys can keep going through these piles, then divide the sweaters you are keeping into colors and use this board to fold them." Peaches was OOC's best client and mostly worthy of the attention she demanded. Lauren held out a stiff translucent plastic rectangle. I hoped I remembered how to use it.

The moment Lauren left, Joanna dropped onto the bed and leaned up against the headrest, piles of blouses all around her. "Where did my water go?" Joanna looked around, eyes unfocused, brow wrinkled with confusion. "It was right on my night table." For the first time, Joanna seemed old to me. Frazzled by small things.

"I'll get you some," I said.

By the time I returned from the kitchen, Joanna was curled up asleep among the piles of clothes, like a bird in a nest. Another victim of Lauren's bottomless energy, worked to exhaustion.

I set the bottle on her bedside table and looked around for the folding board. Only after a couple of scans of the room did I notice that Joanna's face was smushed into the mound of shirts beside her. I moved the shirts away and saw that her face looked so white it was almost blue. Something was very wrong, and stabs of pain seared through my chest.

"Joanna?" I said, shaking her.

No answer.

I tried again, louder and harder. Nothing.

My heart raced and my stomach got tight in panic. Something was very wrong.

Get her OUT OF HERE. Thomas was in a panic.

I grabbed a blanket and shifted Joanna down onto it, knocking stacks of clothes off the bed. I dragged her several feet and then slipped on a silk blouse, falling and knocking my head into the bedpost as I went down. Things went starry and blurry. I got to my knees and gingerly felt my head to find a huge lump.

Get her out! Gas! urged Thomas.

I'm going as fast as I can! Back off, Thomas.

Dizzy, with a pounding head and racing heart, I managed to drag Joanna out through the French doors onto a little patio next to a tinkling fountain. I knelt down and put my hand on Joanna's chest and could feel a faint heartbeat, but nothing I did roused her to consciousness.

Hands shaking, I dialed 911. Feeling like a vise was tightening around my head, I choked out the location. Right before everything went dark, I remembered Mr. Jacko. "Plumber too," I whispered.

Chapter 2

I was sitting upright on a gurney in the Emergency Department when Lauren came flying in, face white, eyes wide, hair messy.

"Izzy!" she said. "I got a call from Jay! In France? That you are in the hospital!"

"Jay? Oh, right, he's still my 'In Case of Emergency' in my phone," I said. "Whoops." I fumbled around for my phone and changed my ICE contact to Vivi. Jay and I were separated. Lauren was too reactive.

"You had a headache, remember?" I said. "It turns out we were breathing in carbon monoxide! Joanna had been breathing it the longest. And then you left, which helped you. And I was late, which helped me."

"Oh my God," said Lauren. She squeezed my hand. "You okay?"

"Yeah," I said, that is, aside from the lump on my head. I squeezed back, staring at Lauren's hair. I don't think I'd seen her with messy hair since she was six. She must have been really worried.

My phone rang.

Jay. My estranged husband. Nothing helped by talking to him. I turned the ringer off and didn't answer, but I texted him that I was fine, just a client issue and he shouldn't worry. Thank God for texting, the savior of separated couples. Communicate without raised voices or escalating emotion.

A nurse came back in with the news that Joanna was alive and on oxygen, floating in and out of consciousness.

"Mr. Jacko?" I asked.

"They are working on him," the nurse said, hurrying off before I could ask any more.

After I had been thoroughly checked out, we wandered down the row of examination bays, looking for Joanna's. Midway down the row, I saw a familiar-looking woman coming towards us.

Lauren stopped. "Emily?"

The woman looked away from the nurse leading her, "Yes?"

Lauren stepped towards her. "I'm Lauren Larsen, used to be Waring. We were working on your mother's house, organizing. This is my sister, Izzy; she is the one who saved your mother."

Emily grabbed my arm and dragged me with her as the nurse pointed to a bay and slid back the curtain with a crisp flick. "Thank you thank you thank you."

Joanna was lying on a gurney, eyes closed, a mask attached to her face, tubes coming out of her arm.

"Oh my God," whimpered Emily, dropping my arm and moving to her mother's side.

A woman in scrubs stood fiddling with a digital screen on the right side of the bed, and, on the other side of the bed, a tall dark-haired man in scrubs was angled over a keyboard, typing. He stared up at a computer screen jutting out from the wall, his face in profile until he turned fully towards us.

It was like a flash grenade went off. A clearing away of everything extraneous. Every cell in my body leapt to attention.

There he is.

As he spoke, I struggled to orient myself to the physical world. His voice was calm and clear and kind. He said that the good news was that Joanna had briefly regained consciousness and was responding well to whatever they were doing. The degree of damage would be hard to know immediately, though.

I could hear him, but I could also feel him, like he was vibrating at a frequency in perfect sync with my entire brain and body. And, of course, I could see him—his broad shoulders, warm skin, kind brown eyes, and high cheekbones that guaranteed he probably never took a bad picture. His dark hair fell just slightly forward onto the side of his forehead, and I had a flash of myself brushing it back. His face looked like someone had taken the best features from a couple of different cultures and combined them. Tall, dark, and mesmerizing.

Emily tearfully asked questions and then turned to me.

"This is Izzy; she found her."

Heat flooded my face as the doctor looked at me. Please God, don't let him be able to read my mind.

"Well done," he said, stepping closer and sticking out his hand. "I'm Dr. Saito."

When our hands touched, energy swirled through me at such a high vibration that my brain went fuzzy.

"What made you take her outside?" he asked. The paramedics must have filled him in.

I let go of his hand, reducing the energy enough to find my voice.

"I don't know," I managed to say. "It just seemed like the right thing to do."

"You must have had the sense that the air inside was poison," Dr. Saito said. His brow furrowed just the slightest, like he was curious and thinking hard. "Good thinking." As he gave a little approving nod, his eyebrows wriggled, almost like a pair of caterpillars communicating that they were pleased with me.

I was ridiculously pleased with his praise. Like Hippocrates himself had nodded in approval.

"Yeah, well, glad I did," I croaked.

I saw him glance at my left hand and look back up quickly. It was the "is she married?" look. Which meant—

My face was already hot, and now my armpits were suddenly soaked because I didn't have my wedding rings on. Scrubbing our nasty grill, I took them off and then found I hadn't really wanted to put them back on. No one had even noticed. Until now.

Dr. Saito turned back to Emily, speaking in an easy, soothing voice, radiating a sense of calm, making it seem like all would be fine without actually promising that.

The loudspeaker crackled with "code blue in sixteen," and Dr. Saito gave a nod and moved quickly out of the bay.

"We should get going," I said, part of my brain focused on Emily and her mother, another part of my brain trailing after Dr. Saito.

"Yes, but uh . . ." Lauren paused.

Emily looked up.

"Well, I'm not sure how this is going to affect the . . . uh . . . job?" said Lauren. "The gala isn't that far off."

How could she be thinking of work at this moment?

"Oh, right!" said Emily. "I don't know. I don't know anything, really."

I pulled out my phone. "Give me your number; we can touch base with you later. So I can find out how Joanna is doing." I couldn't even look at Lauren.

Emily gave me her number and promised to be in touch.

As we left, I could hear a lot of action coming from what I presumed was bay sixteen. I couldn't keep myself from peeking in as we went by, and I recognized that grubby gray shirt. It was Mr. Jacko. I tried to linger and see what was going on, but Lauren dragged me away. I sent up a little prayer for both Joanna and Mr. Jacko.

The moment we were outside the hospital doors, I let loose. "How could you?"

"What are you talking about?" Lauren looked at me with bewilderment.

"All you care about is your precious business. Joanna almost died! She still could! I could have died. You could have died. Looks like Mr. Jacko's not doing so great in there. Aren't you just a little bit freaked out?"

"So I had a little headache. I'm fine. You're fine," snorted Lauren, walking faster as we headed towards her car. "But we have a contract and are on a tight schedule. That house is a big, beautiful mess, and the gala is less than three weeks away."

"Maybe we could wait, I don't know, a couple of hours? A day? The woman wasn't even conscious!"

"Of course I care about Joanna!" said Lauren, snapping her car door open. "But I'm running a business. If she doesn't need us right away, we need to go work on our other jobs. And someone needs to let Wanda know. Even if Joanna can't be there . . . The gala is too far along to be canceled, and no way they find another venue. It's happening with or without her."

I pulled my door shut, still shaking my head.

Lauren's face softened. "Look, of course I care. I just know that Joanna is going to be okay, and we are going to want to be on track. For her."

Lauren glanced back towards the hospital. "I hate those places," she muttered. A brief spasm of pain on her face as she looked at me, and then the cool professional Lauren was back. Ah, she was probably remembering coming to see me when I was in a coma.

The image of Joanna, almost blue, on her bed was going to haunt me. I could feel Thomas's worry and frustration with me for being so slow to respond to him. But then again, he wasn't super clear. It wasn't like he said, "Hey, there's a carbon monoxide leak here; you all need to get out of the house." And I couldn't tell Lauren. She'd never believe me. I wasn't sure I believed it myself. Maybe the carbon monoxide had made me hallucinate.

Lauren had caught a glimpse of herself in the rearview mirror and pulled a brush and a mini hair spray out of her center console. "Oh my God, how did you let me walk around looking like this?" Eyes fixed on the mirror, she fluffed back to perfection.

Lauren started up the car. "I know it sounds cold, but there is nothing else we can do for Joanna right this second. She's in good hands, and if we don't work, we don't get paid."

Before she pulled out of the parking lot, she dialed a number.

A male voice came through the speakers. "Hello?"

"Rupert? This is Lauren Larsen, from Order Out of Chaos. It turns out we have an opening for a consultation right now. Is there any chance you are available?"

Chapter 3

At 6:30 I dropped onto my couch, ankle and head both throbbing. I was mostly recovered from the car accident, but when I overdid it, my ankle got sore again. I carefully touched the knot on my head, tossed back a couple of Advil, and settled an ice pack around my ankle. I caught up on emails related to my various volunteer jobs and then looked at the seemingly endless college preparation emails for Cole. I flagged the emails, planning to come back to them. Then again, I had over 20,000 emails cluttering my inbox, plenty of them flagged. A problem for another day.

Cole wasn't going to be home for dinner. I could feel his attention increasingly focused away from me, which was as it should be—when you do motherhood right, you've worked yourself out of a job. Luke was already in college, and in a few months Cole would be too. One of these days, I was going to have to really process this whole empty nest thing.

Thank God Vivi was on her way with sushi, and all I had to do was open the wine. And find my car keys. According to Lauren, the way you find something is to clean up, which for my house would be a matter of weeks not hours. I decided to start small and do something about the cluttered counters. I stuck the ice pack back in the freezer, then grabbed a laundry basket and dumped everything on the island into it: papers and vitamin bottles and baseball caps and notepad, all jumbled together. I'd sort it later. I did like the look of a clean island, I had to say.

I went to the garage fridge to get some bottles of fizzy water and found my car keys next to the protein drinks in the fridge. I triumphantly talked back to Lauren's imagined criticism. "See? Things I need always eventually show up." I tossed the keys into the laundry basket and admired the clean counters again.

Once Vivi blew in, my mood lightened. As she unloaded her bag of goodies, I held up two bottles. "Red or white?"

"Ahh . . . ugh," Vivi laughed and groaned. "I'm on a cleanse. No alcohol."

"Noooo! I hate it when you're on a cleanse."

"Open it!" she demanded. "I'll smell it. Not your fault that none of my pants fit. I had to lie on the ground and pull this zipper up with a string. If I don't sit just right, I cut off circulation."

Vivi pulled out a container with my favorite rolls plus sashimi, and then a large glass Mason jar of a mustard-colored liquid.

"What is that?" I asked, pinching my nose.

"Smoop," she said. "It's actually really good."

"What the hell is Smoop?"

"Smoothie Soup. Invented by this cool nutritionist, Tracey Ratté. Simmer a bunch of vegetables and bone broth, add good fats and protein, and then puree it, and it is all the stuff you need and none of the stuff you don't, and you can take it on the go. Or you can order it online. This part of the cleanse is easy."

"Whatever you need to tell yourself," I said.

Vivi popped her Smoop into the microwave, and a delicious garlicky, spicy smell filled the room.

"Whatever keeps me off carbs. It's one day at a time," said Vivi, taking the Smoop out of the microwave.

"How many days are you up to?" I asked.

"One if I make it through today," said Vivi. She tilted herself stiff-legged onto a barstool at the island and held up her Mason jar in a toast. "To carbs."

Vivi sipped her Smoop, set down the jar, and rubbed her right shoulder. "Holy Christ, I'm sore. Played that Czech chick, and she nailed me. She was definitely trying for my face."

"Uh-oh," I said. Vivi grew up in Philly with four older brothers and was perfectly nice until someone attacked her, at which point her inner MMA cage fighter took over. A lot of people have been fooled because Vivi is warm and generous and dresses like she owns a boutique. She will bring you a full-course meal if you are sick and then knife you in the alley if you are mean to her kids.

"You'd be proud of me," she said. "I waited a couple of points and then got her in the cooch. Made it look like an accident."

"Who was your partner?" I loved the juicy dramas of tennis at the local country club.

"Shania. Of all people."

My nemesis. Twenty years after high school, and Shania was still a mean girl, angry that I "stole" her boyfriend.

"I'm still mad at her for that 'maid' comment. We aren't maids; we are organizers. Not that there's anything wrong with being a maid."

Vivi and I looked at each other and laughed.

Vivi continued. "I was this close to hitting her in the cooch too. Maybe next time." Vivi meticulously lodged grudges in her mental ledger and just as meticulously crossed them off when avenged. She was fair that way. Shania would get one "accidental" volley in an intimate spot, and that would be it, unless she added a new line to the grudge ledger.

"You aren't going to believe my day—right up there with being stuck with Shania," I said, arranging the sushi on a plate, determined to live a graceful life, not just eat out of containers.

I filled Vivi in on Joanna and the hospital, her every "ooh" and "oh no!" relaxing me more and more. Unlike telling Jay, who could listen for at most thirty seconds before he'd start offering commentary or solutions. And then get mad when I rejected them. Sometimes you just need shared outrage.

"That is wild!" she said, slurping the last of her Smoop.

"I know. But there is something even wilder." If I
could tell anyone about the new ghost development, it
was Vivi.

"You know how I can . . . sense things?"

Vivi nodded.

"Well, it's gone up a notch. Or ten." I paused. "So I
picked up this gorgeous tangerine-colored dress, and it
was like I tapped into some portal or something. Like
touching it activated something. Joanna's dead husband
Thomas was around, I could see their wedding, and he
was trying to tell me to get Joanna out of her room."

"Whoa," said Vivi, eyes wide. "You mean . . .?"

"Yes, I swear it was her husband. And he was right.
There was danger in the house—the gas—and he was
trying to get her out of there."

Vivi slowly shook her head, taking it in. "That's so . . .
spooky." She took a sip of the fizzy water she'd spiked
with ginger and mint. She held up her glass. "The world
has gone mad. You're seeing ghosts, and I'm not
drinking."

"You believe me?"

Vivi shrugged. "I think that stuff happens. And you
did save her life. So, must have been something going
on."

I wriggled, trying to shed the creepy feeling it gave me
to talk about this. "Probably just a one-time thing.
Probably a fluke."

"My mom said she woke up one night and knew her
dad had died. But it wasn't sad; it was like there was this
intense wave of love all around her." Vivi slid a spoon
around the bottom of her jar, getting the last bits. "So,
who knows? I believed her. She said it was at, like, 3:15
in the middle of night and, sure enough, the next morning
that is what the doctors had listed as his time of death.
She said it was incredibly comforting. And then she went
right back to not believing anything woo-woo."

"It was weird, for sure." I wasn't sure how to think
about the whole thing, so did my normal coping and
pushed the whole topic into a back corner of my mind.

I took a sip of wine. "So, there was this doctor. At the hospital." I lifted my shoulders and rolled my eyes. "I'm sure it's nothing, but . . ."

"Oh my God, you met a cute doctor."

"Kind of."

"This is no time to get shy. Give." Vivi poked my shoulder. "Tell me every bit. Start with his face."

"So handsome. Brown eyes that sort of crinkle on the side, like even when he's not smiling, he's kind of smiling. Great hair. Tall. Probably younger than me."

Vivi whipped out her phone. "What's his name? We'll look him up."

"Christopher Saito," I said.

"Already on a first-name basis," said Vivi, tapping away. "Oh yes. He's hot," she said. She pinched the screen bigger and showed it to me. "That's him, right?"

My heart sped up. "Yep."

"Wow. What do you think he is? I'd guess something Latin, maybe Asian, but something else too," said Vivi. "Maybe Mexican? Italian? Some mixture of the gods and mortals?"

"I don't know," I said. "Saito sounds Japanese." It was Japanese; I had googled it.

"Paging Dr. Steamy," breathed Vivi. "So, there was something? A connection?"

"Yes, definitely an energy between us." I fanned myself. "This is ridiculous! I'm still technically married."

Vivi stopped laughing. "You and Jay do anything about the big D yet?"

I shrugged. "We both used the word 'divorce' and then he went to France. And then we haven't done anything about it."

"You're in limbo," said Vivi. "You need to fix that. You guys don't live together. You don't talk. You need to resolve things."

I felt a sense of dread, more at the idea of going through a divorce than actually being divorced. If I could just jump to the end.

Vivi stared at her phone. "You'd have to be in a coma to not react to this guy. Is he married? Before you schedule your bikini wax, maybe we need to find that out."

She tapped some more. "Can't find anything about a wife or kids." She set her phone down and picked at the melon slices she had brought as dessert.

Thinking about Jay just got me angry again. How he shut down emotionally whenever I was upset. How he dismissed my worries about Luke for so long. How he didn't believe me when I told him about stuff I could sense. How he always seemed to blame other people for his problems. I had started to understand that no one has that many bad bosses in a row. It was him. "I know I shouldn't care what other people think, but I don't think people will understand why."

"No one knows what it is like to live inside a marriage except the two people in it," said Vivi. "And even then, it's hard to agree on 'reality.'"

Vivi tossed the melon slice in the sink. "That's no dessert," she said in disgust. "What do you want? What do you really want?"

"Uhhh," I said. "I don't know." I refilled my wine glass. "I was only going to have one, but this kind of discussion calls for more."

Vivi got up, got herself a wine glass, and poured in a hefty amount. "This is no time for a cleanse."

We toasted and giggled.

Falling asleep later in a pleasant haze of wine and friendship, I thought about Vivi. Despite my fears for Joanna never abating, and my marriage issues, and my depleted funds, I was deeply grateful for Vivi. Although I never did answer that question: What did I want? Why was it so hard for me to know that when I knew so much about other people?

Chapter 4

In the morning I spent a little time picking out a nice outfit, mostly to please Lauren and her standard for how we present ourselves. It was more effort than I usually made, but I liked how I looked in my tan pants, scoop-necked t-shirt, and black girly-shaped safari jacket. I even added a turquoise tassel necklace. I made coffee and got a mumbled "hello" out of Cole as he shuffled out for an early workout, his slim frame hung about with two backpacks and a big water jug. Runners run, all the time. I allowed myself a moment of nostalgia even though he wasn't even gone yet.

I texted Emily and found out that Joanna was doing okay and had returned to consciousness, but Mr. Jacko had not fared so well. The carbon monoxide had come from a space heater Joanna had been running to dry out the carpet in the spare room, and Mr. Jacko, working near it for so long, had died in the Emergency Room. My stomach turned, and I felt like my coffee was about to come back up.

That was why Thomas had tried to get me to the spare room! A faulty space heater.

The sick feeling in my stomach seeped into the rest of my body as I tried to fight off the guilt. As I searched for my car keys, I couldn't shake off the guilt. My God, someone died. It didn't matter that Mr. Jacko was so unpleasant; he didn't deserve to die. If only I had gone into the room, maybe? If only I had— if I had what? What else could I have done? I felt awful but couldn't figure out what I could have done differently.

Where were those keys?

Eventually it occurred to me to retrace my steps from last night, and I found the keys in the laundry basket.

Of course, the key search made me late, yet again. Heading towards today's client, every spin of my tires ratcheted my anxiety up exponentially. Accident-related driving anxiety? Mr. Jacko's death? Fear of ghosts starting to find their way into my head? Or something about the house I was headed towards?

The most obvious explanation for my anxiety was that I was headed to a house with . . . reptiles. On our initial consult, I had seen a room lit up with heat lamps over big glass enclosures. I pushed the images from my head.

When she saw me pulling up at Rupert's, Lacey bounced out of her little green Kia. She was twenty years younger than me, three times better at organizing, and effortlessly stylish. Today she had on wide-legged green pants topped with an asymmetrical striped shirt tied at the waist.

"Sorry I'm late," I said.

"No worries," said Lacey, pulling her long black hair up into a knob on the top of her head. "Whoa," she said, turning to take in the lumpy brown yard, the stick remains of rosebushes, the peeling brown trim on cobwebby windows.

"She did tell you, right?" I said.

"About the reptiles?" said Lacey. "Yeah."

I waved a Chipotle gift card at her. "This is yours if you do that room."

Lacey snatched it from my hand. "Done," she said, slipping it into her little cross-shoulder pack. Lacey could always be bought with food. "Who're we working with here?"

"Rupert, a St. Claire professor, single guy in his forties, inherited the house from his grandparents. A total time capsule, nothing's been cleaned for years. He wants to fix it up because he's got a girlfriend now."

I didn't tell her about sensing that he was a virgin and desperately horny. Lauren had been annoyed when I told him to buy new bedding and wipe down the bathroom, and she had reminded me it's not our job to decorate. But his bedroom was old and gross, and I felt for him.

"This looks like a lipstick-on-a-pig kind of situation," Lacey said as we got our essentials boxes out of our trunks. We had bags for recycling, for trash, for donation. We had rubber gloves, marking pens, and all the other tools of the trade.

"Wait until you see the inside," I said, my throat closing as we started up the walk. The danger felt similar to Joanna's spare room—horror waiting in a room nearby. I felt a growing sense of dread with every step. I tried to tell myself I was probably just paranoid.

Rupert had the door open before we got to the porch.

"Hello!" he said, a tall scarecrow of a man, nodding and bowing over and over.

I introduced Lacey and told Rupert we'd start in his bedroom, fighting the urge to run back to my car.

As we walked past the reptile room, I held my breath, heart racing, stomach churning. I felt like I was in a horror movie, jumpy, waiting for Godzilla to spring through the closed door.

"All right," I said, breathing out when we had made it into Rupert's bedroom. "Let's see what we can do with the closets."

Dumping the stuff from the closet onto the bed, it became clear that Rupert had a uniform. Shirts were cotton button-downs or plaid flannel; pants were jeans or khakis. Countless washings had merged all the clothes into a narrow range of faded color.

"Do you keep clothes anywhere else?" Lacey asked, knowing we were to pull from every room when working on a category.

Rupert nodded and brought several armfuls of jackets and sweaters from somewhere else in the house.

"Shoes?" Lacey asked, and Rupert produced a pile of boat shoes and tennis shoes in various stages of decomposition. Lauren says we tend to buy the same things over and over, and the abundance of white shirts in my closet confirmed that Rupert wasn't the only one.

Two hours later, there was very little left that Rupert actually wanted to keep. The closet and drawers were almost empty, and bags in the hall that were headed for the dump were piled as high as the Grinch's sled.

Lacey narrowed her eyes at Rupert, "Joseph Banks and lululemon," she said.

"Huh?" said Rupert.

"Joseph's for a good professional look and lulu for some casual outfits. They have great stuff for guys. It's not a waste of money to invest in quality."

"Thank you!" said Rupert. "Very helpful." He opened his nightstand and grabbed a pen and notepad.

I glanced at the open drawer and saw a box of condoms. Eek.

It hadn't taken me long to realize how intimate this job was, being exposed to the hemorrhoid cream and ratty underwear, the junk drawers, and the recycling spilling over with beer cans. I was realizing that everybody was putting on a good front.

"I love it!" Rupert enthused, looking around his bedroom. "And I just can't believe you found my alligator belt."

"If you want to find something, clean up," I quoted Lauren, thinking about how long it had taken me to find my keys that morning. "Now the bathroom."

Lacey pointed towards the jumble in the hallway. "Maybe we should load some of the bags in the cars?"

"Right after the bathroom," I said.

Looking at the stuffed cupboards under the double sink, Rupert said, "You can throw it all out; it's all my grandparents' stuff." There were bottles of ancient mouthwash, used razors, half a bag of Epsom salts, and a shoebox full of various-sized Band-Aids that were so old the paper had become translucent. There was a bag of ratty Ace bandages, boxes of brown hair dye, and two bags of pennies. I told Rupert to take the pennies to a coin counting machine as soon as we finished today.

"Put them in your car now," I added, and he grabbed them and disappeared.

Several items later, Lacey pulled out a bulky white thing that looked like papier maché. "What's this?" she asked, flipping it around. I gagged. It was a mold of a man's genitals. And they weren't small.

"Holy shit," I said. "If Rupert takes after Grandpa . . ."

Lacey chortled and peered into the cupboard. "Where's Grandma's? Would only be fair."

"Rupert's got some deviant grandparents," I giggled, then turned to see Rupert standing looking at us, slack-jawed and red-faced.

I felt a flood of shame. I try so hard to be kind; how could I have done that? Not to mention, Lauren would not appreciate my acting so unprofessional.

"Have to make a call," spluttered Rupert, darting away.

"Crap," said Lacey. "We're going to hell."

"Rupert!" I yelled, jumping up and limping after him with my throbby ankle, Lacey on my heels.

I cut the corner into the hall too close and ran into a pile of bags. Lacey banged into me and knocked me over the scattered blobs of black plastic, arms flailing. As I went down, I careened into the next door, and it flung open as I landed face down in the mess. Something scurried over my back and I heard Lacey scream.

And then scream again. And then it escalated into a pitch and volume I wouldn't have thought possible.

I flipped over and watched in horror as Lacey flung her leg back and forth with a huge lizard clamped on it.

Oh my God, that was the thing that had scurried over my back.

"Who opened the door?" cried Rupert, appearing above me from inside the reptile room.

Screaming, I scrambled on all fours down the hall. Once I was free of the garbage bags, I somehow made it to my feet and flew out the front door and into my car.

Doors closed, heart pounding so hard I thought it was going to explode, I leaned on the steering wheel, gasping for air.

Lacey pounded out of the house, still shrieking, but mercifully, lizard-free. She ran to her car and yanked on the door, only to find it locked. She stumbled to my car, pulled the passenger door open, lunged in, and scratched frantically at the door to get it closed.

"Ohmygodohmygodohmygod," Lacey sobbed.

Rupert appeared by Lacey's window, and I hit the "lock" button.

He could die a virgin for all I cared.

When Lacey didn't respond to him, Rupert came around to my side.

"Tell the doctor that was a green iguana lizard," he yelled through the window.

The doctor?

Holy shit. It was poisonous?

"No no no no no!" sobbed Lacey.

I tried to open the window, but I didn't have the car key. I opened the door a crack and held it from going further.

"What the hell are you talking about?" I said to Rupert.

"It is so rare for him to bite," Rupert said. "You must have scared him."

"No! The part about a doctor!" I yelled.

"Oh, right. They are poisonous. I don't think you can die from a bite, but you better take her to a doctor."

"Jesus Christ!" I yelled. "Go get our purses. NOW!"

Rupert jumped, then ran into the house and returned with our bags. I opened the door to get them, and he said, "See you in an hour or two?"

I grabbed the bags, shut the door, and took off for the hospital.

Apparently, they'll give a Ph.D. to any old idiot.

Chapter 5

"She's been poisoned!" I yelled as we ran into the ER. I had left the car in the "Dropoff Only" lane out front. "And she has chest pains!"

Lacey gave me a side look, but chest pains get the fastest attention, and I wasn't above lying. I looked around—yep, good decision to lie. The waiting room was packed with people who all looked like they had made bad decisions.

They took Lacey quickly, and, after I parked the car, I collapsed onto a waiting room seat. I leaned forward with my elbows onto my thighs and stared at the floor, trying to slow my breathing.

On the plus side, I had forgotten my driving anxiety during the rush to the ER. Good to know that bigger dangers squashed smaller ones.

"You okay?" came from a woman sitting on my right side.

I sat up and looked at her. She was well into her seventies and dressed in a full denim jumpsuit, her white hair permed into a dandelion halo that stuck out at least five inches. Bright pink lipstick nicely complemented the hair. She patted my leg. "Take some deep breaths. I heard you guys come in—that gal really poisoned?"

"By a huge lizard," I said.

"Oh good Lord, have mercy," said jumpsuit lady. "I'm going to add her to my prayers," she said, closing her eyes and mumbling softly.

My phone quacked: Lauren. I grabbed it and punched "Accept" to stop the sound. Wouldn't want to interrupt jumpsuit lady's prayers.

"What's going on?" Lauren sounded angry. "Rupert says you LEFT?"

"One of his lizards got loose and BIT Lacey," I said.

"Oh my God," said Lauren. "Ew. Is she okay?"

"I don't know yet," I said. "We're at the ER."

"What did you do? You weren't supposed to go in that room."

"*I* didn't do anything," I said, angry that she would somehow imply it was my fault. I was still feeling sick with guilt over Mr. Jacko. "And guess what? The plumber at Joanna's? He died!"

"Oh my God," said Lauren. She got silent, perhaps finally understanding how close we all had come to dying. "I don't know what to think about that," she said.

"Yeah, me either. I'll call you later," I added and hung up. How could I keep getting this all so wrong? I ignored Thomas, and Mr. Jacko died. I ignored the feeling of doom going to Rupert's, and Lacey got bitten by a poisonous lizard.

Moments later, Lauren texted: *Headed to Rupert's to calm him down. UR doing afternoon consultation, will send address.*

Ha! She could have Rupert. Then I typed back: *Make sure the lizard's been caught.* Lauren could be so annoying, but the thought of the lizard coming after her lasered through the thick rind of my anger. She was my little sister, after all.

I turned my ringer off and went back to leaning on my knees, staring at the ground, focusing on my breathing.

A pair of beat-up running shoes appeared in front of me. I looked up to see Dr. Saito, smiling.

"Is it Lacey? Is she okay?"

He nodded. "She'll be fine. We were able to give her some antivenom. She was very anxious for me to let you know."

I sat back and took a deep breath. "Thank God."

Dr. Saito sat down in the empty seat to my left. "This is two days in a row."

I closed my eyes for a moment in agreement. "Yes." I laughed, too high-pitched to be cute, then opened them. "Crazy."

"One more visit, and I'll start to think this is no coincidence," he said, twisted sideways to look at me.

My heart started beating faster. "These days I seem to be surrounded by drama."

"Must keep life interesting." I loved the sound of his voice. I loved his eyes on me. I didn't want it to stop.

"You could say many things about me, but the fact that my life is interesting these days is probably the most true," I agreed.

"'May you live in interesting times' is actually a Chinese curse. Did you know that?" Dr. Saito said, standing up.

"That fits," I said, taking another deep breath. I just couldn't seem to keep enough oxygen in these days. Either out of panic or attraction. My poor lungs.

"Here's hoping it's not a curse for you," Dr. Saito said, running his hand through his hair.

I smiled inside; I thought only women touched their hair when they were interested in someone. And, for once, my extra senses were welcome, because I knew he was interested.

"Thank you, and thanks for taking care of Lacey," I said.

Dr. Saito gave a little nod and almost a half bow. "My pleasure," he said and, with a last lingering bit of eye contact, walked away.

"Whew!" Jean jumpsuit lady was fanning herself with a magazine. "What's your health care plan?" she asked me, eyes glued to Dr. Saito's retreating figure. "I may need to trade up."

Chapter 6

After Lacey's boyfriend arrived to wait for her, I found the non-highway route to the consultation and headed to Matinsville. Twenty minutes later, I pulled up in front of a cute, one-story bungalow painted pale gray with white trim, its windows shaded by old-fashioned, blue-and-white-striped awnings. The awnings and paint were both faded, but there was a dignified neatness to it.

At my ring, the door opened about six inches, and a puff of white wavy hair edged around the frame, just above the doorknob. "Hello?" A pair of bright eyes peered up at me.

"Hi, Mrs. Maccoby," I said. "I'm Izzy Bishop from Order Out of Chaos."

Mrs. Maccoby pulled her head back and swung the door open. "Come in."

The owner matched the house—good bones, cheerful, but weathered by time. She was maybe four-six and looked like she was the great-grandma matriarch of the Keebler elves, an impression strengthened by the delicious smell of baking permeating the house. A big smile pushed shiny red cheeks up towards friendly eyes as she smoothed her faded white apron.

"Call me Lucille; Mrs. Maccoby was my teacher name."

No wonder I felt immediately at ease with her. "What grade?"

"All of elementary at one point or another, but mostly third," said Lucille.

I'd bet all the cookies in her kitchen that Lucille was beloved by legions of students. I wanted to crawl up into her lap and have her read me stories. For the first time all day, my heart rate slowed to a pleasant tempo.

"Can I get you coffee? Tea?" asked Lucille.

"No, thank you," I said.

"How about some cookies? Fresh out of the oven."

"Yes, please," I said.

Like a cartoon character floating towards a cooling pie, I followed Lucille to the kitchen, a small but charming yellow-and-white room. Along one wall a white display hutch was packed with fancy dishes and whimsical baskets, lined across the top with artificial flowers; in the opposite corner was a hutch with much the same; the counters were surprisingly clear. Obviously, her baking space was a priority. The round pedestal kitchen table was covered in stacks of papers, the tallest almost a foot.

"Obviously, I need help with these papers," said Lucille, gesturing towards the table. "Mostly medical statements, insurance and the like. They just . . . accumulated."

"It can get really personal," I warned. "Will you mind if we see the details?"

"Goodness no, I don't care." She picked up a cake stand cover to reveal a stack of gorgeous chocolate chip cookies. They were huge and lumpy with chocolate and nuts, and I was desperate for one.

"Here you go," she said. I took a bite, and it was everything the smell suggested it would be. Crisp on the outside, chewy in the middle, flavored out the wazoo.

"Mmm," I hummed as I ate. "Unbelievable,"

I tried to remember Lauren's instructions. "We're pretty booked, but since your project is small, we could probably squeeze it in sometime in the next couple of weeks. Can we call you back with a date?"

"I am going on a big trip in three weeks, so it would have to be before or after that." Lucille radiated a childlike excitement. "A tour of the Greek islands. Have always wanted to go."

"That sounds amazing. We will definitely fit you in before then." I didn't care what Lauren said. I wanted to work here.

Lucille stared at me, quiet and intense. Finally, she said, "Hmm," like she approved of something.

My body buzzed, like electricity was trying to come through my skin.

Without breaking eye contact, Lucille said, "You have the sight."

Lucille was so warm and loving that, for the first time ever, I didn't feel like a weirdo admitting it. "Sort of."

"Me too!" she said, laughing with glee.

I sank onto a barstool by her little counter. "All your life? I need help! How do you know? How do you do this stuff? Has it ruined relationships?"

Lucille pulled a barstool around the other side of the counter to face me. "All in good time, my dear. Tell me about it."

"I've always had some kind of weird sensing," I said. "I'd just have an impulse and then it would turn out to mean something. Like, for no reason, I refused to go to a sleepover I had looked forward to, and then the sleepover house caught on fire." I could barely breathe with the need to tell her everything.

Lucille interrupted me. "Slow down. We have time."

"It just made me feel . . . so weird," I said. "Why was this happening to me and no one else? And if I sensed something bad, I felt like I was supposed to somehow prevent it, but I couldn't."

What a relief to tell someone whose face didn't tighten with disbelief, like my mother, like Jay. "So I just ignored that stuff. Managed to keep it from happening much. Then, a year and a half ago, I had a car accident on my way to pick up my son Luke who was drunk at a party. And he ended up getting help with his addictions, so that was good. But I was in a coma and had a near-death experience, and when I woke up, it was like the sensing was turned way up. But not in any specific way. Like, I couldn't tell if I was just thinking something on my own or picking up something from . . . somewhere else. And then this week, a dead man appeared in my brain when I touched his wife's wedding dress."

Lucille slowly nodded. "Sounds like you have a couple of the clairs. Clairvoyant, which is gathering information from other than your five senses. And there are specific ones—sounds like you have clairtangency, which is when touching an object brings information."

"Yes! I touched the dress, and the dead guy came through."

"You need to know this is a gift, a lovely wonderful gift," Lucille said.

I struggled to not burst into tears. It had felt so weird and isolating.

"And there's a contract there, you and Luke," said Lucille.

"Meaning?" I asked.

"Some believe we have made contracts with people in our lives. Some, in particular, can be . . . dramatic. I sense a deep connection there. The two of you, for each other."

"He was on a really bad path," I said. "And he felt awful about my accident. So if I had to do it all over . . ."

"You would." Lucille smiled and patted my hand. "You are a light. You have a gift. Don't let anyone tell you any different."

My whole body started to unclench.

"I'll bet people are drawn to you," said Lucille. "I'll bet you've read people really well all your life."

I nodded in agreement.

"People can feel that you see them."

"Yes," I agreed.

"In fact," she said, "you read other people so well that you don't know where they leave off and you start."

"Yes! It's like I don't really even know who I am. Like, is it the ghost who is anxious or me? Is it my friend who is depressed or me?"

I filled her in on how I had ignored the signals from Thomas and the plumber died. How I ignored my fears about Rupert's house and Lacey paid the price. How I had talked myself out of feeling what I felt. How deeply guilty all of that made me feel.

I licked my finger to pick up a stray crumb on the plate she had slid under the cookie. "I don't like how this is all going now. How I get a fear about something but I can't tell exactly what it is, but then something bad does happen and I didn't stop it."

Lucille nodded in empathy. "Yes, that stings."

"What am I supposed to do?" I asked.

"Hmm." Lucille stared at me, thinking. Finally, she said, "I'm sensing that you don't pay attention to yourself. You don't trust what you think about yourself, your own life."

I nodded. That was true. "But how does that relate?"

"You aren't going to be able to know about other people if you won't let yourself know about yourself." Lucille stopped, letting that sink in and then continued. "You are coming to a fork in the stream, of a sort. And you can let other people paddle the canoe, or you can pick the direction."

"How do I do that?" I asked. I've never been a planner. I just react in the moment and get what I get. Which, until now, had seemed fine.

Well, if not fine, okay.

Or, if not okay, tolerable.

Or maybe it wasn't even tolerable.

Lucille put her hand over her heart. "Deep down, you do know what you want. You are afraid of acting on that knowledge."

"I feel more compelled to act on a fear for someone else," I said.

"Same, same," said Lucille.

I looked through the window at Lucille's tiny backyard. Pink flowering bushes lined the fence and pots of herbs sat on either side of an old-fashioned bench swing with a fluttery canvas awning over it. I wanted to be five years old and sit in that swing and do nothing but read and sleep with the sun on my face. I sensed the pot of rosemary longing for the sunniest corner.

I gestured outside. "That rosemary would rather be in the sun."

Lucille laughed. "When I put her there, she complains it's too hot. But back to you."

"The problem is that I can't control the senses," I said. "They just come or don't come."

"To know about other people, you are going to have to let yourself know about yourself," Lucille said. "Know like the rosemary knows. It really can be that simple. It wants the sun. And then it wants the shade. We are allowed to change our desires. It happens all the time. What do you want?"

"I'm not sure. I guess I'll pay more attention?" It was a weak answer, and we both knew it.

"You'll get there," said Lucille.

Chapter 7

The next morning was devoted to a playroom cleanout that initially triggered a deep nostalgia but quickly made me grateful to be past the toddler age. Seemingly, every toy was battery-operated, and the cacophony of testing to determine whether they were working left me with a jangly head.

I had stayed up late reading about sensing beyond the five senses and was overwhelmed by the variety of descriptions of senses, not to mention the volume of crazies. I hadn't come up with much more of a plan than to just really pay attention to what I was picking up about different people and try to discern if it felt like it was coming from regular or extrasensing.

As I finished, Lauren called. "Joanna is out of the hospital. Go over and see how she is doing and get a feel for when we can get back to work."

Annoying but, for once, it was exactly what I wanted to do anyway. I breathed a sigh of relief when I turned into Joanna's driveway, toddler toys and anxious driving behind me.

I rang the bell, and eventually the door cracked open and a man with dark hair and blue eyes narrowed in suspicion peeked out. He said a disdainful "Yes?" and managed to seem like he was looking down on me even though he was my height.

"I'm Izzy Bishop, here to see Joanna," I said.

"She's had a recent health scare; she can't see you," the man said, starting to close the door.

I stuck my hand over the door frame. "She asked me to come," I said, as the door was pulled open wider to reveal Emily.

"Izzy! Come in," Emily said, giving the man a dirty look. "Marco, this is Izzy. She saved my mom's life!"

Marco shrugged and stalked away.

"Sorry about that. He's not very friendly," whispered Emily, closing the door behind me. "Thomas was my mother's second husband, and Marco is one of Thomas's kids, which technically makes him my stepbrother but I don't think of him that way." Emily shook her head. "Acts like he owns the place—which they all will at some point, but not yet. Thank you again for saving my mother. It's so scary, I still can't believe it."

I felt a pang of guilt that I let it get as far as it did.

Emily led me past the big showy rooms at the front of the house. "Mom's better but, apparently, it is common to have memory loss, so she wanted to find out what you remember."

I let my mind wander around Emily and felt a reserve in her that bordered on prickliness. Also something illicit, a heat that was hidden and in some way wrong. I couldn't get much more than that.

"You met Marco, and this is Karl," said Emily as we reached a smaller living room where Joanna was slumped in an armchair. "Another one of Thomas's sons. This is Izzy," she said to Marco and Karl.

Karl jumped up. "Here, take my seat," he said, even though this "small" living room was four times the size of my living room and had plenty of seating. Like the bigger rooms, this one was full of dark wood, heavy furniture, and lots of stuffy oil paintings, but there was more of a feeling that people actually lived in here. Every surface and shelf was crammed with books and tchotchkes. I itched to open the heavy curtains to get light into the room and clean out at least seventy-five percent of the stuff. I felt like the room was suffocating and begging for help. Could a couch tell me what was going on around here? I asked, but the couch stayed silent.

"I need to move around. Can't sit still," Karl flashed a smile and wandered towards the wall of overflowing bookcases.

Although I could tell they were brothers, Marco seemed more of a carefully curated broker type, with his short haircut, bland conservative clothes, and stiff lean posture, while Karl was more of a rebel, with ripped jeans, a black hoodie that strained against wide shoulders and muscles, and wavy dark hair that must have needed a lot of product to get its height and swoosh. Although the charm and energy I could feel coming off of Karl seemed intentional—manipulative, even—it was more appealing than Marco's dour scowling. A lot of girls would go for his type. Grown women too. Marco was handsome in his own way, but he'd be too much of a project for me.

I wondered why Marco and Karl were here. I had had the impression that they weren't really around Joanna's life, and there was an unsettled vibe in the room, almost like Joanna was the one who didn't belong here.

Joanna looked ten years older than the last time I saw her—hair flattened against her head, face ashen, energy muted.

"Don't get up," I said, leaning down to give her a hug. "I'm just so glad you are okay."

"Thank you," said Joanna, her voice wavery. "Bless you."

"I won't stay long," I said. "I'm sure you could still use rest," I added, hoping to give others the hint.

Emily compressed her lips. "That's what I told her, but she wanted to wait until she saw you." I felt Emily's irritation that her mother liked me so much. Then her reluctant manners took over. "Would you like some coffee? It's Ethiopian Dimtu. Mom's got a million flavors."

"No, but thanks," I said.

"So, what happened?" asked Joanna.

"We were cleaning out your bedroom," I said. "Then Lauren got called to another client's house. Do you remember that?"

Joanna nodded yes.

"Then you were feeling tired and sat down on the bed. When I came back from getting you water, you looked asleep but . . ." I felt a spasm of guilt, and my whole abdomen tightened up. I got an image of Thomas, arms folded, shaking his head at my failure to notice Joanna's state fast enough. "Then I noticed your face too close to a pile of clothes and when I moved it, I could tell something was wrong."

Joanna stared intently at my forehead. "Are you hurt?"

Everyone stared at the bump on my head.

I flushed. "I, uh, slipped, getting you out to the patio."

"Oh no," said Joanna. "I'm so sorry."

I waved a hand. "It's nothing, I'm fine." Marco couldn't hide his smug contempt, looking at me like I had confirmed his idea that I was a bumbling idiot.

"How did you know to take me outside?" asked Joanna.

The million-dollar question. I was tempted to wipe the contempt off of Marco's face by telling them it was his father who told me what to do. I felt a stern *No!* from Thomas. "I guess I had the idea you needed fresh air."

"Thank you," sighed Joanna.

"And then I called 911, and that's about it," I said. I'd have to tell her about Thomas later, when no one else was around.

"Poor Mr. Jacko," said Joanna.

"I know," I said, and everyone made little sad murmurs.

"Crazy that a space heater could be so deadly," said Karl.

"Why a gas one?" asked Emily. "That seems dangerous."

"I'm not sure where it came from, but I found it in the garage," said Joanna. "When the bathroom flooded and the carpet was all wet, it started to smell mildewy, so I thought it would dry it."

"You just found it?" Emily asked.

"I think it was with the tennis team garage sale stuff," said Joanna.

"Why are you holding that anyway?" asked Emily. "Don't let people take advantage of you."

"I canceled it," said Joanna, her voice faint. "Lauren convinced me garage sales are not worth it. She'll get rid of the stuff. And I'll make a donation to the tennis team."

Joanna turned towards me. "Tell Lauren we can work on the garages tomorrow. It will be a good distraction."

"What are you doing in the garages?" asked Karl.

"Just making space to move some furniture during the gala," said Joanna.

"The gala?" asked Marco, his voice tight. "The Heart Gala?"

"Yes, I told you all about it. I bought a table for the family to attend," said Joanna.

"It's going to be *here*?" said Marco.

"Yes. Since the fire at the Saint-James Hotel, they can't have it there," said Joanna.

"We were never told it was to be moved! All those people in this house?" said Marco, eyes flashing with outrage.

"In a tent in the backyard. But access to the house . . . Since Thomas died from heart disease . . . I mean, it's actually *named* after him, as you know." Joanna shrunk further into her chair.

Marco glared at me. "I suppose this was your bright idea?"

"I would love to claim it, because I think it is brilliant, but I'm not that bright." I could feel a flash of amusement from Joanna.

Karl had been opening cabinets, brushing his hand along shelves. He picked up a little battered medicine tin. "Dad and his collections. Are you really afraid someone is going to steal this, Marco-boy?" Karl snickered at his brother.

Marco shrugged, a pretense at calm. "Who knows? Could be something priceless in one of those collections."

Looking at Karl, an image of a baby stroller popped into my mind. Hmm, I didn't see a ring on his finger, but that didn't mean anything. I wasn't wearing one either.

I realized I had stared too long when Karl smirked at me. Oh my God, he thought I was attracted to him. That came in loud and clear. How embarrassing.

Marco shook his head at us. I could read that perfectly too. Jealous of Karl for so easily attracting women and contemptuous of anyone falling for his smarmy charm.

"I didn't think anyone would mind," Joanna whispered, her eyes finding me for help.

"I'm going to my room, see if there's anything I should move out of here," said Marco, standing up, his implication clear.

"I might as well look around for my notebooks," said Karl, setting the tin back in the collection.

After Marco and Karl disappeared, Joanna said, "Oh dear. It didn't even occur to me to ask anyone . . ."

"This is too much stress," said Emily. "Tell them to have the gala somewhere else."

"How did they even know I had the . . . incident?" Joanna asked.

Emily looked sheepish. "I panicked and texted them. And Kimberly. Just felt like family should know. Even though they haven't been around since . . ." Emily trailed off and Joanna winced. Since Thomas's funeral, I'd bet. A wave of sadness confirmed I was on the right track. Interesting that Thomas was around but wasn't trying to contact his sons. I invited him to weigh in on that but got nothing more than a tingle on the back of my neck.

"Mom, you should go lie down," Emily said.

"Are you sure you are up for working again tomorrow?" I asked. "Are you sure you are up for the gala?" I didn't know why I asked it. That train was long out of the station and speeding at us.

"Absolutely!" said Joanna.

"Oh my gosh, I just realized, we never finished your room," I said, looking at my watch, I was already late for my next job.

Joanna shrugged. "Maybe tomorrow before the garage?"

We agreed on that, and I gave her another hug and then hustled out.

Chapter 8

Twenty minutes later, I was parked and stepping over an impressive array of kiddie toys in a driveway at the end of a cul-de-sac. A disheveled woman came out of the front door, wearing a dark blue t-shirt and jeans, her brown hair in a messy high bun.

"Hey, Patty!" I said, my mood lifting at her cheerful smile. I had met Patty while working for the Montavilla Education Foundation—unpaid parents perpetually fundraising to supplement the inadequate state funding for public schools. Privately, I thought we should just increase the one time "donation" of every parent and be done with it. It still would be cheaper than private school, by far.

"Where are you headed?" I asked.

"Staying here, just moving to a bigger house." Patty gestured towards the overflowing garage. "I'm out of room; the garage is my shipping warehouse and the kitchen is just too small for my business anymore."

"Oh yeah, you have a keto thing going, right?"

"Gluten-free," corrected Patty. "But adding keto soon. I started a couple of years ago when the twins were diagnosed gluten-sensitive. Hah, they are everything-sensitive." She sighed and then perked up again. "My cookies always were popular, and then I, uh, entered a new space." Her eyes gleamed.

Practice the senses. What was she thinking about? I let my focus go soft. Something green, maybe plants? Vegan?

"I now make gluten-free edible cookies," grinned Patty. "Very popular."

"Aren't all cookies edible?" I asked, and then I got it. "Oh! Edibles."

"Plenty of people in California like their weed but don't like their gluten."

"Brilliant," I said.

Patty rolled her eyes. "There's only so much tennis and book club/wine club shit I can take. And with all the volunteering, I realized if I'm going to work that hard at something, I might as well make some money."

Patty continued. "Anyway, I never did organize this place well, and Kimberly told me about Order Out of Chaos."

"I'm going to have to do something nice for Kimberly," I said. Kimberly was not only my physical therapist and Joanna's niece, she was also apparently Order Out of Chaos's best publicist.

"Let's start in Charlie's room," Patty said, leading the way. We stared at the clothes covering every surface.

"I guess we could start with the clothes." I laughed. Impossible to do anything else.

"We can do the drawers first; he doesn't use anything in them," Patty said. "I've given up." She paused. "I'm not sure I'm ready for a teenager. Charlie is super grumpy and angry all the time."

"Teens are tough," I agreed, pulling out the top drawer. "Pick whatever you want to save for Tommy and Mark. The rest gets given away."

"Huh!" said Patty. "I already gave some of these clothes to Mark but I can't keep it straight in the laundry. So it ends up back in here. Same thing from Mark to Tommy."

"I've got you," I said. "The Sharpie dot system! We'll put one dot on the label of all of Charlie's clothes. When you give the shirt to Mark, add a second dot. And a third dot when it goes to Tommy."

"Genius," said Patty.

I pulled out a couple of Sharpies, and we made quick work of adding dots. With every piece of clothing I touched, I got a stronger impression that Charlie was gay. Afraid to even let himself think it, let alone tell anyone. No wonder he was grumpy. Poor kid.

The information just came. I didn't know how. I also didn't know what to do about it. Maybe I could find a way to help without actually telling Patty what I was sensing.

As we worked on the floor clothes, Patty said, "Hey, is your mother doing okay?"

"She's had a series of mini-strokes," I said. "She's not as proper as she used to be."

"That explains it!"

"What did she do?" I asked.

"It was at church, at Moms' Council, and Cindy Lassiter was talking about how she can't stop snacking at night and your mom told her to have more sex. Said that's what she does."

"That's the disinhibition," I said, laughing.

"I have a feeling your dad is happy at home," said Patty, more at ease now that I was laughing.

"Mom *is* in great shape," I said, giggling.

"I'm going to give you some edible cookies for her— might help," said Patty.

"Okay." Seemed like a bad idea to add to the disinhibition, but I didn't want to offend her.

We looked around the neatened room.

"If we kept things this neat all the time, we wouldn't have to move," said Patty, laughing. She pulled her hair down from its bun and reworked it. "Glass of iced tea?"

I looked at my watch to check my time. "Yes!" I said and followed her to a small galley kitchen that was barely more than a hallway.

"You get all those cookies made here?" I said, impressed.

"Yes, but I'm moving into an industrial kitchen." Patty looked around. "Shoot, I need more bags from the garage." She pulled a Ziplock bag out of a drawer and slid two cookies off a baking tray into the bag. "Not the fancy packaging, but give these a go for your mom."

Patty launched into an enthusiastic description of all the benefits of weed, finishing with "I don't even drink alcohol anymore; it seems so toxic. Time comes, I'm going to tell my kids I'd rather they have weed than alcohol. That can just ruin lives."

"Mm-hmm," I said.

Patty clapped her hand over her mouth. "Oh I'm sorry; I forgot about Luke . . ."

"It's okay," I said. "You aren't wrong about alcohol. Of course, there are so many things that can be going on for kids that parents don't pick up on."

"Right?" said Patty, taking a sip of her tea.

"But, you know, some parents get pretty creative. Like, I saw a story about a dad who was pretty sure his son was gay, and he called a gay bar and asked for help in how to be supportive when he talked to him about it. One person after another got on the phone with him to give him advice."

"What a great idea," said Patty.

"It wouldn't bother me if Luke or Cole were gay, but I'm afraid I wouldn't know what to say right away."

"Yeah," Patty said. "But I guess I'd just hug them and say I love them, no matter what."

"Yes," I said. "Just love them. No matter what."

Maybe it was possible to use the skills without anyone knowing.

Chapter 9

In the morning, I remembered I had meant to do laundry. Whoops. I sniffed my way through a pile of shirts on the chair, finding a blue and white checked cotton shirt with no stains or smell. I fished a pair of tapered dark jeans from a pile on the floor and was rewarded by finding my missing favorite shoes under the pile. I slipped on the gray Dr. Scholl's espadrilles, the gateway drug for comfy shoes, then dug around my jewelry box to find an old pair of solid gold earrings because my ears were reacting badly to the cheap stuff these days. Compression socks and readers couldn't be far behind.

When I arrived at Joanna's, Vivi had just pulled up next to Karl's blue Nissan. What was he doing here again?

Vivi and I climbed out of our cars and high-fived. I loved it when we got to work together. Even when she refused to drive me.

As we walked up the steps, Vivi looked around, then whispered, "Is he here?"

"Who?"

"The dead guy," she said, hitting the doorbell.

"Not yet."

"Actually, I'm not sure if I want to know," she said, uncharacteristically meek.

Karl opened the door. "Hello," he said, smiling but cool. His charisma was like a neon light blinking in the window of a bar—something that catches your eye, but doesn't necessarily promise anything good.

"Karl, this is Vivi," I said, and as he nodded, his eyes blinked an up-and-down look at Vivi so fast it was almost imperceptible.

"Nice to meet you," he said, pushing up the sleeves on his hoodie, like he was trying to reveal his muscles.

"Charmed," said Vivi, as we all walked towards the kitchen.

I managed to bump into Karl as we walked and was hit with a wave of disappointment and sadness. There he was, Thomas reacting to Karl.

Do you miss him? Are you disappointed? I silently asked Thomas.

More cool air on the back of my neck, but no answer from Thomas.

Why don't you want to connect with Karl?

Again, no answer.

The kitchen was large, with creamy-beige cabinets, warm honey hardwood floors, and French doors leading onto a flagstone patio. OOC hadn't gotten to this room yet, and the counters were almost as cluttered as my own. Added to the normal mix of papers, canisters, and bags of coffee were four foil-covered casserole dishes. Word must have gotten out that Joanna had been in the hospital.

Joanna was sitting at the long table, still in her robe, hair uncombed, face pale.

"Sorry to start so early," I said. "Hoping to finish up your room before we start on the garage. This is Vivi; she's going to help. Lauren will be here right after her parent-teacher conference."

"Nice to meet you," said Joanna. "Sorry I'm not dressed. Karl surprised me this morning," she added, a fake cheer to her voice.

"I don't have a gig tonight, so I've got all day," Karl said, pulling out a chair, sitting down and man-spreading his legs.

"Are you in a band?" asked Vivi.

"Yep," said Karl.

"That's cool," said Vivi. "Would I have heard of you?"

"KalKrew," said Karl. "With two Ks."

Vivi shook her head in disappointment. "I've got to get out more. Was a day where . . ." Her eyes went hazy and a faint smile appeared.

"Karl's a really good musician," said Joanna. "Works so hard; he even drives for Uber."

Vivi glanced around at the huge mansion we were standing in.

"We are house-rich but cash-poor," Joanna said with a faint smile, picking up on her unasked question.

Karl shrugged. "You do what you need to do," he said.

"And who you need to do, I'll bet," whispered Vivi, low enough that only I could hear it.

"I better get dressed so you can get in my room," Joanna said, using both hands to push herself up from her chair and shuffling out.

"I'm going to go poke around the garage," said Karl, popping up and sauntering out the other direction.

"Stop it with the comments," I said. "He could have heard you!"

"You know he's killing it out there. In a band? Looking like that? Please. I wasn't married, I would be all over that."

"You talk a big game," I said. "You're the happiest married person I know."

Vivi shrugged as we walked towards Joanna's room. "Don't tell anyone. It's kind of embarrassing now that half of Montavilla have split up."

I winced.

"Whoops," said Vivi. "Sorry not sorry."

I stopped walking and looked around as if suspicious.

Vivi stopped too. "Is the ghost here?" she whispered.

I jumped at Vivi and said "Boo!"

Vivi screeched and staggered against the wall. "What? Was that him?"

She saw me laughing and slammed her fists to her hips. "Not funny."

"Sorry not sorry," I said.

Joanna was dressed, and we settled her on the couch in the TV area of her suite to supervise. Vivi found the plastic folding board and made quick work of the sweaters, arranging the perfectly folded stacks into a rainbow wall. Stepping back from admiring her work, she looked at my efforts with the hanging clothes and shook her head. "By type and then, within that, by color," she said, quickly fixing my error. Sunglasses, jewelry, scarves, and other accessories were organized into the drawers under the hanging racks, and then we went to work on the active wear.

"You really have a knack for this," I said to Vivi as we slid the last pair of yoga pants into its vertical stack in a drawer.

"With four boys, it was just survival," she said.

We brought Joanna into the closet, and I pointed out the backwards arrangement of the hangers. "After you wear something, hang it back up over the front of the bar. That way, you'll be able to tell which clothes you don't wear. In two months, anything still hanging backwards gets the boot."

Someday, I'd have to try that myself. Not sure what the procedure was for the clothes on my floor, though. Or the chair. Or Jay's side of the bed, which had turned into a storage pile.

"Look at this closet! I love it!" Joanna slid open a drawer. "My sunglasses, all in one place!" She opened the scarf drawer. "Perfect!" She ran her hand along the skirt of the tangerine dress which we had hung on a hook for display. "So nice," she murmured.

Lauren appeared in the closet doorway. "This looks great—now, time for the garage."

In the kitchen we found a man standing next to a box on the counter.

"Hello!" he said. "Reinforcements are here! Put me to work."

"Oh, I was out of Yield. Thank you," said Joanna, moving to give him a hug. She pulled back. "This is Jacques, another one of Thomas's sons. He's a vintner! His wine is so good." She pointed at the box.

Like Marco and Karl, Jacques had blue eyes and brown hair; in his case, the hair was brushed back from his face in a wave and left longer around the ears and back. He was dressed in well-fitting jeans, a checked linen shirt, and a copper-colored suede jacket. He looked like a gentleman farmer.

Why were Thomas's kids showing up to "help" when they had ignored Joanna for so long? I knew they had been mostly grown by the time that Joanna and Thomas had married, and my impression had been that they weren't really around her much.

Jacques moved over toward the coffee maker. "Let me just fuel up." Seeing it empty, he said, "I'll make more. Marco and Serena are on their way too." He picked through the bags of coffee. "Wow, so many choices. But yuck, blueberry coffee? Definitely not that one."

"Maybe you could move a comfortable chair to the garage for Joanna to sit in," said Lauren. I kind of admired her bossiness, the way she leaned in and made it a superpower.

"I'm on it," said Jacques, disappearing as water started gurgling in the machine.

"So, Jacques works for a winery?" I asked Joanna, thinking about Thomas's alcoholism and sobriety. "Was that a concern for Thomas?" Even as I asked it, I felt a stab of pain go through my chest and the back of my neck prickle. Of course it was.

Vivi saw my little wince, and her eyes got big. She looked over both shoulders, as if there was a chance she'd see Thomas floating towards her.

"Oh yes. Part of the reason Thomas didn't invest when Jacques asked. Although he really didn't have that kind of money anyway. People see this house and think Thomas was rich, but he spent a lot on his dad when he was sick and then, of course, gave half to his ex-wife when they divorced. But yes, he was worried that Jacques could end up like him."

"And has he?" I asked.

"Not that I can see," said Joanna.

Chapter 10

In the garage we discovered Karl had opened all four bay doors and already pulled a bunch of stuff onto the driveway.

I felt like I could see blue electricity zigzagging out of Lauren's head. Interesting to start seeing actual colors around people. "Ahh, we need to organize how we do this," Lauren said, pulling out her plastic cheery voice. It was going to be a long day.

"Right!" agreed Karl.

Lauren stalked out to the driveway. "Trash over here." She pointed to the far left. "Recycling here." She pointed at an old basketball hoop across from the garages. "And consignment or Goodwill here." She pointed to the far right. "First, we go through the tennis team garage sale pile. Doesn't belong to anyone here, so we can sort that more easily."

Lauren looked at the heaps Karl had made. "Which of these is garage sale stuff?"

Karl shrugged. "I don't know."

Joanna got out of the wing chair Jacques had brought for her. "Um, let me see . . . that, I think." She pointed at a box of pots and pans. "And maybe that?" She pointed at a trash bag with clothes spilling out.

Vivi poked Karl's shoulder. "Dude, you've just made a shit-ton more work. How would you like it if I rearranged your equipment on stage?"

Karl's eyes flashed. "I think I'd like it a lot."

Vivi grinned back, unfazed. "Well, maybe right now leave the organizing to the ones getting paid?"

"You're right, so sorry," said Karl. "I'm at your service. Just tell me what to do."

"Me too," said Jacques.

Lauren pointed at a box of wicker baskets and said to Joanna, "Garage sale?"

When Joanna said yes, Lauren pointed to Karl. "Put that in Goodwill pile."

Joanna sat back down and answered Lauren's rapid-fire questions about every item already out of the garage, all of us scrambling to do her bidding as she pointed at piles.

Almost all of the tennis team donations ended up in the trash pile. Vivi kicked at a broken plastic cart. "What is wrong with people?" she griped. "How could they possibly think someone would want this?"

As Jacques rolled a decrepit push mower into the middle pile, a woman came around the corner talking on a cell phone. She was buxom and dressed in various layers of black, with her long, dark hair pulled into a loose ponytail. She poked at the phone to hang up, shifted her huge pink purse, and looked at me and Vivi.

"I'm Serena," she said. "I guess we're cleaning out the garage today?" She sounded like she hoped we'd say she'd gotten it wrong and could leave. I could see her resemblance to her brothers, but she was either older or had lived a harder life or both.

"Yep, cleaning out. That's Lauren, Vivi, and I'm Izzy," I stuck out my hand, and the second Serena took it, I felt myself deflating, like all hope and energy were being sucked out of me. I had an image of someone holding a smiley mask up in front of a sad face, a swirl of resentment and anger mixed with the sadness, and got an image of Serena lying in bed with a man, facing away from each other. I saw her surrounded by a purple so dark it was almost gray. Then my chest got tight—definitely Thomas. No words from him and no sense he wanted to communicate with his daughter.

"Nice to meet you," I lied, letting her hand go and wishing I could shake my body to shed her depression, like a cloud of fleas had landed on me.

Serena looked behind her. "Where did Marco go? He was right behind me." She walked towards Joanna, and it was like a switch flipped her energy. "Joanna! I'm so sorry to hear about the carbon monoxide thing! So scary." She shivered and leaned down to hug Joanna.

"Thank you, dear," murmured Joanna.

"At first I thought maybe you were cleaning out because you might be thinking of downsizing." Serena paused. "This is a lot of house!"

As she spoke, Marco came around the corner of the garage and his head immediately snapped towards Joanna, presumably hearing what Serena had just said and wanting to see Joanna's reaction.

Joanna's eyebrows rose. "No, the gala just seemed like a good excuse to get things cleaned up and organized."

Serena's shoulders dropped. "Right."

I could feel Lauren's impatience. "Since you are all here, we will clean out some of the family stuff. Put whatever you want to take with you in your cars. And if there is anything you want to keep here, stick a label on it." Lauren whipped out sheets of colored dot stickers. "Marco, you're green; Jacques, yellow; Serena, you can be purple; and Karl, here's red."

"I'll be right back," said Serena, heading into the house while Marco wandered to the back of the last bay.

Jacques grinned at Joanna as he dropped a pile of tarps in the recycle pile. "We should have done this a long time ago. Sorry to have left you with all this." He seemed like one of those people who aggressively point out the positives in any situation.

Jacques picked up a stack of flattened and dusty pool floats and got an unfocused look in his eyes. I could feel waves of nostalgia floating through him.

"Trash pile," barked Lauren, startling Jacques out of his reverie.

"Right, right," he said, complying.

"Does everyone collect this much stuff?" Jacques asked Lauren.

"Yes. And everyone asks if they are the worst," she said, laughing.

Serena wandered back in, coffee cup in one hand, phone in the other. "Let me just finish this and I'll help," she said but continued sipping slowly on her coffee and looking down at her phone.

"My clubs!" exclaimed Marco, dragging a set of golf clubs out onto the driveway. "I've been looking for these!"

"Those are mine," said Karl, stepping towards him.

"No, they aren't!" said Marco. "You don't even like golf."

"But they are mine. I think I'll take them," said Karl, a smile hovering around his lips. You didn't have to be psychic to see that Karl got a kick out of needling Marco.

"I don't know how they got so buried," said Marco, brushing cobwebs off the bag.

"Thanks, dude, I'll take it from here." Karl grabbed a strap on the bag and flicked a glance at Vivi.

Vivi muttered something about apes beating their chests.

"You will not," said Marco, gripping a strap on the other side of the bag.

"Oh dear," Joanna murmured.

Karl gave a quick yank, catching Marco off guard and he fell forward as Karl dragged the bag a couple feet.

"You're a dick!" hissed Marco, righting himself and jerking back on the handle, but Karl was too strong and he couldn't get it to move.

"Oh my God, what babies," said Serena. "Are you really fighting over some moldy old golf clubs?"

"Golf clubs, women . . . poor Marco, never getting what he wants," said Karl with an extra gleam in his eye.

"Shut up!" roared Marco, his face red, the veins on either side of his forehead enlarged and pounding. "They shouldn't even be here."

"Jesus, he's going to stroke out," murmured Vivi, coming up behind me.

Jacques glared at Karl. "Really?" he said.

Karl shrugged and let go of the strap. "Douche sport, anyway."

Once again, Marco was not ready, this time falling backwards. He managed to stay on his feet and spun towards his car dragging the clubs.

I could feel Joanna's distress coming at me in waves. I looked around for a distraction and felt drawn towards an old hammock, crumpled and dusty in the back. I grabbed it and was hit with a flood of joyful memories. Laughing, shrieking children, a rocking and spinning motion, warm summer sun, the smell of freshly cut grass.

I dropped it near Karl. "Was this from when you guys were young?" I said innocently.

Serena and Jacques joined Karl by the hammock.

"Oh jeez, yes!" said Jacques.

"That thing was evil!" said Karl, laughing. "You guys used to spin me on that until I flew out!"

Marco was back and, for a second, his face looked at ease. "You were the best," Marco said to Serena. "The hammock queen."

"You doofuses have no balance. It wasn't that hard," said Serena. Her face was lit up, and I got a glimpse of the happy person she might have once been. "Remember when we launched Dana? She was on crutches for a month."

One fun summer memory followed another one. "Remember when we hid Karl in the woodpile and got the babysitter fired?" "Remember when we tricked the new babysitter into drinking Tabasco?" Real laughter from all of them.

Joanna looked relieved.

Maybe I could use these senses for good. Without anyone being the wiser.

"Okay! Into the trash," said Lauren, dragging the hammock to the trash. Of course, Buzzkill Lauren broke the spell. Then again, that was why people hired her, to keep them focused. She was like a personal trainer who seemed annoying and then ended up making you look like a million dollars. I was probably going to have to learn to be more like her if I was going to be any good at this.

The Sullivans stood staring at her, fragmented back into pieces.

"You can always buy a new one," said Lauren, misunderstanding their disappointment. "People actually rarely need to, but their garages and attics overflow with 'just in case.'"

Kind of like a husband in France. Not here but not completely gone, just in case.

Serena wandered over to the Goodwill/consignment pile. "Where is this stuff going?" she asked.

"Goodwill or consignment, depending on how valuable," said Lauren.

"I could use these pots," said Serena. "And maybe the hoses?"

"Of course!" said Joanna. "Take anything you want."

As I watched Serena pull item after item out of the pile, Karl said something about looking for stuff in his old room and Marco and Jacques both said they were going to do the same.

"Vivi, start loading the flattened cardboard into my car," directed Lauren.

As Lauren turned around, Vivi saluted her back and then winked at me and Joanna.

Joanna giggled. "You guys are so fun. Izzy, could you grab me a sweater? There's one on my bed."

"Of course!" I said. "Do you want a break?"

"I'm good, just a bit cold," she said.

Heading towards Joanna's room, I heard noise in the large living room. I detoured past it and saw Karl on his knees in front of a cabinet with its doors open. Definitely looking for something.

In Joanna's room, I grabbed the sweater and took a quick detour into the closet to touch the tangerine dress, hoping to get more from Thomas. This time, I wouldn't be taken by surprise in front of people. This time, it would be under my control. Sort of.

As I held the skirt of the dress, I noticed a bit of a stain near the hem. I'd have to ask Joanna if she wanted to get it dry-cleaned.

Why are you still around? What do you want? I asked, both hands scrunched into the material.

My neck tickled with cool air, and I felt a wave of love and sadness mixed together, with a dose of fear too. Then I got an image of a desk, like an office desk, near a window with light streaming in. There was an office in the back of the house, if I remembered.

I let go of the dress and then made my way down that wing and as I got closer, I heard angry voices, so I hovered outside the closed door.

"Go away," Marco grumbled.

"Not until you do. You have no business being in here," Jacques said.

"You're the one who insisted we come, anyway. I'm just looking around to make sure Joanna isn't hiding anything from us."

"Sounds like projection to me," said Jacques.

"Ooh, 'projection.' Aren't you fancy." said Marco. "You're no better than me; we both know that."

"I never said I was," said Jacques.

"Going the 'we are all sinners' route?" said Marco. "I haven't noticed any confessions coming from you.

"I'm going to," said Jacques, but his voice had gotten higher and weaker. "Not that I expect you will."

"Nothing to confess," said Marco.

"I did it once. You did it repeatedly," said Jacques. "Mom and Dad might have been drunk and clueless, but I'm not."

"I have no idea what you're talking about," said Marco. His voice sounded closer, so I dashed across the hall into a guest room and pulled the door quietly shut as I heard them come out and then walk away.

What were they both hiding?

***

"My spidey senses started going off this afternoon," I said into the speaker in my car as we both were driving home.

"Yikes," said Vivi. "I'm glad you didn't tell me. Maybe you were just remembering what happened when you and Joanna passed out."

"It felt different than that. Like a small, dark cloud floated in and then got bigger and bigger until it was all dark and scary. And then when we left, it faded, like the cloud is there at that house."

"What did the dead geezer have to say?" asked Vivi.

"It didn't feel like it was coming from him. I mean, I felt him around, but he seemed—I don't know—reluctant. Like he didn't want to communicate with his kids, which seems odd to me."

"Yeah, Marco was my son I might not be in a rush to talk to him either," said Vivi.

"I feel like something is off with this family. I mean, I felt the sense of danger about the space heater, and then the feeling was gone when the heater was gone. But now it is back, a scary feeling. But bigger, darker, scarier. Something is still bugging me about this family. Like there is evil there."

I heard Vivi suck in air through her teeth. "I don't like that." After a few moments of silence, she added, "But I do trust your instincts. I'm playing with some LaSalle tennis ladies tonight. I'll find out about the Sullivans. Subtly."

"Ha! You subtle?"

"You know I can be; I just don't normally choose to be."

Chapter 11

At 6:00 a.m. the next morning, I met Vivi in the parking lot behind the Village Green Bistro. She adjusted her headlamp, I turned on the light around my waist and we started at a brisk walk to warm up my ankle.

We passed the early morning women's boot camp on the basketball courts, evident only from the grunts and bouncing individual little headlamps, like fireflies jiggling in midair.

There's not much more bonding than forcing yourself out of a warm bed on a cold, dark morning to work out with a friend. We've done it for so long it feels like our bond is unbreakable. If only I had something like that with Jay.

"This never gets easier," I said, complaining being part of the bonding. "I'm so cold." It would take at least half a mile to get my ankle warmed up and another half mile before my muscles started cooperating with each other.

"But your ass has never looked better," said Vivi.

"And yours," I said.

"Ha! We both know my ass hasn't shrunk in twenty years. I run so that I will have stamina for Brian."

Vivi made a lot of jokes about having a great sex life with her husband but didn't ruin it by actually giving details. The woman knew her boundaries.

"I've got some Sullivan scoop," said Vivi. "Specifically, Connie, the ex-wife."

"Ooh, what've you got?"

"You owe me. I broke my cleanse, again, to get this info," said Vivi.

"I think I can run now," I said, ankle mostly warmed up.

We turned off onto a dirt path that wound up and around a hill, which then would lead to another hill, and then a ridge along the top with an amazing view if the sun was up.

"First, I've played Connie and she's batshit crazy," said Vivi. "Maybe even crazier than Shania. She's getting older and I think her rating dropped, which absolutely sent her ballistic."

"Give me the tennis-for-dummies version," I said.

"In USTA tennis you get a rating, and that determines who you play against. It would kill Connie to drop down."

I grabbed a branch and pushed it away from my face as I slogged by.

"Connie is one of those people who yells at their own partner. And that's before she gets to the bar, although she's been known to hit the Fireball before some matches."

"No wonder Thomas divorced her."

"When Thomas got sober, it just didn't work to stay married to someone who wasn't. So he and Connie split up, and then he met Joanna."

The path narrowed, and I moved in front of Vivi so I could hear her.

"Apparently, Connie is still super bitter." Vivi was breathing heavily but didn't stop talking. "Claims Joanna stole Thomas even though they didn't even meet until after the divorce. She used to be a bigwig at Tires2U and either got fired or forced out. Sued over it and lost and sounds like she's run through most of her settlement. Didn't make her any less bitter. Lives in a condo in the country club and racks up huge bar bills but took in a roommate, which means she probably needed money."

"And the kids?" I gasped.

"Jesus Christ, who made the hill steeper?" Vivi huffed. "Hold on."

When we hit the plateau, I said, "ankle . . . need a break," so we slowed to a walk along the ridge.

When Vivi had her breath back, she said, "Connie's tried her best to turn them against their dad. And Joanna. Says Thomas cheated them out of money, that Thomas's dad had a lot of money and Thomas was hiding it from them."

"Huh," I said.

"Apparently Karl butted heads with his dad a lot. Got in some trouble in high school, not exactly sure with what. Marco, they didn't know so much about."

I thought about Marco and Jacques fighting in Joanna's office. And Serena seemed interested in Joanna downsizing. Karl was driving an Uber so he obviously wasn't rolling in money. After meeting with Lucille, I had looked up the "clairs" she had talked about and, right now, was hit with "claircognizance," which is when you just know something that is otherwise unknowable. I just knew that Joanna was back in danger. Like, someone-wishing-her-evil kind of danger. Could it be a Sullivan, current or former?

"Anything else about Connie? " I asked. "Relationships?"

"A bunch of crash and burns. It's been, what, 16,17 years since she and Thomas broke up, and she is still blaming Joanna for ruining her life. She tells everyone that Thomas hid money so it couldn't be part of their divorce settlement."

"Wait!" I said. "Joanna plays tennis too. Do they play together?"

Vivi chortled. "They're both on the LaSalle Country Club team. Joanna's really good. I guess she didn't play for years but when she started again, she ended up playing on the same team as Connie, and Connie threw a fit and broke a racket and then lost her match. Then got blasted afterward. Didn't make her like Joanna any better."

We slowed to look out over the line of hills above our town. From here, it looked like we lived in Italy—rolling green hills and little villages tucked into valleys where you could only see the Mediterranean red tile roofs of the town.

The Connie story had a certain guilty pleasure, but I could feel Connie's rage coming through Vivi's words, and it worried me for Joanna.

We headed down the trail, which seems like it should be easier than uphill, but my thighs were burning with at least a mile to go. Could Connie have stashed the space heater in Joanna's garage? Her own old garage. With the tennis team garage sale collection, anyone and everyone had been dropping stuff off there.

Nagging question, though: If someone intentionally tried to gas Joanna with the space heater, how did they know she would even use it? Connie didn't sound like a patient woman. Seemed like a reach to kill someone with a space heater you couldn't even be sure that they'd use.

"Anything new on the delicious Dr. Saito?" asked Vivi as we rounded the last bend.

"I wish," I said. I'd already filled her in on the Saito sighting on the Lacey ER trip.

By the time we got to the parking lot, the boot camp had just finished. The young and cute instructor bounced among the women rolling up mats and laughing with each other. No wonder the women were getting up early to work out. Burn off some calories and get in a little harmless flirting. Or maybe not harmless. Not my business, though.

"Hey, Samantha," I said, seeing a familiar face walking with her yoga mat in one hand, kettle bell in another.

"Izzy! Just the person I wanted to see!" Samantha was bouncing with energy, even post-workout.

I knew Samantha from when our sons had been on the same soccer team. Many years and sports ago. A former soccer player herself, she had coached the team and still gave off that wholesome athlete vibe, short dark hair, no makeup, glowing skin. "What's up?" I asked.

"I hear you're psychic," Samantha said, dark eyes shining. "Can I have a reading with you? I lost my dad a couple of months ago . . ." She paused. "It was complicated, and if I could know some stuff . . ."

"I'll get you a latte," said Vivi, peeling away.

I had vowed to keep this all quiet to protect Order Out of Chaos, but I also needed to practice the skills. I didn't want someone to die because I missed a sign. I didn't like the odd stuff I was picking up around Joanna. Maybe I could practice with Samantha.

I checked my watch. There was still time before my PT appointment with Kimberly.

"Maybe in your car?" I said, not wanting an audience.

"Sure!" Samantha said, clicking a remote to open a trunk a couple of cars away from us. She stowed her mat and kettle bell in the back, and we climbed into the front seats.

"Here's the thing," I said. "I sometimes sense stuff, but it isn't something I can do consistently. And I don't think my sister would like for her business to get a woo-woo reputation. I'll try it with you, but you can't tell anyone."

"Got it. No problem!" Samantha chirped, eyes filled with hope.

"I can't promise anything," I warned. "It comes and goes. I don't really have control over it."

"It's okay!" Samantha said. "Just get to it, just try."

I took a deep breath. "Give me your hands."

She reached across the console, and I held her hands and stared down at the console, letting my vision go soft. Imagined my mind opening, softening.

I felt a stab of recognition. Samantha felt distant from her husband. I felt my mind pull back, fighting with itself, tune in and don't tune in. I didn't want to feel her sadness or loneliness, too familiar. Focus. Feel around for her father. Not much was coming.

Samantha shifted around, restless.

"I don't know if this is your dad? Something about basketball? Trophies or awards?"

Samantha looked puzzled. "My dad wasn't really into basketball."

I nodded. "Okay. Must not be him. Hmm," Maybe I was trying too hard. The stuff always seemed to come when I didn't want it. I felt Samantha's unhappiness again and again felt myself fighting to stay open.

"This is not specific, but I'm feeling a lot of nostalgia. Was your dad nostalgic? Sensitive?"

Samantha nodded, "I guess, I mean he liked talking about stuff with us, reminiscing." She looked disappointed.

"I'm sorry, I'm not getting a lot. Just the trophies things, and it seemed related to basketball. And a sense of happy memories with that. Like, 'oh yes, that was great; I enjoyed that.'"

"He didn't play, so . . . I don't know," said Samantha, pulling her hands back into her lap. She wiped at her eyes.

"I'm sorry," I said.

"It's okay," said Samantha. "Worth a try."

I resisted the urge to say, "He loves you and is at peace," because I didn't know if it was true, and there was no quicker way to be labeled a fake than to be a fake.

As I got out of the car, I said, "And I'm sorry he passed. Sorry for your loss."

Samantha gave a dejected nod.

I walked away, feeling Samantha's sad eyes on my back. Vivi handed me a skinny vanilla latte as she stared at the bootcamp instructor loading the last of his gear into his Jeep. She sipped on her coffee. "Maybe we should sign up for bootcamp. They start in the dark and end up sweaty and happy. Gotta be more going on than burpees."

Chapter 12

Back at home, the Samantha failure echoed around my brain as I filled two huge Gatorade containers for Cole's track meet later in the day. I made quick work of it, dumping in the packets of Gatorade powder, adding water and ice, leaving them by Cole's old Jeep for him to take along. I laughed, thinking about the first time I got assigned the job and bought up half the aisle of Gatorade bottles at Safeway to dump in the cavernous barrels before another parent told me about the packets. I'd miss all this. I didn't want to think about Cole off to college and me left with . . . what?

Me alone?

Me and Jay?

Both filled me with dread. Back to Joanna.

I couldn't shake the sense that Joanna was in danger, and I could feel swirling tensions with Thomas's kids hanging around her. Perfect timing to have a PT appointment since Kimberly was Joanna's niece and the one who had connected me and OOC with Joanna to begin with.

I had set up spongy mats and a selection of weights and bands in the garage, spending way more time arranging my workout space than actually working out. I sheepishly admitted to Kimberly that I had not done anything since our last session. And that sometimes my ankle still hurt at the end of the day.

"No problem!" Kimberly chirped. "We'll strengthen that ankle right up." She was a noodle of a woman, slim and tall with no hips and no apparent bones either since I had seen her bend herself completely in half. I thought about how I had started picking up on colors related to people and tried to imagine a color around Kimberly. It was odd; my first thought was a really dark purple, almost black. I wondered what that meant—was there a book somewhere I could look up colors? Was that passion? Creativity? Something wrong?

"Let's start with the toe raises," Kimberly said.

My phone buzzed and I glanced down.

"Do you need to take that?" asked Kimberly.

"No, thought it might be Joanna, I'm trying to keep a close eye on her."

"I talked to her this morning. She's feeling okay," said Kimberly. "So scary!" Kimberly shivered. "I just couldn't believe it when I heard it."

I hung the back of my feet over the step leading into the house, held onto the garage refrigerator beside it for balance, and started moving up and down. I could feel the refrigerator asking to be cleaned out. Like my house didn't call to me enough already.

"You were there, right?" said Kimberly. "Emily told me about it."

"Yes, it was scary. Lucky that the paramedics got there in time," I said, losing count.

"Ten more," said Kimberly.

"So is Joanna your mom's or dad's sister?" I asked.

"Mom's, but . . . my mom hasn't been around for a long time. Dad gone for even longer. Joanna has been kind of my everything. And Emily is like a sister."

"So you would have been around when Joanna married Thomas?" I asked.

"Yes." Kimberly directed me to sit on the bench along the wall and grip a towel with my toes, scrunching it towards me. "I was so happy for Joanna. He was the nicest man, and he adored her."

"Sad to lose him that early," I said.

"And so unfair! Joanna lost her first husband too. It was such a great second chance for both of them." Kimberly nodded encouragement for my footwork. "Other side now."

I wanted to know Kimberly's take on Connie. "Thomas's first wife Connie sounds like . . . a lot, and Thomas sounded so nice. What brought them together, do you think?"

Kimberly took a gulp from her water bottle. She was a fiend about hydration, and I felt a stab of guilt. One more thing I was failing at. Then again, there were lots of things I was good at. Then again, keeping my brain focused was not one. "From what I understand, Connie was really successful in her career—worked for some tire company, like, as an executive. Thomas was good at his work too, so I'm guessing they might have had that in common. And then maybe the alcohol just took its toll, turned them into different people." Kimberly wiped her mouth and continued. "She's a work-hard-play-hard kind of person, enjoyed being the only woman in a man's kind of business. Seems like it fit her to be aggressive— probably good and bad sides to that."

"Sounds like you know a lot about her. Do you know her?"

"Well, if I did, as a client, you know I couldn't say." Kimberly practically winked. She had worked with Connie. "I can tell you that Joanna had nothing to do with their breakup, but Connie acts like she caused it. Connie tried to turn his kids against him."

"Was she successful?" I asked.

"Both sides, again," Kimberly commanded, pointing at my feet on the towel. "Seems like it. Thomas was trying to reconnect with all his kids, but . . . who knows? Jacques and Serena were in college when Connie and Thomas divorced, but Karl and Marco were still home. Sometimes, I think those two had it harder because they were literally back and forth between houses."

"Mm-hmm," I agreed as we moved on to band work. I slid the stretchy band over my thighs and started my side leg raises.

Kimberly continued. "Of course, the house they grew up in was so much nicer than the condo Connie moved into in the country club, but on the other hand, she didn't enforce any rules. Lots of arguments about that."

"Oh yeah, the house," I said. I had so many directions I wanted to go in. That sense of danger was real but unfocused. What if it was something dangerous about the house itself? "That house is amazing. It was Thomas's? In his family?"

"Yes. I think his dad built it, but maybe it was the granddad," said Kimberly. "It will eventually go to the kids. Other side now," she added, and I switched legs. The exercises weren't really that bad, not when someone else was directing them. Maybe I could look decent in yoga pants. Or walk without pain.

"What was it all like for Emily?" I asked.

"It was tough. She was happy for her mother but still missed her dad. To be honest, I don't think she has ever let herself really deal completely with her dad's death. Lots stuffed away. It's an amazing house, but I don't think she ever felt really at home there. And I don't think the Sullivan kids were that excited to welcome a stepsister. Although it was just Karl still home when Joanna and Thomas married." A little smile passed over her face.

I finished with the band. "What was that like? All of a sudden living in a new house with a stepbrother."

"And a stepsister, at least part of the time," Kimberly added. "At some point Serena lived with them while she got going with teaching. But the stepbrother part . . ." Kimberly giggled. "Em did not like it, but all the girls at school did. Including me."

"I've met Karl," I said.

"Then you get it. We all had crushes on him. I mean, not Em, but the rest of us. I always hoped he'd be there when I was over. But he was at Connie's a lot of the time. Lots of partying."

Kimberly got more business-like. "Okay, some arm work? How's that wrist feeling?"

"Still twingy at times. Stiff in morning, but okay,
mostly," I said as we started range-of-motion exercises.

"Ten more on that wrist."

I pulled my fingers back with my other hand and held
it, letting the tendons stretch. "Must be a bit odd for
Joanna, alone in that big house."

"Aside from missing Thomas, she doesn't mind that so
much," said Kimberly. "Emily and I both go around a lot,
and she's got lots of friends and neighbors. She's very
independent."

Kimberly knelt down and moved my foot around,
testing my ankle. As she touched me, I was flooded with
a feeling of dark fear, like it was pouring out of her
hands. I flinched, and she mistook the flinch.

"That hurts?" she asked.

"No. I mean, a little," I floundered. It hadn't hurt but
how to explain myself? It was like depression itself had
just flooded the room. All light and happiness gone.
Come to think of it, that would fit with the dark purple I
had imagined around her. I wondered if Kimberly would
have any motive for hurting Joanna. Was she close
enough to be in her will?

"I mean, I guess it makes me think of the accident," I
said and realized maybe that was the connection with the
sudden darkness. Probably had nothing to do with
Kimberly.

No wonder I didn't want to do my PT. It just brought
up pain.

Chapter 13

I hurried off to get in a couple of hours at a job before the track meet, lucky that both were in my home town today. The ever-demanding Peaches had commandeered Lauren for the morning, so it was me by myself pretending to know how to organize an office. Then the plan was to get to Joanna's at some point in the afternoon to pack up the little artifacts in the public space rooms.

Three hours later, I had a feeling I had just made the office situation worse, but I assured the client that "it always looks messy before it looks clean." Before she could say anything, I rushed off to Cole's track meet.

At the stadium I saw my mother sitting at the top of the stands and wove my way past clumps of people standing talking along the bottom walkway. A muffled bullhorn voice called for warm-ups for a group I couldn't make out, a starting gun went off, someone bumped me without even apologizing. Track meets are chaotic and yet somehow work.

"Well, well, hello, Izzy," I heard that brain-grating voice and saw Shania clomping towards me on her three-inch wedges, flanked by Shania-wannabe's on either side. They all wore skintight jeans, variations of Shania's wedges, dry-clean-only shirts and full makeup, which didn't cover the predatory facial expressions that no amount of Botox could erase. More "lipstick on a wolf" than "lipstick on a pig."

I looked up at all six feet of the smirking Shania. Long strawberry-blond hair, today in two side braids that should have looked ridiculous but somehow looked sporty. Like she just stepped off of the ski slopes. I subconsciously smoothed my ponytail, wishing I'd taken the time to style it. Or at least dry it. Or throw on some root cover-up.

Shania was living proof that some Mean Girls never grow up or forget "stolen" boyfriend grudges.

"Hey, Shania," I said, coming to a halt, unable to get around her because the clones stayed tight on either side of her. What was this, West Side Story? Were we about to have a gang fight? A dance-off? Shania gathered unhappy women looking for people to feel superior to, and they all mistook that commonality for friendship. The Schadenfreude Sisters.

"How's that *cleaning* business going?" asked Shania. The clone on the right giggled.

I didn't take the bait. "Great, actually, but, hey, need to get to my seat." I stepped backwards, but they all took a step closer.

"Yeah, how's the cleaning business?" echoed the clone on the left, pity-patting my shoulder. The second her hand touched me, I was flooded with images.

Everyone in her life was mean to her. Husband, mother, father, kids, a constant barrage of yelling and criticism. Shania's faux friendship was the best she could do. I searched around the images, was there anyone at all who was loving to her? I felt a grandmotherly presence, not dead, but lost in all the pain.

Patting her shoulder, I gently said, "Jules, go see your grandmother. Stay with her if you need to."

"What?" Jules said, her face briefly losing its mask-like appearance.

"She loves you," I said.

"What the hell are you talking about?" asked Shania.

"Got to go!" I said brightly, stepping around the motionless Jules, and Shania poked at me as I slid by.

The poke was enough to hit me with another image: Shania rolling around a karate studio mat with the instructor. Naked. I turned back towards Shania. "Those karate mats have all kinds of bacteria, you know. Very bad for bare skin. Have Josh put down a towel next time."

Swaggering away, I heard gasps behind me, and it was all I could do to not turn around and gloat.

I felt a flush of pride climbing the steps towards my mother. Her mostly silver hair shone in the sunlight, cut in a short chic style that emphasized the fine bone structure of her face. She was always nicely dressed in what Lauren called "Chico's 'Professor line,'" which usually meant something dark, something jewel-toned, and a chunky piece of jewelry. She was a woman who had very few regrets, nothing left to prove, at ease with the wrinkles she had earned. Other than the mini-strokes, she was glowingly healthy.

"You made it!" Mom exclaimed, looking at her watch.

"I did," I said, ignoring the implication that I might have been late.

I gave her a quick hug, sitting down next to her. "Dad's game?" I asked. I hadn't had a chance to check the score.

"Up 7-2 in the bottom of the fourth when I left," she said.

With my dad coaching the local college baseball team, our spring weekends had been all about baseball for as long as I could remember, and then when Luke and Cole started playing sports (neither lasted in baseball), it took a back seat. I was really going to appreciate something to fill my weekends next year. Better make sure Dad didn't retire for a while.

Mom was scanning the track oval. "I can't find Cole," she said.

"He's never missed a start. He'll show up," I said, staring down at Shania and her gang. I saw Jules peeking back up at me, pain on her face making her look more like a real person. Shania was in animated conversation with Clone Two, poked at her, then stomped away. Clone Two darted over to a group of women and started talking, arms waving. The gossip was spreading right in front of me. Didn't Shania know that Josh slept with every karate mother he could lure into the dojo? What a cliché.

"How's the work going?" Mom asked. She was proud of Lauren for starting the business and had pressured her to take me on as a partner, no doubt worried for my financial situation and puzzled by my lack of ambition.

"You know what? I am actually liking this work. It is way more interesting than I would have thought."

Mom smiled serenely, secure in her knowledge that she had known what was right for me before I did. Everyone knows me better than I know myself. "How are you and Lauren getting along?"

My turn to smile. "How do you think?"

"Probably a bit bumpy until you both come to appreciate what the other one is bringing to the business."

"I appreciate what she can do!" I protested. "She just doesn't see the value of what I'm good at."

"If she's smart, she will figure it out soon," said Mom. "And so will you."

"What does that mean? I'll figure it out?" I got defensive so quickly around her.

"I've said it a million times, I don't care at all if a woman decides to work or stay home. But I've always felt like you had more to offer the world. So many skills."

Her words sounded complimentary, but the effect on me was deflating. Like telling someone they have "potential," which means they aren't doing something great now.

"What do you think I'm bringing to the business?" I asked.

"Social skills, for one," Mom said, pulling a water flask out of her bag and taking a sip. "You are warm and friendly and get along with people easily. People like you. That is a huge asset in a business like OOC. Lauren is fabulous at organizing, but she is nowhere near you in the social stuff."

"Is that it?" I asked.

Mom looked at me. "Are you feeling insecure?"

I shrugged. "Maybe."

"It isn't fashionable to use the word 'smart' anymore, but you are really smart. You can figure anything out." Mom chuckled. "All those detective books, you figured out the mystery every time. Any puzzle, any crossword. You put things together really well."

Mom took another swig of her water. "And you are incredibly resourceful. You'd be the winner on those survivor shows. You'd figure out how to cook a meal with a tin can and a roll of tape."

Mom had never said this stuff to me before. Maybe the mini-strokes had loosened her up.

The 3200 was called over the loudspeaker, and my heart sped up in anticipation. I am cursed by way too many mirror neurons. I feel everything everywhere, especially when one of my people is involved. The boys lined up; I found Cole in his green uniform, legs and hair golden in the afternoon sun; the gun popped; and they were off.

The 3200 is a long time to be anxious, but I'm good at it. Cole got himself in the front part of the pack quickly, then stayed there for a lap. The pack stretched out leaving Cole a step behind the leader, Tommy Timmons, his closest competitor from the high school a valley over.

My mother grabbed my arm. "Why is he not in front?"

"That's his strategy," I said. "He always does it that way."

When the cowbell signaled the last lap, I watched expectantly. This is where Cole would make his move.

Cole didn't make his move; in fact, he seemed to be fading. What was going on? He hadn't lost the 3200 the whole season. The parents in front of me got silent. Something was wrong.

Cole barely held on to second place, falling over the finish line with the rest of the pack right behind him. He doubled over, throwing up onto the grass of the field inside the oval.

My mom grabbed my arm again. "Is Cole all right?"

I shrugged. Not the first time he'd thrown up from running, but it was odd he had faded at the end. I reminded myself it was just a race, that he was human, that I didn't have to live in his reflected glory.

My phone quacked—Lauren.

"I need you at Joanna's right now!" commanded Lauren. "Marco showed up and is telling her she can't have the gala here, and she's crying, and he won't listen to me. Bring those famous people skills."

Before I could respond, she hung up.

"Speak of the devil," I said to Mom. "I've been summoned."

I said goodbye to the people around me, ignoring the sting of "second is always good!" and walked with Mom to the parking lot. Getting into her car, she said, "Let Lauren do her thing. Just focus on what you do well."

What I was doing well these days was channeling a man two years dead. My uber-scientific mother would never believe that one.

Chapter 14

At Joanna's I slipped in through the slightly ajar front door and found Marco standing in the largest living room, glowering at Joanna. The room was littered with boxes: maybe ten closed and taped, five or so open and partially filled, and a flattened stack of unused boxes ready for assembly. Joanna was shrunk back into the depth of a huge maroon couch, clutching a gold tasseled pillow tight to her chest, like a shield.

"Hey, folks! What's up?" I said in my breeziest tone.

Marco turned his glare on me.

"Joanna can't have a gala here. It is an absolute no," Marco barked, his face and neck so tense that the ligaments from his shoulders to his jaw were sticking out.

"I promised," Joanna said in a faint voice. "I signed a contract. Tickets have been sold. It's in less than three weeks."

Marco looked around the room. "It's ridiculous! There are a lot of valuable things here. No way the public should be in here."

I tried to breathe slowly and not get sucked into Marco's emotional state. "Yes, I can see how that might worry you," I said, nodding as if I was in complete agreement.

Marco stared at me suspiciously.

Tactical skill number one: find something to agree with.

"Not many private homes are used that way," I continued. "No matter how nice they are."

"Exactly!" Marco said, expanding like an angry lizard puffing up to show dominance.

Tactic two: find their concern.

"What is your main worry?" I kept my voice slow and easy.

Marco looked at me like I was an idiot. "Strangers in the house! That they'll take stuff."

I nodded again. "I can see that. It would feel weird to me to have strangers wandering around my house."

Lauren's face was blank, but her head was angled just enough sideways that I could tell she thought I was making things worse.

"Someone who gets it! Finally," said Marco.

I gave Joanna a big smile so she'd know I wasn't siding with Marco. "If I understand it, the plan was for the tents to be set up in back, right? Like, it's mostly outside?"

"But they are going to need to use bathrooms! And Wanda was so excited about the house," said Joanna.

"Who is Wanda?" Marco asked.

"The event planner. She's very persuasive." Joanna winced at the memory.

Lauren nodded. "I know her. She is very persuasive."

"They make trailers with complete bathrooms—like, tiled floor, nice counters, the works," I said. "Keep the glam, but keep people out of the house?"

I heard footsteps, and Serena schlepped in. "What's up?" she asked. She was dressed in loose, dark-gray sweatpants and a shapeless beige sweatshirt, her hair stringy, face with no makeup.

I wondered why Marco had called her. I wouldn't have pegged her as the one in the family who got things done.

"Why are you bringing this up now?" Lauren asked Marco.

Marco fumed. "The more I thought about it, the worse of an idea it seemed. Joanna should have asked us."

There it was. The idea that Joanna should ask them about doing something with the house she lived in.

Serena sat down beside Joanna. "How are you feeling?" she asked.

"I'm okay. I just didn't think . . ." Joanna trailed off.

. "What if we make sure everyone stays outside?" I said to Marco. "It would be nice to do this, given how your father passed away. Given that it is actually, you know, named for him."

"Even if you have outside bathrooms, how are you going to make sure people don't come in?" Marco asked.

"We'll post people at the doors," I said.

I could feel Marco's anger looking for a place to go, like it was a flamethrower he couldn't just turn off. After a tense silence he stepped towards Lauren, looming over her. "Figure out how to keep it outside! And stop boxing this stuff up; one way or another, no one is going to be in here. Put it all back!"

I half wished Vivi was here. It would have been fun to watch a Philly girl take Marco down. In my peacemaker role, I couldn't do it.

"Whatever you say, Joanna," said Lauren, looking pointedly at Joanna, not Marco. Good for Lauren, emphasizing that Joanna was the paying client and probably enjoying thwarting Marco.

Marco walked over to a box and pulled a heavy gold clock out of it. "I think this goes here," he said, setting it on a mahogany sideboard. He walked back to the box and pulled out a smaller box full of antique medicinal tins. "And these were arranged here, on these shelves," he said, plopping one after another onto a set of narrow shelves.

"I don't know about you, Joanna, but I never got lunch," I said. "Should we go find something to eat?"

Joanna smiled gratefully. "Okay."

Lauren murmured that she would try to track down Wanda and, poking at her phone, wandered out.

In the kitchen Joanna pulled a cinnamon roll off of a paper plate. "It's the last one. Want to share it?" she asked.

"No, I'm good," I said.

Joanna slid open her trash drawer to drop the empty plate. "Oh dear. Could you maybe take this garbage out for me? I keep meaning to, but I'm just too tired."

"Of course!" I said. I yanked at the sides of the bag, but it was so heavy and full it was stuck. After I wrestled it out of the can, I lugged it, banging against my ankles, outside.

The outside can was also overflowing, the lid propped half open over the piled bags. With the craziness of the week, Joanna probably missed her garbage day. I eased the bag I was carrying down on the ground and opened the lid the whole way. I shifted a bag on the top of the can to make more room and saw the black edge of something metal. I got an immediate flash of danger, my heart started beating fast, and my chest tightened. I pulled back the bag to find the space heater.

I stopped myself from reaching for it. What if there were fingerprints on it? What if someone really did try to kill Joanna with it and we could find out who? It felt important to keep it, somewhere hidden, maybe.

I went to my car and got a pair of gloves and a new trash bag. Back at the garbage can, I put on the gloves and eased the space heater into the bag. Touching it was creepy, a feeling of death vibrating out of the heater and into my body. I felt sad for Mr. Jacko and scared for Joanna. I stowed it on the floor in the middle row of seats in my SUV, threw a couple of big empty garbage bags over it to hide it, and tossed my used rubber gloves beside it on the floor.

I hurried back to the garbage can to add the kitchen bag. It was so heavy I gave it a swing, trying for some momentum to get it up into the can. At the top of the arc of its swing, the thin plastic tore and the bag ripped open, spilling its contents down the front of my body and all over the ground. Cucumber peels, shreds of something that was brown and gooey, and remnants of lasagna marked a trail down my shirt and onto my pants. Swearing, I picked up all the pieces of garbage from the ground, wishing I still had gloves on but not wanting to waste any more time. I tried not to focus on the texture or smell and just shoved it all back in the can.

Back in the kitchen, I washed my hands and scrubbed at my shirt and pants with a towel.

"Oh dear," said Joanna. "What happened?"

"Just me being me. Accidentally broke the bag and got some on me."

Lauren came walking back in, a smug look on her face, Marco trailing behind her.

Lauren wrinkled her nose at me and raised her eyes. Critical but not surprised, I'm sure.

"Well?" asked Marco. "Did you talk to her?"

Lauren directed herself at Joanna. "Wanda was not happy about it, but we worked it out: no one inside. I had to listen to her vent, but bottom line is that she can get the fancy Portapotties. We'll finish unpacking that room and then figure out what else you might need from us before the gala."

"This really kind of simplifies things, doesn't it?" I asked.

Lauren nodded. "Yes, mainly we need to get the kitchen ready for the caterers, but everything else can be done without a rush now." She spun around and walked back towards the living room, Marco behind her.

Joanna stood up. "I'm going to go to my room, maybe read a bit."

"Oh, I meant to mention it to you, I noticed your wedding dress had a little stain around the hem. If you want me to take it to the dry cleaner for you, I will," I said.

"You are so thoughtful," said Joanna. "That would be great."

I went with Joanna to her room, she handed me the dress, and as I made my way back to the kitchen to set it with my purse, I could feel Thomas appear with a whoosh. *Stick close to her,* he urged me.

And do what? I asked. No answer.

Back in the living room, Lauren was busy.

"We've got this," Lauren said. "It'll all be back where it started."

Serena smirked, looking around the room. "Good luck with that. I'm sure you can't remember where it all goes."

Serena leaned over and picked a strand of spaghetti off my shoulder and handed it to me. "Need this?" she asked.

I shoved it in my pocket.

Lauren whipped her iPad out. "I'm sure I can. We have pictures of every bit of the room for exactly that purpose."

Lauren looked down at the iPad and then at the shelves she was standing beside. "For example, this set of Swarovski figures is in the wrong place. It goes on the shelf below. And one over to the right."

Marco pulled his phone out of his pocket. "I've got to take this," he said, stalking out in the direction of the back of the house. Maybe the office again?

"I'm going to go look in my room for something," said Serena, also heading out.

Why were Marco and Serena still hanging around? I didn't like it and decided not to leave until they were gone. I felt such a strong sense of danger but could not figure out anything more specific. I thought of Joanna's pale face, passed out. I thought about Mr. Jacko dying. The dread grew.

Thomas? Anything you have to say here?

A vision of him shaking his head no.

Why don't you want to talk to your kids?

Another head shake. *Joanna. Pay attention to Joanna. Any hints?*

A shrug.

I was going to have to look at every possible source for the danger. Which meant everyone around her. The Sullivans. Emily. Kimberly. Any cleaners or gardeners. Friends.

Chapter 15

I heard a buzzing noise as Lauren put down an armful of books and pulled her phone out of the fanny pack that never left her waist.

"Mm-hmm," she said. "Yes, of course."

A pause.

"I'm just finished here," Lauren said in the extra-soothing tone that meant she was either talking to her kids or Peaches.

She hung up. "Shit. Peaches is having a meltdown. I have to get back there and finish today's project."

"What was it, labeling the hubs and kids?" I said. "There can't be more than that left."

Lauren giggled. "Right? Hey, Peaches is at least forty percent of my business. If she wants to label my tush, I'll ask how big the font."

She handed me the iPad. "You can put this all back, right?"

"Sure," I said. Plus, I wasn't leaving until I was sure Joanna wasn't surrounded by people who might want her dead.

Lauren left, and as I worked on the unpacking, I wondered if I could get the police to fingerprint the space heater—if I could convince them it wasn't an accident.

As I finished the last box, Cole's ringtone blasted out of my phone, and my mom antenna shot up. He never called, only texted.

"Hey Mom," Cole gasped. "I'm on my way to the hospital. Feel like shit."

"You aren't driving, are you?" I said, my whole body instantly lit up with adrenaline.

"No. Can barely breathe. Stomach, side. Appendicitis, I'll bet," he said, his voice strained. Cole was a stoic; I'd never heard him like this.

"On my way," I said, hanging up. Ohh, that was why he lost his race and threw up at the end. Already sick and ran anyway.

I grabbed my purse and the tangerine dress lying on top of it. Once again, Thomas appeared. *Don't leave her!*

I've got to get to my son! I thought to Thomas, but I called Vivi to see if she could come over. When I got no answer, I texted Emily and struck out again.

Shaking with the need to get to Cole, my fingers trembled as I called Kimberly.

A rush of relief when she actually answered and said she could come right over. I felt Thomas's relief. At least I think that is what that was.

I got on the highway. It was a blur, but I changed lanes several times, lasted the five or so miles and exited, sweating, shaking, willing to do anything to get to Cole. Even face my driving fear.

I got to the hospital at the same time as Cole, his friend Sanjay pulling up as I was running in from the short-term parking. "I've got him, thanks!" I said, as Cole lurched out of the car and slung his arm around my shoulder.

Within thirty minutes, Cole was on a gurney, blood drawn, IV started, but still writhing with pain. The track star was gone, replaced by a boy in pain who clung to his mother's hand.

Two nurses worked on either side of the gurney, a female on a computer, a male fiddling with the IV. The female nurse looked up and said, "All of a sudden, I'm hungry for Italian."

I cringed. "Sorry, that's me. Had a little altercation with a lasagna."

"I hope some got in your mouth," she said.

"Sadly, no," I said, embarrassed but relieved that she could be joking around. Things must not be so dire with Cole.

I felt the change in the air before I even saw him. The curtain pulled back and there he was, Dr. Saito.

He took in the bed and me beside it, and his eyes showed a flicker of something. Attraction? Amusement? My whole body flickered too—definitely attraction, on my part. "Hello again," he said as he walked towards Cole. "So, what's going on?"

"The trash bag broke," I said.

His mouth was held tight like he was trying not to laugh. "I mean with Cole. Cole, what's going on?"

Cole mumbled out his symptoms: nausea, vomiting, felt hot, stabbing pain all through his abdomen but worse on the right side.

"When did it start?" asked Dr. Saito.

"Yesterday . . . maybe two days?" said Cole. Two days! And he had run a race today.

Dr. Saito said, "I'm going to feel around your abdomen, okay?"

Cole let go of my hand and said "It's okay, you can keep going. Ow!"

Dr. Saito asked more questions about when the symptoms started and how they developed. "Looks like it's probably the appendix. Going to get a scan and look at the blood work, but he's showing all the classic signs."

I nodded. "Okay, what's next?"

"I'm guessing surgery. We're probably going to want to get that thing out, sooner rather than later. We'll get some painkillers going in the IV," he said, motioning towards the nurse. "And the surgeon will be here soon."

I took a deep breath. "Okay."

Dr. Saito smiled—oh my, he had the nicest white, even teeth. And adorable crinkles at the sides of his eyes. "You know there's no loyalty card here, right?"

"I could swear there was a Groupon for this place." My laugh came out high-pitched.

"Must be for Alta Bates; they'll do anything to get new patients." Dr. Saito held my eyes for just a fraction longer than he probably should have.

Cole gave another moan. What was wrong with me? My child was in severe pain, and I was flirting.

My phone started quacking, obviously Lauren. I hit "end" quickly and turned off all the sounds.

Then it vibrated; Lauren was persistent.

"They should be coming any moment to take him to get scanned," said Dr. Saito. He glanced down at my shirt. "We could give you some scrubs if you need them."

"No thanks, I'm good," I managed to say.

He nodded and stepped out.

I texted Lauren to let her know about Cole.

These extrasensory skills were so weird. A cute doctor, and I know he's noticed me. The dead husband of a client tells me his wife is in danger. And yet I had not gotten any sign of Cole's appendicitis.

After the tech came to take Cole to his scan, I texted Jay to let him know what was going on. I hoped he wouldn't feel like he had to come home—and immediately felt guilty for that thought. But really, by the time he could get home, the surgery, if necessary, would be done.

The phone buzzed immediately: Jay calling back. I answered as I did the math; it would be after ten at night there.

"What the hell is going on?" Jay said. "What's with all the ER visits? Every time I look at my phone, someone's in the hospital."

"Hello to you too," I said, wanting to cry. His angry tone took away the hope we could manage this family crisis together. And yet, why would I have thought we could? We didn't with Luke.

A big sigh. "I'm sorry. It's just hard to be this far away when something goes wrong. Tell me what's going on."

I filled him in while I shoved my hurt feelings back in their cages. As I finished, Dr. Saito popped back in. "Hold on, I'll call you back," I said, poking "end" on the phone.

"No need to interrupt your call," said Dr. Saito, but it was too late.

"It's okay, I can call back," I said, feeling the mental whiplash of anger at Jay while looking at the handsome, calm Dr. Saito.

Dr. Saito tossed me a green scrub top. "Just in case."

My shirt must look even worse than I thought. "Oh, uh, thanks?"

Dr. Saito broke into a full grin. "It's just that the whole department is now craving Italian, and I need them to focus."

I guess I was lucky it wasn't rotten fish that had slimed down my shirt.

"Anyway," he continued, "I just wondered if you had any questions or concerns. Thought I'd check in while Cole was getting scanned."

"Well, of course I have concerns," I said. "I mean, surgery . . ."

"Yes, it's very straightforward—possible even to do it laparoscopically, which they can tell you more about. He's a healthy teenager and should recover well."

I nodded, then closed my eyes and took a deep breath in and out. I opened my eyes and gave a weak smile.

"You've had quite the week," said Dr. Saito. "Is this normal for you?"

"No! But not much is normal for me anymore."

Dr. Saito's eyebrows raised. "Oh?"

I sighed. "Too much to explain, really."

"I'm happy to listen," he said. He reached into a pocket and pulled out a business card and a pen and wrote on the card. "Here's my office and cell number if you need anything. Or just want to explain what isn't normal." He bowed, threw me a warm smile that lit up his whole face, and said "Take care" before he walked out.

Jesus Christ.

I looked down and noticed I hadn't actually ended the call with Jay.

Double Jesus Christ.

I cringed and put the phone back to my ear. "Hello?"

"Well, hello," said Jay, his voice sarcastic. "Who was that?"

"A doctor," I said.

"Quite the care. . . . 'Happy to listen,'" Jay said. "Why do I feel like he's not some fat sixty-year-old doc? And what the hell was the "craving Italian" thing?'

"I spilled lasagna on my shirt," I said. No need to say it came out of a trash bag.

"So you're having a hard week," Jay said.

"Well, yes," I said. I had an image of him sitting at a sidewalk cafe in Paris, wine glass in front of him, attractive brunette across the table. Was that a made-up fear or something real I was picking up? We had mentioned divorce but hadn't done anything about it, so we were in odd territory.

At that moment Cole was wheeled back in. His face was relaxed, in a doped-up kind of way.

"Here's your dad," I said, holding out the phone.

"Heeyyyyy, Dad," Cole said, his voice slowed-down. "I feel like shit."

I couldn't hear Jay's answer.

"I came in second today," Cole said in the same drowsy voice. "Worst time in two years."

A pause.

"Yeah, me too," Cole said and handed me back the phone.

I agreed to keep Jay updated on Cole, no matter how late it got, and hung up. And double-checked that I had hung up.

I read the card. Christopher Saito, M.D., Emergency Medicine Doctor. A color appeared for him, blue-gray, like the ocean, the color itself full of depth. I slid the card into one of the slots on my phone case, feeling a silly pleasure at its presence.

Chapter 16

Five blurry hours later, I was slumped at Cole's bedside, dressed in my new scrub shirt. My prayers were finished, Jay updated, and my parents here and gone. Cole had scored a private room, and the nurses had turned a blind eye to my presence. One of them had mentioned that the complicated wood and vinyl chair was supposed to unfold into a sleeping arrangement. For once, the answer to a puzzle eluded me, and every part of my body was uncomfortable.

Cole looked so vulnerable, swaddled in hospital blankets, surrounded by machines blinking with mysterious numbers. I stared at his peaceful sleeping face, and the self-pity witch landed on my back. Why was someone in our family always ending up in the hospital?

The door opened and Vivi silently waved.

I slipped out into the hall so we wouldn't wake Cole.

"You join the staff here?" she asked, looking at my scrub shirt.

I rolled my eyes. "The garbage bag broke on me. I was covered in lasagna and I don't want to know what the rest was."

"They just gave you a shirt?"

I blushed. "Dr. Saito did."

"Ah! Dr. Dreamy is on the scene!"

I filled her in on Cole and Dr. Saito and Jay's call. As we giggled, a passing nurse gave us a stink eye.

"I better get back in there before they throw me out," I said.

Vivi handed me a lavender tote bag. "Here's a few things you might need." She hugged me and slipped away.

In the room I dropped back into the torture chair and opened up the tote bag to find a charging cord, a soft wrap, a puzzle book, a toothbrush with a tiny tube of toothpaste, snacks and even a mini bottle of white wine. I skipped the wine but made use of everything else, amazed at how Vivi had stomped the self-pity witch into dust. The puzzle book worked its normal magic, getting my brain focused somewhere else, giving a little hit of mastery.

I settled back and closed my eyes, only to be hit by panic—I had never checked in to see if Kimberly made it to Joanna's or if Joanna was okay.

I remembered the darkness I had sensed around Kimberly. What if *Kimberly* was the danger? She was practically a daughter; what if Kimberly was in Joanna's will and knew it? And I had invited her over.

My brain spun. What was extrasensory and what was just my fear?

I squirmed around in the chair.

Focus on the breath. In and out. Let your body relax.

In the morning, assuming Cole was doing okay, I'd go to check on Joanna myself. I had a visceral need to get back to that house.

I finally drifted off and then, bang! My eyes popped open, my heart racing with fear. It was 3:00 a.m.

Cole was sleeping peacefully. None of his machines was going off. What had woken me?

My whole body was lit up, like an electrical storm skimmed through my nerves.

Something is wrong, get over to Joanna's.

Rational brain came online. You had a crazy day. Your son had emergency surgery! Of course you're anxious.

I mostly believed it but still felt like there was something I was supposed to be doing.

Rational brain said, mothers always feel like it is their job to keep people alive. But even mothers need to sleep. Besides, I wasn't about to leave Cole.

Eventually I drifted back to a sort of sleep.

***

In the morning, I texted and called Joanna, then Kimberly, then Emily, getting no answer from any of them.

Cole woke up, groggy and in pain.

"How're you doing?" I asked when his eyes came into focus.

"Ok," he croaked. "Hungry."

Always. But it seemed a good sign.

"Good morning," my mother said, as she and my dad came into the room carrying balloons and a pink cupcake bag.

Cole closed his eyes. He loves his grandparents, but they are kind of relentlessly energetic. I played along.

"Good morning," I whispered. "Let's go out in the hall."

They set down the bag, wrapped the ribbon from the balloons around a chair and tiptoed away. I slid the bag closer to Cole; he could open it once we were gone.

In the hall my dad shook his head. "I told your mother, let him sleep!"

"It's okay," I said. "He's just snoozing. Everything seems fine."

"We don't have time to come later," explained my mother. As usual, she was perfectly coiffed and dressed in khaki pants, a red top, and a chunky gold necklace. My dad was in baseball pants and a fleece. Years ago, he found that it was just easier to put his uniform on first thing in the morning. It kind of cracked me up.

"Good morning," I heard from behind me.

My body sparked with electricity, hearing that voice.

"Thought I'd check in on Cole before I left," Dr. Saito said.

My dad stuck out his hand. "I'm Dutch Waring, Cole's grandfather. Thank you for doing such a great job with him."

"I'm not the surgeon, but I saw him in the ED," said Saito.

"Well, thank you anyway," said my dad. "It takes a whole team, and we are just grateful he is okay."

My mom looked back and forth between me and Dr. Saito. "I'm Nell, and you are handsome. Are you married?"

I wanted to sink through the floor.

My dad laughed. "You'll have to excuse her; she's embracing her new uninhibited self. Courtesy of some mini-strokes."

I couldn't speak.

"I am not married, as it turns out," said Dr. Saito, smiling and acting like it was a normal question, like "where did you go to college?"

"My daughter is not really married right now either," said my mom.

Dr. Saito's eyebrows went up, managing to look curious, warm, and amused all at once.

"He's living in France right now, and they are separated," my mom added.

Dr. Saito nodded. "I see. Sometimes things are just not normal for a while, yes?"

Using my words from yesterday.

"That doesn't have much to do with Cole, Mom," I said.

"It is life, though, isn't it?" said Dr. Saito, looking at me, his eyes bright and friendly. Stubble darkened the bottom of his face, making him even more attractive. As did the smile hovering around his very kissable lips.

"Isn't Izzy beautiful?" said my mom.

Dr. Saito gave a little bow, "Very."

"Don't you need to get to the field?" I looked at my dad, desperate.

"Yes, we'll check back with you later," said my dad, taking Mom by the arm. "Goodbye."

I couldn't look at Dr. Saito.

"Divorced four years, no kids, love my job, moderately active, and a foodie," said Dr. Saito. "Does that even things up?"

I finally looked at him. "I'm so sorry; my mom's not herself anymore. And she's only a small part of what's not normal."

"I'm glad, actually. I was trying to find a way to ask you out without being unprofessional."

"I don't know," I said. "We're separated and supposed to be divorcing but haven't done anything about it yet."

"I get it," said Dr. Saito. "It's complicated. No rush, but the offer is there. If you ever decide you want to, you know, date. Or not date, just get coffee or something that isn't a date."

"Well, coffee that isn't a date wouldn't be bad," I said. What was I thinking?

"You have my number," he said. "If we get coffee-that-isn't-a-date, I'll tell you about Bibi Saito."

"Who is Bibi Saito?" I asked.

"My mother." Dr. Saito said, his eyes like a dance all by themselves. "Your mother may be recently disinhibited. My mother has always been. You can't imagine what it is like to be born to a Mexican mother and a Japanese father."

That explained his perfect face. The best of two cultures.

Back in the room, Cole seemed okay and I felt so drawn to Joanna's that I told him I was going to run an errand and would be back soon.

When I got in my car, I saw the tangerine dress on the front seat. I touched it and felt Thomas appear almost instantly. *Stop wasting time! Get to the house.*

Chapter 17

I pulled up to Joanna's to find a police car parked next to Kimberly's car.

I was too late.

I haphazardly parked and ran to the front door, which was cracked open. I pushed it. "Joanna?" I called, heart pounding.

I was met in the foyer by a police officer with his hand up to stop me. "Who are you?" He was tall and thick with salt-and-pepper hair cut close and a fleshy face that was both stern and calming.

"I'm Izzy. Is Joanna—?" My heart was racing, chest tight.

"Oh my God, Izzy!" Joanna wailed as she ran past the police officer and fell into my arms, hair wild, face puffy and tear-streaked.

"Poor Kimberly," she cried into my shoulder.

I looked at the police officer.

"A young woman who was here last night has unexpectedly died," he said.

"Oh my God," I said. "What happened?"

"I'm here to go over those details with Mrs. Sullivan right now," he said. "I'm Officer Barrett. Maybe we could go sit down?" he said softly to Joanna.

I walked with Joanna to the little living room and settled her on the couch. She stared blankly ahead, then looked at me, the grief in her eyes almost unbearable. "Izzy, I just . . . It was so..."

"Start with when Miss Selleck arrived," Officer Barrett said, leaning forward in the chair he'd taken across from Joanna.

"Kimberly came around 4:30 or 5:00," started Joanna, wiping her eyes.

Officer Barrett nodded in encouragement.

"I can tell you when she got here," I said, pulling out my phone. "My son had just called me." I found Cole's call from the day before. "He called me at 4:35 and I called Kimberly to come stay with Joanna, so I'm guessing she could have gotten here by 5:00 or so."

Officer Barrett noted that down. "To stay with Joanna?"

"Joanna, Mrs. Sullivan, had a health scare this week and she seemed really tired and I didn't want to leave her alone, but I had to get to my son."

"So no one else was here?" asked Officer Barrett.

Joanna and I looked at each other.

"Marco and Serena were here," said Joanna, looking sideways.

"Who are they?" asked Officer Barrett.

"Stepkids," said Joanna. "I was married to their dad before he passed two years ago. Marco Sullivan and Serena Reed." She looked at me. "They, uh, were going to have to leave, so Izzy called Kimberly for me."

"And Kimberly is what relation to you?" asked Officer Barrett.

"My niece," Joanna's voice broke. "But more like a daughter."

Officer Barrett paused while Joanna got control of herself.

"Kimberly got here, and then what happened?" he asked.

Joanna wiped her eyes with the ends of her sleeves. "Marco and Serena left, Kimberly did some PT on my shoulder, and then we had some of the lasagna my neighbors dropped off." She paused.

"Did you both eat all the same food?" Officer Barrett asked.

Joanna nodded. "Yes, both had salad and lasagna."

"Did you feel sick at all?" asked Officer Barrett.

"No," said Joanna, shaking her head. "Just the tiredness that I've been having since the carbon monoxide thing."

"What did you have to drink?" Officer Barrett asked.

"I had sparkling water. Kimberly had maybe a half a glass of wine. She wanted to try the Yield that Jacques brought." Joanna got tearful again. "I had actually opened the bottle the night Jacques brought it and then realized I better not drink any until I'm fully recovered from my carbon monoxide thing."

Joanna stared off into space. "We were just talking; had finished eating. Kimberly got up and was clearing the table. She was standing by the sink and said she felt dizzy, and then she passed out. I couldn't wake her up and called 911." Joanna paused. "They took her and . . . on the way to the hospital, she died."

Heavy footsteps pounded down the hall and Emily appeared. "Oh my God, Mom, I'm so sorry. My phone was off. What happened?"

Emily sat down beside her mother on the couch. "Kimberly *died*?"

Joanna nodded, mouth trembling.

"What happened?" Emily asked Officer Barrett.

"That's what we are trying to figure out," he answered.

"Did she have an accident on the way home?" asked Emily.

"No, she collapsed here," said Joanna, a fresh wave of tears forming and spilling down her face. This time, she didn't even bother to wipe them off.

"Did she seem high or out of it?" asked Officer Barrett.

"No," said Joanna.

"Did you see her take anything?" he continued.

"No, nothing," said Joanna. "We ate, talked for a while, and then it happened."

"Could it have been the wine?" I asked.

"We are checking on that, to see if she had any allergies, see if there was anything in the wine or the lasagna or salad, although both of you ate the lasagna and salad," said Officer Barrett.

I was thinking that something must have seemed off about her death since the police were already here.

"Could it have been her asthma?" asked Emily. "It was really bad."

The full impact of Kimberly's death hit me. I had called Kimberly to come over. Whatever I feared for Joanna had happened to Kimberly.

Panic rose through me, my head getting so buzzy that I thought I might pass out or start screaming.

"I'm going to use the bathroom," I mumbled, standing up.

I made it to the nearest powder room, shut the door, closed the toilet seat, and sat down, just as darkness descended. I leaned forward, elbows on my knees, head down, slowing my breathing.

Staring at the white marble floor, I could not shake the feeling that if I had been here, Kimberly would still be alive. That somehow I could have sensed enough to prevent the death.

I knew there was danger but I hadn't known how to prevent it. Trying to use the senses was making me feel like a horrible failure. Maybe I should go back to being "only" an organizer. Stay in my lane. Not that it was really my lane. I was a failure at everything.

I hadn't kept Luke from addiction.

I hadn't made my marriage work.

I hadn't ever done any kind of meaningful career.

I had barely ever even made money for our family.

And now, I had gotten someone killed.

There was a soft knock on the door.

"Izzy?" It was Emily. "Are you okay?"

"I'm okay," I lied. I stood up and opened the door.

"Officer Barrett wanted to talk to you before he leaves." She pointed. "He's by the front door."

"Okay," I said.

Officer Barrett had his little notebook out.

"Your full name and address?" he asked, and I told him.

"What is your relationship with the family?" he asked.

How to say that I'm Joanna's guardian angel, appointed by her dead husband?

"I work for Order Out of Chaos, an organizing company," I said. "We are helping her organize her house, but I also knew Joanna from when I used to work at a book store, so I'm kind of a friend too. I am worried that someone is trying to hurt Joanna," I added.

"Has someone threatened her?" he asked.

"Not exactly. It's just, I don't know, a sense," I said. How could I tell him that I didn't like Marco, that Serena had a scary darkness, that Jacques seemed fake positive, that Karl had the charisma of a serial killer, that all four of them could use money? "She almost died from carbon monoxide poisoning from a defective space heater. In fact, the plumber did die. You could fingerprint the space heater, see who has touched it," I said.

"Fingerprint it to see if someone in the family touched an item that belongs to the family?"

"Only Joanna lives here. She didn't know where it came from. I just thought . . ."

"Why don't you leave the thinking to us?" he said.

"What if someone was trying to poison Joanna but accidentally poisoned Kimberly?" I asked. "When Joanna dies, the stepkids get the house. What if someone wants her gone now?"

Officer Barrett stared at me. "Or maybe a young woman with severe asthma died from ingesting something that set off her asthma."

There must have been something suspicious about Kimberly's death, why else would the police even be here?

"I'm just hoping you are testing the wine? Sounds like that was the only thing Kimberly had that Joanna didn't."

Officer Barrett stared some more. It must be his favorite interrogation device. Little did he know he couldn't make me feel worse than I already felt.

"The coroner will be doing an autopsy," Officer Barrett finally answered.

"A number of people had a chance to do something to the wine," I added. "All of the stepkids have been here this week," I said.

"And you know they were here how?" he asked. His head was pulled back, almost to the point where his face went straight into his neck, like he doubted everything I said.

"Because I was here," I said.

"Uh huh, uh huh, you were here too," said Officer Barrett, eyebrows raised. "I won't tell you how to clean, you don't tell me how to detect," he added, closing his notebook and walking towards the door.

"We don't clean, we organize," I said to his back.

I went to the kitchen to see if I could sense anything. The wine bottle was gone, the wine glass on the table empty. I reached towards the wine glass and then stopped before touching it. Maybe not a great idea to put my fingerprints on it. I held my hand close to it but sensed nothing.

I walked to the sink and stood in front of it, where Kimberly must have been standing when she collapsed. I took in the whole scene: the dirty dishes in the sink, the silverware, a coffee cup, a big spoon with remnants of lasagna on it, a paring knife beside cucumber skin peels. A half-full plastic container of cherry tomatoes sat on a cutting board, along with the bottoms of romaine lettuce stems. I closed my eyes, imagined I was Kimberly, and was overcome with an extreme feeling of heaviness, then a sense of not being able to breathe.

I am so sorry, Kimberly. So sorry, I thought.

My intuition was telling me that Kimberly had eaten or drunk something that killed her. Must have been the wine. But was it just my general intuiting of things or was there any otherworldly help here? I couldn't tell. I couldn't tell the difference between my own thinking and, for lack of a better description, help from another world.

Chapter 18

With Emily there, I felt like I could get back to Cole. "I need to get back to the hospital. Please call me if you need anything," I said, hugging Joanna.

The second I was alone in the car, tears came. By the time I was halfway down the driveway, they were flowing hard enough that I had to stop, unable to see clearly enough to drive. Flooded with guilt, I wiped and blinked until I could focus on the flowers lining the driveway.

I had the feeling of intrusion again, like ancient spirits were telling me I didn't belong here.

I shivered. What if this was some kind of old sacred ground, like a burial ground? And the bad stuff that was happening was because of that? If someone who died two years ago could come through, why not someone who died two hundred years ago? I stared at the live oaks. What had they witnessed? Were there spirits still here, hovering, protecting?

I remembered the sense of darkness around Kimberly. It seemed too obvious to me now that my feeling of dread when she was working on my ankle wasn't because of my accident; it was her impending death.

These senses were a curse. If all I sensed was "something bad is coming," I was going to live a horrible life. Always trying to figure out what the horrible thing is, always vigilant to prevent it. Without enough information.

I wanted to give it up.

But.

If I had any doubt before this, I had none now. Someone was trying to kill Joanna. It was a deep knowing that pervaded my whole body—what Lucille would call claircognizance. I knew Kimberly died by mistake. I knew it was supposed to be Joanna. She was still in danger.

I couldn't live with myself if something happened to Joanna.

"Not on my watch," I said to the flowers outside my window. I was Joanna's protector now. I was an organizer second. All decisions filtered through that: Joanna's safety first.

I was going to have to use the senses, and I was going to have to get skilled at using them, quickly. No matter what Lauren said. Two people had already died; I could not live with myself if anyone else died. Maybe I could keep Lauren calm if I started doing a better job as an organizer. Be super professional. Great at my job. Then she'd have to keep me if I veered off into woowoo territory once in a while.

I grabbed a handful of the tangerine dress. *Thomas, do you have any way to help with this?* I could say it out loud, here alone in my car.

I had an image of Thomas with his hands on his head, like he was grabbing his hair in frustration. *That's not much help,* I said.

My phone quacked, making me jump. Thomas disappeared.

"Hey, any chance you can get over to Peaches's house with me for a couple of hours?" asked Lauren, not bothering with hello.

"Oh my God, Lauren," I said. "I'm at Joanna's. Kimberly died here last night."

"What?"

"I came to check on Joanna, and the police were here." I filled her in on the rest.

"Oh Lord," said Lauren. "That is just tragic. Poor Kimberly! Maybe she had a condition no one knew about, like heart disease or something. Is Joanna's daughter there with her?"

"Yes, but she's devastated too. Kimberly was like her sister."

"Oh, that is so hard." Lauren paused, maybe remembering almost losing me. I could feel her brain turn away from the thought. "I guess it is a good thing all we have to really do before the gala is get the kitchen organized. I mean, it's so awful, someone dying and all, but . . . well, just keep in touch with Joanna, I guess. So can you come help me out at Peaches's house?" said Lauren.

Even if I understood why, it seemed heartless to move on so quickly. Then I remembered I was going to prove how professional I was and tried for a soft tone. "Not today. I'm just so sad. And I have to get back to Cole."

"Of course it's sad," said Lauren. "I know you think I'm being cold, but sad things don't change the fact that we have contracts to work for a ton of people. Lacey is taking a few days off, which I get—that lizard thing scared her. Vivi is busy. I need someone to help move heavy stuff. Peaches is my best customer."

"I'll do it tomorrow, I promise." My phone buzzed with a text from Cole, asking for a charging cord. "I've got to go," I said, hitting "end."

***

Back at the hospital I found Cole scrolling on his phone. I tossed him the cord from my car and found a place to plug it in.

"You're welcome," I said, mentally writing off this cord. Even though I technically should get it back, I knew I never would. Like "lending" someone money. Just call it a gift, so it doesn't get added to the grudge ledger.

"Thanks," he said. "I'm bored."

My phone buzzed: Lauren. "Vivi can help. I'm going to need the two of you to meet me at Peaches's in the morning and move the big stuff; then she wants her pantry redone. I've got to go finish up for Rupert, and I KNOW you don't want to go there, so you and Vivi will do the pantry. I'll send instructions."

"Fine," I said. "And by the way, I'm going to need to get paid more often. Like every week.

"You realize you haven't finished one job yet?" said Lauren. She was laughing, and I couldn't tell if it was with me or at me. But I wasn't laughing, so it must have been at me.

* * *

Slouched in the torture chair, I woke repeatedly in the night, anxiety bubbling. At 4:00 a.m., wide awake, I looked at the peacefully sleeping Cole and felt a welling of nostalgia. Soon he'd be off to college and I'd be . . . alone? Stuck with Jay?

I loved being a mother. I had never had career aspirations, never felt a sense of rightness in the world until I had kids. And now I was about to be out of the only job that had ever fulfilled me. The empty feeling sent me back to when I was about to graduate from college. Not sure what I wanted to do in life.

And then Jay proposed. In the moment where he went down on his knee on the rose petals he had scattered there, there was a split-second pause, where a teeny part of me wondered if perhaps I was just saying yes to avoid the not-knowing. I pushed that part of me away, slipped the ring on, and never looked back. Until now.

All these years later, I was back to that unanswered question: What do I want?

It was too agitating to think about. I needed to move. Anything to keep from thinking. Or feeling.

Peeking out of the room, I saw the nurses' station to the right and slipped out to the left. No need to advertise my presence and get anyone in trouble. I shuffled along, peeking around corners, a little mood boost from feeling so stealthy, ending up almost full circle to the nurses' station from the opposite direction. I saw a familiar profile leaning on the high counter, head on his hand propped on his elbow.

Saito!

I jolted fully awake. Was that head lean flirting? Or was he just tired? Not wanting to be caught, I backed up, still looking at him, and ran into an IV pole on wheels. The pole crashed into a rolling metal cart, knocking the top tray off. The clattering sound of a metal tray bouncing onto a hard floor in an otherwise silent hallway sounded like a bomb going off. Saito turned and saw me as several nurses and techs came running from the other side of me and, with a deeply red face, I apologized and speed walked back in the direction I'd come, irrationally hoping to slip into Cole's room before anyone caught up with me.

As I came around the last corner, I saw Saito leaning against the doorjamb, arms crossed, face blank, but eyes spilling with laughter.

"Hi," I whispered. It was the middle of the night, after all.

"Hi," he whispered.

"I don't suppose we could just pretend I'm coming back from the bathroom," I said, still soft-voiced.

"We could," Saito said. "But then I'd have to find someone else to deliver Nurse Marla's lecture to."

"Not Marla," I said. Marla had come in at the beginning of the shift and winked while she gruffly informed me that, under no circumstances, should I be seen past visitor hours. That should a visitor be found, Marla would be the one in trouble so . . .

"I told her I would take care of it," Saito said, finally letting himself grin.

"I don't want to get her in trouble," I said. I looked down the hall towards the nurses' station but no one was peeking out of it.

"Why do I feel like trouble hangs around you?" asked Saito.

I shrugged. "Because it does. I can't seem to help it." I looked at the door to Cole's room. "I better get back in there before I burn down the hospital."

Saito stepped to the side. "Just so you know, I hate being bored. And I was bored. And now I'm not." He did a half bow. "Thank you. Goodnight."

Chapter 19

In the morning I took Cole home and set up the couch as a bed, with everything he might need on the wide ottoman beside it. He eased himself onto it and let me kiss the top of his head before I left.

I picked Vivi up on the way to Peaches's house, tossing the tangerine dress into the back seat to make room for her. I was going to have to find time today to stop and leave that at the dry cleaners.

"I know driving freaks you out, but you seem even more wound up than usual," said Vivi. "Either kick Jay out or sleep with him. You can't tolerate this level of stress."

"Even worse," I said. "You know Kimberly Selleck? My physical therapist? Joanna's niece? She died the night before last. At Joanna's."

"Oh my God, what happened?" said Vivi, hand to chest.

I gave her the details, adding, "I sensed darkness around her. Like a really heavy darkness. Now I know it was her death."

"Shit," she said.

"But nothing stops Lauren," I said. "Not effing lizards! Not sudden death! On to the next job!"

"It is kind of how you have to be when you own a business," said Vivi.

I hated it when Vivi was right. Especially about Lauren.

Peaches opened the door of her McMansion, greeted me, and then stabbed a finger at Vivi. "I know you! You play for MCC."

"I was not part of any of that," Vivi held her hands up in the air in surrender. "I mean, I was there, but I didn't hit anybody. And I thought it was a bad call."

"Huh," huffed Peaches. "I didn't see you pulling anyone off anyone." Peaches was a hair over five feet, more than a hair under a hundred pounds and looked like she could fit in a chihuahua carry bag. She had long beige-and-brown-streaked curls and a tight black top tucked into painted-on, high-rise jeans, tapering down to four-inch platform shoes. We followed as she tip-tapped to the kitchen.

"You try to stop Shania when she's got a couple of Sea Breezes in her," said Vivi.

Peaches glanced back, an unwilling smile appearing. "I guess we all have our team nut. You've got Shania; we've got Connie."

The massive kitchen looked like it had manifested straight out of a design magazine. Twenty-foot-high ceilings, custom white cabinets and white marble countertops, dark wood, and wrought-iron accents—modern minimalism meets ranch chic. Not a piece of clutter to be seen.

"You know Connie?" I asked.

Peaches rolled her eyes so hard I was afraid they'd get stuck in her Bambi-length lashes. "Dated her son in college."

"Which one?" I asked.

"Jacques. My luck I caught him during the divorce. Connie was hell on wheels then. I'm not sure she's improved much since. Let me show you what I want," Peaches said, sliding back a refinished barn door hanging on one side of the kitchen. It revealed a room at least ten feet deep and eight feet wide, lit by a chandelier. Built-in cupboards and shelves lined the room, every surface stuffed with cans, bags, boxes, haphazard bins. The center was piled with flats of drinks and Costco-sized packs of paper towels and toilet paper. Now I understood the pristine kitchen; the real life lived in here.

Peaches said, "I keep shoving everything in here. But I just can't stand this pantry one more day."

Peaches's inability to stand things one more day kept OOC in business.

Vivi nodded. "We've got it. No problem."

Before I could ask Peaches more about the Sullivans, I heard a "Hello!" and Lauren walked into the kitchen. She looked around. "You are doing amazing, Peaches! It looks so good!"

Peaches smiled, flashing perfect white teeth and an otherwise unmoving face.

"We'll get that stuff arranged upstairs, and then we'll get going on the pantry," said Lauren.

"I'll be gone but feel free to text me if you need anything," said Peaches, picking up a purse bigger than her whole torso. "The Container Store stuff is out in the garage. We leave the door propped open for access, but please don't let Blanca out of her crate. She's still a puppy and is not allowed in the house."

Peaches grabbed a bottle of Prosecco from a Subzero refrigerator twice her height. "Don't freak out if a grumpy teenager comes through," she added. "My, uh, bonus child, he's not very talkative."

After Vivi and I pushed and hauled the furniture in the upstairs playroom into place, we went back to the kitchen where Lauren handed us the pantry instructions, told us to behave, and left for Rupert's. Better her than me.

We looked at the first instruction.

1. Take everything out of the pantry.

"Hold on, let me get the before pic," I said, and snapped a couple.

"I just can't believe that poor girl died," said Vivi, dragging two bales of toilet paper to the kitchen counter. I hated to mess up the pristine kitchen but it had to be done. As Lauren said, often something has to get dirty so something else can get clean.

I dumped a flat of chicken broth cans beside the toilet paper, my chest heavy with guilt. If I had just been there. "Poor Joanna. First the carbon monoxide and now her niece collapses right in front of her."

I filled Vivi in on Kimberly and then the Saito sightings.

Vivi dropped an armful of half-eaten chip bags on the counter. "You think someone actually . . . killed Kimberly?"

"I think someone meant to kill Joanna," I said. "And accidentally killed Kimberly. It couldn't hurt to learn more about everyone around Joanna, right?"

"I'm in!" Vivi exclaimed. "Let's investigate the shit out of those Sullivans. My money's on Marco, but who knows?" Vivi rubbed her hands in anticipation.

"Discreetly, though!" I said. "How am I going to justify it? 'A dead man told me you're up to no good'?"

An hour later we stood looking at the piles of food spread over every counter. Half-used everything, bags of chips, cans of nuts, cereal. Lots of unopened canned food, dry pastas, granola bars. A couple of Costco-sized coconut oil drums.

"No wonder Peaches is so thin," said Vivi. "No one actually seems to eat the snacks here. I'm gaining weight just looking at it."

I looked at the instruction sheet.

2. Throw out anything open or expired. Keep a list of things to be replaced.

I heard a grunt behind us and whirled around to see the back of the presumed "bonus child" facing into the open refrigerator.

The door clicked shut, and he turned around, a sleepy-looking kid, maybe sixteen or so, with wavy, dark hair covering most of his face.

"Hi," I said, "I'm Izzy; this is Vivi. We're doing some cleaning out."

"Hey," he mumbled, ambling over to look through the food scattered on the counters. "Nothing to eat around here," he said, and as he flipped his hair out of his face, I froze. For a split second his eyes reminded me of Luke when he was using. The hair fell back over his face. He was probably just sleepy.

The bonus child left, and we heard the sound of a car start and drive away.

"That sounded familiar," Vivi said, continuing to organize the preposterous amount of food that had seemed so unappetizing to bonus child.

Two hours later everything was neatly arranged. Vivi and I stood back to admire our work.

"It looks fantastic," said Vivi, and we fist-bumped.

I took a bunch of pictures and sent a couple to Lauren, feeling proud.

Lauren texted back immediately.

Lv xtra org stuff in garage. P will check.

I took the leftover organizing bins to the garage.

The dog whimpered, and I went over and baby talked at her. She was adorable, a white lab probably half grown, alone in a crate. It just didn't seem right.

"Hello, cutie patootie," I said.

The puppy stuck her nose through the grid of the crate, and I petted it. Her whimpering hit right in my heart. The poor thing was lonely.

I opened the door of the crate, and the dog jumped on me, wagging its tail and licking my face.

"Hi Blanca! Hi cutie," I said, kneeling down and scratching it.

Vivi came through the door, which was blocked open with a huge bag of dog food. "We were supposed to add a chalk board; is that out here?" Before either of us could blink, Blanca took off towards Vivi, knocked her into the food bag, toppling both before disappearing into the house. Free of the prop, the door clunked shut behind the dog.

"No!" I yelled, scrambling towards the closed door. To my horror, it was locked.

"Goddamn dog," said Vivi, rubbing at her knees. "This is linen for Christ's sake."

I tugged on the door and fiddled with the handle. Nothing doing. We were locked out.

A quick circling of the house revealed no unlocked doors or windows, so I ended up using a ladder from the garage to climb in a second-story window. I ran through a massive bedroom suite so neat it looked uninhabited and eventually found Blanca destroying the pantry, pawing at the shelves, the floor already littered with a mix of the previously organized items. Blanca grabbed a bag of chips in her mouth and darted past me. I turned to see Peaches staring in disbelief.

"Why is Blanca IN THE HOUSE?!" screeched Peaches, face red and eyes shooting daggers.

"I'm so sorry," I babbled, running past her. "I'll catch her. I'll put her back."

By the time I managed to get hold of Blanca's collar and drag her back to her crate, Peaches was standing next to Vivi in the pantry, looking at her phone, then looking back at the pantry.

"Lauren sent me this lovely picture," Peaches said in a fake sweet voice. "I checked the security cameras for a quick peek and imagine how I felt when I saw Blanca running through the house!"

I looked around the kitchen. It hadn't occurred to me that she might be watching us. Sure enough, perched directly opposite the pantry, on an open shelf with artfully arranged cookbooks, was a little white camera with a blue light, focused right at us.

"But this," she flung her phone up at me, "is not what I'm looking at now, IS it?" Not even sarcastic sweet was left.

"No ma'am," I said.

"Did I not tell you to leave the dog in the crate?"

"Yes, you did," I said.

"And yet, here I stand, hundreds of dollars later, with a more fucked-up pantry than I started with!"

"We'll fix it," I said. "No charge. For any of it." Lauren was going to kill me. I had screwed up for her best client. Our best client. I was going to have to start feeling more ownership of this business.

"You'll fix it." Peaches pointed at me. "She will leave and never show her face here again." She pointed at Vivi.

I was about to protest when Vivi gave a little shake of her head. "I'm so sorry I let the puppy out," said Vivi. "You were right; I should have ignored her. I am truly sorry." Vivi grabbed her purse and left, having fallen on the sword for me. Unless, of course, there was a camera in the garage, in which case it was my ass on the chopping block.

"I'm so sorry, it must have been so frustrating to see this on the camera," I said, quivering and feeling a lot like a chastised dog myself.

"Yes!" said Peaches.

"Such a beautiful home, things in such a nice order, and then to see the dog you told us to keep in the crate go running by." I shook my head, doing my best to empathize with her, bring the emotions back down.

"Yes," said Peaches again. "I was so excited by the pantry pictures."

"You've made this kitchen a jewel and were so wise to get that pantry organized too." I thought about the perfect bedroom upstairs and about living with a teenager who isn't your biological child. "Must be hard to get everyone else in the house to keep things neat. I mean, I have kids. It's not easy. And teenagers? Don't get me started."

"Right?" said Peaches, her tone softening just a bit. "No one puts anything away!"

I shook my head in agreement. "They just drop it wherever. Let me get this cleaned back up," I said, moving into the pantry. "And so sorry for making you come home."

Peaches waved a hand. "I was bored. Bunch of ladies just bitching about their husbands."

As I scooped granola bars off the floor, I asked, "So you dated Jacques Sullivan? Are you still in touch with him?"

"Not really, but I hear he's doing well with the winery. We dated at Cal Poly, and he was already obsessed with wine. Made for some fun parties." Peaches smiled. Then her face got serious. "He took a wrong turn but, from what I hear, he has stayed clear since then."

"A wrong turn?"

"Got caught up in a gambling thing," said Peaches.

"Ended up in debt?" I asked. Seemed like the end point for anyone who gambled too much.

Peaches shrugged. "I don't know. He was super stressed and then it all worked out. I always assumed his dad paid off his debt, although Jacques said he couldn't or wouldn't."

What was it Jacques said to Marco? "I did it once, you did it repeatedly." Could that be gambling? Gambling seemed like something Jacques would have done repeatedly.

After I finished, I slunk out to the car where Vivi was scrolling on her phone and laughing.

"I owe you," I said.

"Got that right," said Vivi.

Lauren called right after I dropped Vivi off.

"Not only did you screw up the Rupert job, you screwed up a job for my best client!" She sounded like she was about to start crying. I heard the Excedrin bottle rattling. "I'm done with you. You. Are. Fired." The phone went dead.

Chapter 20

I stared at the phone. She'd get over it, right? Lauren needed me, at least until she found more employees. When I finally made myself add up our debt, I was staggered. Luke's rehab, my medical bills, Luke's tuition, Cole's upcoming tuition, Jay's company cutting his division and switching him to a lower-paying job, a depleted retirement account. I liked working, but I didn't have any marketable skills. Lauren was paying me more than I could get anywhere else. Plus, I was actually liking the work. I was sure I could get better at it.

I saw the flash of an email notification and caught "Saito" in the words. Sure enough, it was from him. Checking on Cole, then something more.

I'm feeling bored again. And I'm feeling an unaccountable desire for coffee, would love company. I'm off work today and tomorrow. Then his phone number, again.

Pant, pant, pant. My whole body lit up with a zingy kind of energy. "An unaccountable desire." Whew.

I started to type a text to his number and then stopped. I was still married, recently unemployed, and on the trail of a murderer. This was no time for romance.

As my energy deflated, the devil on my shoulder protested. You deserve some attention, some excitement. Jay had a sort of affair. You are separated, headed for divorce. It's just coffee.

I typed *funny, I was thinking about coffee a lot today too*; suggested a coffee shop and time tomorrow; and hit "send" before I could stop myself.

I tossed and turned all night, toggling between immense guilt over Kimberly and buzzy excitement over Saito. I woke up exhausted, but my excitement at seeing Saito sprung me out of bed. It was just coffee, right? And I was due to shave my legs anyway. And why not put on a nice outfit in case Lauren rehired me?

I settled Cole on the couch again. On the ottoman I set down a tray with a travel mug of hot chocolate and a bagel with cream cheese. "I've got, uh, an appointment," I said, plumping the pillows and folding the fluffy blanket into a neat rectangle over him. I was really getting into this neatness thing.

Cole grunted a grumpy "Thanks." Aware that he was facing a boring day and no running, I perched on the side of the couch and asked about his friends and school. Then I remembered. "Hey, I was working at a really nice house yesterday, and she had these little cameras around the house that she could watch from her phone."

Cole nodded. "Yeah, probably an Arlo or Ring or something."

"How does that work?"

"Easy. Just plug in cameras and connect to an app on your phone. Why? Are you going to start spying on me?" Cole laughed.

"No, just wondered."

"Yeah, I kind of appreciate that we don't have them, if you know what I mean," he said.

Did Cole have parties here that I didn't know about? I doubted it; the cross-country kids were the straightest in the school. What was I going to catch them doing, chocolate milk shots? Girls maybe, though.

I laughed, glad his mood had lightened at least a little bit. "Okay, text me if you need anything."

As I started to back out of the garage, Lauren called.

"I'm sorry, okay? I shouldn't have fired you. I'm just
so worried. I feel like I've taken on more than I can do,
but I hate to turn down clients. I can't make myself say
no. I really need you back at the Hathaways today; the
moving truck is coming tomorrow. Lacey is still out, Vivi
won't answer her phone, and Rupert paid us triple to
finish his place this morning. If we get behind, we'll
never catch up."

As she talked, a big black SUV pulled up along the
end of the driveway, blocking my way. The door opened
and Jay climbed out of the back, a small duffel bag in one
hand and a briefcase in the other.

"Hello?" said Lauren.

"What? Oh wow, holy cow, Jay just pulled up."

"Jay? From France?"

"I'll call you later." I hung up before Lauren could say
anything else.

Shit.

I stepped a foot out of the car as it drifted backwards
and I realized it was still in reverse. Good job, Izzy, you
almost ran over your husband. I slammed it into park and
got out.

"Hey," I said, as the SUV pulled away.

"Hey," said Jay. His dark hair, gracefully sprinkled
with gray, was cut short but just long enough to spike
straight up from his face in a kind of punk meets
sophisticate cut. It was smushed on one side and his face
was shadowed by overnight stubble. Even rumpled and
tired, he still could have gotten second or third looks from
women. We used to laugh about women looking at him
like I wasn't standing right there. It did nothing for me
now.

He set down his bag and briefcase, and we hugged,
awkwardly.

Once again, my premonition skills had failed me;
nothing had warned me he was on his way. The place the
skills could be most useful, my family, seemed blacked
out most of the time.

"Cole's going to be so happy. Let's go in," I said.

"He's doing okay?"

"Yes. You didn't need to come," I said.

"Of course I needed to come!" barked Jay. I had forgotten how quick his anger could be. "What kind of father do you think I am?"

Before I could answer, he laughed sarcastically. "Don't answer that."

He picked up his bags, and we walked towards the house. I let him go in front of me as I looked down at my phone.

"Were you headed somewhere?" said Jay, glancing back as I stopped.

Oh, right. That. Hard to ignore the fact that I was married when my husband was standing right in front of me. Even if we'd talked about it, we weren't divorced yet.

"Just a job with Lauren. I can be a little late."

Jay peered more closely at me. "Are you okay?"

"Just distracted—with Cole, and I messed up a job yesterday." I was babbling. I felt like my airway was closing up. Jay shrugged and headed towards the door from the garage into the house. Me being emotional and distracted was nothing new to him.

Screw it. I was going to coffee. It was just coffee. My throat relaxed. I started to breathe more easily. I wondered if this was how Kimberly had felt, her airways closing up. I pushed the thought from my mind.

I texted Christopher that I was running late. Odd to think of him as anything other than Dr. Saito. But I wasn't going to coffee with a doctor; I was going to coffee with . . . a possible friend? Who was I kidding? I was going to coffee with someone I wanted to see naked. Time to think of him as Christopher.

My phone pinged with Lauren's To Do list for the job. I texted back that it would be at least two hours.

Christopher answered back immediately. *No worries. Can I order you anything?*

I felt ridiculously pleased. With Jay, I had been so determined to prove I was self-sufficient that he never got in the habit of doing stuff like that for me. My fault, really.

I hurried into the house and found Jay and Cole hugging. I could see Cole's face buried in Jay's shoulder and a flash of tears. I love my sons so much, and seeing Jay make Cole that happy did what his good looks couldn't; it opened up a trickle of affection. We disagreed on many things, but there was never a doubt that he loved his sons.

Cole wiped his face along Jay's shoulder as he pulled back from the hug. "Can you believe it?" he said, face lit up with joy.

I smiled. "It's a good surprise, for sure."

Jay raised his eyebrows, like he didn't believe I thought it was a good surprise.

"How long are you home for?" asked Cole.

"Depends," said Jay. "I can figure that out later."

I felt heavy inside, not ready to deal with our problems. So much easier to put him out of mind when he was out of sight.

I went into the powder room to pull myself together—a disturbing stew of emotions: anger at Jay, frustration at him for ruining everything, annoyance at his presence, grief over Kimberly, guilt over longing for Christopher.

I thought about how happy Cole had been to see Jay, and I thought about meeting Christopher for coffee and suddenly the guilt took over everything else. I imagined how happy Cole and Luke would be if Jay and I could work things out. How could I be so selfish as to throw away a family that had just barely re-formed after Luke's troubles and my accident? I had to at least try.

With a tired soul, I texted Saito to let him know I was so sorry but something suddenly had come up and I couldn't make it. I on purpose thought of him as Saito, not Christopher. Just a doctor.

Chapter 21

"I'm going to leave you two to catch up," I said to Cole and Jay when I got back to the kitchen. "I need to get to a job."

I stuffed down the disappointment over no coffee with Saito and filled my Yeti with coffee and sugar-free vanilla creamer. Fake energy, fake sweetener, fake organizer, fake life.

On the way to Patty's, I lectured myself. Enough with the self-pity. Put on your big-girl panties and do the job. Focus on Cole's happiness.

My chest got tight. Thomas. Great, even a ghost was angry at me.

Don't worry, I won't forget.

I called Joanna before I got out of the car, but there was no answer. I would check in again right after Patty's.

Patty was waiting in the driveway, dressed in yoga pants and a sweatshirt, her hair tied back in a pony-tail.

"Ready?" I said, laughing in anticipation. Being around Patty was always fun. Upward mood contagion was the positive side of my extra sensitivity.

"Ready!" Patty said, literally pushing up her sleeves. "Fair warning, the damn shed is stuffed."

We walked around the side of the house to a long wooden structure built in the same style and materials as the house. It was about ten feet long and six feet deep, with two wide doors.

"Everything out to the driveway," I commanded.

As we dragged baseball and wiffle ball bats to the driveway, Patty said, "Oh my God, I'm sure you heard about Kimberly? I wonder if she had a medical condition no one knew about."

"So awful," I agreed.

"She was such a fan of OOC, talked you guys up all the time," said Patty. "Said Joanna loved your work. Poor Joanna."

I shuddered, "Can you imagine? Having someone collapse right in front of you like that?"

"So unlucky," said Patty. "Thomas dies and now this." Patty kicked a hose out of the path. "It's such a small world. I'm in Joanna's Walk the Reservoir group, and her stepdaughter was actually Charlie's first grade teacher."

"Serena?"

Everyone knew everyone in this area. Uncomfortable as the target of gossip, useful to me right now.

"Yes. Charlie loved her. Such high energy, so organized, and kept the kids disciplined, but in a completely loving way. It was a big loss to our school when she moved to Sacramento. She was devastated at having to move, but they couldn't afford to buy a house here. Then I think they moved back this direction, maybe Matinville? "

Sounded like a different Serena.

I shook my head as I dragged a sack of stuffed animals onto the driveway. "Real estate is ridiculous here."

"Yeah, even with all our fund raising, we still don't pay teachers enough. It's a crime." She saw the stuffed animals. "Oh Jesus, I forgot about those. When we cleaned out their rooms, I let them keep ten stuffed animals each and these were extra, if you can believe it!"

"Yeah, they expand exponentially," I said, feeling a stab that my boys were past the stuffed animal stage. Past so many stages.

Patty rolled her eyes. "Me and stuffed animals, can't seem to stop procreating. Maybe I could donate them somewhere. The stuffed animals, I mean."

"The police will take them. They keep them for when they have a child they need to comfort."

"Do you know the other Sullivan kids at all?" I asked as we went back and forth with bags and boxes and old toys and broken sports equipment.

"Know of them, mostly," Patty said, wiping a hair out of her face. "I just ran into a friend of mine who got recently dumped by Marco, one of the younger two. I mean, it was never going to work out. Jenna is older than Marco, and he's got mother issues."

I was going to have to meet Connie one of these days.

"And he's wound pretty tight, from what I hear," she added. "But those Sullivans are all good-looking, and he's successful in his job, so I guess desperate women would overlook a personality flaw or six."

An angry ex-girlfriend was just what I needed. "What's your friend's name?"

"Jenna Long. Had a quickie marriage that bombed, now out in the dating world again. Better her than me." She gave me a quick guilty look, like she knew that Jay and I were separated. We hadn't announced it, but we also hadn't really hid it.

"I don't know her. Is she in Montavilla? LaSalle?"

"Oak Creek. She runs the Barre Method."

"I've been meaning to check that out. I keep hearing good things about it," I said. Sort of true. The hearing good things part, anyway.

"Tell her I sent you!" said Patty. "But be prepared to get your ass kicked."

From the back of the shed, Patty pulled out a white box with a picture of security cameras on it. "Oh jeez, we never even opened this. Put this in the Goodwill pile, the new house is wired for security already."

"I think those are expensive. We'll add it to the consignment or resale box," I said. Then I had a brilliant idea. "Actually, I have another client who might be interested in buying it from you."

"Just give it to them," Patty said, waving her hand. "Present from Dan's parents that we didn't need."

I picked up a heavy picture with an ornate frame and was hit was an onslaught of images and smells. Without even turning it around, I knew it was a wedding picture. I felt a rush of time, within seconds moving from a happy, sunny, jasmine-smelling wedding day, through years of disintegration, ending in bitterness.

"What are your plans for this?" I asked Patty, flipping the frame around to see a full-length portrait of a young woman stiffly posed in a big starched wedding dress, lost in all the layers, like the dress had taken over her entire life.

"Ugh, that's my mom's wedding picture. My parents were divorced a long time before my mother died and she didn't want it. She gave it to my sister, who gave it to me, and I just buried it in here."

"You can let it go. It's a nice frame; I'll take it to the consignment store."

Patty looked uncertain. Easier to throw out shin guards than a wedding picture.

Cool air on the back of my neck, and then I felt her mother's approval. She had moved on from the marriage in life and definitely was over it in death.

"It has negative energy," I said. "I'm sure you have much happier pictures of your mother."

Before I could second guess myself, I said, "Your mother gives permission to get rid of it."

Patty stood up from the box she had been sliding out from the wall. "Huh?"

"I feel like she is right here with us, telling you it's okay; you can let it go." I was getting clear communication, and Patty was a kind person, and I needed to get better at these senses.

"I heard you were doing some psychic stuff." Her face was blank.

I shrugged. "Sometimes I pick up on stuff. I can't really know if it is true or not. I just felt that with this picture."

"Is she telling you anything else?"

I held the picture tight, opened mind and body. I was noticing that it was a matter of letting my whole body sense things, not just my mind. A completely different portal than the intellect.

"I'm seeing the most beautiful lilac bush," I said. "So fragrant and dripping with dew. Just lovely."

Patty's face lit up. "Oh my God. Yes."

"She loves it that you think of her when you see the lilacs."

Patty smiled. "Yes! In fact, I already had a bush planted at the new house. We have a gorgeous one here but it is too big to dig up. Izzy, it's true! You are psychic!"

"Maybe don't say anything to my sister?"

"Too late for that," said Lauren, stepping into my view outside of the shed.

Patty swiveled. "Don't be mad!" she said. "This is the greatest thing ever. I'm so glad my mom knows I still think about her! Lilac is our forever connection." Patty slung her arm around my shoulder. "Izzy is the best. I'm going to want her to help me set up everything in the new house. As many hours as it takes."

Patty looked at the portrait. "Yes, take that to the consignment store. I don't need it."

Walking the picture out to the driveway, I thought about how nice it was to tune into something positive instead of all the dark stuff around Joanna. Maybe it wouldn't be so bad to use the skills if they made people happy.

Lauren stalked after me. "Why did you have to do that? I don't want this weird voodoo business associated with Order Out of Chaos. We are trying to *remove* chaos, not add it. It is just so unprofessional."

"It made her happy," I said. "She wants even more hours with our business. It's a positive." I stood and faced Lauren, hands on hips. "I'm not hiding it anymore." I felt a burst of anxiety flow through me but didn't take the words back. I had to save Joanna.

Lauren crossed her arms tight against her chest and sighed. "Why do you have to be this way?"

The question I'd asked myself my whole life. "I wish I wasn't. Truly. But I'm just so afraid someone is going to die and it will be my fault."

Patty lugged a heavy box towards us and dropped it at the end of the driveway. "All these are piano books that can go to a new home." She pulled up the top flap. "No one in my family is going to want the sheet music for *Moonlight Sonata*." She laughed and glanced at Lauren.

"Hey Lauren, I think it is awesome that Izzy is psychic. You guys will never run out of clients!" said Patty. "Clean out your house and your family dysfunction at the same time. You could charge double."

Lauren forced a half-assed smile in response to Patty's enthusiasm. "You are right! It's just, I'm not sure everyone will be as . . . understanding as you."

"Fuck 'em," said Patty. "There are SO many who would love it."

Lauren put on the full plastic smile. "I will definitely think about that! But maybe, until, uh, we decide what to charge, not let people know?" With that she wheeled back towards the shed.

"Of course," Patty said to Lauren's back, then grinned at me. "Lauren could use some of my cookies," she murmured.

Chapter 22

As I was driving away from Patty's, the worries flooded back. Joanna, Kimberly, Jay, and, of course, Saito. Saito's text back had been understanding, but I doubted he'd wait around for long.

Still no answer from Joanna so I decided to drive to her house and check on her before visiting the Barre Method.

Joanna's gate was, for the first time, closed. I pushed the intercom button and waited. I pushed it again. After another long wait, there was a crackle.

"Hello? It's me, Izzy."

Something garbled came back. Not Joanna's voice, but female. Emily?

"Hello? I couldn't hear you," I said. "This is Izzy, here to see Joanna."

This time it was clear. "This is Serena. Joanna is sleeping. Maybe come another time." Her voice was cool. No first-grade teacher love for me.

"Uh, okay," I said.

Was I really going to give up that easily?

I pushed the button again.

"Yes?"

"How is she? I just was wondering."

"Tired," Serena said, and then in a bright voice, "but thank you for stopping by!" The intercom went dead.

I reached into the back seat and pulled the tangerine dress forward into my lap.

What now, Thomas? I asked. *Hey, want to talk to your daughter?*

An image of him shaking his head. *Later. Joanna first.*

I couldn't force my way in, and feeling his irritation with me, I put the dress down in the passenger seat and headed towards Oak Creek and the Barre Method.

As I drove my little side route, avoiding the highway, Lauren called.

"The more I think about it, the more I am sure I do not want you using your psychic senses in my business."

"I told you, I feel like I have to use it. I won't be able to live with myself if someone is hurt or dies and I ignored the information."

"Well, can you use them on your own time? Promise me you won't bring them into any client interaction?"

"No. I can't promise that," I said, anxiety flowing but knowing it was what I had to say and do.

"Then you leave me no choice," said Lauren. "You can't be part of Order Out of Chaos."

Silence from both of us.

"Well, goodbye then," I finally said. I was pulling up to the Barre Method and would have to sort that all out later. She couldn't mean it. She had too many job commitments because she refused to say no, afraid she'd lose out on the business forever.

I found Jenna working the front desk. If she was older than Marco, she didn't look it, her face smooth and glowing, her brows nicely shaped, a hint of mascara her only makeup. Her black hair was pulled into a tight bun, and she was dressed in black yoga pants and a black sleeveless top with complicated crisscrosses in the back. A line of words was tattooed sideways from her shoulder halfway down her bicep. I couldn't make it out without turning my head sideways, so I just smiled and told her I was friends with Patty and asked if she had a moment. Assuming I wanted a tour, she started a walk around the facility.

Dance studios had come a long way since I was a kid. The place was spacious and very sleek, but the energy was too peppy and pressured for me.

"The classes sound cool, but I have another reason for wanting to talk to you," I said to Jenna as we exited the locker room. "It's kind of personal."

Jenna pushed on a door across from the locker room. "Here's my office."

In the office she gestured for me to sit down on an exercise ball mounted on a base. "Umm, very comfy," I said as my nonexistent core wobbled me side to side. "I'm working for Marco's stepmother, Joanna, and there's been some drama in that family. Patty mentioned you had been dating Marco and that his mother was kind of an issue . . .

Jenna was happy to unload. "Connie? She's a lot. Big energy that just steamrolls people. She has Marco wrapped around her little finger, like he's ten years old or something. Any time I've been around her, it is all victim stories. Unfairly treated in the divorce, unfairly treated at work, and she's got her kids believing her. She HATES Joanna, hates her."

Jenna vented for a good ten minutes, the gist being that, away from his mother, Marco was a good guy— really ambitious, obsessive about work, exercise, fairness. A health nut, which was how they met. Probably had a problem with commitment, which Jenna attributed to Connie. He said he couldn't "abandon her like everyone else." Jenna said the last with air quotes and a violent eye roll.

"Would you call him an angry guy?" I asked. That's all I had seen of him.

Jenna frowned, thinking. "It's more about fairness; he can get very angry when something is unfair. Like, how his dad helped Jacques and Serena out with money but not him or Karl. He was very bitter about that. Thought his dad would make it right in the will, but they all got the same amount."

"What did he want help with?" I asked.

"He wants to be a developer," said Jenna. "He's a mortgage broker but says that owning land and developing it is the way to make big money. He and his partner had some property they were buying, but I think the financing fell through. I don't know what's happened since we broke up."

"Do you mind if I ask why you guys broke up?"

"Connie! She had it out for me." Jenna shook her head, disgusted. "I don't know that it was ever going to be serious, but I would have enjoyed him for a while longer."

Jenna looked down at her nails, holding her hand out to inspect each finger, then shrugged. "I'm old enough to learn to move on when a guy has too much shit he's still carrying. Too bad, though; I liked him."

"Does he spend much time with Joanna?" I asked.

"Not while I was with him. I knew about her but never actually met her."

That was interesting. Now, all of a sudden, Marco was interested in Joanna's well-being?

Jenna glanced down at her fitness watch and stood up. "I probably need to get back out there." No doubt her watch had notified her she had sat still for more than five minutes.

I rolled awkwardly off of the exercise ball. "Thanks for your time. You've got a great place here. Oh, and what does your tattoo say?"

Jenna held out her arm and said, "'Right in the difficult.' It's from Rainer Maria Rilke. The whole quote is 'Right in the difficult we must have our joys, our happiness, our dreams: there against the depth of this background, they stand out, there for the first time we see how beautiful they are.'"

"Oh," I said, pausing to take it in. "That's so good."

"Yeah, it's helped me get through a lot. Like right now, it's a good reminder that I can let go of all the Marco bullshit." Jenna broke into an easy grin that made me think that there was something to all this meditation/yoga/core work after all.

"Yes," I said. "Very wise." With that, I hustled out before anyone could sign me up for a membership. Although I'll bet this place could shrink my pooch of a stomach.

On my way home Vivi called. "I've got some good gossip for you."

Just hearing Vivi's voice lifted my mood.

"So I was in Boopsies, you know, just looking around."

"Ha ha," I said. "'Looking around,' my ass. I'm sure you bought three-hundred-dollar silk camo pants or something."

Vivi laughed. "I have to buy things. There is no way that place stays in business without me."

"It's a vanity boutique. That place stays in business because Tina's husband needed her out of the house. It's a tax write-off and a way for Tina to 'express her creative side,'" I said. "There's like four items at a time displayed there." To be honest, I was jealous, although if we had "keep her out of trouble" kind of money, I'd probably pick something besides a boutique. I'd write a mystery novel or design crossword puzzles or something.

"Lucky for you, it is also info central. The LaSalle ladies get their lavender oat milk lattes and wander in to 'look around' and 'catch up,' which is code for 'gossip their brains out.'"

"What did you hear?" I asked.

"I ran into Virginia Forrester—you remember her? Older lady who used to teach English at the high school?"

"Yes, never had her, but I remember her. Always really sharply dressed," I said.

"Yeah, still is. Looks great for her age. Anyway, we got to talking, and I told her I was working for Order Out of Chaos and that we had just done a big garage cleanout at Joanna's."

"Shouldn't be disclosing clients, but go on," I said.

"Turns out she used to go to parties there, back when Thomas was still married to Connie and still drinking. She said there were some wild ones. And then they suddenly stopped. And I said, 'Yeah, I heard it's because Thomas stopped drinking.' And she got a funny look on her face." Vivi was enjoying herself, I could tell. "I could just see, something was up, so I said 'unless you know something else?'" Vivi stopped for a second.

"And?" I prompted.

"Virginia said that something dramatic happened at a party. She was there. One minute, everyone is partying and laughing and the next, Thomas was stomping through all the rooms, telling everyone that the party was over and they had to get out. She never found out what it was but said it had never happened that way, that those parties usually went late into the night, and that was the last party they ever had. And not long after that, Thomas and Connie divorced."

"Huh," I said. "And Thomas stopped drinking right before he and Connie divorced. Maybe something happened at a party that made him stop drinking. Jesus, it would have to be something big, I would think."

"Maybe he caught Connie with someone," said Vivi. "Maybe she's super deviant, was dressed as a dominatrix and banging the caterer in Thomas's closet or something."

"Wow, you are very specific in your . . . ideas," I said.

Vivi giggled. "I'm imaginative. Anyhoo, who knows if it is related to whatever is going on now. But it seemed important."

"Definitely," I said. "Thanks for joining the investigative team. Which, of course, Lauren cannot know about. Although I am currently not working for her."

"What?" said Vivi.

"Not to worry, she'll need me," I said. I had to believe that.

"You know what? We need a murder board or whatever they call those things. Let's get it all up on notes and get some red string," said Vivi.

"That's not a bad idea," I said. "Spoken like a true organizer. We need to organize what we know."

Chapter 23

I walked in to find Jay and Cole both asleep on the couch, feet overlapping at the corner of the L. Cole's blanket was twisted and half on the floor, take-out containers were jumbled on the tray beside the bagel plate and hot chocolate cup, newspapers on the floor, plates and containers scattered across the kitchen island. So much for my clean counters. I know clean counters aren't permanent, but I would have liked a little more time with them.

I poured a glass of wine and took it upstairs to shower off the grime of the cleanout. I was relieved to see Jay's bags piled on the guest room bed but cringed to see how junky the room had become. It had accumulated all the stuff that didn't have a home, which actually made it perfect for Jay.

I detoured into Luke's room, thinking about the corkboard that hung over his desk. Since he was off at college, I was thinking his room could be turned into my murder-solving office. The corkboard was covered in pictures and participation ribbons and posters and papers. I took a picture and texted it to him. *Mind if I take this stuff down to use the board? I'll keep the picture to put it back if you want me to.*

By the time I was out of the shower, Luke had responded. *Throw it all out except the Jimi Hendrix poster and pictures. But fine to take them down.*

I did a quick clear-off of the board and then stuck a couple of Post-it note categories across the top of it. Suspects—Opportunity—Motive. It looked like a pitiful start, but I would add everything I knew when I had more time.

Back in the kitchen, I was surprised to see the mess cleaned up.

Jay was sitting at the counter, beer in hand, a hint of a sheepish smile. Cleaning up was a new behavior for him.

Cole was awake and grumbling. "I'm hungry! What's for dinner?"

"Let's order out," said Jay. "If you want, Iz?"

Somehow his efforts were annoying.

"I was going to make spaghetti. I have some sauce thawing in the refrigerator," I said, pulling a Tupperware container out.

"Yes!" said Cole, doing a fist pump.

Jay sighed. "I've missed your cooking."

"Really? You live in Paris. I imagine there's plenty of good food," I said.

"Tons. But it's not the same," said Jay.

The three of us sat at the end of the long table, right back in our normal spots.

"Comment se passe ton français?" Jay said to Cole.

"Je le parle plutôt bien," said Cole, not as fluidly as Jay, but not halting either.

They carried on a conversation in French, losing me after that first exchange. I tried to feel happy for Cole that he could learn and practice another language, but I just felt left out. I mean, I've had all these years to learn French if I really wanted to but never managed to get past the first lesson in Duolingo. Which reminded me I needed to cancel the membership. Which reminded me I should look through our credit card statement for all the subscriptions I wasn't using. I've helped OOC clients do it and always mean to do it for myself.

I listened to Jay and Cole *parlez vous*-ing and realized I had forgotten how the energy of our family was so male-dominated. Maybe I hadn't ever really paid attention until it was just me and Cole, but it was irritating now.

I heard the name "Olivia" a couple of times and couldn't help it. "Who's Olivia?" I asked.

"Just someone Cole—" started Jay before Cole cut him off. "No one important."

"Fine, no problem," I said. Cole and Jay exchanged amused glances. They were talking about stuff Cole didn't want me to know, right in front of me.

Screw them. I could use my senses and figure it out. Except that it didn't work. I let my brain get fuzzy and felt around to see if there was anything about Cole and this girl. Nothing.

Figures. The senses only seemed to cause problems or get me anxious. Never seemed to calm anything down. I took a big gulp of wine, knowing it was not a real answer but not knowing how else to calm my growing agitation.

While we all contemplated dessert, Jay pulled out his phone. "Let's Facetime Luke! He doesn't know I came home; we can surprise him."

"Wait, let me do it," said Cole. "He might actually answer."

Luke actually did answer, and it was so great to see his face. He looked good, not pale and out of it like he did when he was using. His eyes were alert, like he was really there. I wondered if there would ever be a time I wasn't looking for signs of relapse.

"Dad! Cole! Mom? Wait, what?" Before I had kids, I tended to think of college students as kind of grown-ups, but now that I had my boys, I knew that they were a messy mix of grown-up bodies and unfinished insides.

It was fun to see Jay and the boys interacting, but it also twisted me inside. It was all I had ever wanted, this feeling of family. My parents loved me, but they had both been very devoted to their careers and I was lonely a lot. I had on purpose set out to be more present, more available, than my parents had been. I had always thought I succeeded, but right now the family I had created was leaving me out.

When Cole turned the phone towards me, I automatically shifted my wine glass out of view.

"Mom, it's okay." Luke laughed. "I see alcohol all the time around here. I'm good. You don't have to hide it."

It felt odd, all the same, drinking in front of Luke.

After we finished talking to Luke, Cole got up, washed his plate and put it in the dishwasher. "I'm going to my room," he said, looking back and forth between Jay and me. Clearly, he wanted to give us time alone. "I better look online for my homework. Wouldn't want to get too far behind." He added, "Thanks for dinner," and left.

Jay jumped up. "Don't get up. I'll do it."

He took our plates and set them in the sink, then opened the refrigerator and pulled out the Pinot Gris. "Want some more?"

"Sure," I said. With Cole out of the room, my tension soared. Just Jay and I.

"Feels good to be home," repeated Jay, as he poured.

"I'm sure it does," I said. "How's work? How's Paris?"

Jay shrugged. "You know, they always stick me with the worst staff." He vented about several co-workers—nothing new to me. Either Jay was profoundly unlucky or built to notice other people's flaws.

Jay stopped moving and stared at me. "I've kind of just done what I needed to do, but coming home and seeing Cole . . ." He shook his head a smidge. "I underestimated how hard it would be to be away from him. His last year at home." Jay's voice broke a bit on the last sentence.

"Yeah," I said. "I can see how that would be hard." I bit back a sarcastic comment about how close they clearly still were. Seemed immature to be jealous of that, and yet I was.

Jay leaned down, both hands on counter. "I don't want to go back," he said, staring intensely at me.

I felt my insides turn cold.

"How can I do this?" he continued. "The more I think about it, the more it is bullshit that I've had to move during his last year. I don't want to miss this stuff." Jay teared up. Jay is not a tear-up kind of guy.

I understood. In a million years I wouldn't have agreed to live in another country during Cole's last year of high school.

Cole missed his dad. Jay missed his son. I noticed Jay hadn't mentioned our marriage or the "D" word.

Jay got control of himself. "I'm going to talk to Glenn about moving home somehow. I've done everything they've asked of me. It's time they returned some favors. No one else was able to just up and leave home that fast. There is a lot I can do remotely, especially now that I've got my relationships set up there."

As he spoke, the coldness that had started in my center got heavier and colder and expanded to my entire body. I felt pinned to the earth by dread.

I wished so much I could feel something different but that was it.

Dread.

Chapter 24

"I'm exhausted," I said to Jay. "I'm going to go to bed."

Jay glanced at the clock. It was barely eight. Then he shrugged. "Okay." He walked over to the couch and plopped down. "I guess I'll try to catch a little sleep before my workday starts"—he looked at his watch—"in four hours."

In my room I checked my phone and was relieved to see a text from Joanna asking me if I had time to come tomorrow. I had nothing but time, until Lauren realized she needed me back.

I slipped into Luke's room and cleared off the corkboard, setting aside the poster and pictures. Stared at the blank board, wondering how to organize what I knew about Joanna and her family. I wrote each person's name on a Post-it and put them down the left side. Feeling like that was enough of a start, I did my ab exercises, retinoled my face, brushed my teeth, and snuggled into my bed.

I turned on the TV and found Tyler Henry and watched an episode. I wondered if I could schedule a session with him. What happened when both people could channel the dead? Did different dead people start talking to each other through us? But then, why would they need us?

In the morning, I tiptoed past Jay asleep on the couch, computer open, papers scattered around him.

As I drove, I thought, yet again, about telling Joanna about sensing Thomas. Immediately my shoulders got tight, my arms stiff like someone was literally holding me back. *No!* I could feel from Thomas.

Hey Thomas, most spirits want me to tell their loved ones they are around. What's wrong with you?

That brought a grumpy feeling and one word, *focus.*

Maybe another spirit would be more help.

Hey there, Kimberly, so sorry . . . Can you help me find out what happened to you?

Nothing.

Maybe I could find something to touch that was Kimberly's; maybe that would help connect me with her.

At Joanna's the gate was open, a good sign. I rang the bell and when there was no answer, I tried the door and found it unlocked.

"Hello?" I called as I went down the main hall, anxious as I flashed back to Joanna being gassed.

In the kitchen I found Joanna propped in a chair, barely awake, wrapped in an old pale blue robe. Unwashed dishes sat on the counter, and the table held a jumble of mail, books, and a vase of wilted tulips. The normally cheerful kitchen felt dull and lifeless. As did Joanna.

"Are you okay?" I said, setting the Arlo box on the counter.

"Tired. And groggy."

"We don't have to work today," I said, sitting down across from her. "You can take it easy. And I've got some security cameras if you want them." I gestured at the box. "One of our other clients didn't want these."

"Okay," said Joanna. "I like staying current."

"Can I get you anything?" I asked.

"I was just trying to get up the energy to make coffee."

"On it," I said, jumping up and walking over to the coffee maker. The second my hand touched the carafe an intense fear hit me, and the deep purple color I had associated with Kimberly floated around it.

My brain went back to the day after Kimberly had died. I saw the kitchen as it had been that day and, like a "zing!," my attention focused in on the coffee cup that had been in the sink.

"Did Kimberly have coffee, by chance, the night she . . .?"

"Hmm?" Joanna said, eyes foggy as she stared out the window at the weak sun filtering onto the patio.

"Just wondering," I said. "I remember seeing a coffee cup in the sink the next day."

Joanna's eyes opened wider and she finally looked awake. "Actually, now that you ask, yes. Kimberly did have coffee. Said she needed it because she had reports to write. I forgot."

The vibes coming off of the coffee maker were so strong, I was sure something had been added to the coffee. "Have you had any since then?"

"Yes," said Joanna.

"Do you remember what kind Kimberly had?" I asked, looking at the jumble of open bags on the counter.

"Hmm," said Joanna, face going blank. "Let me think."

I picked up the bags of coffee, one by one, to see if any of them gave off a bad vibe. None of them stood out over the others.

"It was Saturday," I reminded her. "Marco was making the fuss about the gala. Serena came. I got a call from Cole about his appendicitis. I called Kimberly to come over. Imagine yourself back there."

Joanna closed her eyes. "So unpleasant," she murmured. Her eyes flew open. "The blueberry coffee! Thinking about 'unpleasant' made me remember! After you left, I made some and then didn't get around to drinking it and then when Kimberly wanted coffee, she insisted I just warm up the blueberry."

"Good job," I said, searching through the bags on the counter. No blueberry. I looked in the cabinet. Also no blueberry. "Was there any left?"

"Most of the bag," said Joanna. "It should be there. Plenty left because no one else likes it."

No blueberry coffee.

My senses were humming. Someone added something to the blueberry coffee, thinking only Joanna would drink it, then got rid of the bag after Kimberly died.

I wondered if anything had been added to the other open coffee bags. It wasn't worth taking a chance.

"Maybe we should give all this coffee to the police too, see if there is something in it that might have, uh, set off Kimberly's asthma," I said. Joanna agreed, maybe not wanting to follow the reasoning too deeply.

I found a used grocery bag and dropped the open coffee bags into it. "I'm going to run down to Starbucks and get us something."

"You don't need to," said Joanna.

"I want one too. What do you want?"

"I like the vanilla lattes," said Joanna.

"I'll be right back," I said, grabbing my purse.

I wanted to tell her to lock the door behind me, but that was a waste. Too many people knew how to get in here. When I got back, I'd suggest she change all that.

I stuck the bag of coffee next to the space heater in the back seat of the car, hoping the police might be interested in it. This couldn't be good for me, driving around with a double dose of death. I'd have to do something with them both.

I pulled the Post-it notepad out of my purse and scribbled down my new bits of information. "Coffee! Blueberry coffee missing. Pot of blueberry coffee made on Saturday" all got their own notes. Eventually, I'd fill in all the stuff I already knew, but this felt like a good start.

At Starbucks I bought two vanilla lattes, making sure mine was decaf, and two bags of ground coffee to replace all the bags I had confiscated. I hadn't seen breakfast food among the neighbors' offerings and thinking Joanna might not have eaten yet today, I added sous vide eggs and two pastries.

At my car I set the tray with the coffees on the roof and fumbled around for my keys.

"Izzy?"

My heart sank. It was Samantha of the boot camp ESP failure. "Hi," I said as I found my keys, beeped open my door and set the bag with the coffee beans and food onto the front seat.

Samantha was bouncing. "I'm glad I saw you! You were right about my dad!"

"What?"

"The basketball thing! My mom was going through a box of my brother's basketball trophies and said how much my dad loved watching my brother when he played. My dad must have been thinking about that when you tried to contact him!"

"Ahh. Good! Glad it made sense," I said.

"Anything else you can come up with?" She looked hopeful.

"I'm kind of in a rush, am working and need to get back with this coffee before it's too cold."

Samantha deflated. "Right, okay."

"Maybe another time?" I said, mad at myself as I said it. My skills were very erratic these days; why would I offer that?

"Yes! I'll call you," said Samantha.

I asked her to keep the sensing thing quiet for now, pulled the coffees off the roof and climbed into my car.

Back at Joanna's, I put the food on plates and set it on the table. "I got you some new ground beans."

"Oh Izzy, you are so thoughtful." She took a big sip. "Ah yes, that's good. I wish I could get my old energy back. It's just been hard—Kimberly and, of course, the carbon monoxide thing."

"I'm so sorry," I said.

Joanna gave me a wan smile. "It's so nice to have you here with me. You are so easy. Everyone else makes me tense these days."

"I'm glad to be here. Although I came by yesterday, and Serena wouldn't let me in."

Joanna rolled her eyes. "She showed up as I was about to nap and wanted to look around in her old room, but I'm not sure why. Actually, they've all been here this week. And last week. It's like they are making up reasons to be here."

Any of the Sullivans could have taken the blueberry coffee away. Or put something in it to begin with.

"Patty Hathaway told me that Serena was her son's first-grade teacher," I said. "Said he loved her, that she was energetic and fun."

"Yes, kids loved her," said Joanna.

"But . . ." I wanted more.

"She's had some hard years," said Joanna. "She hated Sacramento, and then she had post-partum depression after both babies. She got fired over it at her last job and probably should have sued. And her husband Jared keeps losing his job."

"What was all that like for Thomas?" I asked. I was answered by a hollowness in my chest and a wave of sadness.

Joanna took a gulp of her coffee. "This stuff is like crack. It's delicious." She was perking up, like an almost dead plant that was watered just in time. "It was hard for Thomas. Serena lived with us her first year of teaching, right after we got married. She loved it, but Thomas wanted her to, you know, move on to being an adult on her own." Joanna took a bite of a chocolate croissant. "Thomas actually helped her out with her first apartment. He must have had extra sympathy for her because he didn't do the same for the boys, at least as far as I know. And he didn't have as much as they all thought."

I looked around the kitchen. "It would be hard, I would think. Growing up in a house like this, you'd probably come to believe there is lots of money around." I sipped some more of my latte. My heart was racing and I wondered if they gave me caffeinated instead of decaf.

"Thomas's father had a long illness that ate up most of his fortune, and Thomas was happy for him to use it all. Thomas made a good enough living, but he paid for all the kids' colleges and, of course, had to give Connie half his money. This house is really all that was left."

"In fact," Joanna looked slyly at me, "no one knows that I have paid for the upkeep on this house."

Chapter 25

Joanna leaned back, triumphant. "I sold my house when we got married, and it seemed fair for me to pay for stuff, living here."

Joanna brushed the fallen tulip petals into a pile in front of her. "In fact, without my money, Thomas would have sold the house years ago. It's a lot of maintenance."

"And his kids don't know this?" I asked.

"No. I'm glad they all inherited something when he died—it would have been nothing if I hadn't been taking care of the house. Then again, if he had sold the house, he would have been able to leave them more."

"I think you should tell them," I said. Maybe it would decrease the chance of someone wanting her dead. Then again, Joanna was still sitting on their inheritance.

"That feels too braggy." She wrinkled her nose.

I got up and brought the Arlo box over to the table. "Maybe we should take a look at these cameras before we start on the spare room."

"Sure," Joanna said.

"I heard Karl had some kind of trouble in high school. Must have been hard for Thomas," I said, pulling the three cameras out. My chest got tight, and I felt a flash of anger. Thomas was ornery today. "What happened?"

"I'm not exactly sure. Ran away, I think. Thomas was still drinking, so he probably didn't handle it well."

The cameras seemed pretty straightforward. Plug in, connect through wireless, and set up app on phone to manage them.

Joanna continued. "Thomas had a lot of guilt about how his drinking affected his kids, and he was trying to make up for that. Then there was all the stuff with Jacques."

"What stuff was that?"

"Jacques got in trouble with gambling while he was in college. Ended up in huge debt. We were together at that point."

"Did Thomas have to bail him out?"

"No, Thomas was adamant he wouldn't do that, but somehow Jacques got it settled. Worked it off, maybe? And went through a program. He hasn't had any problems since."

Or has he?

"Thomas and Jacques were the most reconnected by the time that Thomas died. Jacques had gotten religious and apologized for the pain he caused by the gambling. And forgave Thomas for his drinking stuff."

"And how about the others?" I asked.

"Not as much."

More sadness seeping through me from Thomas.

I thought about Jacques and Marco arguing in the office. "We need to get this kitchen done, and of course the spare room, and then if you want, I could help organize the office." Maybe I could find whatever was so interesting to Marco.

"Yes! I should hire you full time!"

"You can," I said. "Lauren actually fired me."

"Why would she do that?"

I paused. "We have different styles. She'll hire me back, but for now, consider me your personal assistant."

"You're hired," Joanna said, holding up her coffee cup as a toast. "This is exciting! I always feel so happy with you around, Izzy." Joanna gave the full wattage of her sunny smile. "I'll get dressed, and we'll do the spare room."

"We maybe should work on the kitchen?" I said.

"Lauren has that scheduled," said Joanna. "I'm just really feeling ready for the spare room." She smiled a bit sadly. "Might not keep feeling that way, so . . ."

"Okay," I said. "We'll do the spare room. While you're getting dressed, I'll put these cameras up," I said. "Maybe one here in the kitchen? One out in the front hall? And the other where?"

"Wherever you think," Joanna said.

After Joanna left, I scribbled furiously onto my Post-it
pad, excited to get home and get my information up on
the corkboard. Then I got to work with the cameras.

The first camera went between a soup tureen and a
curvy pitcher on some open shelves. The second in the
foyer peeking from under a dried flower arrangement. As
I plugged it in, the doorbell rang and I opened it to find
an older couple, the man holding a covered casserole, the
woman a big Tupperware bowl.

"Hi! We're the Newcombs, live across the street," said
the man, dressed in a warm up suit from the 70s, red with
a thick white stripe down the sides. His gray hair was
thin, and his face covered in age spots, but his body
looked like it hadn't changed since he bought the suit.
"I'm Lou and this is Marion."

Marion looked like Rod Stewart if he'd partied harder.
She had spiked shag hair; a puffy, lined face; and eyes
that had seen everything, twice. "We heard about the
gassing. How is she?" Her voice sounded like rusty
wheels rolling over gravel. Had to be a smoker.

"She's recovering. Seems to be doing okay," I said. In
the driveway behind them, a convertible Chrysler was
still running. I could understand why they drove if their
driveway was as long as Joanna's; it would be almost a
mile front door to front door. Ron looked like he could
run that far in his sleep, but Marion wouldn't have made
it twenty yards.

They walked past me and set their containers on the
side table.

"We brought salad and lasagna," said Marion. "Joanna
was so good to us when Lou had his surgery."

The third set of lasagna and salad. I made a note to
myself to take lasagna off my good neighbor offerings.

"Tell her we missed her Tuesday night at The
Wildhorse," Marion said. "But we'll see her at the gala."

I flashed on an image of Marion and Lou line dancing
with Joanna and felt a happy giggle bubble up.

"I can go get her," I said.

"Nah, got to go, got a leathercraft class we can't be late for," said Lou, twitching his warm-up jacket sleeve up to look at a huge and ancient Timex.

"That sounds fun," I said.

Marion shrugged. "We take turns picking. Next one's mine. We're going to do the tantric thing."

My surprise must have shown on my face because, as they went down the steps, I could hear Marion say, "The world is full of prudes, isn't it?"

Lou squeezed a handful of Marion's behind. "Lucky that's not us."

I put the third Arlo on a bookshelf in the office, doing a quick glance around to see if anything interesting jumped out at me. I wasn't going to find anything without snooping through drawers, so I joined Joanna in the spare room. As she got comfortable in an armchair, I told her about Lou and Marion's visit.

"They are so much fun." Eyes twinkling, she added, "You just have to know your boundaries with them."

"I'm afraid to ask."

"You'd be surprised how many swingers there are around here," she said. "It's not for me, but . . ."

"Wow," I said.

"You'd be surprised," Joanna repeated.

"Let's see if we can get the cameras working on your phone," I said, ready to move on. Marion was right; I was a prude.

"It's in the kitchen," said Joanna. Her watch beeped. "Oh, time for my pills, I'll take them and get my phone."

When she got back, Joanna tapped her password into her phone and handed it to me. "Go for it."

I downloaded the app, and asked her to put in her wireless password.

"You do it. It's 'Sunny,'" she said with a little sad smile. "Capital S."

"Now you are going to need a password for this account," I said.

"Just use 'Sunny' again," she said. I had a sinking feeling that was her username and password for everything.

"Maybe add something, a number?"

"15," she said. "For years married."

"Let me test them." I went and held the buttons on the various cameras and, presto, they worked.

"All right! The closet!" I said, sliding open the doors. "There are some beautiful clothes here," I said, as I dumped a pile of suits on the bed. "Would Thomas's sons want them?"

"No, I already asked them," she said.

"Consignment, then," I said.

We worked our way through the closet and a dresser and in the bottom drawer of the dresser I pulled out a display case of six watches. There were several with leather bands, one all silver, and one all gold.

"Thomas's company was really into incentive watches." Joanna laughed. "He didn't want those. Take them all."

"I'm going to get them valued by a jeweler."

Joanna waved her hand, "Do what you need to."

"Let me take a couple of loads to the car," I said. "Give us some more room to work with."

"Okay," Joanna said. "I'm just going to close my eyes for a few moments."

"Are you okay?" I asked. She was back to looking pale and weak.

"Apparently, the aftereffects come and go," she said, leaning her head back against the top of the chair. "I'll just grab a quick catnap."

I draped a throw blanket over her.

"Thank you," she murmured, eyes closed. "That feels nice."

As I hefted the stack of suits into the back of my SUV, a lavender-colored pocket square dropped onto the ground. I picked it up and tried to really tune into Thomas. Maybe it would help even more than the dress. I felt a deep sense of regret, of time lost and relationships damaged.

Come on, Thomas, help me out here. Who is trying to kill Joanna?

Thomas disappeared.

I went around to the front seat and touched the dress and asked the same thing, but Thomas wasn't going to help me. I left the pocket square by the dress. Maybe once I dropped off the dress, I could use the square to try to connect with Thomas.

Back in the house I found Joanna asleep, head canted awkwardly forward. I touched her arm. "Joanna, let me help you to lie down."

When she didn't wake up right away, I shook her arm.

"Huh? What?" she mumbled.

"Let's get you lying down."

She flopped onto the bed across from the chair, curling up on her side. I put the blanket back over her.

"Are you sure you're okay?" I asked.

"Just tired," Joanna managed, without opening her eyes. "Doctor said to get plenty of rest."

"I'll check back."

I was feeling an overwhelming desire to talk to Lucille and realized this might be the perfect time. I left a message and while I waited to hear back, I grabbed my Post-it pad and headed upstairs to look at the kids' rooms.

I started with the room right across from the stairs. It was pink and childish and had to be Serena's first room. Immediately, I felt sadness, followed by loneliness and detachment, oddly mixed with childish playfulness, as if all the versions of young Serena were still hanging around. The room was pretty, with pink and white striped walls and stuffed animals everywhere, and yet it felt nightmarish. I touched a pillow on the bed and got the image of a middle-aged man, balding and sweaty, his face hovering above mine. He didn't feel dead to me, so I wondered if he'd been an intruder. It felt so creepy I left to look at another room.

I found Serena's second bedroom on the opposite side of the house, far away from the first room. The childish pink and white stripes had been replaced by shades of purple everywhere. I looked at high school pictures still pinned to a corkboard. Typical stuff: cheerleader, laughing with friends, some tropical settings with the family. One stuffed animal and an oversized teddy bear, propped on the lilac-shammed pillows at the head of the bed. I picked up the teddy bear and felt a sense of comfort along with an image of many tears absorbed by his fluffy fur. ,

I scribbled some notes and then my phone rang. Lucille, saying she'd welcome a visit. I told her I'd be there soon and did a quick tour through the boys' rooms.

The first room had a banner from Cal Poly San Luis Obispo, pictures of a younger Jacques, and a jumbled dresser top. It was dusty, and I realized I hadn't seen any cleaners here. Joanna must have some for a place this big. I'd have to ask her about that. Jacques's desk was a jumble of old high school notebooks, and his closet was filled with out-of-style clothes. I ran my hand along them and felt a sense of seeking, also a stab of guilt. There was a flash, like light catching on something—maybe a chandelier? Something crystal? I jotted it all down.

Marco's room was neat and lacked personal mementos, except for a string of cross-country bibs thumbtacked in a precise line along the wall. I couldn't resist and checked the times written on them. Competitive, but not as good as Cole. I picked up a half-filled bottle of cologne and felt an anger and a secretive kind of defiance mixed with triumph. Marco had done something wrong.

A room with amps and wires and music posters lining the walls had to be Karl's. I touched an amp, and a feeling of hazy fun came over me, like being at a weekend concert during the day with nothing to do but relax and drink beer. I was anxious to get to Lucille's, but I stopped at Karl's desk, picked up a chunk of thick rope with a knot at the end. I was hit with ocean smells and overwhelming grief and dropped it. This was definitely connected to a death. Was it related to the danger around Joanna? I picked it up again. Felt a mermaid-like presence who then slipped away. I put it back down and left, carefully closing the door behind me.

Chapter 26

As I pulled out of Joanna's driveway, my chest tightened and my gut roiled.

Don't go. Stay here.

Great, *now* Thomas was ready to communicate. Well, too bad. I had promised Lucille I would drive on the highway that was sending my anxiety sky high. I couldn't spend any more time on Thomas right now; I needed to focus on my driving.

I let myself imagine having coffee with Saito, imagined us laughing together, pretended it was excitement pouring out of my skin, not anxiety.

Lucille was waiting at the door for me, the heavenly smell of baking wafting out. My reward for going on the highway.

"You did it!" beamed Lucille, holding the door for me.

I was still jittery. "Too much cortisol zooming around my body, but yes, I did it."

"Come have some Snickerdoodles," Lucille said, walking to the kitchen.

I sat down at the counter, and Lucille pushed a plate with two large cookies on it towards me. "Coffee?"

"I've had too much today. Maybe milk?"

"Got it," Lucille said.

The sun was coming into the cheery yellow kitchen, the cinnamon smell of the Snickerdoodles was like a shot of Prozac, and the warmth of Lucille's smile was so calming. Everything started to unclench.

I guiltily wondered what it would have been like to have Lucille as a mother. My mother went back to school right around the time I hit first grade, and these kinds of warm, peaceful moments disappeared.

I tried not to look like a savage eating the cookies. "These are unbelievably good," I said, my mouth full. They were chewy and sweet and worth any weight they might add to my thighs.

I finished the second cookie. "Let's get down to business. Let me at those papers."

I peeked into the small dining room beside the kitchen. "Any chance we can use the dining room table?" It was covered with a pale blue linen tablecloth and, aside from a centerpiece of cut flowers, it was empty.

"Of course," said Lucille.

We sorted by type of bill, ending up with stacks around the entire perimeter of the table. "Now, let's put each stack in order of date, putting the duplicates in the shred box," I said. "Most recent on top, to oldest on the bottom." Maybe I'd do the same with my bills at home. Just sort them. I could do that step.

As we worked, I told Lucille about trying out the skills with Samantha and Patty. "I can't make them happen. They just seem to happen or not. But I do get a sense that when I'm trying to communicate with someone who is dead, it really helps if that person *wants* to communicate."

Lucille nodded in agreement. "Yes. Eventually, you may be able to tune in whether they want that or not, but I don't like trying to sense something from someone who doesn't want that. It seemed invasive."

"Here's my other problem," I said. "Thomas won't stop bothering me, but he won't tell me much. Just 'she's in danger' and 'stay' or 'go' kinds of things."

"Maybe he's still stuck somewhere he can't get through very well," said Lucille. "Or maybe it's a clue, like he has mixed feelings for some reason."

"It is almost like he just wants me in front of her as a bodyguard, but doesn't want me to actually figure out who is doing it." I could feel Thomas sadly agreeing. Keep Joanna safe without revealing who wanted her dead. A hope that it would just go away. Which made me even more suspicious of his kids.

"And how do you know when you are feeling your feelings versus someone else's?" I asked. "It's so confusing. It's all in my head and in my body, my stuff and other people's all mixed together."

"That takes practice too," said Lucille.

"Like, coming here today, I was so anxious. And I know that part of that was my being afraid of the highway, but I wonder if part was Thomas not wanting me to leave Joanna alone. But my body can't tell the difference."

"It can get muddy." Lucille paused, a clutch of papers in her hand. "And how is Lauren reacting to your using these skills with clients?"

"She fired me," I said.

Lucille looked around the table at our stacks and raised her eyebrows.

"She'll hire me back. And then I'll be ahead of my work," I laughed. "Or it's free. Or whatever. I did want to get this job done, but I also wanted to ask you more questions."

Lucille giggled. "And?"

"And I wanted some more baked goods," I said. "Your cookies are amazing."

I looked at my watch. "I better get back to Joanna's; she's probably awake by now."

"We've made a lot of progress!" Lucille said, looking around the table. "This is great. Thank you, dear." She walked to the kitchen. "Let me pack up some cookies for you to take home."

I'd be stupid to turn down Lucille's cookies, so I stuck the Ziplock she gave me in my purse. "I have plenty of free time, for now, anyway," I said. "I'll come back soon."

"You're welcome anytime," said Lucille.

Impulsively, I gave Lucille a hug. Just touching her brought such a sense of peace and kindness I almost cried. I wished she wasn't going away so soon.

The peaceful feeling lasted until I pulled alongside Emily's car in front of Joanna's house. Something in my chest fluttered with fear.

As I walked down the main hall towards the back of the house, Emily ran towards me. "Where is my mother? I can't find her!"

"She's in the bedroom next to hers," I said, hustling towards the spare room.

Emily pushed past me and got there a step ahead of me.

Joanna was still asleep on the bed, completely still and very pale.

"Mom!" said Emily, her voice loud and scared. She shook Joanna's arm, but there was no response.

"She was okay this morning," I said, panicked and guilty. "She got sleepy and seemed too tired to make it to her room, so I helped her lie down here."

I bent closer. "She's breathing. That's good."

No matter what Emily did, she couldn't get her mother to wake up.

"We should call 911," I said.

"Do it!" Emily said, still shaking Joanna. "Mom! Mom!"

I called 911 and then Emily questioned me. "When did you leave? Was she still coherent?"

"A couple of hours ago. She was just sleepy, said it was the aftereffects of the carbon monoxide poisoning."

"Why did you leave?" Emily said. "You should have stayed here with her!"

She was right. I hated myself sometimes. Nothing was clear to me.

The doorbell rang, and Emily ran to let the paramedics in, where they made quick work of getting Joanna onto a stretcher and moving her out.

"I'll see you at the hospital," I said, trailing after Emily as she followed the stretcher.

"Don't bother!" she snapped, whirling around towards me. "This is all your fault! She doesn't need your kind of help." She spun back around and ran out the door.

Chapter 27

I told you not to leave. This time Thomas's words were completely clear. I was back at my car, holding the dress.

You are going to have to give me more than that, I thought back at him, angry at his lack of help.

And angry at Emily. How could she be mad at *me*? I was the one trying to keep her mother safe. I was getting tired of this family.

I took a couple of calming breaths. What could I do on my own?

I could take the coffee to the police. No, it would need to be from Joanna. I got the coffee out of the backseat and hid it in a half-full bin labeled "table cloths" in the garage. Fingers crossed Joanna would be okay and could make the call.

It occurred to me that if someone poisoned the coffee, they could have poisoned other food in Joanna's house. Back in the kitchen, I opened the refrigerator and slowly touched each thing, picking up nothing. Same with the cabinets and pantry. When we organized the kitchen for the gala, I would convince her to throw it all out and start fresh.

Driving home, I wished I could start fresh too.

I found Jay sitting at the long table where I had left him this morning, papers scattered, two computers set up, the TV droning in the background. I had forgotten about his constant need for background noise. Seemingly soothing to him, mind-grating to me. When he saw me come into the kitchen, he leaned back and stretched. "Whew. Good timing. Time for a break."

Jay got up and went to the refrigerator for a beer. "Want one?" He laughed. "I am so turned around I don't know if I should have breakfast coffee or evening beer. My sleep is for shit too."

"No thanks," I said. "I'll be right back."

I ran up to Luke's room and stuck my Post-its up on the corkboard. It seemed kind of random at this point, but later I'd spend time trying for some organization.

Before heading back downstairs, I sent a quick text to Emily. *So sorry about Joanna! Pls let me know how she is doing. I should have stayed to make sure she was ok.*

I left out that Joanna hired me as her personal assistant since the first thing I did was leave.

Back downstairs, I dropped onto a barstool. "I didn't make a plan for dinner."

"Cole's going to be late, so it's just us," said Jay. "I ordered from Guido's."

Good, no dinner decision. Although we couldn't just keep pretending we could afford stuff like that. I pushed that thought away. I was good at pushing stuff away. Hence our money problems. And our relationship problems. And my cluttered house.

Jay was facing me across the island, leaning back against the counter behind him. "Did Raymond not come this week?"

"I stopped the gardeners to save money," I said. "I've been meaning to get out there and mow."

Jay winced. Dual finance denial. Although I'm sure it causes conflict, it's better if every marriage has at least one financially responsible partner.

"I'll do it," said Jay. Then he took a big breath in and let it out. "Where are you with, you know, us?"

I felt my body close in on itself, like a roly poly bug folding into an impenetrable ball. I managed a shrug. "I guess we need to get started with the, you know, details." I couldn't say the word "divorce."

"Yeah, about that," said Jay with a sheepish smile.
Oh no.
"I want to come home. Everyone thinks it would be so awesome to live in Paris, but not like this. I miss my family."

I stared down at my phone, then looked sideways, unable to make eye contact. I reached around and squeezed the back of my neck to try to relieve the tension that was petrifying my muscles.

Jay ended the silence first. "I miss you, Iz. I don't want to end things."

I snuck a glance; he was crying.

Shit.

I stared down at the counter.

"I miss the old Izzy, the one from before all the shit with Luke," Jay said.

I looked up, anger stomping out sadness. "What? Like I'm someone different now?"

"No. Yes. I don't know," Jay wiped his tears with the back of his hand.

"So sorry I didn't handle my son's addiction perfectly," I said, neck and shoulders rock hard.

Jay rolled his eyes and head. "There! That's what I mean. So hair trigger! I didn't mean anything personal. You don't have to be so sarcastic."

"'You turned into a bitch' isn't personal? Guess what? I'm a nice person without you here." I was done keeping it in. "I'm never angry anymore. You've been here less than a day, and I'm angry again. I don't know how to get past it."

I got up and pulled out a half bottle of Chardonnay from the wine fridge, poured myself a glass and went back to my barstool. With Jay home, I'd have to go back to buying full bottles.

"If I work it out to move back, am I moving back in here or getting a place?" said Jay, staring down at his feet. His turn to avoid eye contact.

Hadn't we already decided this? Why was he making me say it again? Then again, there was no way we could afford another place.

I took my time to answer. "That would be great for Cole." I paused. "And it's not like we could afford another place."

"I want to work on things," he whispered.

"Maybe," I said, not meaning it. "Right now I'm just so stressed with working for Lauren, and there's a big problem with Joanna, one of our clients."

"Like, counseling kind of working on it," Jay added.

I looked at him in surprise. He had resisted it before, tried it once, and quit.

"Izzy, I haven't given up on us. I don't want you to give up."

The gentle voice undid me.

Jay walked around the island and wrapped his arms around me from behind. "Just tell me you want to try . . . please."

I felt myself disappearing inside, like everything was shrinking in towards my center to hide. Like he was a threat. How could I even think that? He was a good dad and wanted to keep his family together. I was the messed-up one. "I want to want to try," I mumbled.

The part that was hiding inside rose up in protest, pounding tiny hands on the inside of my chest. Stop! You don't want him back here!

My brain reminded the little creature that Jay was actually trying, that we weren't yelling at each other, that I owed it to the boys to try. The little creature huffed and sat down hard on my intestines, reminding me she was not going to go away.

The doorbell rang, and Jay went to get the dinner. I saw a reply from Emily on my phone.

No thanks to you she will be ok. Vitals r good, just deep sleep. Won't need U for a while.

I answered back: *Think someone put something in coffee that Kimberly drank, so maybe the other food or drink stuff at your mom's shouldn't be eaten. Seems like something is making her sick? Kimberly drank coffee (blueberry) not just wine and now that bag is gone.*

Saw the bubbles. And then:

U R not a dr Maybe someone who almost died fr CO poison might not b all better.

"Thank God," I sighed as Jay came back in.

"What's going on?" he asked as he unloaded chicken parmesan, veal Marsala, veal piccata, and salad.

"Wow, you went all out," I said.

"Some for Cole for later, second dinner," said Jay. "Why 'thank God'?"

"Joanna. Our client who had the carbon monoxide poisoning? She's back in the hospital! But it looks like she'll be okay."

"Yeah, what's that whole story?"

"Sit down," I said, sliding a piece of the veal piccata and a piece of the chicken parmesan onto a plate. "I'm going to be my full honest self. I've always just kind of ignored my extra senses. They were subtle and easy to push away. But the accident set off a bunch of new stuff, and it won't go away. I didn't ask for it. I don't want it. But. It. Is. Here. And I'm tired of pretending it is not."

I inhaled a couple of bites of the veal Marsala. Nothing stops me from enjoying good food, and I took a moment to savor it. "I really can sense stuff other people can't. I almost never get stuff on our family. But . . . you were emotionally involved with Sarah Melville. I knew it from picking up your pants. Sometimes when I touch objects, I just know stuff."

I held out my hand in a "stop" position. "I don't want to know about it."

"Okay." Jay said.

As we ate, I told him the whole Joanna story. Thomas and his urging me to protect her. The way I had known she was in danger, the impulse to go into her house and save her, the knowledge it was the space heater, the coffee, the works.

For once, he actually listened. By the end, we had finished dinner, he had drunk two more beers, I had finished off the half bottle of wine, and we were sitting on the couch, me cross-legged in the deep corner of the L with a pillow in my lap, him with feet stretched out onto the ottoman.

"What next?" asked Jay. "Sounds like you need to go visit Joanna tomorrow."

At least, he wasn't trying to talk me out of what I knew.

Jay added, "I don't understand it, but I really do believe this is happening to you."

We sat in silence.

"And I'm sorry," he said.

"That could cover a lot of things."

"I'm sorry I didn't listen when you tried to tell me before. Sometimes I'm an ass." Jay gave a sheepish smile. Could be genuine but, then again, he was very good at getting what he wanted from people. "I'm really glad you want to try."

I actually said "I *want* to want to try," but I didn't correct him.

Later, alone in bed, I thought about how Jay was trying, which should have brought relief but just left me frustrated. And annoyed. I thought about Saito, the intense connection I had felt so immediately, his unnatural and mesmerizing calm. Could I just step away from an old, complicated relationship and into a simple, new one?

I know you can't just run away from problems; they so often follow you. Because maybe it was me that was the problem.

Chapter 28

I woke up in the morning feeling odd and then realized that my chest wasn't tight. As if Thomas was feeling more relaxed about things. I kind of felt like my old self, which should have felt more comfortable but felt less so.

No word from Lauren. She must be really mad this time.

I slipped into Luke's room and filled in a bunch of Post-its with notes I hadn't gotten written down yet. I stuck all the possible people I could think of under "Suspects." I filled in a bit by each person under the next category of "Motive," then what I knew of "Opportunity." After some thought, I added a section for "Victim" and added Mr. Jacko, Joanna, and Kimberly. Then I added "OOC" and "Lauren" and "Izzy" under "Victim." It seemed a stretch that we were the target, but it had occurred to me that someone could be targeting OOC. Seemed like something all good detectives did— look into the victims.

I was scheduled to take Cole for a follow-up appointment with his surgeon. Of course, Jay wanted to go too, so the three of us climbed into Cole's Jeep, as my car was too full of undelivered castoffs from Joanna's cleanout. At the hospital we walked into the building, me hoping to see Saito, but dreading it with Jay by my side. Though he was scruffy-faced and puffy-eyed from working in the middle of the night, Jay was cheerful and kept bumping shoulders with Cole.

After we found Cole's doctor on the third floor and Cole was pronounced "looking good," I told Cole and Jay I wanted to go check on Joanna.

"We'll find something to eat while you do that," said Jay, hitting the elevator button.

In the elevator Cole stood, arms crossed, face stormy, furious at the running restriction the doctor had just laid down. Jay slipped his arm across Cole's shoulders, and Cole relaxed just a smidge, leaning into Jay. Of course he missed his dad, and I was happy for Cole that he was home. We stepped out into the large, round lobby that looked more like a high-end hotel, with its shimmery tiled floor, deep couches, and scattered towering orchids. Convenient to all the doctors located in the hospital setting.

Without any extrasensory warning, Saito stepped out of the elevator next to ours.

His eyes lit up when he saw me. And then they shifted to Cole, and then Jay, and the light got careful.

"Hey Cole, how are you feeling?" Saito asked.

"Oh hi," Cole said. "I'm good. Can hardly even notice I'm missing an organ."

Saito's eyes crinkled in the most adorable smile. "It's not one you need."

Jay stuck his hand out. "I'm Jay Bishop, Cole's dad. Did you take care of him?"

"Yes, in the ED. Not much to do, he'd already diagnosed himself." Saito gave Jay a friendly smile.

Worlds. Must. Not. Collide. Even as my brain turned to mush, I could admire Saito's calm, his easy way of introducing himself to Jay. Just another patient's dad. Like he hadn't asked out his wife.

Jay's eyes squeezed the slightest bit at the sides, and I could see his brain working. Putting it together that this was the doctor he had overheard when I forgot to hang up the phone in the ED.

"Yes, hello, Dr. Saito," I said in a fake cheery voice. Probably emphasized the "Dr." too much. I talked too fast. "Jay and Cole are getting food, and I'm going to find Joanna Sullivan—remember the one with carbon monoxide poisoning? She's back, and I'm worried about her. Good to see you. Bye."

I walked away, feeling like an idiot. I turned down the first hall I found, just wanting to get out of Jay's line of sight. Before I could go back to the Information desk, Saito appeared at my side.

"Need help finding her?" he asked, a smile hovering.

I looked backwards, no sign of Jay and Cole.

"I'm sorry," I said, shoulders slumping. "I'm an idiot."

"A cute one," said Saito, then clapped his hand to his mouth, pretending to be shocked. "Did I say that out loud?"

"Dr. Saito, that is inappropriate." I laughed, feeling better. He wasn't mad. He still liked me. He was trying to lighten my mood.

Saito pulled out his phone. "Let's see where Joanna is. I'll take you."

"I'm sorry about the coffee," I said.

"It's okay. I think I can see what happened," said Saito.

"No, I mean, I'm sorry, for me," I said, heart racing at my daring.

Saito looked up from his phone. Those eyes, so hypnotic. Telling someone he had brown eyes would give no sense of the warmth, the good humor, the brilliance of the person shining out. The rush of energy looking into them almost felt indecent. "I'm glad to hear that," he said.

I looked away before I did something embarrassing, like throw myself at him. I spoke in a rush. "We are supposed to be divorcing, he came home from Paris to see Cole, I didn't even know he was coming." Jay believed I had agreed to work on things, but right now I wanted nothing more than to spend more time with Saito. He was the definition of "attractive." Like I was being physically pulled towards him.

"Your mom kind of already said that, remember? So, Joanna is in Building D." He gestured down the hallway. "This way."

We walked down a long hall, into another lobby and to another set of elevators. The whole time we walked, I was hyper-aware of him next to me. His height, probably a good four or five inches taller than my five-eight; his broad shoulders above mine; his easy gait. We glanced at each other a couple of times, and I was glad Jay wasn't around—anyone could have seen the attraction.

I told him the latest on Joanna (minus the extra sensory information) and asked if she could really be having aftereffects of the carbon monoxide poisoning.

"Sure," he said, hitting the elevator button. "It's a hard thing to predict. I have seen patients do better and then get worse. It can take a long time to recover." He glanced at me. "I wasn't the one who admitted her this time, so I don't really know anything, not that I could tell you if I did." He softened the last bit with a mischievous grin.

"I'm really worried about her," I said as we stepped onto the elevator. "I'm afraid her stepkids might be trying to speed up her, uh, end of life."

"Really?" Saito said, eyes widening. "That would be awful."

I loved it that he didn't doubt me. Then again, he probably saw just about everything in the ER.

We found her room and Saito knocked. "Hello? Mrs. Sullivan?"

Joanna was asleep in bed, hooked to several monitors. Emily was sitting reading by the bed, looking like she'd aged ten years in a week. A sick mother and the sudden death of your cousin will do that to you. At the sight of me, she jumped up, closed her book around a finger to hold her place, and pulled me into the hall with her.

Saito stayed in the room, no doubt understanding I should talk to Emily alone.

"What are you doing here?" Emily asked, decidedly not friendly.

"I wanted to see how she's doing, what they've figured out," I said.

"They are worried about her heart now, so it's hard to know. They are doing tests. Not that it's your business."

Emily dropped her book, and I leaned down to grab it for her. As I handed it back, I felt around but picked up nothing about her. Come to think of it, the world was feeling muted, like the extra senses had taken the day off.

Emily gave me a hard stare. "Why are you hanging around us?"

"I'm worried someone is trying to hurt your mother," I said. "I think her coffee was poisoned and Kimberly drank it instead. And if that's true, then she's still in danger."

"That is ridiculous. Although," Emily tilted her head, "this is the second time you have been around when she passes out. Maybe *you* are doing something to her!"

"Me! Why would I have any reason to hurt Joanna? I'm the one worried about her. I just wondered, what if one of Thomas's kids wants that house sooner rather than later?"

"Don't leave me out of the crazy accusations," said Emily, crossing her arms over her book.

I had just been about to tell how I had stashed the coffee, but held off. What if she was involved?

"I looked up Thomas's will. That house is worth a couple of million dollars. And his kids get it when she dies."

"You looked up his WILL?" screeched Emily. A passing nurse jumped at the sound and gave us both a dirty look.

"Just for a second, think about it," I pleaded. "What if someone is trying to hurt her? And accidentally hurt Kimberly? I just have this really strong feeling so I started wondering who might have a reason."

"They get the house. So what?" Emily said. "We all knew that. Why do you care?"

"I care about your mother!"

"Maybe you should just go," she said as Saito came out the door.

"We need to finish organizing the kitchen before the gala," I said.

"Don't worry about that. Either Wanda can do it or I will. Just go."

"Okay," I said. "But please watch out for her until it gets figured out."

Saito and I walked back towards the elevator.

"What was that about?" he asked.

"Her daughter didn't believe me when I said I thought someone might be trying to hurt Joanna. Then she said, if someone was trying, it was me."

"That seems ungrateful." He looked at his watch. "I need to go. And I'm guessing your . . . family is waiting for you."

We rode down the elevator, painfully aware of each other's presence, and as he turned to go left and I to go right, he grabbed my hand and squeezed it. "I'm patient," he said, his eyes locked on mine. "I can have coffee now or I can have it later. So . . ."

I squeezed back. "Okay."

I stood still for a moment to watch him walk away and savor the energy his hand had left.

"Mm-hmm," said a woman waiting for the elevator a couple feet away from me. She was maybe sixty, dressed in scrubs, with wise eyes peeking out under a matching cap. "I don't know who you are," she said, "but I haven't seen him look at anyone like that before. Watch out—half this hospital will be hatin' on you if they find out."

"He's kind of cute, isn't he?" I was almost giddy at her words.

"Cute ain't the half of it. He gets marriage offers a couple of times a day. Other propositions too. You must be something special." She cackled in a deep, raspy way. "This is good. I'm definitely winning the pool. I said no one here was going to bag him."

I shrugged like "who, me?" but couldn't stop smiling as I walked away. Coming into the building where Jay and Cole were, I put on the bland business face Lauren had taught me, shoving my crush energy into a mental locker.

Chapter 29

Back home, I tried to tune into Thomas for help with Joanna but couldn't sense anything. Odd. I pulled out the tangerine dress and held it but only got the faintest sense of him, like he was there but far away. Or not even there, and I was just imagining something. Not a good time for the senses to go on the fritz.

Fine. I'd just figure it out myself. I'd ask Joanna about anyone around her house, like cleaners and gardeners. I could visit Jacques's winery. I could find out where Karl's band was playing. Before I could come up with how to talk to Connie and Serena and Marco, my phone quacked.

"So, uh, it turns out that we have a bunch more consultation requests," Lauren said.

"Uh-huh," I said.

"Vivi is great but refuses to work full time, and Lacey is not back, and I haven't found other people yet," Lauren said.

"And?"

"Okay, I need you. In fact, people are asking specifically for you," said Lauren. "Samantha Rollins was so insistent that you are scheduled to meet with her tomorrow morning."

"You do realize that Samantha wants me to channel her dead father, right?" I said, panicking because the senses didn't seem to be working.

Lauren sighed. "Yes. This is so against my better judgment, but I'm willing to give it a try. Of course, you must realize the readings are in *addition* to the organizing. The *organizing* is the focus."

"I'll think about it. I have other options. Joanna hired me as her personal assistant."

"You can't do that!" said Lauren. "She's an OOC client."

"Maybe," I said.

"What do you mean?"

"Emily is upset with us. Joanna is in the hospital again, and somehow Emily's mad at me."

"Jesus, Izzy. One easy phone call, is that too much to ask?"

"Yeah, sorry. Anyway, I'm not listening to Emily. I'm trying to keep Joanna safe, so if you want me back, I have to be allowed to do my sensing and do whatever Joanna needs. And I want a percentage of the business."

"Fifteen percent," said Lauren.

"You're hysterical. Forty."

"Now you're the one being hysterical. Twenty," said Lauren.

"Twenty-five," I countered.

"Look, we were supposed to build this together. And I get it—you had Luke's stuff and the accident and the whole Jay thing, but I built this myself. Now you want to just jump in on the profits?"

"I'm recovered. Luke's good, Jay's not an issue. But it turns out I'm a good personal assistant so . . ."

"Fine!" said Lauren. "Twenty-five percent. I'm still boss. And any Joanna stuff goes through OOC."

"Okay," I said.

"I need you to swing by the Ryans and grab the last load of stuff for the kiddie consignment store. I left it stacked in the garage." With that, Lauren hung up.

After dropping off the kiddie clothes, I googled Karl's band and discovered they were playing in Oak Creek at Xave's.

I should have taken Thomas's clothes to the adult consignment store next, but the traffic was bad and it was two towns and a highway away. I'd do it later. I thought about dropping off the tangerine dress at the dry cleaners but realized then I would have no way to connect with Thomas. Maybe it could wait a day or two.

***

Vivi expertly wedged her SUV into a tight spot on the street and flipped off the driver of the car who honked at her for cutting in front of him. She yelled a good Philly slur and laughed in delight.

"I forgot what it was like to go out with you at night," I said as we headed towards the bar.

A pack of girls in their early twenties passed in front of us, trailing a cloud of good smells—perfume and hair products and skin creams—laughing and talking over each other. I felt a pang of jealousy; they had nothing to worry about beyond who would buy their first drink.

Xave was dark with the exception of the bar, the top of which was glowing in a Mediterranean blue, the two-story wall of liquors behind it lit to showcase the bottles as if they were jewels. Vivi and I grabbed drinks and one of the last open tables in the back.

The band was good, and Karl was very good. Kind of a Lenny Kravitz feel, both in sound and his appearance: ripped form-fitting jeans; a tight t-shirt showing muscles; tattoos; and a couple of silver link chains of varying lengths around his neck. Something about the glint of the chains reminded me of something, but I couldn't catch it. Lots of women in front giggling and preening for him.

Thinking it might be harder than I had expected to talk to him during the break, I went back to the bar.

"Can I help you?" asked a bartender, her scoop-necked "Xave" black shirt showing an expanse of colorful tattoo that spread across her entire chest and up to her chin. She was Latina, probably mid-thirties and constantly undulating to the music.

"What does the band do when they take a break? I was hoping to talk to one of them."

The bartender smiled knowingly and a mouthful of braces shone in the bar light. This was a woman who knew exactly what she wanted to look like and was making it happen.

"No, not that, I just know his family and wanted to say hello. How should I catch Karl?"

"Buy him a drink. I'll tell him it's from you. He likes the IPA."

"Give him a big one," I said, and told her which tab was mine. "Very cool tattoo," I said leaning in to see a riot of flowers and twined vines. "Did it hurt?"

The bartender laughed. "Like a motherfucker." I felt boring and predictable compared to her, just another blond in a pair of jeans. She looked like someone who could put Shania to the floor with one hand and catch her flipping cocktail shaker with the other. I wouldn't be surprised if she owned the bar. "You Xave?"

She nodded yes, her eyes friendlier than they had been before. "Point for you. That beer will be on the house."

We shared a smile, and I headed back towards Vivi, not really paying attention until I collided with someone. "Sorry!" I said.

"No problem," said the man.

"Rupert!" I said.

"Izzy, a delight," said Reptile Rupert. He was wearing new clothes: a pale cotton shirt that fit him well, over slim black pants, possibly lululemons?

"Izzy, this is Adley. Adley, this is Izzy. She's one of the organizers."

Adley was six feet tall and built like a Humvee. She had short platinum hair spiked up into points, a wide, tanned face, and a slash of red lipstick for makeup.

"Nice to meet you." I stuck out a hand.

Adley smiled, teeth blindingly white against the red lipstick. "Same."

A slow song started.

"Ooh, I love this one," said Adley. "Bye." She dragged Rupert onto the tiny dance floor and pulled his head against her chest.

Finally, the band took a break. Women swarmed the stage, but my tattooed friend followed through, handing Karl a pint and pointing in my direction. Karl's eyebrows raised, and he smirked.

"Hey, girls," Karl slid into a seat across from me.

"It's women, and you guys are great," said Vivi, standing up. "I'm hitting the bathroom."

"Thanks for the beer," Karl said.

"It's girls' night out—I mean, women's—and your band is great, and then I thought, why not chat a bit?"

Karl seemed to be trying not to laugh, which annoyed me. "It's like that, huh?"

I felt myself blushing. "Like you're available. Popular band, lead singer? I'm sure you are set."

"Matter of fact, I am," said Karl, warm and genuine for a second.

"Wife? Girlfriend?"

"Something like that," he said. He sipped the beer. "That can't be why you came."

"Honestly, I'm worried about Joanna. I wondered if the family had any kind of thoughts on her."

"In what way?"

"Like maybe that is too much house for her."

Karl's eyes flickered with interest. "Hmm, it just might be. She didn't sound like she was ready to downsize. Has she looked at anything?" His voice was casual, but I could feel the energy rise in him.

"No," I said. "But at some point, maybe that would be right for her?"

"Yeah, probably," he said, leaning back and clasping his hands behind his head, muscles flexing.

"Has anyone asked her about that?" I asked.

Karl brought his hands back down and drank more of the beer. "Not me. After Dad died, we kind of drifted away."

"What is bringing you all back now?"

Karl looked embarrassed. "We should have been more in touch. And then Jacques called us all up . . . kind of laid on the guilt."

Serena had said the same thing.

"And I realized I would kind of like something of Dad's to remember him by, so I thought I'd look through his collections."

He was lying and smiling, like "aren't I just adorable?"

"Sorry you lost your dad. And it must have been hard when your parents divorced too."

Karl shrugged.

"You were still at home then?" I asked.

"Yeah, so, what does this have to do with Joanna moving or not moving?" Karl said.

I leaned forward. "I'm kind of, well, maybe divorcing, and I'm wondering what that's like for the kids, you know?"

Karl's eyes flashed. Like he had just switched my category in his brain.

Whatever it took.

"Sorry," he said. "Or is it congratulations?"

I shrugged. "Little of both. What was that like?"

Karl drained his glass and set it down hard. "Some sucky parts, but so what?"

"Was there anything you wish your parents had done differently to make it easier?"

"Almost everything," said Karl. He slid back his chair and stood up. "Probably better to not call your ex 'a fucking loser' to your kids. I would start there."

"Right," I said. "Was that your mom or dad?"

"Mom. Thanks for the beer." He paused. "Let Joanna know if she decides to downsize, I'm happy to help move stuff."

"Got it. Hey, you guys are really good. Sort of a Lenny Kravitz vibe."

Karl's face lit up. "Thank you! I love that dude." With that, he swaggered away.

Vivi slid back into her seat, eyes bright. "I've got some excellent intel! Karl's girlfriend is pregnant!"

"I knew it!" I said, thinking of the image of the stroller I had seen attached to him.

"I was in the bathroom and heard someone throwing up and talked to her when she came out of the stall. Karl is kind of stressed about the baby. You know, money-wise." Vivi sat back, triumphant.

Karl's need for money was more pressing than he let on. And I still felt like he was looking for something at Joanna's. I didn't buy his "I want something of my dad's to remember him by' bullshit. His eyes had lit up at the idea of Joanna moving out of the house. Was any of that enough motive to try to kill her?

Chapter 30

The next morning my phone buzzed as I was lying in bed, trying to convince myself to get up and do my PT exercises. Happily, it was Joanna.

"Am I catching you at a bad time?" She sounded completely lucid.

"No, it's great to hear your voice," I said.

"I'm feeling so much better. I'm going home today."

"That's great," I said, relief coursing through me.

"I was wondering, though, were you here yesterday? I feel like I'm going crazy, losing track of time and people."

"Yes, in the morning. You looked like you were asleep, and Emily was there. She came out to talk to me in the hall."

"That's a relief!" said Joanna. "Emily left before I could ask her. Were you serious about being my personal assistant?"

"Yes," I said. "I'm back with Order Out of Chaos, but Lauren agreed I could still be your personal assistant." Sort of.

"I have so many calls from Wanda about the gala. I just can't handle it all myself. Can you come help me?"

"Of course! Happy to," I said.

We agreed I'd come by in the afternoon.

On my way to Samantha's, I stopped into the Village Green to buy a scone and a chai tea latte. Switch up the coffee consumption a bit. After placing my order and stepping to the side, I looked around at the morning crowd. I caught sight of the back of a familiar head and remembered that Jay had said he was going to find a different spot to work. Then my insides burst into flames.

Shania sitting with Jay.

She was leaning forward, face propped on her right hand, head tilted, flirty-focused. Even if I didn't want him, I definitely did not want her to have him. My name was called for my order, and her head shot up. Her eyes found me, and a big smirk appeared.

I shrugged, like "hey you can have him," grabbed my scone and tea, and slid out of the cafe.

In the car I set my tea in the cup holder and it tilted sideways, spilling a bit. I pulled it back out and saw the collection of discarded jewelry. OOC clients would be appalled to see how messy I kept my car. I pulled the bracelet and earrings out of the cup holder, slid them in the slot in the door, and set my tea back into the holder.

What an imposter. A disorganized organizer. I needed to clean up my car. Clients could potentially see it, after all. It was stuffed with things that needed to be dropped off, old takeout food bags on the floor, castoff jewelry mixing with pens and straws and broken charger cords in the side pockets.

Messy car, messy house, messy life. As I drove to Samantha's, I wondered how I could have ever let myself fantasize about another man. It was silly to think marriage stayed wildly romantic for decades. I was just normal. I wasn't going to think about Saito anymore. Jay deserved a chance.

Feeling heavy and old, I pulled up to Samantha's single-story ranch house, surprised to see Lauren's car there. I must be on probation.

Lauren popped out of her car. "Don't make this weird, okay?"

"Izzy!" Samantha called, popping out of the front door. "Come in!"

The foyer and living room were immaculate, not a shred of clutter to be seen. Samantha led us to the kitchen which, though dated, was also spotless.

Lauren looked around. "I'm not sure you need us. In fact, I might want to change this consult into a job interview. This place looks amazing!"

Samantha looked sheepish. "Well, I really am interested in Izzy's talents—you know, the sensing ones." She paused. "But I could use some help with my garage."

We followed her to the garage. It wasn't the worst I'd ever seen, but it was overstuffed.

"You remember Greg," Samantha said as her husband climbed off of a stationary bike wedged into a corner.

"Of course, how're you doing?" I asked. "This is Lauren."

Greg was streaming with sweat and looked like he was constipated. "Right. Hi Izzy," he said, scooting past me into the house without even acknowledging Lauren.

Samantha looked uncomfortable. "He's, uh, not a believer."

I shrugged. "It's okay."

"Anyway," Samantha gestured at the garage. "I really would like help sorting it all out."

Lauren walked around the garage. "Use these much?" she asked, pointing at a jumble of tennis racquets, wiffle ball bats and fishing rods.

"Only occasionally," said Samantha.

Lauren pointed at a pile of baseball equipment. "Use this a lot?"

"Just about every day," said Samantha.

"How many kids?" asked Lauren.

"Three. Plus, of course, all of our stuff."

"How would you feel about clearing out this section?" Lauren pointed to the right side of the garage near a window. "You could either put up a section of peg board on the wall to hang stuff or do something like lockers, one for each family member to stow their gear. Shoe cubbies on the bottom, hooks for baseball bags, that sort of thing."

"Yes! I love it," said Samantha.

"If it doesn't have a home, it just ends up living on the floor, and then stuff gathers around it," said Lauren. "And then, without meaning to, you are using the floor for storage."

"So true," nodded Samantha.

Lauren walked around the rest of the garage. "And what percentage of this stuff do you think you use?"

"Fifty percent, at most," said Samantha.

Lauren beamed. "This place will look great. We'll help you sort and get rid of stuff, and then I have a guy who can put in the cubbies and wall stuff."

Lauren had offered her tease of ideas with the gear lockers. She said she didn't want to give away all the ideas or people would never go beyond the consultation. I could see her calculating. This would be a one-day job, at most. Unless she wanted to split into two half days.

"I'm thinking one day," said Samantha, echoing my thoughts. "But I'll pay you for two, for a session with Izzy.

I could feel Lauren's excitement. That was a lot of money for something that cost her nothing.

"Maybe something right now?" Samantha asked. "Just see what you can tune into? About my dad?"

I hadn't been feeling much connection to the sensing. "Maybe we should schedule it."

Lauren turned to me. "Go ahead, just a little bit right now." My turn to offer a tease.

"I'll try," I said. "But like I told you before, it comes and goes. I can't seem to make it happen, at least not yet."

Samantha moved closer to me. "What would help?" The desire in her face was breaking my heart. I hated this kind of pressure.

"Do you have anything that belonged to your dad?"

Samantha looked around. "Hmm. Oh! These were his golf clubs. Mom gave them to us." She pulled out a club and brought it to me. "Here!"

I held the club and closed my eyes.

Nothing.

I let my brain go soft, like a kind of blank that was an invitation that I was open.

Nothing.

I opened my eyes and saw Samantha's eyes full of hope. I saw Lauren's face tightening.

I closed my eyes again. Hello? Anyone? Samantha's father?

Nothing. I tried harder. I imagined someone playing golf . . . I imagined an old guy playing golf, but it felt like me just trying to conjure up something.

I wondered if being close to Lauren's negative energy was throwing me off. "I'm going to walk around," I said and walked into the house, holding the golf club.

Greg was in the kitchen, chugging a thick, white drink. He grunted at me and left the room. He'd always been fairly friendly, so either he was really freaked out about the senses or he was just generally unhappy. I remember the earlier sense I had that Samantha was unhappy in her marriage. Seemed to be going around.

Then a burst of insight. I had been feeling more like myself. Myself from before the accident. Myself from before Jay went to France.

The senses had faded. Maybe they were gone for good.

Right when Lauren was prepared to give them a shot.

Right when they were about to help our business.

Right when I was in the middle of finding a murderer.

I tried one more time but could get nothing. I wasn't going to try to fake it.

I walked back to the garage, shaking my head.

"Not coming today," I said. "So sorry. Just one of those times, I guess."

The light in Samantha's eyes dimmed, and her whole body seemed to slump from disappointment. "Okay. Well, I get it."

"So when would you like to set up the garage cleanout?" Lauren said, looking at her iPad. "We might be able to fit you in next week. This should be a quick one."

"I'm going to check with Greg on some things. I'll call you," said Samantha.

I had failed the test. No garage cleanout.

Chapter 31

Back in my car, I watched Lauren zoom away from Samantha's, not bothering to answer her call that came seconds later.

What if the senses were gone for good? I leaned into the back seat and touched the tangerine dress. Nothing. Oh no. Not long ago, I would have been happy for them to be gone. Now I needed them.

My phone buzzed with a text from Joanna asking for a ride from the hospital. Perfect timing.

At the hospital, Information directed me towards the C wing, through a beautiful flower-filled courtyard. As I glanced towards a scattering of tables outside a café, Saito walked out beside a woman, both of them laughing.

I felt a stab of jealousy, even though just this morning I had been angry at my husband for sitting with another woman.

Trying to rush past them, I managed to trip on a completely smooth walkway. The stumble, and my little whimper, caught his attention.

"Izzy!" Saito called, hurrying over. "You okay?"

"Yeah, fine. Just getting in my daily embarrassment."

Big, dazzling grin from Saito. God help me.

"What's the injury du jour?" he asked.

"Coming to pick up Joanna."

"Right, okay, good." He was babbling. How endearing. "How are you? How are . . . things?"

I sighed, my shoulders going up and down in defeat. I should be saying, "We're working on it," but the words wouldn't come out of my mouth.

Saito stared into my eyes, also quiet. How can silence be even more intimate than talking?

Without breaking eye contact, Saito reached for my hand. "This feels ridiculous, and completely unprofessional. But I'm not Cole's doctor now." His eyebrows went up, like "here goes." "I feel very drawn to you. It's almost mystical. I know we don't know each other, and I know you are married or separated or whatever, but I will never forgive myself if I don't say something, right now, when you might be . . . trying to decide something."

My heart was pounding, my hand sweaty.

"I have never had this reaction to someone," he continued, with an adorable nervous smile. "I understand things are complicated, but I'm hoping for a chance. I can wait. Take as long as you need to with figuring stuff out, but . . . is there, I don't know, is there any chance?"

I couldn't handle the eye contact any longer and looked down.

He misunderstood and let out a disappointed sigh.

"No!" I said, looking back in his eyes. "I mean, not no. I mean, no, don't think I was saying no."

I giggled at how idiotic I sounded. "I feel it too."

The most delicious smile back.

"It is really hard," I said, not wanting to let go of his hand, unable to say the words that would end this feeling. My brain said, this is not how to save your marriage; my heart said, don't let go of this. I had never felt like this before either. Which seemed insane. He was right. We didn't know each other.

I squeezed his hand. "Yes. There is a chance."

A held breath expelled. "Good. Take as long as you need."

"Okay." I didn't know how I was going to do it. My brain and heart felt like they didn't even reside in the same body.

Saito gave a final squeeze. "See ya."

"See ya," I whispered.

The whole way to Joanna's room I was spinning. Everything felt right, and everything felt wrong.

***

Back at her house, Joanna wandered around her kitchen. "So good to be home. I hate the hospital."

"Me too," I agreed. "What did they find out? Emily said they were testing your heart?"

Joanna frowned. "Yes, when I first came in, something seemed off. The rhythms or something. And then it corrected. Every time, it seems there is a new symptom."

Didn't seem like it could be coffee this time, which reminded me. "Hey, I'm thinking maybe you should give the police the coffee bags that were here. To test if anything in them set off Kimberly's . . . attack."

"If you think so, call the police."

"It might be better if it comes from you," I said.

Joanna called and left a message, although I wasn't convinced that the right person would get it.

"Another thing," I said. "If someone did put something in the coffee, what if they put something in other food around here?"

"Oh no, Izzy," Joanna said. "That can't be. It's just been some bad luck."

Without thought, I blurted, "Joanna, sometimes I sense things. Like a sixth sense."

Whoosh! Thomas flew back into my body. I could barely breathe with the tightness of my chest, and pain stabbed through my rib cage. I wasn't even touching anything related to him, as far as I knew.

Stop stop stop! I felt him saying.

Joanna looked doubtful. "I'm not sure I believe that stuff."

My vision got dark and I grabbed for the top of the chair beside me.

"Izzy! Are you okay?" said Joanna, grabbing my arm and helping me sit down.

I put my head between my knees, trying to stay conscious.

Fine, Thomas! I thought. *I won't say anything. Yet.*

My vision cleared, and my chest relaxed enough that I could breathe.

"Right, maybe fanciful to have these impulses," I said, forcing a light tone. "Just an idea, you know? Anyway, I was thinking, since we need to get everything organized for the caterers to be in here, maybe this is the perfect time for a fresh start? Just toss everything open or expired. Start fresh."

"I guess it couldn't hurt," she said. "Oh, I better take this," she said, looking down at her phone.

I grabbed a notepad and made a list as I cleaned out Joanna's refrigerator. It is pretty fast work when you just throw it all out. I promised myself to do the same thing to my overstuffed refrigerator.

"Hmm. Oh my. Well, that is a puzzle," I heard Joanna saying. "I'm so sorry. So hard to understand. I'll be in touch."

"That was Kimberly's boyfriend," said Joanna. "They found beta blockers in her blood work, which she's never taken. And there was nothing added to the wine. He wanted to know if I saw her take anything, but of course I didn't."

Because it was the coffee, I was sure.

Joanna waved her phone at me. "So many voicemails from Wanda. Can you just look through them?"

She handed me the phone, and I scanned them. "Okay, I've got this, I'll call her. Most pressing is that she wants to get her landscaping people here to make sure everything is all cleaned up. And then they are going to start installing the tent this weekend."

Joanna waved a hand. "Tell her I'll just leave the gate open. They don't need to arrange the time with me."

"Speaking of landscaping, you have gardeners for here, right?"

"Yes, dear Carlos, have had him forever."

"You get along with him?"

"Of course. He and his son, and now his grandson, have been taking care of these grounds forever. They were here when Thomas's father had the house. Carlos is ancient, so his son really runs things now, but Carlos likes to keep active."

"Do they ever come inside?"

"No, what are you getting at?"

"Just wondering, you know, if anyone might have a grudge against Kimberly, or you."

"It wouldn't be Carlos."

"What about your cleaners?"

Joanna shook her head. "Izzy, I don't like where you are going with this. In fact, I'm in the process of getting new cleaners. My old one retired, and I just haven't gotten around to calling the people she recommended to replace her."

"But do they have the garage code?" I asked.

"Yes, but again, like Carlos, Peggy has been coming here forever. She's just lovely and there is no way she would have any kind of grudge against me. It isn't like I fired her or treated her badly or anything."

For the moment, the gardeners and cleaners seemed like a dead end.

Joanna looked at the cluttered kitchen. "I don't know what to do first. I really need to get through these papers. I'm probably missing something important I should be doing."

"I'll help you; we'll do it right now and make a list of all the stuff you need to do. Are there any things on the calendar coming up that you have to get to right away?"

"Well, just the trust meeting next week," she said, shuffling papers around on the counter and pulling out a calendar.

Yes! That! I felt a pinging and a feeling of cold air hitting not only the back of my neck but my whole body, like Thomas was swirling around my body.

"What's the meeting about?" I tried to sound casual.

"Something about a vote."

"Actually, maybe we should start with these papers." Joanna swept her hand over the jumble of mail and papers. "I should find that letter from the lawyer, make sure I have the time right, and read over the stuff I'm supposed to vote on."

Yet again my chest felt so tight I almost couldn't breathe. Thomas was beyond agitated, and his reactions were wreaking havoc on my body.

I abandoned the refrigerator cleanout. "Let's find the most urgent stuff and then sort the rest into piles based on action needed."

Halfway down the pile, she found the lawyer letter.

"Oh yes, here it is," said Joanna. "I remember opening it and putting the date on the calendar."

Joanna handed it to me. "Could you look and see if there's anything I need to do before next week?" She picked up the next paper. "Ugh, another recall on my car; I need to get that into the dealer at some point."

Scanning the letter, I went completely cold.

Joanna was chattering away about car recalls and insurance statements, oblivious to the multi-million-dollar motive for her death. She seemingly had not understood the implications of the upcoming meeting. According to the letter, the Sullivan family held a huge tract of undeveloped land that was in a seventy-year conservancy trust during which time no property could be sold or developed. After seventy years, the trustee would decide whether to move the land to permanent conservancy or sell or develop it. The seventy years was up next Tuesday. Joanna was the sole trustee. For land that could go to Thomas's children.

"So," I said, keeping my voice light even though I was shaking with danger. "This looks like you have to vote on whether to keep the land conserved?"

Joanna looked up from a Blue Shield statement. "What? Yes. But I'm just going to do what Thomas planned. Permanent conservancy. Just a quick signature. Easy peasy." She waved the insurance statement around. "I hate these things. Is this just a statement? Something I owe? Which part do I owe?"

How did Joanna not realize that by voting to conserve the land, she would permanently deny Thomas's kids millions of dollars?

"What do you know about this land trust thing?"

"Thomas's grandfather owned a big chunk of land here in LaSalle, all those hills that back up to Grant Road? Thomas's dad set them up in a trust so they wouldn't be turned into developments. Thomas was the trustee and named me his successor."

"Does the family know about this land? Did Thomas talk about it?"

"I don't think so," said Joanna. "Oh look, my Triple A is overdue. I've got to get on these bills."

"Why wouldn't they know about the land? It sounds like it is family land, and maybe a lot of it?"

"Something about the way the land was acquired," said Joanna. "I never heard Thomas talk to his kids about it. It came up when we were doing all our legal stuff before we got married. Pre-nups and all that."

I felt Thomas sighing, troubled about the land trust.

"Who takes over as trustee if you couldn't do it?" I asked.

"Hmm," said Joanna, cutting off half of a pastry and nibbling on it. "I'm sure the lawyers probably explained all that right after Thomas died, but there was just so much. I don't remember."

Every one of Thomas's kids had been in this kitchen with this letter sitting there, open and available.

And maybe Connie knew the seventy-year term thing; she'd been married to Thomas for a long time.

"Why was it set up as a seventy-year thing?"

"Thomas laughed a bit about how his mother wouldn't marry his father unless he agreed not to use the land. It sounded like Thomas's grandfather got that land in a questionable way. Maybe something to do with the Miwok? Thomas's mother was part Miwok. But she didn't want him to sell it either, didn't want other people to have it."

I heard a rustle in the trees outside the kitchen and felt something cool move through my body. *Not to be disturbed* floated into my head.

Joanna continued. "So, Thomas's father put it into that long trust, and then Thomas didn't want to raise trust-fund kids, so he agreed with his father that he'd just permanently conserve it when the time came. Plus, I'm not even sure it is zoned for any kind of development."

Joanna shuffled more papers, "Oh, there it is!" she exclaimed picking up a large pill organizer. "Don't get old, Izzy. Look at how many pills I take every day." She held the organizer towards me. It was blue translucent plastic and had seven columns with four rows each, labeled 'AM, Lunch, Dinner, PM.' It had a sticker along the side edge that said "Week 2."

"Wow, that's a lot," I agreed, still obsessing about the land trust. I had to talk to the attorney. How to ask Joanna without scaring her?

"Blood pressure meds, arthritis, vitamins, hormones, and a blood thinner," said Joanna, taking the organizer with her to the sink and getting a glass of water. "After you guys came the first time, I was so inspired that I ran out and bought four of these organizers for the month." She opened a drawer and showed me three more organizers, one full, the other two empty. "I'm going to fill the others as soon as I get my refills."

"I love it!" I said. "Any of those beta blockers?"

"Nope. One of the few things I'm not on."

We worked our way through the rest of the papers on the counter, ending with a neat set of folders labeled Urgent, To Do, and File.

"I'm getting a little tired," Joanna said. "Maybe I'll just lie down a bit." She looked around the kitchen. "Feel free to work on this without me. Just toss whatever you think should be tossed."

"Happy to," I said.

She grabbed my hand. "I love having you here. It's like you are family. I feel like I've known you forever."

Thomas fluttered around inside me, as if she was holding his hand and it made him happy. It felt invasive, in the middle of someone else's relationship.

Joanna gave a big yawn, her eyes almost closed. As she stood up, she tilted sideways.

"Whoa!" I said, grabbing her arm. "Let's get you to your room."

Was this more of the aftereffects of carbon monoxide?

Chapter 32

While Joanna slept, I called Wanda and let her know Joanna would leave the gate open for the landscapers. Then I finished tossing all the food that was open or could have been tampered with, opening enough room in the cabinets to move stuff off the counters. Flour and sugar canisters, vitamins and supplements, unopened olive oil—all got stored away. It wasn't finished, but clearing off the counters really gave the kitchen a clean and workable look.

As I worked, I thought about Saito's smile and holding his hand. I thought about Joanna and Thomas and about my senses, seemingly back working. I wondered if I had to be here at Joanna's for them to work or if Thomas was somehow blocking other sensing so I would focus on Joanna. Puzzling but a huge relief to have them back.

I checked on Joanna; she was still breathing peacefully. As I dragged the heavy bags of tossed food to the garbage can, I ran through the people in her life, thinking about what each might want from her, and I remembered Connie. It seemed like a huge oversight that I hadn't talked to her yet.

I knew she lived in the La Salle Country Club condos. I knew she played tennis. I knew she was a drinker. Was she working again?

Back in the kitchen, I spent a few seconds admiring the neat look of uncluttered counters and then called Vivi. "Do you know if Connie has a job? I heard she was fired, but then did she find anything else?"

Vivi was breathing heavily.

"Whoops, did I interrupt something?" I asked.

"No." Ragged breath. "Perfect timing, actually. I needed an excuse to stop this yoga video. It's killing me. Namaste my ass."

"I'll call back," I said.

"No! Truly, I can't do this shit. Us Italians are meant for pasta and walking a lot—that's it. Not this body-bending crapola."

"I need to meet Connie."

"I haven't heard that she's working again, and she's always at the club. We have a match with LCC coming up," said Vivi. "But not sure how much you'd actually get to talk to her." Vivi took a couple of deep breaths and laughed. "I can't even do the damn breathing right. She's always at LCC at the bar. I'd try there first. We must know a million people who belong."

We were both silent a moment, thinking.

"I know, I'll call Ted Jamison" I said. "I'm way overdue to meet with him, and we could meet there." Ted was the financial adviser we had hired after Jay's brother screwed up our retirement investments. We had met once and had a whole list of "action items" that I hadn't taken any action on, so I had never scheduled a second meeting.

Before we hung up, I filled Vivi in on the land trust letter.

"This is getting juicy," said Vivi. "My money is on Jacques."

"Not obnoxious Marco?" I said.

"Plenty of people are obnoxious, but doesn't make them killers. Jacques's old holier-than-thou religious persona seems fake to me. I think he'd do anything to be a full partner in his winery."

"Don't forget Karl with a baby on the way. And Serena who is angry she doesn't live in the area."

"True. Let me know what you find out from Connie," said Vivi.

I tracked down Ted, and we set up an appointment to meet Saturday night in the bar at the LaSalle Country Club.

That done, I turned my attention to Jacques. Thought about visiting him at Yield. That could be interesting. See him in his natural environment.

Maybe Jay and I could go for a wine tasting. A way to show some basic cooperation?

I felt crazy inside. I had just been thinking about how Saito might be my soulmate, and now I was considering a wine tasting to show I **was** making an effort with Jay. I pushed the romantic nonsense aside and looked up Jacques's winery, Yield. I clicked around, booked a reservation for tasting at 6:00, then called the winery to make sure Jacques would be there. Texted Jay to ask him if he wanted to go. Within five minutes, Jay had replied. The plan was on.

I checked back on Joanna and managed to help her wake up enough to have a conversation.

The words *Keep her safe* floated in, joined by a flood of nostalgia and a heaviness in my chest. Hard to believe how relieved I was to have the sensing back.

"Whew, I feel kind of out of it," said Joanna, rubbing her hand through her hair, leaving it messy. She was propped up in her bed, sleepy-eyed, but at least she was talking.

"Your body must need rest." It sounded good but somehow felt wrong. Maybe I shouldn't be giving medical advice.

"Yes," said Joanna, her eyes brightening a bit. "We never give ourselves permission to just rest, do we?"

"Can I make you something to eat before I go?"

"If you really don't mind," said Joanna. "All I'd really like is some soup. There's some frozen creamy carrot soup in there you could heat up for me." She paused. "Unless you threw it out?"

"No, it was sealed if I'm thinking of the right one," I said.

By the time I had the soup heated, Joanna was up and moving around the kitchen, so I felt okay about leaving.

"I left some Snickerdoodles for you," I said, motioning to the Ziplock bag on the counter. "And don't forget, I'm your personal assistant. You can call me for anything."

***

At home I added the land trust information to my corkboard, changed into something more suited to wine tasting than organizing, and Jay and I headed out.

Without thinking, we climbed into my SUV, me in the passenger seat, Jay driving. We looked at each other and smiled a little.

"Kind of automatic," Jay said. "You want to drive?"

"Only if you're tired," I said. And then I panicked at the thought that we'd be in a car for over an hour each way. It will be fine, I told myself.

"I'm two and a half energy drinks into the day. I could probably run there with you on my back," said Jay.

As Jay backed out of the driveway, my phone buzzed with a text.

It was from Saito, and my face started burning.

Even when I'm not drinking coffee, I still enjoy thinking about coffee. Great to run into you. And two coffee cup emojis.

I flipped my phone over and looked out the window, face blank, while my insides squirmed with happiness.

How could I be mad at Jay for sitting with Shania when I was fantasizing about Saito? Actually, that was an easy one. I could always be mad at Shania. She was a horrible person.

Jay fiddled with the radio, flipped between my presets, then looked at me. "Why don't you pick the music?"

Surprises never end. We always argued over which music to play, rarely agreeing. Early in our relationship, it made us laugh; then eventually, it was just one more area of conflict. The differences that seem so cute in the beginning morph, inevitably, into irritants. Maybe that was the problem with marrying too young or fast—infatuation covered an abundance of differences, some of which turn out to be crucial. Or maybe, once you want out, you view everything through a filter of reasons to leave.

"I have an idea," Jay said as I searched my playlists. "We could talk about everything that's wrong—and there is a place for that, But maybe sometimes we should just try to have fun together. Keep it pleasant."

Trapped in a car, that seemed like a good idea. "Okay," I said.

"So, tell me about this Jacques character," he said.

I filled him in on what I knew about Jacques and then googled him. "Let's see what the world knows about Jacques."

I quickly found Yield's website and the "Our Staff" page. Jacques was described as "one of Napa's rising stars who has established himself quickly as one of the most innovative winemakers in an area stocked with the very best."

Yield was started twelve years ago by a brother and sister and one of their friends who didn't seem to be listed with the winery anymore. The website emphasized their use of recent technology, both in the growing of the grapes (e.g., fancy weather sensors helping to cut down on water use) and in the social media marketing. Jacques looked like a perfect fit for the place.

"Joanna said Jacques wants to be a full partner, and he had a disagreement with Thomas over it."

"Because of the wine thing or the money?" asked Jay.

"I think both. Thomas was worried about Jacques working in that industry but also either didn't have the money to help or wouldn't."

"Sounds like a motive," said Jay.

He was definitely trying. Why did that annoy me?

With Jay focused on the road, I snuck a quick reply to Saito: a thumbs up and a coffee emoji.

What was wrong with me?

Chapter 33

We almost missed the turnoff from route 29 into Yield; the sign was small and minimalist, a matte black stone finish with "Yield Vineyards" in silver. We bumped down an unpaved driveway, circled a large structure that looked like an architect's modern re-imagining of a barn, and ended in a small parking lot. Vines grew up and over a pergola along the length of the building, with small metal tables and chairs underneath. The tables were full of people, an array of wine glasses in front of each. Long rectangular planters spilling over with colorful flowers served as a barrier between the parking and the seating.

We parked and went into the tasting room, which was just as charming as the outside. It was small, with a hammered tin bar along the right side. Soft miners' lights hung over the bar and a couple of high, round tables, one of which was in use by a couple so young and so googly-eyed they had to be on their honeymoon.

"Welcome!" said a young man with wavy brown hair pulled into a ponytail. "Here for tasting?"

"Yes," I said. "I made an appointment; I'm Izzy Bishop."

"Right on," he said. "I'm Trevor." He placed two lists on the bar. "Here are the tasting options: we have the Flight or the Reserve. And for $20 more, you can add a cheese accompaniment to your experience. We have a great local selection."

"We'll do the Flight," I said, and thinking about my pooch, "no cheese."

"Inside or outside?" asked Trevor.

"Inside, and I'd like to say hello to Jacques."

"Let me start you out with our Viognier. It's got peach and honeysuckle notes." He poured us each a decent tot. "I'll find Jacques," he said, heading to a door behind him.

I wanted to go warn the giggling newlyweds that infatuation is not love. Maybe I was a tad bitter.

Jacques appeared through the doorway with Trevor. "Izzy!" he said effusively. He was dressed in jeans and a black V-necked cotton sweater, with a little gold cross peeking out the top. Simple, refined.

"This is Jay," I said. "Thought we would try out your winery for date night."

"Good choice," said Jacques. "What have you started with?"

Trevor filled him in on our Flight choice. "I've poured the Viognier."

"Great, I'll take over," Jacques said. Trevor grabbed a couple of bottles and headed out the door.

"This is our Old Vine Zinfandel. It has a medium body, an aroma of blackberry bramble, and a hint of spice," said Jacques, pouring us each twice the size of the last taste. Then he grabbed another glass and poured some for himself.

"Date night to Napa, huh?" Jacques said, expansively exuberant. Sampling his product, no doubt.

Jay gave the wine a swirl and sniffed it, a step I had skipped. France had probably refined his wine tastes.

"Trying to win her back," said Jay, startling me with his honesty. Maybe it was a good strategy—give a little intimate information, get a little intimate information.

Jacques gave me a knowing look. "A woman likes to be pursued!" he gushed. Definitely tipsy.

"Doesn't hurt," I said.

"Plus," said Jacques, taking another sip of his wine and leaning forward, "I know you talked to Karl last night, so I guessed I was next."

"I'd never turn down the chance to taste wine, but yes, I'm worried about Joanna," I conceded. "Wanted to check in with her family, see what you guys all think."

"About what?" asked Jacques.

"If you think that might be too much house for her."

Jacques shrugged. "Not my decision."

I held up my glass. "This is very good."

Jacques nodded in acknowledgment, "It's one of my favorites in this flight." Jay and I had decided he'd drive home, so I was going to enjoy this. Jay dumped the rest of his wine in the spit bucket. I hated to see wine thrown out, but I appreciated his caution as my driver.

"You really think she might not be able to handle the house?" asked Jacques, so casually I couldn't tell if he really didn't care or cared so much he was holding back.

"She's not recovering that well from the carbon monoxide poisoning, and I worry that she can't manage it all." Under the bar, my fingers were crossed to cancel my lie. Immature but felt right.

I tried to tune into Jacques with the extra sensing but got nothing. Why were the senses so unreliable these days? I'd have to figure it out the old-fashioned way. Asking questions.

"That house has been in the family for a long time. My dad grew up there," said Jacques, pouring our next taste. "This is Fonte, a mixed black. It's a blend of 30% Zinfandel, 25% Carignane, 25% Petite Syrah, and 20% Alicante. Have you talked to Emily?" Jacques asked. "She'd be a better judge of Joanna's ability to live alone in a big place."

"Not yet; they are dealing with Kimberly's death right now," I said, watching him for a reaction.

Jacques frowned. "Yes, so tragic. And right after that plumber dying as well." Jacques shivered.

"You ever feel like that house is cursed?" I asked.

Jacques tilted his head in consideration. "The land used to belong to the Miwok, so I always kind of thought there was something special about it." He shrugged. "Cursed, though? Nothing to make me think that."

"Are you guys all good with Joanna living in that house?" I asked. "I assume it comes to you when she is, uh, done with it."

Jacques leaned on the bar. "I'll be honest. I had a difficult relationship with my dad. The divorce was hard, and I was really happy for him to get sober, but he worried about me, what I do." He waved a hand, indicating the winery. "I get it. But Joanna made him happy. And for that, I'm glad."

"Did I hear something about land in a trust?" I said innocently.

Jacques looked puzzled. "No, I don't think so, unless you are talking about the house—that's probably in a trust." He looked at our glasses. "Ready for your next one? This one is our Cabernet."

I thought about Jacques and Marco fighting in the office at Joanna's.

"Nice you can be glad for your dad and Joanna," I said. "Not everyone can be that way. It's hard when a family breaks apart with divorce. Sometimes brothers and sisters kind of bond over that; sometimes they get pushed apart. What about you guys?"

Jacques rolled his eyes. "Like any brothers and sisters, I'm sure."

"I just wondered . . . Marco seems so quick to anger. Was he always that way?" I asked.

Trevor had returned and seemed to want Jacques's attention.

"Ha!" Jacques barked. "Yes. And I'm his favorite target! I'm trying to be forgiving, but Marco makes it hard sometimes. It's like he has a grudge against me, for no reason."

I loved tipsy Jacques.

"Table at the end outside asking for you," said Trevor before Jacques could say any more.

"Right back," said Jacques, picking up his glass and walking a little unevenly out the door.

Trevor watched him, a little smile playing across his face.

"Something about what Jacques said funny?" I asked him.

Trevor nodded. "Everyone but Jacques can see it. Marco's in love with Julia."

"Jacques's wife?" I asked.

"Yeah. Marco comes up here a lot. One night he had too much and was kind of crying on my shoulder. Complaining that Jacques 'stole her.' But even if he hadn't told me, anyone can see it."

"Does Julia . . . return the interest?"

"No. Apparently Marco and Jacques met her at the same time, and she was only interested in Jacques. And believe me, they are the better match."

"Someone driving Jacques home tonight?" Jay cut in.

Trevor nodded. "Julia has his truck and is coming back to get him."

The Julia thing was interesting, but it didn't fit with the argument I had overheard at Joanna's. Marco and Jacques both seemed to know something the other had done wrong.

Jacques returned as we were tasting the last of our flight.

"Your wines are excellent," Jay said to Jacques, holding up his glass as a toast. "I'm working in France, and these hold up to the best I've had there. The Fonte is particularly good. What a texture! And beautifully integrated."

Jacques beamed. "Thank you. I feel like God called me to this."

Jacques's excitement for his work made him seem more likable. Then again, lots of serial killers were known to be charming.

Jay and I talked each other into signing up for the wine club and moved all the Goodwill and Consignment piles enough to fit a case of Yield into the back of the SUV.

"I wonder how far Jacques would go to be successful. He's too good to be true," I said, feeling pretty buzzed as we bumped out of the unpaved lane towards the main road.

"I liked him," said Jay. "He's good at winemaking, and he seems super happy in his job, which most of us can't say."

"You would probably love that job," I said.

"You have no idea," he said, which launched him into a list of what the France office was doing wrong.

I inclined my seat and closed my eyes. "I'm just going to think about the whole Joanna thing a little," I said.

I woke up as we were pulling into the garage.

"Some fun date you are," said Jay, but he was laughing. "See you in the morning. I'll put the wine away."

I trudged into the house, dry-mouthed and gritty-eyed. I poked my head into Cole's room to say goodnight, ignoring the hope in his eyes, giving him a bland "We had a nice time."

In bed, teeth brushed, face washed, retinol cream applied, I allowed myself a thought about Saito. I sighed and rolled out of bed onto the floor and did thirty stomach crunches. Not a good mix with a belly full of wine. Back in bed, it took me no time at all to fall asleep.

Chapter 34

I woke up in the morning unrested and sluggish, too tired to get up.

Hey Thomas, got anything for me?

Nothing. Not even a twinge in the chest.

I felt around for sensing about anything and got nothing. I was scheduled for an OOC consult with my senses as an add-on, and they were gone again. Yikes.

I texted Lauren that we'd have to reschedule the appointment.

The phone quacked within seconds.

"What do you mean reschedule?"

"Good morning to you too," I said.

"What's going on now?" said Lauren.

"Nothing," I said. "That's the problem. My senses are unreliable these days and I'm not feeling it today. I don't know why."

"I can't believe this," groused Lauren. "I finally agree to allow this nonsense, and you flake out. Make something up."

"I'm sorry," I said.

"Why do I let myself fall for this stuff over and over? You're just being so *Izzy*," said Lauren.

That stung enough that I hung up.

Okay, so my sister didn't believe in me. I could believe in me. I wasn't going to give up.

Face the day.

I texted Joanna and got a little surge of energy when she replied that she was feeling good.

Then I called the client. "I wanted to give you a heads up," I said. "Sometimes I really feel myself tuning in to the other world and sometimes I don't feel it, and today I'm not feeling it. If I can't tune into anything for you, we won't charge for that part."

The job was to clean out a recently deceased woman's house. Her middle-aged daughter Kelly had heard about me from Samantha and was eager for her mom to "help."

"Okay," said Kelly. "I hope something comes through. But I need the help either way. I am getting almost nowhere myself. Going through her stuff alone is just too emotional. I'm falling down one memory hole after another."

"Great," I said. "Be there soon."

In the car I touched the dress and, sure enough, got nothing. *What is up with you, Thomas?* I asked. No answer.

***

"You've gotten more done than you think," I said as Kelly showed me through the house en route to her mother's bedroom. Kelly had fluffy, shoulder-length hair, more gray than brown; a kind smile; and an air of someone who gets things done. She gave off long-time school principal vibes, but even the most efficient people struggle with dead parent cleanouts.

We started on her mother's side of the closet.

"You don't have to be diplomatic," Kelly said. "Mom was no fashion plate. She never bought new clothes, so I'm not even sure Goodwill will want this stuff."

"For Goodwill, used is fine as long as it is in good condition, but you are right," I said. "No one wants something stained or ripped. That stuff can just be tossed."

It was when we got to the shoes that Kelly started crying. "I don't know why." She wiped at the tears. "It's so personal, the shoes." She was sitting in the corner of the closet, holding a navy wedge. "It feels so sad to . . . just send it all away. Like she's really gone. Like she was never here."

I sat down beside her. "It feels so final."

I wasn't picking up anything from her mother, but I could feel all of Kelly's emotions like they were my own. I'd had that ability my whole life, and it never faded. I feel everything everyone around me is feeling.

"Of course you are sad. Even if she was ready and in pain, it is still really hard," I said. "Tell me about her. What was her favorite music? What were her quirks?"

Kelly smiled through her tears. "She loved Neil Diamond. I mean, loved. And she was the most amazing cook, and she played soccer with her dog! Literally kicked a ball around with him and would pee herself because, you know, giving birth and all."

"Yep," I said. "The wet underwear club."

Maybe because Kelly's feelings weren't mine, I could hold all of them at once. Deep grief but also deep love. Handling Kelly's mom's belongings had turned into a holy act.

Lauren would have already gotten Kelly back on track, but this seemed a moment made for company in grief.

Just as I thought that, Kelly said, "Let's get back at it. I'll probably keep crying but might as well be productive too."

We stood up and got to work. As I dumped a drawer of socks into a garbage bag, a couple of the balled-up socks rolled to the side and I grabbed them.

"Huh," I said. "One of these is heavy." I unrolled it and a wad of money fell out.

"Holy cow," said Kelly, opening the folded pack. "Holy cow," she said again as she counted. "This is five hundred dollars!"

I remembered Lauren telling me to go through every pocket and drawer looking out for hidden stuff. People hide their valuables in odd places.

Kelly laughed. "This is SO mom!"

We looked around the closet with new eyes.

"Right," I said. "We need to look through every pocket and drawer, to see if anything else is hidden."

Kelly dumped the bag of socks onto the floor and we unrolled every ball, finding a gold necklace and another pack of cash, this time three hundred dollars.

By the end of the closet cleanout, we had netted her mother's passport, a packet of letters rubber-banded together, two more gold necklaces, and her mother's pearls in the deep inner pocket of Kelly's dad's herringbone sport jacket.

Hours later, Kelly walked me to the door and pulled me into a big hug. "Thank you, Izzy," she mumbled into my shoulder. "You made this so much better. Really helpful, even without exactly hearing from mom."

She released me from the hug, and I grabbed her hands. "I feel honored to have helped. It was a privilege to hear about your mom and help do this." I paused. "It seems like an important ritual, almost, doesn't it?"

Kelly squeezed my hands. "Yes. Helps me process it all, I think. And I do believe she was around, right?"

"Yes, I have no doubt," I said, still feeling like a failure.

I wasn't even out of the neighborhood when it occurred to me that Joanna and I hadn't looked through any of Thomas's pockets or balls of socks. I pulled over and parked and went through the suits lying across my back seat. A couple of receipts, a pen, two combs, and three handkerchiefs in the first three suits. And then, a hard object in the inner lapel pocket of a dark brown tweed. I pulled it out: a key. Nothing in the rest of the clothes, so I dumped the wrappers from an old Burger King bag and put the pocket stuff into it to give to Joanna later. I put the bag into my center console so I wouldn't accidentally throw it out. The key was kind of intriguing, I thought, as I drove the rest of the way home. Smaller than a house key and dull enough to seem old.

Chapter 35

At home I found a note on the counter from Jay saying he had gone to the track meet with Cole. Maybe having his dad along would soften the sting of not running, but I doubted it.

I texted Jay to remind him of our appointment later with Ted.

Close to 6:30 Jay and I walked through the massive oak doors of the Mediterranean-style LaSalle Country Club. It looked charmingly like one of the original missions scattered through California, but it had been built less than twenty years ago. This kind of architecture had always appealed to me but ever since my senses got more active, it also gave me a subtle discomfort, a whiff of land stolen from Native Americans and early Mexican settlers. As in "We're keeping the cool white stucco and red-tiled roofs, but you're going to need to go find somewhere else to live."

Seeing Ted in a corner booth, we made our way through the buzzing crowd. I searched for a match to the pictures of Connie I had found online but didn't see a crazy-eyed, sun-baked older woman with hair the bleached green hue of a water polo boy.

"Izzy, Jay!" Ted said, standing up and giving us a hearty handshake. "Good to see you." Ted was the picture of a financial advisor, his dark-brown hair cut short, wearing wire-rimmed glasses, with one button open on his crisp, pale-blue, Brooks Brothers button-down.

Ted launched into a summary of our finances (which sounded dire, despite his calm voice), describing the "buckets" our money should be divided between, several of which were currently empty. I nodded, distracted by watching for Connie.

"So, that should eventually get you back on track," Ted finished.

We could do that? I looked down and saw how many years that was going to take.

Jay looked shell-shocked. "My brother really screwed us, didn't he?" I could see the dark cloud of anger taking over his face.

Ted wisely didn't answer.

"I told you I'm working now, right?" I said.

"That's great. What's the yearly income?" he asked, pen poised in the air over the diagram. Ah, which bucket would my salary not fill?

"Hard to say yet." I explained the OOC set-up.

I heard a burst of loud talking, and a group of people came in, one of whom had to be Connie.

How to talk to her? I hadn't actually planned that out.

Connie sailed towards us, wild-eyed and with a manic smile that reminded me of the Joker.

"Teddy!" she said, weaving ever so slightly as she approached.

Ted smoothly slid the papers in front of him into a folder and folded his hands on top of it. Discreet.

"Connie," Ted said, face blank. "Nice to see you."

"And who do we have here?" Connie stared hungrily at Jay.

"Jay and Izzy Bishop," said Ted, not explaining anything more, perfectly professional.

Connie's smile disappeared, and her eyes swiveled from Jay to me. "Izzy Bishop!" she spat. "Why're you poking around in my kids' stuff?" She took a long sip of the dark drink sloshing around her glass.

I smiled pleasantly. "Their stuff?"

"Everything there is theirs," Connie said.

"Hmm," I said. "Most people are happy to have me help organize their stuff."

"Steal it is more likely," said Connie.

"When was the last time you were at the house—you know, Thomas's house?"

"What?" said Connie, ice cubes clicking against her teeth as she drank. "Not since Mr. High and Mighty got all holier than thou. Why would I go back there?"

She was drunk but sounded like she was telling the truth. Maybe she didn't put the space heater there.

Connie slung an arm around Ted, leaning down on him. "Teddy, dump this loser and come have a drink with me."

"Maybe later," said Ted. Poor guy, trying not to make enemies in a town where he did business with a lot of the residents. Then I realized I was in the same position. Whoops.

"I guess it's all about the trust," I said, keeping my voice light, almost ditzy, but watching carefully to see if Connie reacted to the word "trust."

Connie cackled. "Trust? I wouldn't trust that gold digger as far as I could throw her."

No reaction to "trust" in the financial sense. Either Thomas didn't tell her or she'd never been aware that the land could be released from conservancy.

"You aren't friends with Joanna?" I said, playing confused. "I heard you guys were on the tennis team together . . . oh well, never mind."

"Ha!" said Connie, alcohol and long-held resentment loosening her tongue. "Friends! Like I would be friends with my ex's wife. You're even dumber than you look."

Connie pointed a gnarled finger at me. "That woman is sitting there in my kids' house. She killed the Golden Goose! Of course we aren't friends."

"Connie," said Ted in a pacifying voice. "We all know Thomas died of a heart attack. Joanna did not kill him. You need to be careful of what you say."

Connie leaned back and drained the rest of her drink. "As good as. My kids are all scrounging to make a living, and she sits over there in a mansion by herself. Selfish." She smiled so big I could see the metallic edges of her crowned teeth shining from receding gums. "Such a shame she keeps ending up in the hospital."

What a charmer.

"Funny thing," I said. "Your kids have ignored Joanna ever since Thomas died, and now all of a sudden they are hanging around. What's up with that?"

I could have sworn that, for a second, Connie's eyes got cool and assessing before going back to unfocused. "Like I said, maybe stay in your own business?" she said.

Connie might not be as unhinged as she let herself look. "Well, it's been a treat. Like I said, Teddy, lose the loser and come party with me." She looked back at Jay. "You're invited too, sugarbuns." With that, she turned and weaved towards the long, crowded bar.

"Sugarbuns," said Ted, holding his drink up to toast Jay.

"That's a new one," said Jay.

We finished our drinks, agreed to a bunch more action items, and said our goodbyes to Ted. Threading through the crowded bar, several people clapped Jay on the shoulders and welcomed him back from France. When we were almost to the door, Sarah Melville walked through it.

We all stopped in our tracks. Sarah recovered the fastest. "Hi Izzy, hi Jay. So you're back from Paris?" Her attempt at a casual voice was weak. My senses went off like a smoke alarm. Her longing for Jay would have been clear to anyone, not just someone with extra senses.

If I had to have picked a candidate for my husband to have an affair with, Sarah wouldn't have even been in the top 50. She was normal, bordering on plain; unstyled, light-brown hair; a roundish figure; not a super flirt that I had ever seen. Then again, she was wickedly funny and seemed at ease in the world. Who knew how these things happened? I had felt the lightning bolt before I even knew Saito's name.

I switched to bland work face. "Hi Sarah, good to see you. How's Tommy? And Elana?"

"Great. Well, teenagers, so, you know, moody. But fine." She was babbling.

I could feel a swirling energy between Sarah and Jay. It wasn't just Sarah.

Jay recovered too. "Good to see you, Sarah. Just on our way out. Bye." He slipped his arm in mine, and we left.

In the parking lot I laughed, mostly out of nervousness, but also because life felt so absurd these days. "Well, that was awkward," I said.

Jay looked at me, his face pained. "Sorry," he said. "Sorry I've fucked things up so badly. We never . . . we never did anything."

"Okay." I felt strangely detached. Funny, I couldn't feel much about Sarah, with whom Jay clearly had a connection, but was enraged by Shania, with whom he didn't. Nothing about me was logical.

Chapter 36

My whole body was sore when I woke in the morning, even though I hadn't done any hard physical labor. Maybe it was the constantly held breath of being around Jay.

I had until ten to get back to Kelly Dugan's, so I ran an Epsom bath and sank in. As my shoulders and back unclenched, I thought about Jay and Sarah and the energy between them last night. And how I had the same kind of energy with Saito.

Maybe that lusty energy was just novelty, a new object of fantasy projection. Maybe infatuation was nature's way of pulling someone into your orbit, and then you started the work of real love. Maybe we had failed to transition to the adult version of love.

Nice try, Iz.

Who said that?

Something in my brain. Keep talking, I begged.

Why are you trying so hard to force this? You know Jay well enough to know if you love him. Stop pretending to feel what you do not feel.

This was a new development. Who was this talking in my head? I liked what they were saying, but it also was hitting too close to home. I decided that was enough introspection for the day, I climbed out of the tub, got dressed, and shot off a quick check-in text to Joanna. No sign of Thomas, even when I touched the dress in the car. Maybe he was repelled by Epsom salts.

At Kelly's I was surprised to find how much she'd done since I had left yesterday.

"Fueled by eclairs and a couple of gin and tonics, I just kept working last night," Kelly said. "You inspired me yesterday."

"This is impressive," I said. "What should we work on next?"

"I've pulled out anything I might want to keep, or that I think should go to anyone in the family," said Kelly, gesturing to a corner of the living room. "We really can just get rid of everything else. And I was just talking to a friend who is helping a refugee family get settled here. What do you think of giving them everything they could use?"

I thought that was an outstanding idea. Kelly called the friend, and within an hour a truck and a van pulled up.

Several hours later, the house was eighty percent emptier and the truck and van had left for the third time. Kelly and I sat on the front step, drinking water we had snagged before the pantry items made their way to the refugee family as well.

"Mom would be so happy with this," said Kelly. "She was all about helping people."

I nodded. "I'm going to tell Lauren. What a concept: we have a whole house full of unneeded items and an apartment empty of needed items. Perfect."

Kelly laughed. "Although maybe I should apologize to them for that plaid couch."

"A plaid couch is better than no couch," I said. For all my worrying, I wasn't homeless or starting over in a new country with nothing but the clothes I arrived in.

Just then Vivi called. "I'm at LaSalle Country Club, and I've got some car trouble. Can you come get me?"

"Of course."

I hugged Kelly. "I think your mom is very happy with this."

As I drove, Jay called. "Your mom dropped brownies off for Cole. Was surprised to see me."

Whoops.

"We're going to their house for dinner unless you have other plans," he said.

"That's fine. Got to go," I said. After I hung up, I realized I hadn't even filled him in on mom's mini-strokes. Out of sight, out of mind.

The LaSalle Country Club parking lot was full of tennis ladies and golfers, all wide-eyed, watching Vivi. She was standing by her car, hands on hips, yelling at a woman, visor to visor.

Vivi saw me. "Izzy! Glad you are here."

I slammed my door and hustled over to her. "What's going on?"

Vivi pointed violently at her front tire. "Look at that!"

Her tires were all flat.

"Seems like more than running over a nail," I said.

"Paige here claims to know nothing about it, but gee, coincidence that LCC lost this morning? That it was me who won the match to clinch it? We go for a drink, and I come out to THIS?!"

The woman, thick and muscular in her tennis clothes, stood her ground. "You're ridiculous. I would never do that."

Vivi's eyebrows shot into her hairline. "I didn't say YOU did it. We all know who is capable of that! Where is that cheating bitch?"

I looked around. The women spread out on the sidewalk were a mix of two teams, some in white skirts and green shirts, the rest in navy skirts and white shirts. Most with colored PT tape on their legs or arms.

"Connie? Come out, you coward!" Vivi yelled, then looked at me. "She tried to cheat, and we all saw it, and no one will say anything! And then I won my match and she stomped off and, all of a sudden, all my freaking tires are flat!"

Wild hair sticking straight up from her visor, Connie stepped forward from behind a clump of women, sipping through a straw from a tall plastic cup and talking on a cell phone. "Yes, she's here," she said as she walked towards us. "The LaSalle Country Club parking lot. You know what to do." She ended her call, shoved the phone into the waistband of her skirt, and walked up to Vivi. As she got closer, I could see her eyes, wild and darting around, underneath ridiculously steepled eyebrow arches, like a mad clown.

"What's your problem?" snarled Connie.

Vivi pointed at her tires and took a step towards Connie. "THAT'S my problem."

Connie shrugged. "Bad luck—must've run over some spikes or something."

"Not bad luck. A misdemeanor. At least," said Vivi. She looked around. "I have to believe the club has security cameras. Shall we go take a look?"

Connie turned around and scanned the building. She faced back at Vivi. "Doubt it. This place is a dump."

Nice thing to say about your own country club.

"But tell me how this is somehow my fault." Connie leaned towards Vivi.

Vivi stepped the last step between them and stuck her face down into Connie's. "You're a loser and a cheater, and you couldn't take it and slashed my tires."

"Are you calling me a liar?" growled Connie, shoulders rising like a cobra about to strike. Their faces were maybe four inches apart.

"Yes. You're a cheat and a drunk too!" said Vivi.

"You fat dago." Connie poked a gnarled finger into Vivi's chest.

Vivi lunged at Connie, and I jumped in, pushing Vivi one way and Connie the other. Connie stumbled and bounced into a car before coming back at me.

"Vivi! She's not worth it," I said, putting myself between them, back to Vivi, facing Connie.

Connie shoved me. "Don't touch me, bitch." She looked around. "She attacked me!"

I stepped back, forcing Vivi back as well.

"You probably blew out the tires getting in the car; you really should do something about that blubber," said Connie, looking down at her watch and then towards the long road leading into the country club.

Vivi's phone buzzed, and she looked down. "Oh good, Triple A is finally on their way." Then, to Connie, "Should I call Double A for you?"

The crowd gasped.

"Double A?" said Connie, not getting it.

"You know, AA," said Vivi.

"Hmfph," said Connie. Then she turned and stumbled back towards the sidewalk where she stopped, turned around, and continued to glare in our direction. A couple of women in tennis gear were murmuring to Connie and glaring at Vivi. Very tribal.

"Can you wait till the tow truck gets here?" asked Vivi.

"Sure," I said, looking at my watch. I hadn't heard from Joanna and wanted to go by her house to check on her.

I saw the tow truck pulling up and didn't notice the police car right away. When I saw it, I poked Vivi. "Someone called the police!"

"Maybe that's not such a bad idea," said Vivi.

As the tow truck maneuvered itself into place in front of Vivi's car, the police car parked, and two officers got out and walked towards us. Both were medium height; one on the near side of forty, with a dark crew cut; the other maybe thirty, with thin, blond hair.

Connie was doing some weird waving thing, but I only half noticed.

The dark-haired one, with a name tag that said "Roth," walked straight at me.

"Izzy Bishop?" he said.

Chapter 37

"What?" I was surprised. "I mean, yes. But this is Vivi Ricci; she's the one with the slashed tires."

Officer Roth looked at Vivi. "Your tires were slashed?"

Vivi nodded.

"Ms. Bishop, were you at Joanna Sullivan's house recently?"

"Yes. Oh my God, is she okay?" I panicked. I hadn't been able to get in touch with her. And Thomas was giving me nothing today.

"She's in the hospital," said Officer Roth.

"Oh no, not again. Is she okay? What happened?"

"Her daughter is very upset, says you slipped her cannabis-laced cookies without her knowing it," said Officer Roth.

"What? No I didn't!" Then a sick feeling. Oh my God. I must have given her Patty's cookies, not Lucille's cookies. I had forgotten both were in my bag.

"Then Mrs. Sullivan's son called to tell us that you are here at the LaSalle Country Club harassing other members of the family," he said.

"What?" My head was spinning. Joanna's *son*? Stepson?

Connie stalked forward. "She attacked me! Slammed me into a car."

"Connie was attacking *me*," said Vivi. "Izzy stopped her. All she did was separate us. No attack."

Connie was close to being drunk. If I could just keep my cool, maybe it would be clear who was the crazy one here.

"Wrong!" rasped Connie. "She hit me."

"Plenty of witnesses; maybe ask around," I said.

Silence. Either in support or fear.

Officer Roth looked at Connie. "We will get to that. First, we are here to look into the Joanna Sullivan issue. Did you give Mrs. Sullivan cannabis cookies?"

"BY MISTAKE. I had two packs of cookies in my purse and thought I was giving her plain old Snickerdoodles."

Connie was smirking.

Marco joined the group. "Hello, sir, thank you for coming."

What a tool. That's who Connie had been on the phone with.

I was so frustrated. "*I'm* the one who is worried that someone is trying to hurt Joanna. Like one of her stepchildren. I've been trying to protect her!"

"By giving her drugged cookies?" said Officer Roth. "Some kind of protection."

Connie pointed at me. "Sheesh been harassing me," she slurred.

I kept my voice calm. "I talked to Officer Barrett at Joanna's when Kimberly Selleck died. I think someone on purpose gave Joanna a space heater knowing it gave off carbon monoxide. And then I think someone tried to poison her, but her niece, Kimberly, got it instead. And Joanna keeps getting better and then worse again. I've been trying to get people to believe that."

"We are worried too." Marco stepped closer. "But it's Izzy who is always around when Joanna has an episode. And now we find out she was drugging her! Then she attacks my mother!" Marco's face was red, his whole body tight, like a Komodo dragon puffed up and angry.

"Why would I want to hurt Joanna?" I asked. The crowd was getting bigger again. Vivi stood transfixed, ignoring the tow truck guy. Connie had walked over near my car. All I needed was for her to slash my tires too.

"Maybe you are stealing from Joanna," said Marco. "Get her high and then sneak out the valuables."

"You guys are the ones with a motive, not me. When Joanna dies, you guys get the house and it's worth millions. And then the whole land trust deal."

I saw a flash in Marco's eyes. He knew about the trust.
I filed that observation away for later.

"When were you last at Joanna Sullivan's house?"
asked Officer Roth.

Thursday," I said.

"Tell me what you did there that day," said Officer
Roth.

I filled him in, including the fact that she was feeling
fine when I left.

"Just ask Joanna," I said. "She can tell you what we
did Thursday."

"She is still too groggy," said the blond officer. I
looked at his tag: Melton. "She ate the cookies last night;
then her daughter came by to see her and found her very
loopy."

"Maybe you should look in her car," said Connie,
weaving her way back to us. "Looks like a lot of booty in
there."

Connie must have seen me pull up, otherwise how
would she know my car? Unless she was hiding out,
watching Joanna's house.

"You mind if we look in your car?" asked Officer
Roth.

Oh shit, Thomas's stuff was still in there.

"Don't you need a search warrant or something?" I
asked.

"Not if we have probable cause, but why would you
say no if you have nothing to hide?"

As we walked towards my car, I saw Karl stepping out
of his beater car. They were all converging on me?

Connie followed, gloating and weaving. Drunk in the
middle of the day. Her sons must be so proud.

Vivi was signing something with the tow truck driver
but looking at me anxiously.

I opened the car. "I have all the stuff that Joanna asked
me to get rid of. To take to consignment stores and
Goodwill, etc. You can ask her. Or take it and show her."

Marco, Karl, and Connie watched the two police officers pull Thomas's stuff out. Behind them it looked like the entire country club had emptied, people staring with fascination, like I was being busted as a drug dealer. How could I have given Joanna the wrong cookies?

"Those watches!" said Connie, spying the display box as Roth picked it up. "They are worth a lot of money. Why would you have those? Those should have gone to the boys. She stole those!"

"I am doing what Joanna asked! These are just some incentive watches Thomas got through work. She said she offered all his stuff to his kids right after he died, and no one wanted it. It's been two years!" I said, but I was scared. It looked bad. Lauren was going to be so angry— why had I not dropped that stuff off already? This was my own stupid fault.

Connie narrowed her eyes and leaned towards the watch case. "That's a TAG Heur, worth $5,000! Incentive watches, my ass."

The crowd was rapt, the police officers' antenna was up. I could feel their brains shifting against me. The hot sun and the shame of being the center of attention made my whole body sweaty.

Then Officer Melton pulled out the bag with the space heater.

"Be careful with that! It might have fingerprints on it," I said. "I thought if you ever believed someone was trying to hurt her, you might want it. "

Officer Melton eased the bag down to reveal the dinged-up old heater.

"What the hell?" said Connie, staring at the space heater, shocked. "What's *that* doing here?"

"You recognize this?" asked Officer Melton.

"That was mine!" Connie said, turning to Karl. "I told you to throw tha' thing out."

"What?" Karl was flustered. "I don't remember. It must have ended up with the stuff you told me to drop off for the tennis garage sale."

"That should have been in the throw-out pile." I could see the wheels in Connie's head turning. Either she looked guilty, or Karl did. Would she throw her son under the bus? She took a long couple of sips from her cup. Good, get more drunk.

"This is the space heater responsible for the carbon monoxide poisoning?" asked Officer Melton.

"Yes," I said. "I was working with her after the whole carbon monoxide thing and saw it in the garbage can, and I just have had a bad feeling all along that someone was trying to hurt her, so I took it out of the garbage. No one believed me, but I kept it, just in case. The clothes, I'm embarrassed to say, I just kept forgetting to drop off at the consignment store."

"Maybe she set up the space heater," said Marco. "Maybe she found it and tried to kill her with it."

"How would I have possibly known it was leaking carbon monoxide?" I protested. "I didn't start working with Joanna until after she had it going. My first day there, she mentioned how she had a wet carpet in the other room and was trying to dry it. Ask Lauren, my sister—she was there. We both got headaches but didn't think anything of it at the time."

"And you are?" Officer Melton was writing stuff down now and staring at Connie.

"Connie. Sullivan. The first wife. Karl and Marco's mother. The one Izzy keeps attacking." Connie sucked at her drink, but nothing was coming up the straw anymore. "I want a reshtraining order."

She was literally making stuff up.

"But this isn't about me," Connie continued. "This is about her stealing stuff from my sons and druggin' ole ladies."

"Just to clarify," said Officer Melton. "Your son Karl took your space heater to the second Mrs. Sullivan, Mrs. Joanna Sullivan?"

Connie shrugged. "Could be. He helped me clear out my garage; we got rid of a lot of stuff."

"Why were you getting rid of it?" asked Officer Melton.

"Didn't need it anymore," Connie said, eyes shifting right, then left.

"You didn't know it was producing carbon monoxide?" asked Officer Roth.

"No," she said, but I didn't believe her. She knew. And maybe Karl knew too.

Officer Melton looked at Karl. "And you are?"

"Karl Sullivan," he said. "Her son." He pointed at Connie.

"And you took this heater to Joanna Sullivan's house?"

"I don't remember. I dropped a bunch of stuff there, so I guess I could have."

"And why were you dropping stuff from Connie Sullivan's to Joanna Sullivan's? The ex-wife to the second wife, if I understand things."

"Tennis team garage sale," Karl said.

Connie pointed at me. "She convinced Joanna to cancel the garage sale. Got a racket going on, if you ask me! Gets paid to 'clean out' a house but then keeps the stuff. 's robbery!"

"Just ask Joanna; she'll verify everything I've said." If she ever woke up.

"Hmm," said Connie. "Didn't Order Out of Chaos work at the Monroes'? And didn't someone steal thousands of dollars of jewelry from them?"

Connie was evil.

"When did Order Out of Chaos work at the Monroes'?" asked Officer Roth.

"You'll have to ask my sister; she's the owner of the business. I wasn't working for them yet," I said.

"Check their client lish. The Monroes won't be the only ones who are missing stuff," said Connie. "Read about tha' in the Weekly."

I turned to Connie. "Do you have carbon monoxide sensors at your house?"

"Huh?" Connie said. Her eyes were looking less wild, more sedated.

"Do you have carbon monoxide sensors? Most people do these days," I said in a more chatty tone.

"So wha' if I do?" said Connie.

"Maybe that is how you figured out you should throw out the space heater?" I suggested.

"They went off, but I didn't know what it was," said Connie. "So I just threw out everything it could be. No way to know if it was the heater."

Both police officers were looking at Connie with more interest.

"Officers, I'd like to file a burglary charge against this woman," said Marco, pointing at me. "She is in possession of items that belong to us."

Vivi had finished her business with the tow truck driver and rejoined us. "She is employed by Joanna to dispose of this stuff," said Vivi, jumping in to my defense. "I've worked there too, and she has Joanna's complete approval."

I pulled out my phone and called Lauren. Gave her a brief summary and asked her to bring our contract and donation receipts to the country club. With a furious but controlled tone that let me know that she wasn't alone, she said she was right down the street at Peaches's house and would be over immediately.

"You admit these are not your clothes?" asked Officer Roth.

"I told you they are not my clothes; they are part of the job. I'm to drop them off at consignment stores and Goodwill," I said, frustrated. "Look, take them all if you want, then check with Joanna when she is feeling better. She said she offered them to Thomas's sons, and they didn't want them."

Marco was cold and defiant. "Not true."

Karl looked down at the ground, apparently unwilling to make his brother a liar. Why was he even here?

"He died two years ago, you could have taken those clothes at any point," said Vivi.

"Stay out of this!" barked Marco. "You're just another grifter." He got up in Vivi's face, his voice louder with each word. Vivi leaned in, nose to nose.

"Bring it," Vivi hissed. "I've had just about enough of your family today." She turned towards the police officers. "I would like to file a police report on my slashed tires. Prime suspect." Vivi tilted her head towards Connie. "Poor loser."

Officer Roth put his hand out in front of Marco, who had expanded into full puffy lizard fury. "Simmer down," he said, his voice calm but authoritative.

"I'll simmer down when I'm ready to simmer down," snapped Marco.

"You'll simmer down when I tell you to," said Officer Roth, puffing up to match Marco, his partner moving to stand beside him.

Lauren appeared from behind me. "What's going on?"

"Who are you?" said Officer Roth.

"Lauren Larsen, owner of Order Out of Chaos and her boss." Lauren pointed at me.

"We have had several complaints about Ms. Bishop," said Officer Melton. "One being that she slipped Joanna Sullivan cannabis cookies and may be involved in her episodes of ill health. Now this woman claims she is harassing her," he pointed at Connie. "It came to our attention that she has belongings of the late Mr. Sullivan in her car. She says this is part of the organizing business. Can you help us understand this?"

At the mention of the edible cookies, Lauren's face had gone slack and then turned back into her blank business face. In a tightly controlled voice, she explained. "Order Out of Chaos was hired by Joanna to help her organize her house. Part of that included cleaning out some of her late husband's belongings." Lauren pulled out some papers. "You'll see our contract here. It is quite detailed as to the items we were working on."

The officers looked at the papers. The country club crowd was very entertained. I could feel Lauren's anger at me coming in waves.

"You can just ask Joanna," said Lauren.

"She is in the hospital," said officer Melton. "Not conscious."

Marco glowered. Karl looked down at the ground, shoulders slumped. He was shuffling his feet and moving a bit sideways with each shuffle, like he might just be able to crab his way out of there.

"Could we possibly continue these discussions somewhere else?" I asked.

"Oh, we will be," said Officer Roth. "May I suggest coming to the station?" His voice was sarcastic. "Now."

"We will be following up with each of you," he added, looking at Marco and Connie. "For now, we will take possession of the space heater and the rest of Mr. Sullivan's possessions, until which time we can confirm with Mrs. Joanna Sullivan the disposition of them. Ms. Bishop, you will come to the station. Ms. Larsen, you too."

"Yes, sir," I said.

Officer Roth looked at Vivi. "And you would like to file a report on your tires?"

Vivi stuck her chin in the air. "Yes, very much so." She gestured towards the country club. "I know they have security cameras; maybe check them."

"Can we go?" asked Karl, and when they said yes, he slunk away.

Connie grabbed Marco's arm and weaved her way towards the clubhouse.

"You might want to make sure she doesn't drive," I said to the officers, pointing at Connie. "She's had more than a few."

Chapter 38

In the car, Vivi and I looked at each other.

"Holy shit," said Vivi.

I thunked my head against the steering wheel. "I can't believe I gave Joanna weed cookies!"

"How'd that happen?" asked Vivi.

As we drove away, I explained about Patty's business and Lucille's Snickerdoodles.

Outside the country club, I pulled the car over to text Joanna. "I've got to let her know that was a mistake!"

Vivi giggled. "Life is never dull around you."

"Hello? Could say the same for you," I said, hysteria bubbling up as laughter. "Slashed tires?"

"Yeah, let's get to the police station," said Vivi.

As I drove, I heard the buzz of a text notification.

"Check that, would you?" I asked Vivi.

"Oh jeez, Emily is not happy with you. Listen to this: 'This is Emily. You are done working for my mother. Marijuana cookies? WHAT IS WRONG WITH YOU?'" Vivi grimaced. "All caps. Ouch."

My phone quacked: Lauren. It was not going to get any easier, so I answered it.

"How COULD YOU!" Lauren's screech echoed through the car. "Jesus CHRIST! The whole country club saw that. Cannabis cookies? I don't even know you anymore. And the whole world heard us accused of STEALING. I'm ruined."

"I'm sorry," I said, inadequately.

"Sorry! This, after that Patch article. My business will never recover. You think you are Sherlock Holmes? You are Calamity Jane! You are fired. FOR GOOD."

The speakers went dead.

Vivi and I drove in silence for a beat.

"You might need to get her on blood pressure medication," said Vivi.

At the station Vivi gave a report on the slashed tires, while Lauren and I waited on uncomfortable plastic molded chairs. Lauren sat across from me, eyes down, shoulders around her ears, arms crossed like she was holding her bones together.

Eventually, Melton and Roth brought Lauren and me to a little room and proceeded to grill Lauren on the work we did for Joanna, dates, scope of duties, specifics in how to dispose of items. She had answers for it all and was professional and cooperative. Her refusal to look at me made me feel worse than actual anger. It was like she was really done with me as a sister.

"Did Joanna realize this TAG Heuer watch was in the box she gave you?" Melton asked.

"I doubt it," I said. "She had no idea any of the watches were valuable. Talk to her, and you can clear it all up."

"I'd like to request fingerprints from each of you," said Melton.

"We were cleaning out the house," I said. "Our fingerprints are going to be everywhere."

"Do we have to?" asked Lauren.

"No," said Roth. "But it would make our job easier."

"Did you ask Mrs. Sullivan if she wanted cannabis-laced cookies?" asked Melton. How many ways were they going to ask me this?

"No, because I forgot I even had them! I told you, I didn't mean to give her those. I would never do that. I didn't even want the cookies myself! I just took them to be polite."

More questions about my relationship with Joanna, while I tried to keep bringing them back to seeing that someone else was trying to hurt her.

"How do you explain the cannabis cookies?" Melton asked Lauren.

"Well, if you knew my sister, you wouldn't really be surprised," said Lauren. "She would never intentionally hurt someone, but she makes mistakes all the time."

Great defense—she's incompetent, not criminal.

"Ms. Larsen, you can go," said Melton. "Ms. Bishop, you stay."

Lauren walked out without having ever acknowledged my presence.

Melton turned to me. "Connie Sullivan says you have been harassing her and her family."

That didn't sound like a question to me, so I kept my mouth shut.

He sighed. "Have you been harassing Connie Sullivan and her family?"

"No," I said. "In fact, I just met Connie last night."

"Why would she say that?" asked Roth.

"I have been asking questions about their family, trying to figure out who might have a motive to hurt Joanna. Maybe I'm getting too close. Maybe she knows who is trying to hurt her."

"Maybe leave the investigating to the police," said Roth.

"I have tried to," I said and explained about the space heater and the value of the house and the carbon monoxide poisoning and then Kimberly dying at Joanna's house after eating a meal with her.

No reaction.

Finally, we were done and they let me go.

After dropping Vivi off, I drove home, my mind humming.

Why did Connie call the cops on me? Something about her kids? Maybe she was the one trying to kill Joanna and thought I was getting too close. Or maybe it was Marco in cahoots with his mother. They seemed most aligned of all the Sullivan kids.

I thought about Connie and her relationship with her kids. Karl had been unhappy to be at the parking lot. Why was he there? He resented his mother. I didn't know where that knowledge came from, but I could feel it. And yet she had something over him. And he had left the space heater at Joanna's.

What about Serena and Connie? My gut feeling was that Serena and Connie were not close, but I'd have to investigate that. And Jacques? It would be a sign that the new religious belief was real if he could tolerate Connie's craziness.

My mind shifted to Emily calling the police on me. Emily was now in the suspect pool.

I pleaded with Thomas to help me but got nothing. Not even a chest tightening.

Thanks, Thomas, you got me involved and now you've abandoned me.

Parked in my garage, I looked in the back seat of the car for the tangerine dress and panicked. The back seat was clear of everything, including the dress. The police had it. My best way to connect with Thomas gone, not to mention now Joanna's wedding dress was somewhere in police custody. What if it got lost? I felt awful. How had I messed this up so badly? And how was I going to protect Joanna?

I had just dropped my purse on the kitchen counter when the doorbell rang. I opened the front door to find a man and a woman. She had short, black hair, a serious but pleasant face, was dressed in gray pants and a loose navy jacket and was holding up a badge. The man looked like a former linebacker in a maroon button-down that was working hard to stay buttoned. "Hello, I'm Luisa Miller and this is Devin Martinez," said the woman. "Can we come in?"

"I told Office Melton and Officer Roth everything," I said.

"These are different questions. We just missed you back at the station house," said Martinez.

We sat down in the rarely used living room. I like the furniture and the faded seaside colors I picked, but the room is an awkward shape and doesn't get much light.

"We are investigating a series of local robberies," said Miller.

"My sister Lauren knows more about the business than me," I said.

"We're planning on talking to her," said Martinez, looking at a notepad. "To clarify, your company has worked at the following houses, correct? Monroes, Denisons, Whitmeres and Mahones."

"Mahones?" I said. That was Peaches.

"Yes, that one occurred two days ago," said Miller. She was sitting in one of the pale wing chairs, legs crossed, calm stare on me.

"I only worked at the Mahones." I paused. "What are the names of the other people who got robbed? Not all OOC clients, right?"

Martinez and Miller looked at each other and seemed to conclude it was public knowledge anyway. "Campbell, Dominguez, Pak, and Grinaldi are the other families," said Martinez.

"Tell us about your work at the Mahones," said Miller. "When was it, what did you do, who was there?"

I filled them in, shamefully adding the dog part. "Did you check the security cameras?"

"We did. Nothing helpful," said Miller.

"Were you given an entry code for the house?" asked Martinez, leaning forward from the other wing chair, feet planted in front of him. He seemed to bring the muscle, Miller the scalpel.

"No, we actually locked ourselves out, as I said, with the dog. Believe me, if we had been given an entry code, we would have used it."

"And you got back in how?" asked Martinez.

Oops. "Uh, with a ladder up to the second floor," I said.

Martinez and Miller looked at each other.

"The ladder was in the garage. I don't normally go around climbing into people's second-story windows," I said with a laugh that fell flat. "What was missing?"

"A number of things, including jewelry," said Martinez. Jewelry again. "When you went in the second-floor window, for the dog, did you look through the drawers, maybe look for jewelry?"

"No! I was after the dog."

I was not liking how this organizing work put us at risk of being accused of all sorts of things, especially if we were in the house when none of the residents were home.

"Did you go into the bathrooms?"

"No," I said.

More questions about OOC and Lauren.

"She would never take anything," I said, having said that already in several different ways. "Even if clients wanted to give us their stuff, she didn't allow that at all. She is completely professional, at all times."

They asked the names of all the OOC employees. They asked for the dates of work completed. They asked about the disposal of things like papers that might have private information on them.

Miller made wrapping-up sounds and stood up.

"Before you go," I said, "are you aware of the death of Kimberly Selleck? She died at Joanna Sullivan's house a week or so ago."

"Yes," said Miller, sitting back down.

"I've been working at Joanna Sullivan's house. And I believe someone is trying to hurt her. Joanna almost died of carbon monoxide poisoning and then Kimberly was at her house and drank some coffee that normally only Joanna would drink and then Kimberly died."

"Word is that Kimberly took something that interacted badly with her asthma," said Martinez.

"Yes, beta blockers, someone said," I said. "But Kimberly was not on them. I think someone was trying to hurt Joanna and put them in her coffee. And when I tried to find the coffee she served Kimberly—blueberry—the bag was gone. Joanna did not throw it out."

"Why would someone want to hurt Mrs. Sullivan?" asked Miller.

I explained about the house and the land trust.

Martinez shrugged. "Sounds like a family where some money might be coming in the future."

"The plumber died, Kimberly died, Joanna almost died," I said. "That's not nothing. And if she votes the way her husband wanted her to vote, the family gets none of the millions."

Miller stood up. "The best I can say is that we'll keep our ears open for anything going on with the Sullivans."

Martinez stood up too, right as my phone buzzed with a text from Jay.

Your parents coming here. In 10 mins

There was a knock at the door, then the sound of the door opening.

Oh no.

Chapter 39

"Hello?" It was my dad.

Before I knew it, my dad and mom were standing in the opening between the living room and foyer.

"Sorry we are early." Mom said, clutching a huge casserole pan. "Didn't realize there were other guests. Don't worry, I made plenty."

"We're finished," said Miller.

My parents paused, waiting for me to show the manners they had drilled into me and introduce them.

"I'm Nell Waring," said Mom, setting the casserole pan on the sideboard and walking into the room. "This is Dutch."

Martinez broke into a big smile. "Dutch Waring? I thought that might be you."

Dad nodded. He was a bit of a celebrity in our area. I felt the familiar sense of pride, looking at him—tall, fit, always neatly groomed, whether in a baseball uniform or the khakis and sweater he had on now. Gray hair cut short, wire-rimmed glasses making him, not mom, look like the physics professor. An easy kindness that you would only mistake once for being a pushover.

"Man, it's nice to meet you," said Martinez, bounding to shake Dad's hand. "I'm Devin Martinez. I wanted to play for you!"

"I remember you." Dad had an amazing memory for anything baseball-related. Stats, people, plays. "Amador High School?"

"Yes!" said Martinez. "Ended up at Delaney Community College, then joined the force. But, boy, I loved those days playing."

Dad squinted. "How do you know Izzy?"

"Hello, sir," said Miller. "I'm Luisa Miller. Martinez and I are detectives. Izzy was telling us about an older woman she believes to be in danger."

Mom looked back and forth between me, the detectives, and my dad. "What are you guys up to!" she demanded, angry.

"Mom, it's not you," I said.

"You think I don't know you guys talk about me behind my back?"

Mom looked at Miller. "Are you going to test me or something? Take away my driver's license? This is BULLshit."

"Ma'am?" said Miller. "We are here about some robberies, and then Ms. Bishop was sharing information about a client."

"Remember, Mom? Joanna? Her physical therapist died at her house. And I think someone is trying to hurt her."

"Oh," said Mom.

Mom had always been a brilliant, elegant woman with a great sense of humor. She still was, with a little unpredictable spice thrown in, courtesy of the mini-strokes.

The humor resurfaced. "Well, sorry," she said, smiling wryly. "Apologies for the cursing." She paused a moment. "I've had a series of small strokes, which seems to have freed up my tongue."

Mom looked at Dad. "That's a new one—paranoia."

Dad shrugged. "You've always kept me on my toes, Nell. Don't mind it." The warmth in their smiles at each other made me want to cry. In happiness for them; in sadness that I didn't feel that with Jay. They were smiles of two people who have weathered forty years of ups and downs, and even the changing brain of one of them, and still felt an affection that was obvious to everyone in the room.

"We'll be in touch," said Miller, heading to the door. Martinez gave Dad another handshake. "Honor to meet you, sir."

In the kitchen Dad pulled out a salad and foil-wrapped bread from the bag. "Must have been some day if it ended with detectives in your living room."

I was already opening the wine. "You have no idea."

"I called Lauren to ask them to join us, and, wow, she is not happy with you," said Mom, a smile hovering.

"She fired me. Again."

Mom shrugged. "She cares very much about that business. She's worked hard at it, and she's such a perfectionist."

Mom and Dad looked at each other and smiled. The three of them were the perfectionists of the family. I was the outlier.

Jay appeared in the kitchen. "Nell! Dutch!" he said, hugging them both.

"Good to see you, Jay," said Dad.

"Still handsome," Mom said. "I'll bet the Parisian women are falling all over you!"

Her tone was suggestive, like a man with his friends at a bachelor party, and Jay looked at her in surprise.

"Mom's had some mini-strokes," I explained. "They kind of removed her filter."

"Oh," said Jay. "Sorry to hear that."

My parents glanced at each other, maybe realizing how little Jay and I had been communicating.

Cole wasn't going to be home until late, so it was just the four of us. We sat at the long table, candles lit, fancy place mats, Frank Sinatra on the Sonos speakers. Wine and the buffer of having other people around helped me ignore my tension with Jay.

Mom's phone beeped, and she jumped up. "Time for my pills!" she said, going over to the counter and pulling a small pill organizer out of her purse.

"I found this app that reminds you to take your medicine," she said. "And keeps track of drug interactions and whatever." Mom dumped the little compartment of pills into her hand. "I don't trust myself to remember."

Another loving smile from Dad.

"How is Cole doing?" asked Mom, walking back to the table. "He must be so angry to not get to run."

"Furious," I said.

"Pretty fast recovery, though," Dad mused. "He's already back in school."

"Yes, he got great care," I said.

"Adorable, too!" Mom said. "That doctor was handsome and, boy, did he like you, Izzy."

A rush of red to my face. Jay stared at me. Thanks, Mom.

"I felt sparks when you guys were talking," Mom added.

"Mom!" I erupted. "Jay is right here! Stop embarrassing me." I try really hard to be patient with her, but this was too much.

Mom deflated. "I'm sorry. I don't know what I was saying." She looked at Jay. "I'm really sorry. Ignore me."

Dad looked like he was in physical pain.

I felt guilty for my outburst.

Jay was silent.

At that moment, Cole walked in, a welcome distraction.

By the end of dinner, I was so tired I felt pinned to my chair.

"I've got this," said Jay, picking up plates. I wished he'd stop being so helpful; it just annoyed me even more.

Cole cleared his plate and said he needed to do homework. He hugged and kissed both grandparents, looked happily at the group, then disappeared. Stab of guilt.

Then again, he'd be gone soon. Was I really going to stay with Jay just so the boys could have an intact family to come home to once in a while?

Dad leaned down and hugged me. "Don't worry about Lauren. She'll come around."

Mom leaned close. "Sorry about the doctor comment," she whispered. "I'm sure that was the last thing you needed with Jay."

My parents let themselves out, and I closed my eyes, listening to the sounds of Jay rinsing the dishes.

"You aren't the only one who can sense things," Jay said. "I saw it with the doctor. You guys were into each other."

"I 'sensed' you sitting with Shania at the Village Green, just so you know." It came out before I could stop myself.

Jay laughed. "She sat down uninvited. You should know that."

"Because she's never stopped trying to get you back?"

Jay snorted. "I dated her in high school, for crissakes. A nothing then and certainly nothing now. But you and the doctor . . ."

"I am willing to talk about anything, but not tonight. I've had a shit day, and my brain is exhausted. 'kay?"

"Fine," said Jay, not moving, facing away from me.

"I'm not denying it," I said. "I'm just too tired to talk."

Jay turned around. "Just tell me, before we start working on things. Are you seeing him?"

Way to respect my request not to talk about anything tonight. A spurt of anger woke me up.

"I have had no dates since you've been gone."

"But there's something there?" he persisted.

"Maybe."

"I mean, I don't blame you," he said. "We aren't living together."

"Speaking of 'something there' kinds of things, what about Sarah?"

Jay shrugged. "It didn't go anywhere. Maybe it just was good for the ego to feel like someone wanted me."

I stared into the flickering candle in front of me, my whole torso tight and hollow, like the Tin Man from *The Wizard of Oz*. I hated this feeling, I wanted out.

"You were just always so angry at me," Jay continued. Not fun to be around that."

"I said I was too tired to talk and here we are, talking."

"You're right. I'm sorry," Jay said, his shoulders bunched up. I could see him fighting off the urge to keep blaming me for our problems. I could almost feel him biting his tongue. He laughed like he was trying to lighten the mood. "So, tell me about the guys coming after you since I've been gone. There have to be some. I don't trust half of this town."

A welcome change of topic. Strange times.

"I've wondered who would, you know, hit on you once I was gone. I could make a guess," Jay said, pouring himself a full glass of red wine. When did he open that bottle?

"Really? You think guys hit on me?" He wasn't completely wrong, but I wondered if he'd be correct in his guesses.

Jay sat down across from me, swirling his wine. "This is the Yield Zinfandel. Maybe have a little; it's really good."

"Maybe a little," I said, too tired to argue.

He handed me his glass and went to pour another one.

"Okay, what's your prediction?" I said, taking a sip. It really was good. I hoped Jacques wasn't the one trying to kill Joanna; the world needed his wine-making skills.

"Phil," said Jay.

I laughed. "Bingo. But in a jokey way. Like, when I turned him down, he could jokingly say 'Just kidding, just wanted to make sure you are still feeling attractive.'"

"He's an ass," said Jay.

"I know," I said. "But we all like Shelly so much, what are you going to do?"

"Anyone else?" asked Jay.

How was this the easier conversation? Joking about who hit on me when our marriage imploded? "Just a couple of guys who flirted more than normal. No one coming at me like Shania is coming at you."

I took another sip of the wine. "Instead of investigating Jacques, maybe we should be investing in him."

"No kidding," said Jay, looking at his glass. He looked over at me, and we had a moment. Bonding over good wine and asshat men. Then he smiled, a loving, friendly smile, and I felt myself tense up inside. Too much. Too close. It didn't feel right. I looked away.

"That's it for me. I'm so tired," I said, standing up and trying not to notice the way Jay's smile faded.

Chapter 40

In the morning, I woke early, heart racing, on the hamster wheel of worry. With no chance of going back to sleep, I pulled on yoga pants and a long-sleeved t-shirt and tiptoed past the guest room. I made a cup of coffee, slid on beat-up running shoes and escaped to my car.

I ended up in the parking lot of the park in the dark pre-dawn, listening to boot camp women cheerfully complain as they clambered out of their cars.

Everything felt wrong. Fired by Lauren. Joanna still in danger. Emily blocking my access to Joanna. Unreliable psychic skills. Angry at myself for agreeing to work on my marriage when I didn't want that at all.

I had to figure out who was trying to hurt Joanna before I even thought about the marriage. Time to review everything I knew about all of the Sullivans. I wished I was in front of the corkboard, but I'd look at it again later.

Serena needed money badly. I wouldn't underestimate a mother's need to provide for her children. She hadn't been close to Joanna, but now she was hanging around and seemed to want to live in that house. What did I really sense about her? Her unhappiness came with such a sense of lethargy, it was hard to believe she had enough energy to plot a murder. Then again, despair could be a lethal motivator.

Jacques needed money, but the real question was whether his religion was an act. It gave him an excuse to get involved with Joanna again, saying that he felt like they should be more supportive of her. How far would his desire to become a full partner push him? Any chance he was gambling again? I thought about the conflict with Marco. What were they hiding from the past? What did I really sense about him? So positive, so upbeat, so pious that it was hard to believe it was real.

Marco was ambitious, knew what the house was worth, and needed money to be a land developer. Angry at his dad and felt like he deserved his fair share. Maybe he already took some of his fair share. Maybe he and Jacques both did.

As a struggling musician with a baby on the way, Karl had a clear financial motive. And he was looking for something at Joanna's, maybe something valuable in one of Thomas's collections. What did I really sense about him? A sadness from high school. A charisma he used to manipulate people. Could that make him a murderer?

I jumped when my phone rang, jarringly loud in the quiet car. Happily, it was Joanna.

"Joanna! Are you feeling better?" I hoped it was actually her and not Emily using her phone.

"Yes. I'm feeling much better. Clear-headed again." It was Joanna, but her voice was cold, her words clipped. "I can't believe you gave me those marijuana cookies. I can't believe you would even have those cookies. I am starting to wonder if I even know who you are."

"I'm so sorry I mixed that up," I said. "Patty Hathaway makes those, and she gave them to me for my mother and I forgot I had them! I thought I was giving you the Snickerdoodles another client made. I would never have given those to you on purpose."

"I know it is legal and all," said Joanna. "But to sneak it like that."

"Joanna, you know me, you know I would not do that to you on purpose!"

"Emily has taken some time off work to help me. She'll work with Wanda. I don't need you anymore. Send me a bill; I'll pay whatever I owe."

I felt Thomas panic, and my chest tightened so intensely I was sure I was having a heart attack. *Stay connected!* he begged.

"Again, I'm so sorry. I really didn't mean to give you those. Please let me keep helping you," I said.

"No, thank you," cut in Emily. Must have been on speakerphone. "We are quite done with you and your business. Mom insisted on telling you herself, but this is enough. Goodbye."

They clicked off.

I had screwed it all up. I had ruined Order Out of Chaos's reputation. I had lost the Joanna job. I had alienated Joanna while she was still in danger, and I had no way to protect her anymore.

Sitting there in the foggy dawn, I felt more alone than I ever had in my life. Nothing I was doing was working. No one seemed to understand the sensing part of me except Lucille, and I barely knew her.

I glanced at the time and decided it wasn't too early to call Lucille. I got no answer so left a message asking her to call back.

I gave in to the tears and for about five minutes had a pity party for myself. The crying worked its usual magic, and I felt a little better.

I took a couple of deep breaths.

I have *me*.

That's not nothing.

My head was pounding, so I looked around the car for my Excedrin. It was not in the glove compartment or the center console. I fumbled around in the slot on my door, and came up with the pile of jewelry I'd been shedding lately. I looked at it in the now pale-gray light. Even my own jewelry had rejected me.

I played with the earrings, slid them on my fingers like rings. Held the bracelet up and asked it, "Why don't you like me?"

I had really lost it. I was talking to cheap jewelry.

Because you don't pay attention to what is wrong for you.

Where did that thought come from? Felt like the same voice I'd heard in the Epsom bath.

I looked at the bracelet again. "Hello?"

It wasn't coming from the bracelet, or Thomas—it was coming from somewhere in my head, like a cloud floating by.

We are trying to help you. We send signals all day long, and you ignore them. A headache, tense shoulders, jewelry marks.

"We?"

It isn't that the jewelry is cheap; it is that you haven't been listening. We—which is you—*know what to do. You just keep ignoring it. The body knows. The BODY knows.*

I stared at the windshield without really seeing anything, my mind floating, images drifting in and out, coalescing and breaking apart. An image of sitting in Lucille's kitchen, my body warm and completely at peace; an image of Jay, my body cold and tense; an image of running with Vivi, warm again; an image of Lauren, cooler, tighter.

It was like a game of hot and cold. My own body giving the guidance. This feels warmer—good! This feels colder—bad!

Of course I knew what to do. I just hadn't been doing it. Pushed around by the confusing energy of friends and family and husband and sister and what they wanted. Sitting here, quiet, alone, life completely shredded, I felt my mind connect with my body. Not divided. Not trying to please the world. Trying to please all the parts of me.

Instead of channeling a dead person, I was channeling me. I couldn't see the future, but, at least for a moment, I felt a clear sense of how to direct myself. Warmer, colder—my body could lead the way. Even my jewelry had been trying to get my attention, telling me "You are not being yourself."

What was my body telling me to do?

Stop living divided, stop hiding parts of yourself. Even the inconvenient, not socially acceptable parts. Especially the inconvenient, socially unacceptable parts. Those were the real me, maybe more than any other part. There was nothing wrong with not wanting a career like my mom. There was nothing wrong with wanting to focus on being a good mother. There was nothing wrong with being sensitive to what was going on with other people. There was nothing wrong with communicating with dead people.

Time to stop lying to myself.

I allowed myself to know the thing I had been trying not to know for so long. For years.

Jay was not the one. He wasn't enough for me. There was nothing wrong with me for not loving Jay.

Sadness swirled with an odd sense of relief.

Maybe there was no such thing as "the one," and if there was, it was way too soon to know if it was Saito. But I knew that I felt something way more powerful for him than I had ever felt for Jay. I didn't have to do anything about it yet, but I could let myself fully know.

Now my dim car felt more like a cocoon—a safe, cozy place to grow into something else. I let the knowing just sit there; I didn't try to stuff it into the basement of my head anymore. I noticed how that felt in my body, like a fist unfurling, loosening.

I felt—finally—peaceful inside. Sitting next to the relief was a deep sadness.

But maybe deep sadness was preferable to not liking myself.

An image of Samantha passed through my head, and then Shania's sidekick Jules, and then Serena. Why them?

And then I got it.

They all were questioning their marriages.

I had picked up on that from each one of them and didn't really want to see it because it hit too close to home for me.

I thought about how my senses had stopped working with Samantha. Maybe I didn't want to see what was going on for her because it was too close to me?

And Jules, I had definitely picked up on an unhappy marriage.

And I could feel Serena's sense of being trapped. And feeling like money would be the answer. Money would be an answer for me too. We like to pretend it doesn't matter, but money matters when you don't have enough of it. When you stay somewhere because you can't afford to go. Because then your brain starts talking you into stuff you really don't believe.

I wondered if I had any other blind spots. Places I didn't want to let my mind go and so didn't see in other people.

I sat in a sense of sad peace for a while longer, as the parking lot lightened and the fog burned away.

I felt such a sense of clarity, so clear inside, that the Joanna answer came to me.

Chapter 41

It seemed so obvious I couldn't believe I hadn't thought of it before. Well, I had, but I let Thomas talk me out of it.

I had to convince Joanna that Thomas was around. And convince her she was in danger.

Absolutely not! Thomas communicated.

My chest contracted, and anger and panic started circling, but it was clearly him, not me. Interesting. He was coming through so easily, even without the tangerine dress.

You don't know better than me just because you are a ghost! I told him.

Why had I listened to Thomas? I had assumed that even ghosts know more than I did. Does dying make someone perfect and all-knowing? What if souls could be just as confused on the other side?

Thomas, I'm telling her! I know this is hard because maybe one of your kids is trying to hurt her, but it's the only way.

My phone rang again. This time it was my mother.

"I hope I didn't wake you up," she said. "I forgot my pills at your house. Probably on the counter."

"I'm out, uh, grabbing coffee, but I'll go check," I said. "I'll bring them over." I had nothing else scheduled for today. Just figuring out how to get Joanna to answer my call. And tell her I was communicating with her dead husband. No biggie.

"That would be great. I'm waiting for someone to come to fix the garage door," she said. "Sorry again for saying the stupid stuff about the doctor. It doesn't even feel like me speaking when that happens."

"It's okay," I said. It really was okay. In fact, my mom was on the same path as me. Just saying the truth. It occurred to me that I learned how to stay polite and socially appropriate from both of my parents. It had seemed like a virtue, something to make others comfortable. But maybe it also sent uncomfortable thoughts underground. Uncomfortable truths. "You weren't wrong," I added, feeling a burst of bravery.

"Oh my," said my mom.

"I guess it's complicated," I said. "Or maybe it's not complicated. I don't love Jay. There. I said it."

"Oh Izzy," she sighed. "We love you, no matter what. I just want you to be happy. Don't ever feel like you have to stay for us."

My insides melted. I hadn't realized how much I wanted my mom's approval. "Thank you," I whispered.

I drove home and found the pill organizer under a dish towel. It was a smaller version of Joanna's pill organizer. Was that in my future? Did all old people have varying sizes of pill boxes lying around their kitchens?

And then, like a loud "click" in my head, the answer was there, front and center.

"The pill organizer!!!" I yelped, my brain zinging around in circles like an excited puppy. I found the business card Martinez and Miller had left me. It was Miller's with Martinez's number added in pen. I called Miller first and got the voicemail.

"This is Izzy Bishop. I just remembered something that might be really important. Joanna filled a huge pill organizer, a week's worth of pills; she was on a lot. And you should check it. It would have been really easy for someone to put different pills in there! That would explain why she keeps having episodes at home, but then clears up in the hospital! It is in her kitchen. I cleaned up for her and put it in the drawer underneath the microwave. Please check it before she goes home again. Or tell whoever would do it. Thank you." I hung up, called Martinez, and left the same message.

Then I called Joanna, and predictably, she didn't answer. I left her the same message and then texted the same thing to both her and Emily. I wondered when Joanna would be headed home and hoped she wasn't already there, taking more pills.

I ran upstairs, changed into jeans, put on a bra under my t-shirt, grabbed my purse and mom's pills, and ran out the door.

After I dropped the pills at my parents' house, I zoomed over to Joanna's, barely noticing my normal driving fear, just focused on getting to her house. The gate was closed, and several delivery trucks were pulled up alongside the gate, drivers standing beside the keypad.

"You know the code?" one asked me.

I didn't and tried punching the speaker button.

"No one answering," said the guy. He didn't look completely put out, was smoking a cigarette and sipping on a cup of coffee.

I called Wanda and asked if she knew the code.

"I do. I'll be right there," she said.

"Tell me and I'll let them in," I said.

"I've been instructed not to," she said, apologetically. "Man, Emily is pissed at you!" Wanda gave a little laugh. "No way I'm getting on that shit list. I'll be right there."

I shrugged, told the guys someone was coming, and drove home. On the way I tried Lucille again, and this time I caught her.

"Hello, Izzy dear," said Lucille. "I was going to call you and let you know I'm leaving in an hour for New York. Sudden addition to my trip plans."

"No!"

"Yes, one of my oldest friends is in hospice, and I'm going to spend some time with her before leaving for Greece. I was flying out of New York anyway, so this will work out. It sounds like you are in some distress?"

"I'm so sorry." I felt bad for being so selfish. "It's just that everything is falling apart, and I thought I could figure it out if I could talk to you."

"Hmm." Lucille's warmth and attention seeped through the phone. I could feel her mind reaching for my mind, floating in as easily as a wisp of smoke through an open window. "You have already figured it out. Don't mistrust yourself; you are on the right path."

I knew it and it felt good to hear Lucille say it, but I was panicked at her leaving this soon. I had so much more I wanted to talk to her about.

"You'll do fine, my dear," said Lucille. "I really need to go. I'm getting picked up soon and am not done packing."

"Yes, of course. Have a great trip," I said and we hung up.

Lucille believed in me. I could do this.

Whatever this was.

Chapter 42

I slipped upstairs without seeing Jay and closed myself in Luke's room. Time to organize the corkboard and figure out the pill thing.

Joanna had bought and filled a couple of pill organizers after her first OOC session. The calendar on my phone showed that to be Monday, two weeks ago. A lot of people had been at the house since then. Obviously, all of Thomas's kids, Emily, neighbors bringing food. All four of the Sullivans had been at the garage cleanout, but it would have been hard to replace those pills in the kitchen with people coming in and out. Then again, maybe Joanna hadn't always kept them in the kitchen. If I could get her to talk to me again, I'd ask her. Marco and Karl had come to visit right after Joanna had been gassed. Then there was the time Serena wouldn't let me in. I didn't know about Jacques beyond the garage cleanout. And then I realized any of them could have come when Joanna wasn't even there. They all knew the keypad combination to get in the garage. They probably all even had keys. For that matter, even Connie would have been able to get in.

I thought about the ramping up of activity for the gala. Lots of people were coming and going, landscapers and delivery people. And Wanda. I couldn't come up with a logical reason that Wanda would want to hurt Joanna, though. It would put the gala in jeopardy, for one.

It was going to be hard to nail down when someone had tampered with the pills. Too many people with opportunity, access, and motive.

Come at it from another angle. Kimberly died on Saturday, ten days ago. I looked at my phone again. Joanna went back to the hospital last Wednesday. Almost a week ago. Let's say the pills were switched out close to that time, or it would have happened before. So maybe last Monday or Tuesday? I had been so distracted by Cole's appendicitis and Jay's coming home and the dog debacle at Peaches's during those days. I would have to ask Joanna more about who had visited her around that time. If I could ever get her to talk to me again.

The board was filled with Post-its, and I stared at them, nothing really coming together.

I let my breathing slow down and asked Thomas for help. *Is she in danger right now?* I asked.

I couldn't get any clear sense. Frustrating. Did that just mean that Thomas wasn't coming through well? Did it mean Joanna wasn't in danger? Did it mean she was, and I just couldn't tell? I felt my anxiety rising, with no idea if it was me or Thomas.

I flashed on an image of a dark room, people dancing, loud music. Was it a random bleedthrough? Was Thomas remembering something?

Anything? Can you give me anything? I asked, but it felt like he'd disappeared.

I flashed on Joanna lying still, looking pale, and wondered if that was my own fear or something from Thomas. If I could just peek in her house, see her moving around, I'd feel better. Peek through the window, even.

Then I remembered the security cameras. That I had installed.

"Sunny15" was too easy.

I could get a glimpse! Knowing I was crossing a line, I downloaded the Arlo app onto my phone and signed in to Joanna's account. I had to. What if she was lying on the floor, passed out or worse?

I clicked on all three cameras, but no one was there, in any of the views.

Hmm. Then I noticed a setting labeled "Library." Right, the camera was *recording*. And it was storing the recordings. Maybe I could find a recording of the person who substituted the pills. If the organizer had remained in the kitchen, it would be in view of the camera.

Looking at the first recordings, my heart sank. I had only installed the cameras last Wednesday. The day that Joanna went back into the hospital. Damn. Missed by maybe only a day or two.

So close.

Wouldn't hurt to look through the recordings, though. Maybe I'd find something interesting. Or maybe the person had come back and added more pills.

Very quickly I got irritated with whoever had designed the Arlo setup. The recordings were in little bitty chunks and divided in no obvious way, making it hard to watch anything continually. I made my way through all the chunks and, although I didn't find the person substituting the pills, I did find Marco in the house on Thursday while Joanna was in the hospital. He showed up on the kitchen camera and then the office camera, digging through file cabinets and papers. Then back to the kitchen, looking through papers on the counter. Stared at one for quite a while. Then clearly said, "Holy shit."

Had to be the land trust lawyer letter.

Later that day Jacques also showed up. He came through the kitchen calling for Joanna, either unaware she was in the hospital or pretending he didn't know in case someone was there. He left through the kitchen an hour later, never having been picked up by any other cameras. So, he came in and left through the garage, and I didn't know what he did in the meantime.

If only I'd had the cameras installed before Serena had been there earlier in the week. No Karl sighting but, again, no cameras until Wednesday.

I added all the new information to the board. So many notes but nothing fully coming together. Yet.

Chapter 43

I went downstairs and found Jay working on the long table in the great room, laptop open and papers scattered around him. I immediately felt uncomfortable. In my own home. I couldn't do this, live with someone who made me this tense. I maybe wasn't ready to say it out loud, but it was crystal clear inside me.

"Christ, I'm stiff." Jay stood up and stretched. "Have you had lunch yet?"

"No, but not really hungry," I said.

Jay poked around in the refrigerator, eventually pulling out a pack of sliced ham and putting together a sandwich.

My phone buzzed: Lauren. I hit the red button. Not in the mood for her.

I watched Jay eat his sandwich over the dirty dishes piled in the sink. Somehow one more person in the house made the dirty dishes grow exponentially. I didn't have time for this Jay business; I needed to figure out how to help Joanna.

I let my brain go soft. What was my next step?

Once again, I had the image of a dark place, loud with music and people. I stared off into space . . . what did that remind me of?

Karl!

Yes! From Thomas.

I was willing to take a chance on Karl. Despite the space heater thing, he was lowest on my suspect list. He was basically happy with his life. He seemed at ease with his choices. He was on the rise as an artist. I felt more confirmation from Thomas.

"I need to talk to Karl," I said.

"Huh?" said Jay.

"I'm thinking he could help me with Joanna."

I pulled out my phone and found that his band was playing tonight at Coco's in Berkeley, near enough. I texted Vivi to see if she wanted to go with me.

Two thumbs up came back almost immediately, and the plan was set.

"Good, I'll talk to him tonight," I said.

Jay was back at the table, tapping away at his computer. "What time should we leave?"

"Oh, I'm going with Vivi."

Jay stopped tapping. The air snapped with tension. He didn't speak, just stared, like he was trying to decide whether to say something or not. His eyes were kind of puffy and he hadn't shaved, and there were a few more wrinkles than I remembered.

"You'd rather go with Vivi?" he finally asked.

Obviously, I thought, but I couldn't drop the habit of not saying the truth to him. "She went with me before, and it kind of worked to seem like it was just a girls' night out."

Jay looked at his computer then back at me. "I feel like you don't really tell me the truth. You dance around it. Just say what you want to say. I can take it."

Why was that so hard?

I looked down. Mumbled, "I'd rather go with Vivi."

"Not that," said Jay. "Say what you want to say. Just be out with it."

"Sometimes I don't even know what the truth is," I stalled.

"How could you not know the truth?" said Jay. "It's the truth."

"I don't know," I said, panicked. I just had admitted the truth to myself. I wasn't ready to actually say it.

Jay was completely still, eyes unblinking on me. "What do you want?"

"I don't know," I said, annoyed at being pressured.

"I don't believe you," said Jay, leaning back in the chair and folding his arms. "I think you do know. You just don't want to say it." I could see the challenge on his face. He was going to make me say it. Bastard.

I didn't want to deal with this now. I had Joanna to save. "It's just that it is all so mixed up inside me. I want different things. Incompatible things. I want us to work out, and I don't know how to make us work out. I want to stop fighting, but I don't know how to make that happen."

"What. Do. You. Want." Jay measured each word and threw it at me.

"I want to not fight anymore," I said. "I am so tired of that."

"That is weak," said Jay. "That's obvious. No one wants to fight. What do you want?"

"What are you trying to get me to say?" Put it back on him. "What do *you* want?"

Jay didn't even pause. "I want us. I want you. I want our family. I want to come home."

"What about me is it that you want?" I asked. "What do you love about me?"

Jay's eyes widened like I was being stupid. "I have to spell it out?"

"Yes," I said.

"You're a great mother. You're attractive. You are a good daughter," he said.

"That's it?"

"I don't know what you want me to say, I'm supposed to prove why I love you?"

"Yes. I'm kind of curious. Why me? Why *me*?"

Jay shook his head, rolling his eyes at the same time. Like I was such an idiot to have to ask why someone loved me. "Who knows? I just do." Then he stared me down. "Do you love me?"

His words hung there, sucking the air out of the room.

The conformist, people-pleasing, never-hurt-anyone's-feelings me formed "yes, of course." It was right there, perched on my tongue, but I couldn't release it. It was like a slow-motion fall off a cliff, not answering that question.

Jay didn't break eye contact, not for a good thirty seconds or maybe it was thirty minutes. My mouth opened and closed and opened again, but nothing came out.

Jay stood up and walked out of the room.

What an inconvenient time to stop lying.

Chapter 44

Jay stomped up the stairs, and then the guest room door closed with a bang. Up until this moment, I don't think either of us had really believed we'd really divorce. We'd used the word in anger, as a threat, not as something we really meant.

I had just broken us.

Tears spilled down my cheeks, and for once I knew the exhausting sadness was all mine, not some disembodied spirit's feelings. I flopped onto the couch, turned towards the back, buried my face in the cushion, and pulled the blanket over my head.

This morning's peace was replaced by grief. And crushing, pin-me-to-the-earth guilt.

I heard footsteps down the stairs and then the door to the garage and then the sound of Jay's car starting and leaving.

I cried until I fell asleep.

*****

The buzzing of my phone woke me into a sick sadness. Lauren again. I ignored it.

I wanted to call Jay and apologize, tell him I loved him, make it all right again.

Why are you trying so hard to get a life back that you don't even want?

The thought just appeared. Didn't feel like a ghost, more like my Inner Mystic.

Uh, because I'm scared?

Not a good enough reason.

Because it is killing me to hurt someone?

You need to stop choosing other people over yourself.

What do I do now?

Just the next thing. That is all you ever really can do, anyway.

What is the next thing?

My chest constricted, and Thomas joined the conversation and said, *Hello? JOANNA is the next thing.*

Could I really solve this mystery while my marriage burned?

Yes. Inner Mystic again.

Okay. Distraction by investigation it is.

I sat up, my face tight from the dried tears.

Go wash your face. That is the next thing.

I did it.

Now make tea.

I made tea. Maybe I could make it if the next thing just kept appearing in my head.

Now thaw something for dinner.

I found some sirloin chili in the freezer and softened it in the microwave, then put it on the stove. I added a couple of potatoes in the oven for Cole's favorite combination: a potato smothered in chili, topped with melted cheese. Distance runners needed an insane amount of calories. Maybe not running for a couple of weeks would actually put a smidgen of body fat back on him.

I found that I could actually do mundane things like think about cheese on chili, even though my marriage had just fractured. What an odd sensation. Like a spirit moving around when the body was dead on the couch.

Cole got home, we chatted, I gave him his dinner, and I went upstairs and got ready to go out with Vivi.

Vivi arrived to pick me up, and as I climbed in the car, I burst into tears.

"Whoa!" said Vivi. "What's going on?"

I filled her in.

Vivi reached over to give me a side hug. "Oh Izzy, I'm so sorry."

"I honestly thought I wanted it to be over, but now I feel so awful."

"Of course it hurts! The end hurts. That's okay. You can't force yourself to love someone." Vivi was so gentle.

"It just makes me so sad," I said. "It's a mess."

Vivi grabbed my hand. "Iz, you have tried longer than most people. You have to face the truth."

"Truth," I said. "I seem to be running into that word everywhere."

"What is that line?" said Vivi. "Maybe from Gloria Steinem? 'The truth will set you free, but first it will piss you off.'"

"Oh yes," I said, surprised to find myself smiling. "The truth is a big pisser-offer."

Vivi handed me tissues from the console. "Enough for now. Put it to the side while we go visit the delectable Karl."

"You're the best," I said. "Thank you."

"Lucy and Ethel. Together forever," said Vivi. "I'm here for you. No matter what."

***

We circled the streets of Berkeley, finally finding a parking spot that wasn't in a different zip code. I forgot how different Berkeley felt from Oak Creek or Montavilla. So urban, gritty, full of unexpected delights—a cheese store next to a thrift store with pornographic art in the windows, delicious exotic food smells drifting out of every other restaurant, anything possible around the next corner.

In this case the thing around the next corner was the line for Coco's.

Vivi giggled. "I think my days of blowing past the line are over, don't you?"

"We could try," I said.

"My ego couldn't handle the rejection."

Two young women in front of us holding hands snuck backwards glances, probably interested in seeing this goddess. I could see the humor pass between their eyes.

"Who you looking at? It happens fast," Vivi said, in full Philly mode. "Turn back around."

Once inside we grabbed drinks and squeezed towards the stage. Karl was doing his thing, dressed in extra ripped jeans and a sleeveless t-shirt that showed off his muscles. His dark hair tumbled into and out of his face as he bent forward and leaned back, the hair-flinging part of the act. Two songs later the band stopped and I pressed forward to get to him.

"Could I talk to you, like, seriously?" I yelled.

"Yeah, in about an hour. Over there," he pointed to a side door.

"Can I get you anything?"

Four women were tugging at Karl's back. "I wouldn't say no to a beer," he said.

For an hour we enjoyed the music. Watching people dancing to the music, I could literally see energy flowing in waves around the room, one person's energy connecting with another, connecting with another, weaving us all into a moment of fun. It was so *connecting*, the music. I was going to have to get out and see more live music.

At their break Karl steered me down a dark hallway and outside into an empty enclosed bar area. I handed him his beer, and we sat down on a couple of stools.

"I'm really worried about Joanna," I said. "This sounds ridiculous, but here goes. I had a near-death experience a year and a half ago, and now I, uh, I communicate with spirits. It's your dad; he's worried about Joanna."

I felt an urge to put my hand on Karl's shoulder. That must be Thomas.

"Someone is trying to kill Joanna, but he can't or won't let me know who, and now Joanna cut me off, but I need to get back in and talk to her."

"Whoa," Karl said. "You are saying you are talking to my dad?"

"Yes," I said, realizing I was so focused on Joanna, I hadn't even considered this from Karl's perspective.

Can you help me out here, Thomas?

I felt a little wince, nothing more.

"I'm trying. He's not giving me anything about you," I said.

"Maybe it is him, then," Karl said, bitter.

An image of Thomas with his arms crossed—defensive, almost. Thomas had shown such love for Joanna but with Karl, it felt complicated. I was starting to empathize with the Sullivan kids.

"I don't have great control of these skills," I said. "I kind of have to wait for whatever images come."

Karl glanced at the door, chugged his beer.

"Like, for you, I have an image of a baby stroller. Any babies in your life?"

He looked at me defiantly. "I'm going to need more than that."

"Can I touch your bracelet?" I asked.

He shrugged, and I put my hand over a braided leather band on his wrist.

"Oh," I said. "Does your girlfriend know why you wear it?"

Karl's eyes narrowed just a smidge.

My heart dropped. "I'm sorry. Such sadness."

I was having trouble breathing. I grabbed my chest. "I can't breathe. The girl, she died from something that made her stop breathing."

Karl's eyes widened. "Oh my God."

Just like that, the senses were fully working.

I reminded myself there was plenty of oxygen. That I could breathe fine.

"I'm really sorry. I honestly don't want to know your personal business," I said. Or suffocate. "I just want to prove to you that Joanna is in real danger."

Karl's eyes were wet. "Anything else? About the . . . girl."

"Water, a boat? A little one, beat up, like an old rowboat or something. Shimmering, like the girl was shimmering. Oh, this is why I saw a mermaid connected with you. A water spirit."

Karl nodded.

"It was real," I added. "I don't know what that means, but I think you will."

He nodded again, his eyes latched onto my face.

"She wants you to move on. Like, don't live halfway. The phrase 'don't hold back' comes up."

Karl started full-on crying. "Wow," he whispered. "People said we were too young to be really in love. And then she drowned, and I was just supposed to move on like it was just another high school ex."

This must have been when he went "off track."

"I've been working on a song with those words, 'don't hold back.' Anything else?" he asked hopefully.

I felt around. "Oh," I said.

"What?"

"I'm feeling the loveliest connection to the baby. She's going to watch over her. There's like . . . a fondness for the name you picked."

Karl smiled. "We picked an unusual name. Some people have tried to talk us out of it." He squeezed my hand. "Thank you."

We sat in silence for a minute, and the image of a red stone, like a jewel, showed up. Just then, the door flew open behind us and one of his bandmates peeked out. "Sully, we're starting."

"Give me a minute," Karl said.

The door shut and Karl said, "Okay. I believe you. What do you need?"

"There was this mix-up with a weed cookie," I started.

Karl grinned. "You are full of surprises."

"Emily convinced Joanna to completely cut me off. I never told Joanna about your dad, but now I feel like I really need to. He knows someone is trying to kill her, and I need to help her."

"You don't think it's me?" Karl said, half smiling.

I lied a little. "I don't. I can't say the same about your siblings. Could you help get me in to talk to Joanna? If I could just talk to her and explain, I know I could help her."

"Okay," said Karl. "Call me in the morning. Like, after 11:00? And maybe more . . ." I knew he wanted more connection with the girl.

The door flew open again.

"Dude! Let's go," said a second band member.

"Coming," said Karl. He looked at me. "They know they can't start without me. Can I give you a hug? You have no idea how much this is. Just, wow."

"Sure," I said. We hugged, and I felt Thomas melting inside me. "Your dad does love you," I whispered, and Karl hugged harder.

"Dog, wait 'til after the show," said the guy at the door, shaking his head.

Chapter 45

When I got home, Cole was waiting on the couch.

"What did you do to Dad?" he said, voice mean, arms crossed, head tilted down so that his glare up at me felt almost violent.

"What did he say?"

"That I could ask you why he isn't staying here tonight."

Unfair move by Jay.

I sat down beside Cole, and he shrunk away from me.

"Cole, honey, I'm sorry. This is not easy. I'm really sorry."

"What's wrong with you?" His voice was full of contempt.

He hit me right in my soft spot. Self-doubt.

I couldn't stop my tears. "I've tried so hard. But your dad and I, there is just so much distance."

"I thought France was just work, but you guys have been split up, haven't you?"

"It was a convenient time to try living apart. We told you that."

"No, you didn't," said Cole.

We hear what we want to hear.

"So, you just kicked him out?" said Cole. "That's fucking cold."

"I didn't kick him out. I guess he just felt better leaving."

My poor Cole, such a sensitive soul. The drama with his brother. The drama with my accident. And now this.

"I'm so sorry," I said.

"No, you're not!" Cole said, standing up. "You chased Dad away! It is my last semester at home, and he wants to come home, and you fucking ruined it!" He stomped up to his room and slammed the door so hard the house shook.

I guess the truth pisses everybody off.

No wonder we lie.

***

In the morning I was sad but eerily calm, maybe because I was, for once, on the right path. It was enough to energize me to focus on how to help Joanna.

I was sitting at the island thinking about how to flush out the killer when my phone quacked. Maybe Lauren had cooled off.

"What in the WORLD have you gotten me into!" she yelled. "Do you ever answer your phone? Do you know who I had to talk to AT LENGTH, yesterday? Detectives!"

Shouldn't have answered.

"My business is SUSPECTED in robberies. ROBBERIES!" she moaned.

I switched to speaker and set the phone away from me on the counter.

"I started to actually feel guilty! Doubting me and questioning me about YOU and my business. How could you do this to me?!"

"I didn't do anything," I said. "They will figure out it's not us."

"This is just a CLUSTER," said Lauren. "I honestly hate you right now."

I was still feeling oddly calm. "The truth will set us free."

Lauren huffed and hung up.

I might have to investigate the robberies to clear our name. Right after I figured out who was trying to kill Joanna.

While waiting for Karl, I worked on a plan to catch Kimberly's killer. Unless Martinez and Miller found some kind of evidence, it seemed likely that a trap would have to be set. I doubted that fingerprints on the pill organizer would be enough. Anyone who had been in the kitchen could come up with a rational reason to have touched it.

Thomas hovered, shooting down every plan I considered with a gruff "no."

Give me an idea then, I said to him.

I got an image of him shaking his head no and then nothing more.

Karl called, agreed to pick me up, and we headed to Joanna's. The gate was open, and as we got to the top of the driveway, I could see why. There were trucks everywhere, workers unloading tables and racks and racks of chairs.

"What is this? Why is she here?" Joanna said as she opened the door and I stepped into view.

"You need to hear what she has to say." Karl moved into the doorway so Joanna couldn't close it. "I didn't believe it at first myself, but you really need to talk to her."

Joanna looked uncomfortable.

"You feeling okay today?" I asked. "Clear-headed?"

Joanna nodded. "Emily said . . ."

"Joanna, you know me. You know I'd never do anything to hurt you. Just give me a few minutes?"

"A very few," said Joanna, stepping back.

As we got to the kitchen, I was struck by the view out of the French doors. "Wow! The tent looks amazing," I said. The tent was up, and buzzed with a horde of workers installing lights and tables on the already installed parquet floor.

Joanna sighed. "Yes. It looks great; it's just so much going on." She looked tired and sunk down at the kitchen table, where Karl and I joined her.

"First, did you get the message about the pill organizer?"

"Yes," said Joanna. "I haven't used anything out of it."

"Oh thank God," I said. I took a deep breath. "There is no easy way to say this, but since I first touched that beautiful tangerine dress, I have felt the presence of Thomas. Like, his spirit is here and communicating. Remember how I said 'Sunny'?"

"You're eating too many of those marijuana cookies," said Joanna.

"I saw the two of you dancing; he had on a blue sport coat, there were strings of cafe lights and a swing band, and it was outside, somewhere near water."

Joanna stared at me, unbelieving.

"I keep getting a tight chest when Thomas is around, a sign, like his heart attack. He keeps stopping me from telling you he is around because he didn't want you to worry. But he's been worried about you because he knows someone is trying to hurt you."

Joanna shook her head. "I can't believe this."

Please, Thomas. She knows now. You love her. Help me help her.

I felt a welling up inside my chest, like he was inside me and expanding.

"Joanna, she knew about Amelia," Karl said, his voice catching. "She sensed her from my bracelet."

Joanna looked back at me. "I don't know."

"She knew stuff there is no way she could have known," said Karl.

I closed my eyes, holding onto the handkerchief, waiting for more.

I opened my eyes. "I have an image of you and Thomas in this kitchen. It's dark. And you are both laughing so hard, both covered in something all white and powdery over your faces. You are in a shared pair of pajamas, you in the top, him in the bottoms. Something about pancakes. Laughing so hard you are almost crying."

Joanna's hand drifted up to her mouth. "Oh my," she whispered.

"He is so happy in this image," I said.

Joanna half laughed, half cried. "We made pancakes in the middle of the night and got into a food fight with the flour. We laughed ourselves silly," said Joanna.

"Oh," I said. "I get it. He is showing me he loved being alone with you here, being silly together. That's why he didn't want anyone else living here. He just wanted to be with you."

"Yes. We had so much fun. I miss him so much."

"He knows," I said softly.

"What else?" Joanna asked. "If he is there, is there anything else?"

"Deep, deep love, of course," I said. "And a lot of pain. I think the pain is that he knows who is trying to hurt you, and it hurts him. I think it might be one of his kids." And if it was Connie trying to hurt Joanna, Thomas would have directed me straight to her. Damn, too bad.

"Oh no," said Joanna, glancing at Karl.

"It's not him," I said, even though I wasn't convinced of that. "I don't know about the others, though. I'm trying to figure it out before you get hurt."

"Maybe that is why I have felt so good with you around! Thomas has been here all along," said Joanna, her old sunny smile resurfacing. "Emily thinks you are trying to take advantage of me, but I really don't believe that."

"The weed cookie really was a mistake," I said. "Now back to the pills."

Joanna nodded.

"Where are they now?" I asked, hoping she hadn't thrown them out.

Joanna inclined her head towards the cabinets. "I haven't touched them. I'm afraid to."

Karl and I stood up and walked around the island.

"I put them in that drawer," I said, pulling it out.

"What made you think of the pills?" asked Joanna, following us.

"I kept wondering why you'd get better in the hospital and worse at home. I saw my mom's pill organizer, and it just clicked."

"I can't believe someone would . . . on purpose . . ." Joanna faltered.

"Let's open it and see if any of the pills are different than the ones you take."

Karl reached for the organizer, and I pushed his hand away. "Wait! There could be fingerprints on it."

I used a paper towel to lift the organizer out of the drawer and then to open the long lids covering each day.

We all peered into it.

"I can't tell, I'll go get my bottles to compare," said Joanna, leaving the room.

"There is no pattern to these, different pills every day at different times, just a jumble," I said. "Like, look at Thursday a.m compared to Friday a.m."

Karl nodded. "Yeah."

When Joanna got back, she confirmed that she took the same pills at the same time, some every day, some three times a week. Comparing the pills in her prescription bottles with the organizer showed there were definitely some that didn't match any of her prescriptions.

Joanna shivered and stepped back, like the pills could jump out and bite her.

I pulled out Martinez and Miller's numbers. "I think you should call the police and let them know you'd like them to come get the pill organizer. And oh," I paused, embarrassment flooding my body at the next part. "The police kind of have your stuff, the stuff I had in my car to take to consignment and Goodwill. You could ask them to bring it back. Roth was the officer, I think."

"Oh my," said Joanna. "Do I want to know how that happened?"

Karl had the good grace to look away. "Sorry about that," he mumbled. "Not my idea at all."

"Connie accused me of stealing from you, among other things," I said. "You were in the hospital, so they couldn't ask you about the stuff in the car. Just let them know they can bring it back, I guess." I'd have to try to be here and grab the tangerine dress. I would hate for her to know it had been traipsing all over town.

Joanna called and left the messages. "Well, that's that."

I remembered the key and pulled it out of my purse. "Do you recognize this? It was in the pocket of one of Thomas's suits."

I handed it to Joanna, and her eyes lit up. "Oh, that might be the key I've been looking for! There is a safe deposit box with a missing key. Thank you!"

I felt a swirl of energy in Karl, but his face stayed blank. I wanted to ask what was in the safe deposit box but not in front of Karl.

Joanna looked at me longingly. "Tell Thomas I love him. And I miss him so much." Her eyes welled up again. "I can't believe he's . . . around. I can't believe you can talk to him."

"It's mostly that I get images from him. Emotions, an occasional word or two," I said. "But I know he hears you when you talk to him. I think he tries to communicate with you. If I were you, I would look for signs. Sometimes those on the other side are trying to send us signs, and we just don't see them. In fact, I'm feeling an urge to hug you that I assume is him."

Joanna stepped forward to hug me, and I could feel a joy flowing through me that didn't really feel like it was mine. "My sun and moon," I said.

"Oh my God, it is him," cried Joanna, with another squeeze. She stepped back, shaking her head. "He only ever said that to me in private. Some people knew 'Sunny' but no one knew about the sun and moon."

"Can you convince him to tell us who is trying to hurt you?" I asked.

I felt a swift searing pain throughout my torso. "Or maybe not."

"Thomas, tell us if you can," said Joanna.

I had an image of a stop sign.

No.

I looked at Karl. "That's odd. Something more for you, Karl. Something like 'don't listen to your mother.' Like she's giving bad advice or something."

The briefest of frowns, then I felt Karl switch into his charismatic performer persona. He laughed and shrugged. "That could apply to almost anything she says."

Then Thomas drifted away.

Chapter 46

I heard footsteps in the hall, and then Emily appeared in the kitchen, dressed in jeans, sweatshirt, and no makeup, her hair pulled up into a clip. Anger flared at the sight of me.

"What are you doing here!" she demanded.

"It's okay," said Joanna. "I want her."

"No! Absolutely not! She's the one who is always here when things go wrong!" Emily jammed her hands onto her hips, almost petulant. She reminded me of Lauren fighting for our mother's attention when we were kids. Flash of insight: Emily's irritation with me was an only-child vibe. Only children never really learn to share or tolerate their parents' attention to others. I'd bet if I opened her desk drawer at work, her stapler would be labeled with her name. Must have made it hard to add four siblings.

"She's psychic!" said Joanna. "She is talking to Thomas! He's worried about me."

"Oh my God, this is completely ridiculous!" said Emily, throwing her hands up. "Karl, you don't believe this bullshit, do you?"

Karl nodded sheepishly. "Actually, I do. She has a gift."

"Mom! You have never been one of those old people that gets taken advantage of, but the carbon monoxide must have done something to your brain."

If Emily noticed Joanna wince at the word "old," she didn't react to it.

"Show her," said Karl. "Do her, tune into something."

I knew I was going to get nothing from Emily. She was completely walled off. My mind could find no entrance.

"Go ahead, prove it to me," said Emily, chin jutting out.

I remembered the image I had of Emily having an illicit relationship with someone at work. "Sorry. Not picking up anything from you."

"She knew about Amelia," whispered Karl.

"What?" Emily turned towards Karl.

"She knew stuff she couldn't have known," Karl said.

"And she knew about a night Thomas and I had a flour fight in the middle of the night," said Joanna.

Emily looked back and forth between Karl and Joanna. "I don't know what kind of con she is working on you two, but I don't buy it."

I shrugged. "I wouldn't have either before it happened to me."

"In fact, I came here to get you packed up," Emily said to Joanna. "I think you should come stay at my place. I do believe someone is trying to hurt you." With that, she glanced at Karl and then me.

"No," said Joanna. "I just want to be home." She gestured out the window. "They have a thousand questions a day. Where is the circuit breaker? Water hoses? I can't leave."

"I think it is a good idea," I said. Half the world had access to this house. Who knew what other booby traps might lie in wait? "I think it would be great for you to stay with Emily until the police figure out who is doing this. Or at least until you change your locks and check through all your food."

Joanna looked at Karl. "I agree with them," said Karl, almost apologetically. "Emily's sounds safer, you know, just temporarily."

Joanna's shoulders kind of collapsed. She leaned her elbows on the table and put her head in her hands.

"It sounds to me like lots of people know the garage keypad combo," I said. "Have you given keys to cleaners or anyone in the past?"

"Yes, of course," said Joanna, looking up. "These locks have never been changed. And half of LaSalle knows the garage combo. Almost anyone could have been in here." She stared into space, frowning. I could feel her brain bumping up against one fearful conclusion after another, moving around trying to find an easier place to rest. It felt very familiar.

Joanna took a deep breath, sat up straight, and raised her chin. "The fogginess is over. I want to move forward with the gala preparations, and I need to stay here to do that. Wanda has a million things that need to happen."

"I'll work with Wanda," I said. "And I'll finish organizing the kitchen. You stay at Emily's for a couple of days, just relax. We've got time." Sort of.

"One thing, Izzy," said Emily. "I don't trust you. Why would I let you be alone here, maybe setting up new ways to hurt her?"

"Emily!" said Joanna. "She has saved my life several times!"

"My point exactly," said Emily, her voice rising in anger. "Maybe she knew you were in danger because she put you in danger." She was almost spitting by the end of the sentence.

Joanna shook her head slightly, like she was disappointed in Emily. "I trust Izzy. I will go with you and let her get things organized here."

"Fine," Emily said, icy with fury. She got what she wanted but was resentful at how she got it. I wanted to reassure her that I wasn't trying to steal her mother away but only-child syndrome ran too deep for surface assurances.

I had formed a bit of a plan to try to flush out the killer. With Joanna gone, I could set it up without anyone, even Joanna, knowing. I would need Karl, though. And access to Joanna's house.

"Karl can take me back to get my car, and then I'll get things straightened up here." I looked at Joanna. "If that is okay with you."

"Of course. And thank you, Izzy." Joanna glanced at Emily. "I'm sorry I ever doubted you."

"And I'm sorry, once again, for the cookie mix-up. I really feel awful," I said.

In the car with Karl, I said, "I have an idea to figure out who is trying to hurt Joanna. Is there any way you could call your siblings, maybe to give an update on Joanna's health, and then casually mention the pill organizer? That the police are coming to get it to check for fingerprints."

"Yeah. I'll tell them that now we know Joanna will feel okay for the gala because she figured out that some of the pills weren't hers. And that she let the police know. Would that work?"

"Yes," I said. "And say that she's staying at Emily's while they get all this gala prep done. So if anyone is thinking of coming back to wipe off fingerprints or get rid of the pills, they can." Then I added, "You know, Joanna actually bought two organizers. I'm going to put the real one away, maybe hide it in Joanna's bathroom, and use the other one in its place. That way, the actual fingerprints won't be ruined."

"Are you going to hide and watch?" Karl asked.

"Yeah," I said. He didn't have to know the whole plan. "I'll get it set up with Vivi; we'll take turns hiding out."

"I can take a shift if you want," said Karl. "I mean, not at night, but maybe daytime?"

"I'll let you know," I said, although I had no intention of including him.

"I hope it isn't anyone . . . in the family," Karl said. "I was kind of a shit to my dad. I thought we'd have more time to make up, you know? But maybe I can make it up to him by protecting Joanna for him."

I felt a stab in my chest and then a warm feeling. Thomas. "I feel like he knows and is grateful," I said softly. I had an impulse to pat him, so I reached over and patted his shoulder. "I think that was from your dad," I said.

Karl looked a little teary. "Yeah, that's something my dad would do. Try to reach out but kind of awkwardly."

"Yeah, that was him," I said. "Oh, and he feels so sorry he wasn't more supportive when Amelia died. I'm seeing lots of confusion in his brain around that time."

"Yeah, he was still drinking," said Karl, his eyes red. *So sorry.*

"He says he's so sorry," I said. "And I can feel it."

Karl stared ahead while he drove, a couple of tears sliding out.

Before I got out of the car, I said, "I'll let you know when to make the calls. Give me a chance to make sure it is all ready. I have some other stuff I need to do this afternoon first."

"Got it," said Karl. "And tell Dad—" his breath caught, "I'm sorry too." His smile was so real, so different from the showy Karl charisma. I hoped that was the version of Karl that his girlfriend got.

I sent up the Bat Signal for Vivi and was happy when she called me right back. "Come help me lay a trap at Joanna's," I said. "I can pick you up in ten minutes."

"I'm in," Vivi said. "I have the perfect outfit for trap-laying."

I ran up to my bathroom and found the medicine lock box we bought when Luke was going through his problems. I grabbed everything that was expired and should have been tossed anyway.

Vivi climbed in the car, resplendent in a periwinkle-blue outfit.

"You look fantastic," I said. "What is that? A jumpsuit? A one-piece?"

Vivi wriggled in delight. "A romper. It's so comfortable. No need to lie down to zip anything up." She offered me a bag, "Want some gummy bears? I didn't have time for lunch."

"I'm good," I said. "Already enough sugar on board."

"These are sugar-free," she said.

"Those are allowed on your cleanse?"

"They can't count, right?" Vivi shrugged. "I'm killing it. Look how loose my clothes are."

I refrained from pointing out that loose was the cut, not her weight.

Joanna and Emily were gone by the time Vivi and I got there, so we went in through the garage.

I pointed at the pill organizer in the kitchen. "Joanna bought four organizers, one for each week of the month. But only one was out."

I opened the drawer beneath it and under a stack of unopened mail found two other organizers, one filled with pills, labeled with a #3, one empty with a #1 label. Two drawers down under some dish towels I found the #4 organizer, empty.

Vivi finished the last of her gummy bears and stuck the empty bag in the garbage. "What's the plan?"

I set the #3 organizer on the counter beside the #2 that had been on the counter all along. I pointed at #2. "Don't touch this one; I'm hoping it has some fingerprints." Using a paper towel, I carefully pulled back the compartments on #2 and we did a side-by-side comparison between the completely full #3 and the partially full #2.

"Yep, these are different," said Vivi, peering back and forth.

"See how all the time of day pills match up in #3?" I said. "Like every a.m. slot has the same pills, and every lunch slot the same pills."

We looked at #2, the pill slots were all a jumble.

"I'd bet #3 is still fine but I don't think Joanna should chance it," I said.

Using the extra pills I had brought from home, we set up the #3 box to look like the #2 box, taking out some of Joanna's real pills and adding ones that more matched the substitutions.

I pulled out the empty #4 box and did the same thing, made it a decent match.

"I'm going to hide the #2 box, save it for the police," I said. Using the paper towel to hold it, I took the #2 box to Joanna's closet and hid it deep in the back of a drawer full of scarves. Before closing the drawer, I took the #2 sticker off so I could put it on the kitchen dummy box. Vivi followed me, nodding in approval.

"Just in case Karl isn't who I think he is, I'm putting one of the dummies in the bathroom," I said. We took #3 into Joanna's bathroom and stuck it in the top drawer of the long vanity.

Back in the kitchen I arranged the #4 box exactly where the original tampered #2 box had been and stuck the #2 sticker on, just in case. Three boxes that all looked the same.

"I didn't know you could be this devious," said Vivi. "I might have to make you an honorary Philly girl." There was a gurgle, and Vivi clutched her stomach. "Ooh, that was me."

"Maybe shouldn't have skipped lunch," I said. "Time to set up the cameras." I shifted the kitchen camera enough to get the full view of someone touching the pill box on the counter. Vivi trailed along behind me, as I moved the camera from the hallway to Joanna's bathroom.

"Looks like Joanna might need another tutorial on how to keep a neat counter," Vivi said, as we looked at the spread of bottles and brushes and other beauty implements that had re-cluttered the vanity since we had organized. "Not judging. I've seen worse. Like, for example, your bathroom."

"Haha, it works for our purpose," I said, grabbing a tall bath salt container that was a Moroccan-style stone with cutouts just big enough for the camera lens to see through. I took out the bag of bath salts, dropped the camera in, fed its cord out the back, and faced it so that anyone opening the vanity drawers would be in full view.

Another gurgle. "I'm not feeling so good," said Vivi.

"You are looking a little green," I said.

"Feels like the gummy bears are having a gang war in my gut."

The doorbell rang. "Be right back," I said.

I opened it to Martinez.

"What are you doing here?" he asked.

"I am still working for Joanna. She isn't here, but I can help you. I'm assuming you are here for the pills."

I stepped back to allow him in.

"I am, and to drop off her stuff that was taken from her car. Roth heard me saying I was coming here. I had hoped to talk to Mrs. Sullivan," he said, looking around the foyer at the grandeur. "What's with all the trucks?"

"They are hosting a big charity gala here this weekend. Getting all set up. Joanna is at her daughter Emily's," I said. "I'll call her for you."

Luckily, Joanna answered and confirmed to Martinez that I was supposed to be there, then set a time for him to visit her. He asked if he had her permission to leave the stuff from the car confiscation with me, and she said yes.

The two of us transferred the stuff into the garage and I was thrilled to see the tangerine dress in the pile. I grabbed it and took it along with me as I led him to Joanna's closet. I pulled open the drawer. "The pill box is hidden in here," I said.

I let him handle the box, sliding it into what I presumed was an evidence bag as I hung up the dress. I'd just have to dry-clean it later. I hated the idea of taking it out of the house again. As we walked out of Joanna's closet, a loud groan came from the bathroom. Vivi must have gone in the toilet part, sliding the door closed after her but leaving the door to the vanity area open.

"Who is that?" asked Martinez.

"My coworker," I said, noticing her romper crumpled on the floor by the vanity. Uh-oh.

"Holy mother of god!" Vivi moaned. "Izzy, it's coming out of me like hot lava!" Not the best time to quote one of our favorite movies.

"Is she okay?" asked Martinez.

"Detective Martinez is here," I called to Vivi.

"Does he have a pocket full of Immodium?" she yelled back. "Those motherfucking gummy bears!"

A grin slipped across Martinez's face. "Don't tell me she was eating sugar-free gummy bears."

I nodded. "The whole bag."

"Oh my God." He shook his head, "There's nothing we can do for her now. Except maybe schedule her colonoscopy."

"I heard that!" yelled Vivi. "Just kick my romper closer to the door and go away."

Walking to the romper, I noticed Vivi hadn't quite gotten it off in time. "I'll be back," I said through the door.

I led Martinez back to the kitchen. "Can I tell you what I think?" I said, gesturing to a seat at the kitchen table as I sat down.

Martinez sat down, carefully setting the pills beside him. "Let me ask you a few questions first," he said. "Did you have access to the pill container?"

"Yes, of course! I picked it up when we were going through papers." And then I laid out for him my ideas about a possible timeline of when the pills might have been substituted and who had opportunity.

I noticed Martinez was actually taking notes.

"What did you find out about the coffee? Or the wine?" I asked.

"You don't work for the police," he said. "I don't have to tell you anything."

"Right," I said. How to get him to share information? The words came out of my mouth before I could stop them.

"Mijo," I said.

"What?" said Martinez. "Why're you calling me that?"

"Mijo, tell the girl. Why are you holding back?" I said. Then added. "Sorry, I feel like there is an elderly lady around; she's kinda pushy. Like she wants me to sort of slap the back of your head in a loving but frustrated way. Or, this is weird, take off my shoe and tap you with it?"

Martinez stared at me, unspeaking.

"I had a near-death experience and now I can sense . . . dead people. I understand if you don't believe me. I would never have believed it either."

Martinez winced, and I could feel a spurt of pity; he thought I was crazy.

"I've been worried about Joanna because her dead husband has been at me day and night to protect her. He knows someone is trying to hurt her, and he keeps pushing me to protect her. I never wanted this. But I have it."

Martinez shook his head. "You think you can just throw out the word *mijo* and I'm going to believe you? Every Mexican kid is called that. Got to be in the first lesson for sham psychics."

"Okay," I said, leaning forward. "She's showing me that, when you were in elementary school, you used to walk across the street to her house for lunch. She made you homemade tortillas every day. She knitted you a blue and red beanie, and you wore it until someone stole it on the playground and you came to her that day, crying."

Martinez's eyes were wide. "Holy shit," he whispered. He slid his chair back as if trying to get away from me.

"She still has a grudge against that kid. Says he turned out to be no good, and she knew it all along," I said. "She's a talker, your grandmother."

Martinez laughed, shaking his head in amazement. "Yep, she was a talker. Um, okay?"

"She's proud of you being a cop, being a detective. She never said it, but she always knew you'd be a success. I feel like she is emphasizing something about being humble. Like touching her chest or something."

"Oh my God, that is so true," said Martinez. His eyes were lit up, and his whole face was animated. "No matter how great I did at baseball or school or anything, she always knocked me down a peg. I mean, I knew she loved me, but she just wasn't one to praise a lot."

"Oh," I paused. "I feel like she is telling me that your granddad is coming to be with her soon. They miss each other, and he is in a lot of pain. It's time for the family to let him go."

It was like his grandmother was sitting right beside me, intense and talky. I wondered why Thomas never came through this clearly.

Hey, pay attention to me! I felt the grandmother say.

Martinez's eyes teared. "Yeah. He's been going downhill."

"She's so happy that you have been going over and shaving him. He wants to come to her looking good."

Martinez slid back towards the table and leaned his arms on it, bowing his head. I could see tears dropping onto the surface. It was quiet, and I could feel the energies of the room rearranging. Kimberly's suffering cleared away by the grandma's fierce love for her grandson.

Finally, Martinez sat up, wiping his eyes. "Thank you," he said in a soft voice. "Wow. I never believed in this stuff."

I nodded. "It's odd, for sure. Back to Joanna?"

"Anything more from my grandma?"

I felt her impatience. "She says not until you help me," I said, laughing. "She is kind of scary."

"You have no idea. Okay, let's just say it's true that someone is trying to kill Joanna. I can't believe I'm going to ask this, but does the husband say who?"

"No. I think it is one of his kids and that is why he won't give me more. He just wants me to protect her. Without telling me from what."

"Let's just be hypothetical here," said Martinez. "Let's say someone had beta blockers in their system but wasn't taking them. And that beta blockers interact badly with asthma."

I nodded. He continued. "So maybe, hypothetically, someone just grabbed whatever medications they had around and substituted them into Joanna's pillbox and coffee. Joanna said those weren't all her pills in the box."

"All of Thomas's kids have been around and could have done it," I said, filling him in on what I knew about each Sullivan. "And Connie, the ex-wife, hates Joanna and believes her kids should have the house. Joanna's daughter Emily doesn't seem to have a motive—at least, not a financial one. On the other hand, she's worked really hard to get me away from her mother."

Martinez nodded and finished writing in his notebook. "The stuff from my grandmother was amazing, but that doesn't mean you're on the team."

"It's okay," I said. "Investigate it all, even me. But hurry up. Joanna is not safe."

I laughed.

"What now?" said Martinez.

"Your grandmother wants to know when you're going to get a girlfriend."

The full smile came back across Martinez's face, and he shook his head. "That's definitely her."

After Martinez left, I went back to Joanna's bathroom. "I'm pushing some Immodium under the door," I said.

"I think I've dropped three dress sizes," she moaned. "And I can't believe I'm going to say this, but it is not worth it."

I picked up the romper with two fingers and rinsed the part that had gotten ... dirty, then laid it by the door.

"Your clothes are a little wet but clean now," I said.

"Oh my God, did I . . .?"

"It's all good now. Nothing anyone needs to ever talk about again," I said.

I logged in to the Arlo app and double-checked that the cameras were working.

I went to work on cleaning the kitchen, which was really a matter of putting away some dishes, wiping down the counters, and storing some of the clutter away. I left the desk as it was, pill box casually sticking out from underneath papers.

Eventually, Vivi emerged from the bathroom, pale and shaky. "I think I can make it home now. I'm completely empty. I think I expelled food I haven't even eaten yet."

Vivi stared at me, a shrunken version of her normal self in a rumpled and damp romper. "This may be my most embarrassing moment ever, and I pooped giving birth. Twice."

Vivi and I giggled.

"Go wait in the car, I'll sanitize the bathroom," I said.

"It's official. I'd bury a body for you now," said Vivi. "Person wouldn't even have to be guilty of anything."

Chapter 48

When I got home, I called Karl. "It's all set. You can make the calls. Lots of trucks and stuff still there during the day, but no one should be around at night."

Even though it seemed unlikely someone could get there so soon, I propped my phone on the kitchen counter to watch the cameras. Glancing periodically at the phone, I thawed some frozen tri-tip in the microwave, rubbed it with Montreal steak seasoning, and threw it in the sous vide. Thought about how to add more calories to the meal for Cole and fewer calories for me. Made rice and garlic bread, then picked the gooey pieces out of a bag of lettuce and rinsed the rest, adding cherry tomatoes and a few slices of cucumber.

At 6:00 Cole got home, dropped his backpacks, and tossed his huge empty water bottle in the sink. "What's for dinner?" he said, surly and not looking at me.

"Tri-tip, rice, salad, garlic bread," I said, pulling the tri-tip out of the sous vide and turning on the gas under a cast iron skillet.

Cole grunted then looked at my phone. "What's that?"

I turned it away from him. "Nothing really."

"Looks like someone's cameras."

I didn't answer. Popped the tri-tip into the skillet to sear each side for a minute and a half.

"I don't know you at all," Cole said. "Don't care about your family and now you are spying on people." He reached for the phone. "What are you doing?"

"Nothing," I said, sticking it under my shirt. "Some things are private."

Cole shook his head. "You are acting so weird."

I peeked at the phone. "Someone is trying to hurt a client of mine, and I'm watching to make sure they don't, that's all."

"So you have permission for this?" he said.

"Yes," I said. Sort of. I flipped the tri-tip.

"Is that ready yet?"

"Almost."

"Whatever," he said, scooping rice and salad onto his plate, adding four pieces of the garlic bread and standing expectantly while I pulled the tri-tip out of the skillet and sliced it. "I'm eating in my room," he said defiantly.

"Fine." Good. I didn't need his judgment. While I watched, I started thinking about the local robberies. Were they just targeting rich people or was there some other connection? The buzz around my body told me there was another connection. I just had to find it.

At eight o'clock Cole came back and dumped his plate in the sink.

"Hey, help me out with something," I said.

Cole came up out of the bottom freezer drawer with a pint of ice cream. "Yeah?"

"So you probably heard there've been robberies in the area lately."

"Yeah," he said, dumping huge scoops of cookies 'n cream into a bowl.

"Any connection between these families?" I listed out the names.

Cole squinted while he thought. "Aside from having a kid in high school?"

"Interesting. Do you know any of them?"

"I'm not a narc."

"Well, Order Out of Chaos is being investigated as suspects because we worked in a couple of those homes. The police were here interviewing me, if you must know."

"Is that why you are watching those security cameras?"

"Something like that."

"The ones I know on that list are partiers," said Cole. "Bart Mahone for one. He does hella drugs."

"Peaches's stepson?" I asked, thinking of the grumpy "bonus child" who came through at her house.

"Yeah," said Cole.

"I get that you don't want to tattle, but this is serious," I said. "Anything could help."

"If Bart Mahone is involved, then I wouldn't be surprised at anything you found out," said Cole, before disappearing back upstairs with his ice cream.

Bart Mahone. No wonder he had reminded me of Luke. I thought about Martinez asking me if we went in the bathroom at the Mahones. Maybe Bart was stealing people's prescriptions and other stuff for drug money. Maybe his friends were in on it too. I left a message for Martinez that they might want to look into the teenager connection between those families and that "sources" said at least one of them was into drugs.

****

Karl texted me at 11:30 the next morning, saying he'd talked to them all. I gave up all hope of doing anything else and sat watching Joanna's kitchen camera, live. Even though there were lots of workmen coming and going in the backyard, I wasn't sure that would keep the murderer away. I had to keep an eye out.

Two hours later my shoulders were tight, and nothing had happened inside.

Waiting was too tedious, so I set my phone on the washing machine and reorganized the cabinets above it. Consolidated the three half-used bottles of bleach. Put all the cleaning supplies in one place. Bagged up a bunch of rag towels to take to the dog shelter, knowing they had an endless need for towels. As I worked, I kept checking the camera.

Another two hours later, I had cleaned out every kitchen drawer, tossed unmatched Tupperware, bagged up used batteries for recycling at the hardware store, and redistributed Band-Aids, painter's tape, and a pile of other miscellaneous items to their proper homes around the house, carrying my phone with me the whole time.

I surveyed my kitchen with pleasure. No wonder
people loved Order Out of Chaos. It felt like removing all
the clutter had also removed the dust bunnies in my head.
I felt so light, as if I'd lost weight, and if the scale wasn't
upstairs, I would have checked.

At 4:00 I made a cup of coffee. I needed to stay sharp
and would deal with the poor sleep later.

As I sat on the couch, drinking the coffee and
watching the phone, I thought about how my extrasensory
skills were consistently working now. I wondered what
made them fade and what made them strong. Maybe
because my brain felt so spacious and uncluttered, the
answer arrived, fully formed.

It was Jay.

It was me forcing things with Jay, against my deepest
knowing, that had blocked the senses.

Ever since I had admitted that truth about how I felt
about Jay, the senses had worked. I looked at my
calendar. Yep, they went on the fritz right after Jay came
home and I forced myself to agree to try to work things
out with him.

My body spilled over with energy, like I had uncorked
a fountain of truth. As if admitting the truth to myself
unblocked my insides, and energy rushed like a geyser
blowing. I got up and paced in circles around the kitchen
island, trying to shed some of the energy coursing
through me.

It seemed so clear. Allowing myself to see my truth
had somehow flung open the other-world portal. My extra
senses felt like they could flow easily, nothing stopping
them. Almost like I had been blocking them with my
confusion about myself.

I went up to Luke's room and stared at the cork board.

Help me, I asked the senses. *Anyone?*

My phone vibrated: Vivi.

"Hey, do you have time to stop by?" I asked her.

"Was just going to suggest that, I want to take a look
at your murder board. And I've got tacos. 'Lil treat since
I lost so much weight yesterday."

Vivi and I sat staring at the board. She had already moved Post-its around and added some of her own. I had my phone propped beneath it so we could watch for someone at Joanna's.

"Motive. Personalities. That's what we need to look at," Vivi said, head sideways as she bit into a taco. It fell apart and a mix of salsa and sour cream fell onto her pants. "Dammit. These are dry clean."

"Connie has several motives: hatred of Joanna, money for her kids, generally unstable," I said. "But I feel like Thomas would be only too happy to point me at her if it was really her."

I felt his agreement.

"Serena obviously needs money. Seems mentally troubled," said Vivi, shoving the rest of the taco into her mouth.

I nodded. "I am picking up that she is unhappy in her marriage and feeling trapped since they don't have money. On the other hand, she feels low energy to me, depressed even—seems like it would take energy to try to kill someone."

I felt Thomas drift away. He wanted nothing to do with this.

Vivi unwrapped a second taco. "Jacques. Needs money to be a partner at Yield. Could still be gambling."

"And there is something in his past, or even present, that he did wrong. Marco was holding that over him. Maybe something he is trying to cover up? Plus, I don't know if I buy his religious act."

I felt around for Thomas. Nowhere.

Vivi slurped her soda. "Marco, I hope it's him. He is so easy to dislike. Needs money to do real estate deals. Lots of anger. Seems angry that he hasn't gotten money from his father. I feel like he just has given in to that entitled kind of anger."

"I saw him on the video recordings," I added. "He knows about the trust. He must know that Joanna could vote them all out of millions of dollars. And he also was doing something wrong; Jacques was holding that over him. Like they were holding secrets about each other in a kind of standoff."

Still no Thomas presence.

"Karl." Vivi gave a little sigh. "Don't let it be Karl."

"Karl needs money with a baby coming," I pointed out. "And he's been poking around Joanna's a lot. I can feel it; he is looking for something. There could be some other treasure we haven't even factored in yet."

"Personality-wise, it is hard for me to see Karl as the killer," said Vivi. "He seems more the impulsive, impetuous type. Like, I could see him punching someone in the heat of the moment but not coolly planning a pill substitution. But I could be wrong. Wouldn't be the first time I've been blinded by studliness."

Thomas was nowhere to be felt. Obviously, no interest in weighing in on his kids.

"Emily?" I asked. "She doesn't inherit the house. Joanna said she already has her money in trust from her father. Hard to see a financial motive, and I'm just not picking up on any anger or resentment of her mother."

I picked at the shreds of lettuce left from my tacos and peeked at the phone again. Still nothing.

"Although . . ." I trailed off, not done thinking about Emily. "I do pick up an only-child vibe from her. What if she was jealous of Kimberly? What if *that* wasn't an accident?"

"Hmm," said Vivi. "But you said only Joanna drank the blueberry coffee."

"That we know of. Maybe Kimberly liked it too?"

"Feels like a stretch, but maybe," said Vivi. "Not ruling anyone out yet."

Vivi grabbed the Post-it pad and wrote on it, then folded up the piece of paper and set it on Luke's desk. "There's my guess. Now you do one. Winner buys dinner at Cafe Vino."

I wrote down my guess, initialed it, and set it next to Vivi's. "You're on."

After Vivi left, I got ready for bed, set the phone up facing my bed on the nightstand, and watched until almost midnight, at which point I must have drifted off.

I woke up at six and quickly checked through the recordings: nothing.

A quick shower and dressed: nothing.

Around 6:30 I saw movement on the camera. Maybe trying to beat all the workers who would be arriving soon to work on gala prep. I leaned forward, holding my breath. Seeing the person moving in the kitchen, I felt a wave of sadness rolled together with a surge of satisfaction. I had predicted correctly. I felt Thomas's pain start in my heart and spread out into my body and then felt him drift away.

I heard the person call out for Joanna, probably making sure no one was home, and then go straight for the pill box. Picked up the pill box, dumped it into an open bag apparently brought for that purpose, then grabbed a dish towel and wiped at the box, over and over. Clutched the bag of pills and left.

Pretty incriminating, if you asked me.

I called Martinez, left a message about the recording, and said I could forward it to him and Miller.

I sat back and thought about it all. Put together everything I had found out. Felt sad for Thomas and Joanna. Felt deep grief for Kimberly, which gave me the energy to finish this up.

Then I texted Joanna and asked her if she had time to do a few errands with me. I had a couple of pieces left to finish.

Joanna was happy to hear from me. "That would be great. Maybe you could go with me to the bank? Emily is at work, and we didn't think to bring my car to her place. I want to check out the safe deposit box."

Even better.

Chapter 49

"Here we are!" said Jacques, stepping into Joanna's kitchen carrying a Yield box.

It was Thursday, early evening, and Joanna had summoned the family with a tantalizing message about finding the key to a safe deposit box. Marco had already arrived and jumped to take the box from the woman following behind Jacques.

"This is my wife, Julia," Jacques said to me as he smiled broadly at Julia, getting a bright smile in return. Julia could have been on the cover of a wine magazine advertising the Napa Valley: slim with tanned skin, silky straight brown hair, and white teeth, the picture of a healthy outdoorsy woman.

Watching the fondness between Jacques and Julia made me feel for Marco; this was real affection. Marco stared moodily at Jacques and Julia and switched to a fake smile when he saw me look in his direction.

"Nice to meet you," said Julia, giving me a sense of a bright, happy woman. Definitely worthy of brotherly competition.

"These are chilled already, so you can start with them," Jacques said, pointing at the box he had been carrying.

Vivi pulled out a bottle and started pouring into the tray of glasses we'd laid out. Three different trays for three different wines.

Joanna bustled in from the dining room.

"Julia! Lovely to see you. Thanks for the wine, Jacques. Just thought it might be kind of festive to do some tasting while I share my news."

Marco was almost vibrating with anticipation. "Yeah, about that, what is it?"

"In good time, let's wait for everyone to arrive."
Joanna smiled mysteriously. I could feel her stress
underneath the smile, but she was covering it well.

It didn't take long to get the whole family arranged
around the formal dining room table. The room was
packed with more heavy furniture and thick old rugs,
which would have felt dark and overwhelming except for
the light that poured through a row of French doors along
one side, looking out on an enclosed patio area with
potted palm trees and a bubbling fountain. It all kind of
balanced out. All four Sullivans were there, plus Serena's
husband Jared, Julia, and Emily.

Joanna sat at the head of the table and nodded at the
platters of hors d'oeuvres placed along the length of the
table. "Help yourself. Izzy and Vivi will be serving the
wines, a little taste of Yield's latest."

"I can't take it any longer! What is it?" Serena tried
for a light tone, but her words were rushed and tense.

Joanna took a deep breath. "Okay. Well. Thomas had a
safe deposit box that I had really kind of forgotten about.
I knew he had some valuables in there, but I never really
paid attention to it. He had it before we were married."

As Joanna talked, Vivi and I set glasses with tastes of
the Sauvignon Blanc down by each person.

"Izzy actually found the key in one of Thomas's
jackets, which reminded me of it." Joanna gave me a
smile, and I gave one back with a little encouraging nod.
She could do this.

"Jacques, which wine is this?" asked Joanna, picking
up her glass.

"The Sauv blanc," he said.

Joanna sipped and paused, seemingly waiting for the
others to do the same. When they didn't all pick up their
glasses, she held up her glass. "To Thomas," she said.

Everyone picked up their glasses and toasted, in
varying states of excitement and agitation that she wasn't
moving faster with the news.

"And? The box? You opened it?" Marco prompted as
they all took sips of the wine.

"Yes," said Joanna. She reached under the table and brought up a plain white cardboard box. She opened it and pulled out a pale turquoise leather box that opened into several levels. From the top level she picked up a necklace, sparkling silver with multiple red stones glinting in the light, as it dangled from her upheld hand. "For one, there was the set of Art Deco jewelry that belonged to your grandmother Sullivan."

I had hung back after delivering the glasses and watched Karl. His flashing eyes betrayed him. For sure, that is what he had been looking for. I remembered the red jewel image I had seen associated with him and also how Thomas's message to him had been to ignore his mother. I would have bet a lot of money that Connie sent him looking for that jewelry.

Joanna passed the necklace around and pulled out several other pieces: two bracelets, earrings, a brooch. "Those are rubies."

The family oohed and ahhed. "Obviously, these belong to the four of you," said Joanna.

She stuck her hand back into the box. "A number of documents that might be of sentimental value. Birth certificates, marriage certificates, that sort of thing. Going back to your grandfather."

Marco stuck out his hand. "Can I see those?"

Joanna passed the documents along to Marco, and he quickly shuffled through them. At the last one, his face fell. Not what he had been hoping for.

"That's it?" asked Marco.

"Everyone finished their taste of the Sauv Blanc?" asked Joanna. She nodded at me and Vivi, and after Vivi picked up each person's glass, I replaced it with another taste. "That's the Chardonnay," said Joanna.

Vivi gave me a wink as she disappeared with the glasses, arranged on the tray in the exact shape of the table and seating. We had the fingerprints in case Martinez needed them.

"That's it for the safe deposit box, but there is another issue to discuss," said Joanna. "Your grandfather Sullivan acquired a lot of land around LaSalle many years ago. He did not acquire the land in an honorable way, and when he met your grandmother, she refused to marry him if he benefited in any way from it. He put it into a seventy-year trust and gave the county the rights to use it. He figured that, at the end of that time, it would be obvious to him or his descendants whether the land could be put to good use."

Everyone but Marco looked bewildered. "What land are we talking about?" Serena asked.

"The Ridge Trail area," said Joanna.

"Like, all those hills?" asked Karl.

Joanna nodded. "Clear to the reservoir."

Gasps and exclamations.

Joanna continued. "According to your dad, your grandfather's long marriage to a kind and moral woman led him to believe he should never profit from it, and he planned to permanently conserve it."

"We own the Ridge Trail?" said Serena, her face a mix of excitement and confusion.

I could feel my senses almost pulsing, the faucet open. I could feel each person's energy about the news and, for once, they stayed separate; it wasn't like one big stream. Marco was triumphant and could barely keep himself from leaping up. Jacques and Karl were pleasantly surprised, their brains starting to circle around the implications. Serena was dumbstruck, hope rising out of her chronic anger and fear.

Joanna continued. "Thomas planned to do the same thing, conserve it permanently, but he died before that could happen. And he named me trustee."

I surreptitiously looked at the two cameras I had placed in the room to make sure nothing was blocking them. All good.

"Wait," said Karl. "It's not already permanently conserved?"

"No," said Joanna. "The seventy years is up next week. It's up to me to vote."

"I knew it!" said Marco, slapping the table, furious and excited at the same time.

"What?" "You mean—" "Wait!" They all talked at once.

Joanna held up a hand to silence the group. "I'm curious to hear what you all think."

Again, they all started talking at once.

"Silence!" Joanna said, more commanding than I had ever heard her.

"We'll start at my right and go around," she said, pointing to Karl.

"Are you asking if I think you should conserve the land or develop it or whatever?" he asked.

"Just curious what you think," said Joanna.

"That land must be worth millions," said Karl.

"Yes," said Joanna.

"I could actually really use the money. I'm assuming it would come to us?" said Karl.

"Yes. Although it is unclear how much you could actually develop it. There are a lot of zoning laws in place now. But, yes."

Karl frowned. "I do kind of like the hills and open spaces. I'd hate to take that away from people."

"Are you crazy?" Serena screeched. "You like the *open spaces*?" Her face was flushed and angry, gray energy roiling around her like smoke coming off of a burning building. "Jared and I live in a dump and don't even own it."

Jared's head dropped, and he stared at the table as Serena continued. "Joanna lives in this big house alone. It's just not fair! Of course we should sell it!"

Jacques interrupted, "Easy, Serena. I know it's been hard for you and Jared, and this sounds like a great solution. Of course, I'd love to have the money to be a full partner at Yield. And pay off my house. But I also respect Dad's and Grandfather's wishes."

"This is insane," said Marco. "We are talking about millions of dollars! We'd all be set for life, our kids set for life. Their kids. Why is this even a question?"

"I met with the attorney yesterday," Joanna said. "It turns out that I was able to vote and sign my name early."

The tension in the room became almost unbearable. If Joanna didn't finish speaking soon, I thought some heads might pop off.

"What?" said Marco. "You already signed?" Marco reminded me of a stick of dynamite—hard, tightly wrapped, ready to explode.

"Yes," said Joanna.

The fuse had been lit. "We're fucked," he said. He stood up, menacing and angry, hands clenched in fists. "How dare you!" he spat at Joanna.

I tensed, ready to spring up and protect Joanna. If he so much as moved an inch towards her, I was going to, well I don't know what I would do. Get in his way until Martinez and Miller could get in here.

"That is our family's money, not yours!" Marco yelled.

Serena's eyes were closed in defeat. Jacques shrugged. Karl had an "oh well" look on his face as he slumped back into his chair.

Joanna smiled, amazingly still serene. "In talking with the attorney, I realized that it was not all or nothing. We looked at the land and settled on a section that could fairly easily be separated off and sold. One that is still zoned for development."

Marco was sweating and shaking with the effort to hold himself together. Joanna had the whole room rapt.

"So that's what I decided to do. The trust will sell that section, valued at about six million dollars. Which, of course, all goes to you Sullivans; none of it is mine nor should it be. The rest will go into permanent conservancy."

There was a moment of silence and then whoops and cheers.

"Oh my God," said Karl, hands grabbing at his forehead. "I couldn't have imagined."

Serena's eyes had flown open, and she was crying and holding her chest like she was about to have a heart attack.

Jacques and Julia were hugging. Then Jacques ran to Joanna and pulled her out of her chair into a big hug. "Thank you! This is amazing!"

Marco was leaning on the table, still shaking. "Why didn't you just say so? Why all the drama?" he said.

Karl followed Jacques in hugging Joanna.

Serena wasn't moving, still in shock.

"That was a great idea," said Karl.

"I loved your father very much," said Joanna. "But I never completely agreed with his belief that you should all stand on your own. If there is something to be shared, why not make everyone's life a little easier?" Thomas had actually signed on to this idea and had confirmed it to Joanna, through me, when I accompanied her to the attorney's office. No one needed to know that Thomas and I had also asked the spirits of the land if that was acceptable. Thomas felt a yes and passed that along to me. The majority of the land would remain untouched in perpetuity, and the spirits were pleased. It felt like a fair trade to give up a little in return for preserving the majority.

"Sit down," Joanna said. "I'm not quite done." She paused while they returned to their seats.

"There's more?" said Serena.

"Unfortunately, yes," said Joanna, her face grave. She looked at me, and I nodded in encouragement. "One of you might not have the chance to enjoy that money."

Chapter 50

Another shocked silence.

Joanna looked around the table, her face somber. "Is there anything anyone wants to tell me?"

Tense silence and then Jacques stood up, his face red and sweaty. "I can't take it anymore. I've been trying to find a way for so long."

He looked up at the ceiling like he was asking for celestial encouragement. "Joanna, when we were helping you move in, I took your first engagement ring. It wasn't lost. I owed so much money because of the stupid gambling, and Dad refused to help me. I was so angry at him, and I blamed you." His head dropped, and he started crying. "You can press charges—I deserve it. I can't live with myself anymore."

Julia reached up and squeezed Jacques's hand. Marco looked at Julia and gave a slight shake to his head. I could feel his anguish so clearly. If Jacques's confession wasn't going to turn her against Jacques, nothing ever would.

Joanna's eyebrows shot up. "Well. That is a surprise, Jacques. Thank you for telling me. I imagine you will have enough money now to pay the insurance company back. More on that later. Anyone else have something to say?"

Jacques's head snapped back up. "That wasn't it?"

Joanna sadly shook her head and looked around the table. Julia was smiling softly at Jacques, Emily was staring angrily at Jacques, and everyone else was looking down. Did they all have secrets?

"Anyone?" Joanna said.

Karl sighed and looked up. "I apologize for poking around here so much. Mom convinced me you were hiding the Art Deco jewelry. She said it belongs to Serena, but I think she wanted it for herself. I don't know why I let her talk me into it. I'm so sorry." Karl shrugged, palms up, a sheepish smile on his face. "Obviously, I didn't find it because it was in the safe deposit box."

Serena looked up. "It's jewelry; it should go to me."

"These are interesting confessions, but I'm going to cut to the chase. Someone here has been trying to kill me," Joanna said, her voice even, her head held straight and still.

Dead silence.

"Someone, in trying to kill me, accidentally killed Kimberly. I cannot forgive that."

"No," said Marco. "That can't be true."

"Someone should have just talked to me. See how reasonable I can be? Talked to me about the land trust. Or this house. If you thought I should move out and let you sell it, you could have actually talked to me about that."

"Why do you think someone's trying to kill you?" asked Jacques.

"Izzy? Could you help?" said Joanna.

I stepped forward. "I think it started with the space heater." Karl's eyes got wide. I held up a hand. "I believe it was a mistake. You didn't know it was giving off carbon monoxide. Connie knew, but she didn't mention it to you, and it mistakenly got added into the garage sale stuff."

I looked at the others. "However, Joanna's almost dying gave someone an idea. Someone's problems could be over if Joanna died."

I looked around the table, watching each person's face, noticing swirling auras. "Every one of you could use more money. And everyone knows how much Joanna loves coffee, so someone put poison in the blueberry coffee. Actually medication, but medication known to kill in large doses. Anyone ever hear of beta blockers?" I left out the part about how the spiked coffee was never found.

They were all looking around the table at each other.

"Kimberly drank the coffee, not Joanna." I hoped the cameras were picking this up well; I'd re-watch later to focus in on each person's face. "Tragically, the beta blockers interacted badly with her asthma."

"How do you know that?" asked Serena.

"I've been working with the police." Sort of.

"Not only that, someone switched out the pills in Joanna's pill organizer, adding a bunch of stuff to make her delirious or even kill her. But everyone just thought her episodes were the aftereffects of the carbon monoxide poisoning."

Shocked looks again.

"The police have those pills." I looked at the killer to see the light come on. "And a couple of days ago I leaked word that the police were coming to get the pills while Joanna was at Emily's. Unbeknownst to the killer, we had a security camera set up, focused on the pill organizer. Sure enough, someone showed up, took all the pills, wiped the pill box clean, and left."

I looked around. Intense faces waiting for the rest. One person's eyes fearful.

"Interesting thing, Joanna had several pill boxes. The one this person came and dumped out was a fake. The police already had the box that had been tampered with. And they were able to test the pills in that box, look at the fingerprints on it."

I didn't mention that, when Martinez got back to me to ask me to send the video, he told me they had only gotten partial prints off of the pill box. Although Vivi and I had captured all of their prints on the wine glasses, it still might not be enough to match the partial prints the police had been able to get off the pill box. The killer didn't need to know that, though.

I looked at Joanna. Her turn.

Joanna took a deep breath. "Serena. How could you? Help me understand," she said softly. "It was you who came here and wiped off the box and took the rest of the pills. I saw it."

"Serena?" yelped Jacques. "No."

"I saw the video," repeated Joanna, still staring at Serena. Serena was looking at the table, face flushed, eyes down.

"Funny thing about being a teacher," I said. "These days everyone needs a background check. Fingerprints are on file."

"Serena!" said Jacques. "Tell them you didn't do it."

Serena looked up, eyes wide. "I didn't try to kill anyone!" She looked at each of her brothers in turn. "I just wanted Joanna to seem, you know, a little bit out of it. I swear!"

"What are you saying?" asked Jacques.

"Don't say another word," said Marco, standing up, face dark and forbidding. "Wait 'til you have a lawyer."

Jared looked like he might throw up.

"Just some pills to make her woozy. How could I know Kimberly would drink the blueberry coffee? Only Joanna drinks that! And how could I have known she'd have asthma?!" Serena as the outraged victim instead of the guilty one. "Mom's always talking about how her beta blockers just 'take the edge off.' That's all I was trying to do."

"Why were you trying to make her woozy?" asked Karl.

Serena shot him a withering look. "So people would think she needed to be in a retirement home or something. That this house is too much for her." Her eyes narrowed at Karl. "You're one to talk! You poisoned her with the space heater. On purpose."

Jared had his head in his hands, his body so slumped it looked like he might slide under the table.

"No, I didn't!" Karl jumped up, tensed to fight. "I had no idea it was broken. I didn't mean to put it with the garage sale stuff."

My senses were in full working order. Serena was lying. She meant for Joanna to die. Karl was telling the truth.

I hadn't been completely sure of Karl, even when I teamed up with him. I had stuck the extra pill box in Joanna's bathroom with a camera just in case it was him, letting him think that one of the fake boxes had the real pills.

"So when Joanna got carbon monoxide poisoning from the space heater, you got the idea to stick some beta blockers in the coffee. And when that didn't work, you stuck some different pills in her organizer, is that it?" I asked.

"I wasn't trying to kill her," Serena insisted.

"We saw you taking the pills out of the organizer and wiping it clean, so you must have put them in there." I wanted her to say it, clearly.

"Stop talking!" said Marco, his face red, veins throbbing.

"Why should I? It was your idea!" said Serena.

"What? No way. Uh-uh!" said Marco, his eyes popping.

"You're the one who pointed out how if Joanna had died, we'd all have our problems solved." Serena stared venomously at Marco.

"First, I didn't say it that way!" shouted Marco. "And second, that isn't saying, go try to kill her!"

"That's just it, I wasn't trying to kill her," Serena repeated. "Just make her woozy."

"If you wanted her to move out, why not just ask her?" I asked.

"Ha!" said Serena, her face twisted into an ugly grimace. She pointed at Jacques, "Mr. God Squad over there said we all needed to be nicer to her. And support her, and all that crap. And Dad made it more than clear that he didn't want me here. Didn't want any of us. Like he never even had a family. Said Joanna was to live here as long as she wanted. *Joanna*. Not his own kids."

Jacques eyes were rolling so much I thought he might be having a seizure. "Are you kidding me? Dad loved Joanna. She brought him so much joy and peace. Didn't he deserve that after all the drama with Mom?" Jacques looked at Karl and Marco too. "Why would any of us think we deserve anything more from him? He provided well for us growing up. He sent us all to college. He left us something in his will."

"Big talk from Mr. Steals A Ring," said Karl.

"I'm sorry! I came clean!" said Jacques. "Not like some others." He shot a look at Marco.

Marco had stolen stuff too. I'd have bet the whole land trust on it.

"What family did you grow up in?" shrieked Serena. "Provided for us? He and Mom were completely absent! Drunk every night." Her face was contorted with pain and rage. "So drunk they couldn't even protect their only daughter! So drunk that I get fucking molested in my own bed!"

Shocked silence broken only by hiccupping sobs from Serena.

Jacques broke the silence first. "What do you mean?" he asked softly. "Who?"

"Fucking Rob Limano. Dad's boss. At one of their parties. The last party," Serena cried. "Do you know what Mom said? 'Did you flirt with him?' My own mother." Choking sobs flowed out of her as her nose ran and tears poured mascara into the mix.

"Oh my God," whispered Karl. "Serena, I'm so sorry."

"Is that why Dad stopped drinking?" asked Jacques. "Is that when it happened?"

Serena nodded through her sobbing.

I thought about her first bedroom and the image of the sweaty middle-aged man. I thought about her moving to a new bedroom. It all made sense. Connie dismissed it, but Thomas felt awful. A searing sadness ripped through me in agreement. Thomas still felt guilty and sick from it. My satisfaction at having trapped her as the one trying to kill Joanna sunk into sadness.

Serena shifted back into rage. "Dad gets sober and does he make it up to us? To me? NO! He gives all his new lovey-dovey self to JOANNA." Serena's face was ugly in its pain. "No one ever looks out for ME!"

Jacques looked at Jared. "Jared, did you know about this?"

Jared didn't respond. He might not have known about the pills, but he knew Serena was off the deep end.

"Joanna, how could you do this now?" Serena wailed. "I hate you even more than I hate my dad."

Joanna looked faint at the level of rage and pain directed at her.

Emily stood up, glowering at Serena. "Shut your mouth! You killed Kimberly! I'm tired of your victim act! Lots of people have shitty things happen to them, and they don't go try to kill someone. And, by the way, my mother has paid the upkeep on this house since she married Thomas!" Emily looked around the table. "It's why you still have the house to sell now! And it's worth a ton more now—if they had sold it when they got married like Thomas wanted to, it would have been for like a third of what it's worth now. Shove that up your entitled asses."

Chapter 51

The dining room door opened and Miller and Martinez came in.

"Serena Sullivan Reed, you are under arrest for manslaughter and attempted murder," said Miller. Martinez's physical size and Miller's confident presence took over the room.

"You have the right to remain silent," Miller started, as Martinez came up behind Serena, helped her away from her chair and cuffed her.

Sharp pain contracted my chest, and Thomas's sadness sunk me into a chair, a grief so heavy I was sure I'd never be able to stand up again. Thomas had taken over my entire body, guilt flowing through every cell from not protecting Serena, and then Joanna. A dizzying number of pictures flashed through my head, like Thomas had loaded up a slide projector with all his memories of Serena and was playing it at warp speed. Toddler to murderer in about twenty seconds. I managed to get my hand into my pocket, grabbed Thomas's pocket square, and handed it to Joanna.

It helped. My chest started to relax and the images faded. How could someone already dead be so hard on my body?

As the detectives led Serena out, Jared finally stood up. "Serena," he said, his face twisted in agony.

Serena turned and looked at her husband with contempt. "You win. You get me out of your life. You're free."

Jared stood motionless. He had seemed an insubstantial man even before his wife got arrested, his suit too loose, his limbs folded in on themselves. Like he hadn't stood up straight in years, a man worn down by life.

"Joanna, you all right?" I asked. Thomas was still around, but my body was feeling more my own.

Joanna nodded. "That was hard. I can't believe I did it."

"You were amazing," I said, giving her a hug.

Jared slipped back into his chair, his face wet with tears. "She's never been quite the same since the post-partum depression. Not that I'm blaming the kids or anything, but something in her broke." He looked blankly around the room, unable to meet anyone else's eyes, his head jutting forward like a turtle too far out of its shell. "And the . . . assault when she was younger. It's been coming up again. The older our kids get, the angrier she is at her parents. She's not herself."

Joanna gave him a steely stare. "She killed Kimberly."

Jared started sobbing. "I'm so sorry. I should have gotten her more help." He flung his head down on his arms on the table, crying uncontrollably. "She hated me for no reason. She hated her whole life."

"Joanna, you must be exhausted," I said. "Why don't you go to bed? I'm sure it will take you a while to calm down, but maybe at least get ready?" This drama could get dissected all night, and I felt like she needed an escape. "You've still got the gala coming up. You need your rest."

"Good idea, but I want to say something first." Joanna looked at the sobbing Jared. "I will never forgive Serena. But that doesn't mean I'm cutting you all out of my life. This is your house; you grew up here, and you should feel welcome here. I will do better in the future. I look forward to having relationships with all of you." She nodded in turn to Jacques, Karl, and Marco. "And I am open to talking about when I should move out of this house."

Karl came around the table to Joanna, resting his hands on her shoulders. "I'm so sorry." He hung his head. "About it all. Especially the space heater. I have felt awful ever since it happened. And I'm sorry I was sneaking around looking for the jewelry. My mother wouldn't leave it alone."

"I believe you weren't trying to hurt me," said Joanna.

Karl rubbed his face with its carefully trimmed stubble. "When Izzy asked me for help, I was so happy to have a chance to make it up to you." Karl's charisma was more authentic now. "I'm sorry for how immature we have all been. I know my dad really loved you, and I'm glad he had you in his life. I don't think I ever told you that."

"Rob Limano," Jacques muttered. "I can't even . . ." He looked over at Jared. "Come on, Jared. Let's go down to the police station. I'm sure she's going to need a lawyer."

Jared stood up and stumbled after Jacques.

Joanna picked up a tray of untouched macaroons and walked towards the kitchen. "Izzy, I don't know how I would have done any of this without you. Thank you." After handing the tray to Vivi, she gave the pocket square back to me. "This was yours?"

"It's Thomas's," I said, taking it from her. "It has helped me connect with him."

Holding it, I felt Thomas fully flowing through me but without the chest pain. Just filled with love for his wife.

"He wants to hug you," I said, and she nodded, tears welling up.

I put my arms around her and let Thomas feel the love.

Joanna squeezed. "No wonder I have felt so at peace when you are around," she murmured into my shoulder. "I already liked you, but I can feel Thomas here now. I can."

This was real love, this thing flowing between Thomas and Joanna. This is what I wanted; this is what I never had really felt myself. It was deep and real and easy. So easy.

Finally, she let go. "Well, that was therapeutic," she said, wiping her eyes. "Izzy, how can I thank you? You've saved my life. You are like family now. You have to promise to stay around, even when our work is done."

"I would love that." I stepped back, still holding the pocket square, but it was drained of any Thomas energy. It was just a piece of material. I handed it back to Joanna. "I don't need this anymore."

I could feel Thomas's sadness about Serena at the same time as I felt an overflowing peace that Joanna was safe. I had an image of him bowing towards me, like a thank you, and then he faded away.

Chapter 52

The smell of bacon and coffee woke me in the morning, and for once I felt completely refreshed. I hadn't realized how much Thomas's fears had worn me down, interrupting both sleep and waking hours.

In the kitchen I found Jay cooking breakfast. Before I could say anything, he said, "I'm sorry. I shouldn't have left. I shouldn't have told Cole it was your fault."

"Yeah, kind of a dick move." I slid onto a barstool. "He hates me. But on the plus side, I found Kimberly's murderer."

"I want to hear all about it, but first, I have to say something." Jay put a plate of pancakes and bacon in front of me, poured me a cup of coffee. His hair was wet and neatly combed, but he looked tired, his face puffy, his shoulders rounded a bit more than usual.

"I have to go back to Paris Sunday, temporarily. I'm coming back for the end of Cole's year. I'll find a place to live. I don't see us working anything out with me here."

I didn't see us working anything out, no matter where he was. "We can't afford that."

Jay shrugged. "I'm sure I can borrow someone's pool house or guest house for a bit. Then we'll go from there."

"Thank you," I said. "I'm sorry."

We stared at each other, shared history weaving us together, disappointment pushing us apart. So much sadness in Jay's eyes, but acceptance too. Paradoxically, it made me love him. Not in a "I want to keep him" way, but in appreciation for a moment of grace in the face of disappointment.

Jay held eye contact. "I know. Me too."

I ate a couple of bites of pancake.

"I'm not done with this," said Jay. "I'm sure there is going to be more pain and arguing before it is all resolved. But . . ." He looked away, his eyes red-rimmed and teary. With a shaky voice, he continued. "I talked to my dad last night and, as usual, he was right. Nothing but tough love from him. I love you. And when you love someone, really love them, you want that person to be happy. If you can't be happy with me . . ." More tears and another shrug. The shower went on upstairs, and Jay turned around, facing the stove, to pull himself together.

"All right," he said, turning back around, tears wiped, small smile on. "Let's hear it. How did you figure out who killed Kimberly?"

I filled him in. How I was torn between suspecting Marco and Serena. How I was ninety percent sure it wasn't Karl but had a backup plan. How I got distracted by images of missing jewelry and an argument between Jacques and Marco.

"I was sure Marco knew there was something going on with a land trust, although he didn't know all the details," I said. "He had no affection for Joanna, so it was suspicious he was hanging around so much. Serena seemed the most troubled, but also too depressed to come up with a plot to kill Joanna. But then why was she making the effort to come see Joanna? I picked up on trauma in her past but couldn't see how that fit. The thing that stood out, though, was how unhappy she was, especially with her husband."

I didn't say out loud that she became my top suspect when I realized she didn't want to be married to her husband anymore but had no money to leave. It hit too close to home, which was how I had actually figured her out. Once I admitted to myself that I didn't love Jay, I could see that part in her more clearly.

Jay winced. He got it anyway.

Jay forked into a stack of pancakes. "For Serena, it was about the house? She didn't know about the land thing?" Jay asked.

"The house, but it was really more about her anger at her father and Joanna. She felt unprotected by him and so angry that when he got sober, he gave so much attention to Joanna, not her. She gets molested in her own room, with her parents in the house ignoring her. And then her mother dismisses it. And blames Serena for the divorce! That's a lot of trauma."

I dragged my last bite of pancake through the remaining syrup. I was desperate for money myself. I knew how it could take over your brain, this worry about supporting your family, the feeling of being stuck. I could never go that far, though.

Cole stumbled in, hair wet, eyes puffy, heading straight for the coffee pot. He filled a cup and sat down. "Dad!" he said, as if it took him that long to realize Jay had come home.

Jay flipped a stack of pancakes onto a plate, added some bacon and set it down in front of Cole.

Cole grunted, "Thanks," and dug in. His head stayed down, but I could see him glancing back and forth between us.

Three pancakes in, Cole came enough awake to talk. "When do you have to go back?"

"Sunday," Jay said, smiling to soften the blow.

"Shit," said Cole.

"I'll be back," said Jay. "I'm talking with my boss about it. He needs me to go back now but said he'd work with me, let me live back here soon."

Cole popped up and hugged his dad. "Awesome!"

I felt a swirl of emotions watching them hug: happiness, love, sadness, guilt—all the colors of the rainbow, it seemed.

"Your mom and I have some stuff to work out. When I come back, I'll probably live somewhere else, maybe in the Densons' guest house," Jay said into Cole's hair.

Cole pulled back and looked at me. "Great job, Mom," he said sarcastically.

"Hey!" Jay's voice was firm. "I was wrong to blame her. Marriage is two people. We both are responsible for it. You are not responsible for it. We will do our best to work stuff out, but that is not your concern."

"How is that not my concern?" said Cole.

"None of this stuff is easy," said Jay. "But one part IS easy. We both love you. We will always be a family, no matter what."

"Whatever," said Cole, slouching back to his seat.

"And you will be respectful of your mother. She deserves it," said Jay. "Focus on the fact that I am coming home for your last semester."

My phone buzzed: Lauren.

"I better answer this," I said, knowing she'd be wanting a full explanation of yesterday.

I took the phone to the living room and gave her the shorter version.

Then she gave me the work schedule for the week.

"You fired me. Remember?"

"We both knew that wasn't for real," said Lauren. "Plus, I have really good news. Turns out that they found out who was robbing houses. It was a group of teenagers! And you'll never guess who was part of it.

"Bart Mahone." For once I rendered Lauren speechless. "Yeah, well, it just might be me who told the police about it." Let Lauren think it was my extrasensory skills, not Cole who helped me. "You can't keep firing me. We have to find some way to work together where you aren't always angry at me."

Big sigh from Lauren. "I know. It just worries me that the whole psychic thing will make people not take us seriously. But I get it; it is real. And there are lots of people who are interested in it. I'm going to try, really I am. To see if I can tolerate that part."

We hung up, and I went back to the kitchen where Jay and Cole were still talking about school stuff.

"And then, you know, we can still do a trip after graduation, if you want—have you come over to Paris," Jay said to Cole.

Cole reached for the stack of bacon. "Yeah, that's coming soon."

For a moment we were just a normal family, having breakfast and talking about school.

Just a normal family with a psychic mom, separated parents, and huge debt.

"Holy shit," said Cole, looking at his phone.

"What's up?" asked Jay.

"Bart Mahone was arrested. And, like, three of his friends." Cole shot me a look.

I shrugged, like "what do I know?"

"Aren't they minors? They can't publish those names," said Jay.

"Nah, saw it on a group chat," said Cole. "People are freaking out. Not sure how many are going down."

"You got any worries there?" asked Jay.

"Nope," said Cole. "Not my thing."

Look at me, solving two mysteries in one week. Maybe I should go into crime solving.

Chapter 53

It was Saturday night. The shuttles were smoothly dropping off the black-tie guests onto a red carpet lined with palm trees and uplighting, leading to the entrance to the tent. The tent was huge and magical, like a castle had ballooned up in Joanna's backyard. It was filled with chandeliers and twinkle lights and miles of folded silk gracefully swooping out from the center poles and lining the walls. Here and there, openings to more silk-lined hallways led to outdoor seating areas and an outdoor dance floor, and the promised fancy Portapotties. The passage into the house was not obvious, hidden behind a zigzagging set of silk screens and manned by Vivi and Lacey, both with clipboards and walkie-talkies. They had instructions on the exact list of people allowed into the house and were more than up to the task of facing down anyone who questioned their authority. Even the caterers didn't seem to need access to the kitchen, having arrived with their own set of trucks. I had never seen an operation of this size up close, and it was impressive, more like a military operation than a party.

As promised, Order Out of Chaos was here to make sure no one went in the house. I was also here for any emotional support Joanna might need. She had been very clear that she did not want the Serena arrest to ruin the gala, but feelings were still raw.

Joanna and I stood in the kitchen as she gathered her energy to go out and face the crowd. She was wearing the tangerine dress and looked spectacular. She'd had a professional blowout, and her hair was smooth and shining, her makeup enhancing the glow of her face and emphasizing the deep blue of her eyes.

"You look like pure sunshine," I said, giving her a hug. Touching her in the dress brought back the images of her wedding night, the soft, dark sky, the sparkling lights, the love and comfort of Thomas with his arms around her, joyfully dancing.

"He's here and so proud," I said, giving her an extra squeeze.

Joanna stepped back and nodded. "I know. I've got this."

Lauren appeared from the bathroom where'd she'd gone to check her makeup and hair.

"Could you two do a little walk around, kind of check the temperature, so to speak?" asked Joanna. "Before I go out there, I'd kind of like to know how much people are talking about . . . the whole Serena thing."

"No problem," said Lauren. "Can we bring you anything? A drink from the bar?"

Joanna smiled. "I've already got something. Going to sip a little while you check it out."

Lauren and I wandered through the crowd, listening in. Out of eight conversations, the Sullivans were in two, but no one seemed to be mad at Joanna at all. Mainly a sense of relief that the gala hadn't been canceled.

"Here comes Peaches," whispered Lauren. "Apologize again about the dog if you have to."

Peaches shimmered from every angle. Her form-fitting black sheath dress seemed designed to showcase the diamonds that shined on her ears, neck, and wrists. They almost matched the brightness of her teeth, and under the chandeliers hanging from the peaks of the tent, she was a perfectly showcased jewel.

"Lauren! Izzy!" Peaches gave Lauren a big hug and kiss and then did the same to me. Definitely the type to become effusively friendly when she was drinking.

"Izzy, have you met my husband, Mason?" Peaches asked as she grabbed a flute of champagne from a passing waiter, seamlessly handing him her empty one at the same time.

Mason flooded me with his TV anchor smile as he stuck out his hand. "Delighted," he said, blue eyes warm and bright. His smile felt genuine, like he was truly happy to meet me, like I had made his night. No wonder he had so many fans. "Excellent job on our house. We couldn't be more grateful."

Peaches smiled up at her husband, who towered over her by at least a foot. "Mason loves neatness even more than I do."

Mason squeezed around Peaches's waist. "'Cleanliness is next to godliness,' as the quote goes."

I laughed. "Which one of you is cleanliness and which one is godliness?"

Peaches giggled. "Isn't Izzy funny? Of course I'm godliness. Goddess-li-ness."

Mason beamed at his wife. "You got that right."

You'd never know Mason's son had just been arrested. I wondered if it was a rich person thing, this ability to effortlessly deny real-life problems. Or maybe just good compartmentalization. Why ruin a good gala with parenting failures?

The band kicked in to "You Make Me Feel So Young," and Peaches squealed, "Our song! We have to dance!" She dragged Mason away, and Lauren smiled, her head shaking back and forth.

"I don't know what your magic is, but that woman should hate you instead of thinking of you as a bestie."

"She will if she finds out I'm the one who ratted on her stepson," I said.

"Hmm," said Lauren. "Might make her like you more." She sighed. "I get it, Iz. I guess sometimes I'm just jealous."

"You? Jealous of me? I'm a mess. In every category. You're the one perfectly dressed and organized, and your kids behave, and your husband adores you."

"And yet you're the one everyone wants to be around." I could hear the hurt underneath her light tone. "Obviously, we'll have to figure out how to make our working styles fit better. I know I can be kind of controlling."

I liked this more self-aware Lauren. It reminded me of how much fun we actually had together as kids. "I know I can be kind of all-over-the-place." I matched her light tone. "Hey did I ever tell you what we found under the sink at Rupert's?" As I told her the story, we made our way back towards the house. We brought Joanna back out through the passage to the tent. Vivi and Lacey gave thumbs up, and Joanna made her way towards the stage. The band finished their song, and Joanna took the microphone as the crowd finished settling into their gold-painted bamboo chair seats. "Thank you all for coming to the Thomas Sullivan Heart Gala. Thank you for your continuing support of heart disease research. Thank you for honoring my husband Thomas Sullivan this evening. We all know how devoted he was to this cause and what a tragedy it is that he died from the very thing he worked so hard to prevent. I have a feeling he is here with us tonight, still giving his support." Joanna found my eyes and gave me the slightest smile, then got serious again. "I am going to address the elephant in the room. Our family has had more than its share of trouble lately, and there is, hopefully, a lot of healing in our future, but that should not stop anyone here from having a wonderful time tonight. This evening is meant to honor the work of so many people who have been tireless in raising money for heart disease research and to honor those on the front line doing that research and treating patients. With that in mind, I'd like to turn the microphone over to the ever delightful Mason Mahone who has agreed to emcee, as well as serve as auctioneer."

I watched the crowd as Joanna finished. Right back to laughing and drinking, minds at ease that there would be no more uncomfortable reality to face, at least not tonight. We all drift in and out of denial, to misquote a common phrase. I'm no one to judge; I do the same.

"Hey, Izzy." Patty Hathaway appeared at my side. She was in a maroon silk dress, her hair down and curled and looking good but not really like herself.

"Hi, Patty." I gave her a hug. "Good to see you."

"I keep thinking about that conversation we had about parenting; I'm not sure why. I just keep thinking about it." Patty took a little crab claw off of the tray of a passing waiter. "Delicious," she said, popping it into her mouth. The waiter took the shell from her and moved on.

"Oh?"

"Made me wonder about Charlie, like if he was gay. I realized I'd be okay with it and, I don't know, somehow I don't think I'd be surprised."

"Huh," I said, as if she had come up with that all on her own. "Well, it's always good to be ready for something, even if it doesn't happen."

"Yes! That would be a rare feeling as a mother, though, wouldn't it?! Being prepared."

We laughed together.

Patty's face lit up. "Oh, here comes my best customer."

I saw a couple coming towards us, a frail, barely moving old man hanging onto the arm of none other than Shania. Fully decked out in a sequin dress of shimmering blues and greens, hair cascading in luxurious curls. Towering over her hunched spine husband.

"Shania is your best customer?" I asked.

"No, her husband. Claims it's medicinal, but I'm guessing he needs to be high to live all the time with her." Patty giggled. "I think she married him thinking he'd die soon and she'd have all his money. I think he's keeping himself alive out of pure spite. Whoops, did I say that out loud?" She pretended to slap her own hand. "Bad Patty."

"How many cookies did you have tonight?" I asked.

"Just enough," she said, laughing. "My husband is driving, in case you're worried."

"Rock on," I said.

Shania noticed me and changed direction, which was a bit like turning a tortoise. "When you marry for money you earn every penny," I said, watching Shania inch him a little right and then a little more right until they had a trajectory away from me.

"You got that right," said Patty.

I looked at the sham of a marriage inching away. I thought about the pure love I had felt flow through me from Thomas to Joanna. I thought about my own marriage, somewhere in the middle. I had a basic affection for Jay. But I wanted what Joanna and Thomas had. I knew how it felt now. I wanted that for myself.

It would have been so convenient if that came from Jay. But it didn't. We met and married so young. He was handsome and likable, and I had no next step in life planned. I hadn't known how to send it all in a different direction.

Marrying Jay hadn't actually solved the problem. It was right here, bigger and scarier than ever.

What did I want in life?

It wasn't so simple as just trading Jay for Saito. That wasn't the answer then, and I had grown enough to know it wasn't the answer now.

I needed to face the abyss.

I said goodbye to Patty and made my way out of the tent and past the outdoor seating area and along a garden path until I found a bench tucked into a bed of flowers. I sat down, breathed in the cool night air heavy with the smell of jasmine and just let myself relax for a moment.

Mixed in with all the feelings over Kimberly's dying and Serena's being taken away was a sense of satisfaction that I had not given up on Joanna. That I had been the one to make sure it was resolved. My mother was right; I was resourceful. I liked figuring things out. I liked putting things together, metaphorically and literally. I liked solving things. Whether it was how to arrange a laundry room or who murdered Kimberly, my brain longed for stuff to solve.

I wanted to be brave, to take chances and feel anxious about them and if they fell flat, try something else. To let myself be drawn towards what I liked. What fulfilled me.

Maybe I would learn Spanish. I had always kind of wanted to, and during all these years Jay worked for a French-based company, I kept trying to convince myself to learn French, but I wasn't drawn to French. So, I learned no second language at all. Maybe I would see where my psychic senses would take me. Maybe I would sign up for my first race in all these years of running. Maybe, after reading hundreds, if not thousands, of mystery novels I'd write one of my own. Maybe I would get a cup of coffee with someone who made my whole body vibrate.

I grabbed my phone and texted Christopher.

Coffee tomorrow?

Chapter 54

Having at least taken a peek at the abyss, I made my way back into the loud and hot tent. I found Joanna standing near the bar, chatting with Lou and Marion. As I approached, they both gave me pitying looks and said their goodbyes to Joanna.

"I guess I'm a little straitlaced for them," I said, giggling.

"Don't feel bad, so are ninety percent of the population," said Joanna. "But they have hearts of gold, truly. Just salt-of-the-earth people once you get past the . . . experimentation." Joanna's eyes narrowed. "Oh no. Look who showed up. Of all the nerve."

I looked in the direction she was staring and couldn't see anyone in the crowd of people that stood out to me. "Who?"

"Rob Limano. Of all people," said Joanna, her voice filled with disgust. "I don't think I can bear to even look at him."

"He's headed straight for us. Oh no," said Joanna. "Of course he has no idea what I know."

It was the man I'd seen in the image in Serena's room. Older, less hair but just as sweaty, and crammed into a tux that maybe fit twenty years ago but was straining at every seam now.

"Joanna! What a party! This is just amazing," he said, grabbing her hand and pulling it up to kiss it.

Joanna winced and pulled her hand back.

Rob saw the distaste. "Not a touchy-feely type, eh?"

I jumped in. "Hi Rob, you don't know me, but I'm here as a little fun psychic act for the event." I grabbed his sweaty hand and flipped it over to look at his palm, pretending to read it. "Hmm, so interesting, not a super long life line, I'm sorry to say. And hmm, what is this? Why am I getting an image of you in a pink and white bedroom here at the house? Pretty stripes. Lots of stuffed animals." I dropped his hand. "Whoa, what are you doing in there? No, *that* is something I definitely don't want to see. This is supposed to be a fun night."

Rob glared at me and then looked at Joanna. "What kind of show you running here? Who is this weirdo?"

I continued. "That was Serena's bedroom. Oh my, Serena was there. So young. So unwilling."

Rob's face got red. "I have no idea what you are talking about. I've been to lots of parties here. Probably been in every room at one point or another, so has half of LaSalle."

Joanna stared daggers at him, not moving, not breaking eye contact. "We know what happened."

Rob shrugged. "I have no idea what you are talking about. Whatever. I'm going to get a drink," he said, turning away and running into Connie, who had come up close behind him.

Connie chested into Rob, pushing him back. "Not so fast, Robbie-boy," she growled. Connie actually looked attractive, not crazy, her hair smoothed into soft waves, her makeup perfect, her tan set off by a pale blue strapless designer gown.

"Connie, a pleasure, as always," said Rob, inching back even more.

"It's never been a pleasure," said Connie. "I didn't believe her back then, but I have had some long talks with my daughter the past couple of days." Connie leaned in to Rob's face. "I know what you did. You are a piece of shit, and I promise you I'm going to make your life hell."

"I have no idea what you bitches are talking about, but if it was something from the past . . ." He spread his hands, like "what can you do?"

Karl and Jacques appeared on either side of Connie.

"You've got some nerve showing up here," said Karl. "Fucking pervert."

Rob laughed nervously. "I have no idea what you guys are drinking, but you are crazy." He spun his finger around in circles near his head.

"We know what you did to our sister," said Jacques, his voice menacing in its quiet calmness. Both he and Karl took a step forward.

"I don't even know your sister," said Rob. "But I do know a lot about slander, so you better back off."

"You can leave now or we can make you leave," said Karl. "You are not welcome here."

Rob leered at Connie. "Connie here may beg to differ. She was always happy to have me, if you get my drift."

Like lightning, Jacques's fist flew into Rob's face, knocking him down. Karl put his foot on Rob's thigh and both Karl and Jacques leaned down over him. "He's not even the brother who knows how to fight," said Karl, his voice slow and mean. "So, this is what you are going to do. You are going to get up, walk straight out of here, and never come back."

I was still processing that it was Jacques who punched him, not Karl.

I heard a grunt that must have satisfied Karl, and he took his foot off of Rob.

Connie leaned down and spit on Rob. "It might be too late to press charges, but it isn't too late to get revenge. My specialty."

Rob rolled onto his knees and then unsteadily stood up, blood running out of his nose onto his white shirt. "You won't get away with that."

"I'd welcome the chance to go again," said Jacques.

"You're going to have to get in line," Karl said to Jacques. Karl gave Rob a little shove. "Start walking."

Rob staggered away, people staring at him, hands over their mouths.

Karl and Jacques and Connie and Joanna all looked at each other, a mix of emotions swirling.

There was a sound of crashing glassware and shouts. We looked over to see Rob, bloody and yelling, covered in red wine, a tray of broken glassware scattered around him. That had Vivi written all over it, and I searched around for her grinning face. Instead, I saw Lauren, smiling like she was five again and giving me a big thumbs up.

"Nice punch," said Karl, giving Jacques a little brotherly shove. "I thought I'd get to do it, though."

"I'm actually quite in awe of your restraint," said Jacques, rubbing his fist as if he might have hurt himself. "It was all I could do not to dive onto the ground and pummel him into dogmeat."

"Very Christian of you," said Karl.

Jacques shrugged. "I haven't learned the 'turn the other cheek' part so well, I guess." They grinned at each other.

"Let's go get a drink," said Karl, slinging his arm around Jacques.

They walked away, leaving Connie with Joanna, as I hovered on the edge.

"That son of a bitch," said Connie, still staring in the direction Rob had exited. Her face sagged with a mix of pain and anger.

"A lot of pain," said Joanna softly.

Connie looked at the ground. She sighed, then looked up at Joanna. "I've got a lot to be sorry for."

Joanna crinkled her eyes in a kind of sympathetic wince.

"Thomas isn't the only one who can change, you know," said Connie.

Joanna nodded, quiet for a moment. Then, her voice soft, she said, "I hope that's true. For Serena's sake, if no one else's. She's going to need some help."

I could feel that Connie had reached her limit of self-reflection. She sniffed, almost as if she was angry at herself for being vulnerable. "Time I went for a drink with my sons." With that, she spun and walked away.

Joanna and I looked at each other.

"I hope she meant it," said Joanna. "Serena needs to face the consequences of what she has done, but I'm not without compassion for what happened to her." She smoothed her hands down the sides of the tangerine dress. "I can feel him with me, you know."

I nodded. "I can tell. Like, I don't feel him with me anymore, but I can sense him around you."

I had an image of Thomas standing next to Joanna, bowing to me. Then he turned in a complete circle, bowing four times as he went, almost like the points of a compass.

I felt a cool breeze across my shoulders. I had a feeling it was the whispers of the Miwok, that the decision to keep the main areas of the land and the trails preserved was the right one, that there was a gratitude that the land was forever preserved for all people to use. The phrase *Take only as much as you need* floated through my head, and I had a sense that the spirits were at peace. Thomas and his father had managed to preserve sacred ground, and the small amount of land they had kept was the fair exchange.

As I made my way towards the fancy Portapotty trailers, Emily came up from behind me and touched my arm.

"Thank you for, uh, protecting my mother." She stuck her hand out for a shake. It felt so formal, like we should be hugging instead.

I thought about the image of Emily in a passionate embrace with someone at work. "You know, your mother is one of the most understanding people I've ever met," I said, squeezing her hand. "Doesn't judge, does she?"

"You're right," said Emily.

"I'm just guessing that she'd be happy to hear more about your work life," I said.

Emily tilted her head, considering. "Maybe."

"Or non-work life," I added. "You two are lucky to have each other. I'm probably going to duck out early tonight, but I know you'll be around to make sure she is okay."

"Of course I will be," she said. She paused, and I could feel her trying to decide if she should apologize for not trusting me. It was right there, swirling in her head, but she couldn't choke it out. Still too jealous. Over nothing.

Not my problem to fix. "Enjoy your evening," I said. "I've got to check out these bathrooms. I hear they are amazing."

I felt like my work was done. Joanna was okay, Emily was on the job, Connie sort of neutralized by a common enemy. It was time to go home. After checking out the Portapotty and finding it very plush, I worked my way back through the crowd. Jacques and Karl saw me and beckoned me toward the bar.

"Do a shot with us!" said Karl.

"I don't think so, I'm good," I said.

Jacques turned to the bartender. "Three fireballs," he said.

"Under one condition," I said. I leaned in close to Jacques and whispered. "You have to tell me what Marco did wrong years ago. I heard you guys arguing in the office."

I leaned back and stared, waiting. Karl was talking to someone on his other side, so we had a moment. "I promise I won't say anything. It's just the last piece."

Jacques shook his head no.

"Don't make me use the skills on you," I joked. When he didn't answer, I said, "Let me guess, then. He sold your dad's stuff without him knowing it. Lots of bits and pieces around that house, and I'll bet he figured some of it wouldn't be missed."

Jacques didn't need to say a word. I could tell from his face I was right.

"I'm not saying you are right, but even if you were, it was an immature teenage thing to do," Jacques said. "Something I am sure that person stopped doing a long time ago."

"Got it," I said as the bartender set down the shots and Jacques punched Karl's arm to get his attention.

Jacques handed me my glass, and we held them up to each other to toast.

"To Karl and being a dad!" said Jacques, full-on smiling at Karl.

I was so glad the word was out. "To Karl!" I said and tossed it back.

Karl beamed. "I don't know why I was trying to keep it a secret. It's the best thing that has happened to me."

I knew why he'd kept it a secret. Amelia had given her blessing, and now he could be unreservedly happy.

I squeezed Karl's hand. "She's so happy for you. She's going to be like a special godmother."

A little wetness around Karl's eyes and a nod.

"Where's my shot?" Connie pushed her way into the group.

I wasn't ready to party with Connie. "Enjoy!" I said to the family and slipped away.

I could feel the ghosts relaxing. I could feel the peace of problems faced, if not completely resolved. I could feel the very land around me sink into a contentment.

Time to go home.

Chapter 55

The next morning, I met Vivi for an early run, afraid I'd be too nervous if I didn't burn off some energy first. And there was the job of shrinking the pooch.

"We should go to Jacques's winery one of these days," Vivi said, as we hit the turnoff to the hill.

"Definitely. His wines are amazing."

"Might go see Karl's band again too," said Vivi. "Get myself all hot and bothered and take that home to Brian."

"Brian's a lucky man," I said, starting to get breathless.

"I'm a lucky woman," huffed Vivi.

We plodded our way up to the flatter section, still shrouded in an otherworldly fog. I loved how different the same trail could look, depending on the weather and the light and the season. Just the right amount of novelty laid over a base of familiarity. Enough different. Enough the same.

"I want to feel like a lucky woman too," I said, as we slowed to a recovery pace. "I want what you have."

"You deserve that," said Vivi. "*Jay* deserves that too, from someone."

"He does." I thought about the long road ahead of us. "It's going to suck for a while. But it's the right thing."

"Know what you know," said Vivi.

"Yeah. I think I've known for a long time. Just didn't let myself see it."

"You and Dorothy," said Vivi.

"Dorothy?"

"Yeah, in *The Wizard of Oz*, she had the ruby slippers on the whole time. She had the ability to go home the whole time."

"If I'm Dorothy, who does that make you?" I laughed. "Tin Man? Lion? Scarecrow?"

Vivi snorted. "Please. I'm Glenda."

We made the slow turn towards the downhill.
Although there was more light filtering through the fog,
as the trail wound through a thick span of trees, it got
darker again. Mornings like this, it felt like Vivi and I
were the only people in the world, like the world was all
starting over, new.

"So, did you convince Lauren to take you back or did
she convince you to come back?" Vivi asked.

"Probably a little of both. I need the money. And I like
the work. I can't believe it, but I do."

"It'll be fun to keep working together," said Vivi.
"Lucy and Ethel organize houses."

"It's not boring, I'll say that," I said. "Lizards and penis
molds and loose dogs."

"Don't forget horny old virgins," Vivi added.

"You think Rupert's a virgin?" I asked.

"Not anymore," said Vivi.

* * *

I had picked a coffee place tucked away on a side
street not too far from the hospital. It was funky, with soft
lighting and mismatched wood tables, the type of place
you could linger. I fiddled with a stray newspaper, then
moved it to a chair when I saw Christopher headed
towards the glass door. He had the night shift stubble of
no-shave but had changed out of his scrubs into jeans and
a cream-colored pullover that was thin enough to show
his muscles underneath. He ran his hands through his hair
before reaching for the door, giving it an appealing
unkempt look.

He stepped in, looked around, maybe taking a second
for his eyes to adjust to the dim lighting, then saw me at a
corner table. He smiled.

I smiled.

Without breaking eye contact, he walked over, slid
into his seat, and put his hands across the table towards
mine.

I pushed my hands forward and we held hands. The Joanna drama, the Jay tension, the bills, Cole's surgery—it all disappeared for the moment. Just a lovely, pure stream of energy from his hands through mine. He gave a squeeze and let go, leaning back.

"So, coffee-that's-not-a-date or coffee-that-is-a-date?" he asked.

"Coffee-that-is-a-date," I said.

His melty eyes lit up. "Good."

The End.

As many have said before me, it takes a village. There have been so many teachers and supporters and helpers along the way that it would be impossible to name them all, but here are the superstars. My longtime writing group gave invaluable support and read countless versions of this book. Ann Hutchinson, Kat Panos, Michael McGreevy, Louis Pearl, and Hagar Scher have known Izzy a long time. My incomparable teacher (and friend) Shirin Leos took me from a dabbler to someone who believed she could be a professional. Lisa Manterfield provided the best book coaching and developmental editing, strengthening the book immeasurably. I was extraordinarily lucky to get several edits from the inimitable Susan Chang. David Bloom's cover art is divine. Fellow cozy mystery writer Wendy Adair was a fabulous beta reader. Big thanks to Steve and Celeste Bates for contributing some funny bits (you know which ones). My sister Alison, an uber-reader, a one-woman Goodreads (local librarians ask *her* for suggestions) was an enthusiastic and helpful reader (and not afraid to tell me she hated an early version of my first chapter). My kids, Elle and Xavier, will always be my inspiration for doing my best (I am trying to live up to them!). I can't begin to describe how grateful I am to my husband Dave who gave me a one year "Esquer grant" to take time off of work and write. That grant has been renewed too many years to count, and he has never lost one ounce of belief in me. And finally, I have to thank Dash, my white lab who sits on my feet, and who I suspect is the real muse here.
I am at work on the next book in the Order Out of Chaos series, and I can promise you that Izzy has not quite got the hang of organizing yet. Or her psychic skills. But she is having a lot of fun, and Dr. Saito is not going anywhere.

It really is true that authors LOVE (and need) reviews, so if you liked the book . . . (Goodreads, Amazon, wherever).

If you'd like to be informed when the next Order Out of Chaos book comes out, please let me know at my website: **https://lynnrankin-esquer.com**

Or via QR code:

Check out my blog: **https://lynnrankinesquer.wordpress.com/**

Visit me on Amazon:

https://www.amazon.com/author/lynnrankinesquer

FB author page: **https://www.facebook.com/lynnrankinesquer**

Blue Sky: **https://bsky.app/profile/lynnresquer.bsky.social**

Instagram: **https://www.instagram.com/lynnresquer_/**

Contact me: **lynn@lynnrankinesquer.com**

About the Author

I'm a California girl (transplanted from Pennsylvania via North Carolina). Well, girl might be stretching it, I'm a mom (Thing One is 22 and Thing Two is 21), a baseball coach's wife, a runner (slogger is more like it; I jog very slowly), an obsessed pickleballer, and a lapsed cook. My whole world lit up the second I deciphered *Fun with Dick and Jane*, and it has never dimmed. I am endlessly enthralled with how stories come out of someone's head into my hands then into my head. Every book feels like it is enchanted. I love the beach, Lemonheads, and baseball. I've sampled several professions including psychologist, college professor, rat lab tech, and waitress (not in that order). And these days, I am a writer, taking pieces of everything I know and love and putting them together in one place. Sometimes that place is imaginary (my novels), and sometimes that place is my twist on the real world (my blog). It is a most delicious way to live life, tinkering with words, occasionally glimpsing magic.

Previous Books

My Paperback Cape: The Unlikely Odyssey of a Bookworm

https://www.amazon.com/My-Paperback-Cape-Unlikely-Bookworm-ebook/dp/B00GT1VXS2

The Unmooring of Mrs. Mango

https://www.amazon.com/Unmooring-Mrs-Mango-Lynn-Rankin-Esquer-ebook/dp/B08HHBPHK8/

www.ingramcontent.com/pod-product-compliance
Lightning Source LLC
Chambersburg PA
CBHW020246010826
48973CB00006B/1683